# WHEEL OF THE FATES

*Book II of the Carolingian Chronicles*

J. Boyce Gleason

**Yet A Little While**
PUBLISHING

ISBN: 978-0-578-88078-5 (sc)
ISBN: 978-0-578-88079-2 (e)

*To my mom, Janet Gleason who has been an inspiration and a force for good in my life. Her love and devotion to our family runs deep and the older I get, the more impressed I am with her intellect, her drive, her compassion and work ethic. She has been an enormous influence on all her children's lives - every bit as powerful as my dad, who was the greatest role model a human being could have. To my sons, Brendan, Brian, and Brady, who make me proud every day of their lives and have kept my life interesting (to say the least). To their wives, Rachael, Ali, and Colleen, all brilliant women, who keep their homes and mine full of love and laughter; and to each of my granddaughters who fill my life with great joy.*

# CONTENTS

## Acknowledgements

Many people helped make this book possible: the editors at Writer's Ally who helped me organize Wheel's chapters into a coherent structure; my two dozen beta readers who (sometimes brutally) let me know what they thought of my novel; and the scores of readers who have queried me wondering when "Book II" would be published. None of this would be possible without the endless patience and support of my wife Mary Margaret. My debt to her is unfathomable.

Area more or less under FRANKISH dominion in the time of CHARLES MARTEL

## *People of the Realm*

### Royalty

Childeric (heir to the throne, son of King Chilperic III)

### The Church

Pope Zachary (His Holiness the Pope)
Bishop Boniface (counselor to Charles Martel, Legate to
the Holy See)
Bishop Sergius (Legate to the Holy See)
Bishop Aidolf of Auxerres

### Regional Nobility

*Alemannia*
Theudebald (son of Godefred)
Scales (a commoner)

*Austrasia*
Charles Martel, mayor of the palace (dec.74)
Childebrand (stepbrother to Charles Martel)
Carloman, mayor of the palace (son of Charles Martel &
Chlotrude)
Pippin III *(Pippin the Short)*, mayor of the palace (son of
Charles Martel & Chlotrude)
Hiltrude (daughter of Charles Martel & Chlotrude)Gripho
(son of Charles Martel & Sunnichild-imprisoned 741)
Theodoald, mayor of the palace (deceased 741, murdered
son of Pippin II)
Hamar (a knight loyal to Carloman)
Gunther (a knight loyal to Pippin)
Arnot (a knight loyal to Pippin)

*Aquitaine*
>Duc Hunoald
>Waifar (son of Hunoald)
>Compte de Loches
>Comptesse de Loches (Catherine)
>Compte de Vieux-Poitiers

*Bavaria*
>Duc Odilo (son of Godefred)
>Sunnichild (wife of Charles Martel – sent to Abby at Chelles 741)
>Kovrat (an Avar General, allied with Odilo)
>Hans (son of Eta)
>Eta (a commoner)

*Hesse*
>Hodar (a local chieftain)
>Rasling (a local chieftain)
>Ucher (a local chieftain)
>Einbeck (a local chieftain)
>Immelt (a local chieftain)

*Neustria*
>Bertrada (daughter of the Compte de Laon)
>Aude (daughter of the Compte de Laon)
>Charibert, Compte de Laon
>Lord Ragomfred the Younger
>Lady Ragomfred (Miette)
>Lady Hervet
>Lady Dricot
>Lady Trinon
>Duc & Duchesse de Tricot
>Lady Hélène
>Agnès (a commoner)
>Salau (a knight loyal to Childeric)

*Lombardy*
    King Liutbrand
    Prince Aistulf (King Liutbrand's son)

# CHAPTER ONE

*Laon, 742 A.D.*

Pippin stood at the rampart, broadsword across his back, scowling at the sun as it fell toward the horizon. Although not a tall man, he was an imposing figure with the shoulders of a blacksmith and the casual grace of a swordsman. Those passing gave him a wide berth and some even chose a different path. The people of Laon had had enough of warriors. And from the looks Pippin received, they blamed him as much as Carloman for their plight.

Although Pippin's brother had never taken the city, Carloman had breached the walls and killed nearly a third of its defenders to arrest their half-brother, Gripho. The hectare-sized burial mound on the south plain was a stark testament to the cost of the siege.

Inside the city the devastation was no less evident. Scores of newly widowed women filled the main plaza, selling their household goods in a vain attempt to sustain what was left of their families. From the din of their pleading, their need was palpable.

He should have left weeks earlier but had refused to go without Bertrada. She had broken their courtship over the siege, stating she wanted nothing further to do with the brutality of his family. She had hidden in her father's house and refused all of Pippin's entreaties. And while Pippin had made it clear that he wouldn't leave without her, he was running out of time. His knights were assembling for the spring campaign. He would have to leave for Paris in the morning.

The standoff was taking a heavy toll on him. He had taken to drink and couldn't remember the last time he had slept through the night or eaten a decent meal.

Tonight, would change everything, Pippin promised himself. He even had bathed and donned fresh clothes. When he looked down over the rampart at the burial mound below, however, his confidence faltered. *Why did you have to hang that boy, Carloman?*

Something caught the corner of his eye, triggering his senses to high alert. His eyes searched the entryways on the street and checked the windows, the rooftops and alleyways. Keeping his stride casual, he changed vantage points and searched again, but failed to identify the source of the movement.

His nostrils flared and his skin prickled in the cold wind. His hand moved to the dagger at his belt. Where was the threat? His sense of jeopardy stabbed at him like sunlight off an enemy's shield.

*You're stalling*, he scolded himself. The day was ending; it was time. With a grim determination he began his trek through the city while a familiar litany gnawed at the corners of his mind. He tried to ignore it, tried to keep it buried and hidden from sight, but it rose, nonetheless, to assert itself. *What if I am not worthy?*

As he drew near Bertrada's home, his pace began to slow. And then, he stopped moving altogether. He had known knights in battle like this, too wounded to continue fighting and yet too proud to retreat. They turned to face their opponents as if the sheer force of their will could sustain them. It never did.

He turned into the forecourt of the Bertrada's villa and whispered a short prayer that this night would be different.

The Compte's servant, a portly old man, ushered Pippin into the courtyard before the villa's main door. Pippin tried to appear confident while he waited. His back was to the door when it opened. His stomach clenched at the sound. Slowly, he straightened, took a deep breath, and turned.

Bertrada stood in the courtyard, the last rays of sunlight illuminating her face and blond hair. She was dressed in a simple white robe and clutching a blue shawl to ward off the cold.

"Pippin–"

Relief surged in him as he took her in his arms, wrapping himself around her, clinging to her like a drowning man. "Oh God, Bertie. I thought I'd never see you again. I've been so lost–"

It took him a moment to realize that Bertrada stood with her arms at her sides, as if waiting for him to finish. Despair flooded through him, and he let her go.

"Bertie, I–"

"Shhh." She held her fingertips to his lips. "Please let me speak."

Bertrada bowed her head forward until it rested against his chest. She was so close he could feel the warmth of her body through his clothes.

"I will always love you, Pippin. From the day I met you I have never looked back. Do you remember the first time I kissed you?"

She looked up at him. He nodded, too afraid to speak.

"You were so surprised! A son of the great Charles Martel, you had fought dozens of battles and led armies to conquer the kingdom, but you could barely bring yourself to look me in the eye. You didn't have even the courage to take my hand."

She gave him a wry smile. "I kissed you, because if I hadn't you would have taken another month to formally court me."

Even in his anguish, Pippin smiled at the memory. It had been the best day of his life. He had been so surprised by her boldness. He still remembered marveling at the softness of her lips and the thrill that suffused his entire being.

Bertrada's hand traced the line of his jaw. "God knows I love you, Pippin. But I cannot stay with you."

Pippin tried to speak but the look she gave him brooked no interruption.

"When Carloman hung that boy, it – it changed me." She shuddered. "I finally understood how much blood was on your family's hands. Your father didn't just rule all the tribes for the Merovingian kings; he conquered them. He butchered thousands and you were right there with him."

"That boy was no innocent." Pippin objected.

"How old was he? Ten? Twelve? He was *playing* soldier. Had he been anyone else he would have lived. But Petr was the son of the opposing general. Carloman killed the son to break the father."

"I didn't hang him, Bertrada. I tried to stop the siege!"

"That doesn't absolve you of your sins. I've heard the soldiers boast of you. I've listened to the stories. They say on a battlefield you're a better warrior than Charles, better than Carloman. They say you're violence incarnate."

"Ah, Bertie!" Pippin threw up his hands, his frustration getting the better of him. "The nobles have been at war for hundreds of years! I didn't start this. But, Charles, Carloman and I have brought an end to most of it. We brought order and rule to a world in chaos since the time of Clovis. The Merovingian Kings didn't do that. We did it, in their name. I won't apologize for being good at what needs to be done."

Pippin's voice sounded loutish even to him, but it was the fury in her eyes that silenced him.

Bertrada's voice dropped to a whisper, each sentence a death knell. "Justify it however you want. I can't be part of that. I can't live my life like that. I won't marry you Pippin. I won't have your children. I won't live with the potential of seeing them hung by one of your rivals. I want a simpler life. Now that Charles is dead, you and Carloman can be mayors and carve up the kingdom, but I won't be there to wash your wounds when you get home."

Her voice caught in her throat; she was crying, "Good-bye, Pippin. Please know that I do love you." She kissed him on the cheek and turned away.

Before she reached the door, it opened, and her father stood in the doorway. He watched Bertrada escape inside before turning back to Pippin.

"I'm sorry, son."

Pippin opened his mouth to speak but his face began to falter as the full weight of her words fell upon him. He tried to compose himself, but there was nothing more to say. She was gone. He nodded his acceptance and gave himself to the darkness rising within him.

"She's just so shaken," the Compte began, but Pippin's hand rose to halt the explanation. Unable to speak he bowed to excuse himself. As he walked away, he heard the door close behind him.

❋ ❋ ❋

Pippin found himself sitting on an overturned barrel, the kind used to store arrows and rocks during battle. His back was to the rampart and his sword across his lap. He wasn't sure how long he had been there, only that his will to live was draining from him like blood from an open wound.

He had expected to feel something more - sadness or pain, rage or sorrow - something equal to the loss of a love so great. Instead, all he felt was shame.

In the space of a month, everything he loved had been taken from him and there was nothing he could have done to stop it.

First, Charles had died. While his death had shocked the kingdom, it had ruined Pippin. His father had been the lodestone of his life. And now he was gone. Making matters worse,

Charles had snubbed him at the end, making Pippin the mayor of the smallest share of the kingdom – even smaller than Gripho's. Pippin could have borne the humiliation, but his anguish stemmed from the knowledge that Charles died believing him unworthy.

As if that wasn't enough, Carloman had destroyed what was left of their family by imprisoning Charles's widow and their half-brother, Gripho. Pippin had tried to stop it but had arrived too late. There too, he had failed.

Even Trudi was gone. One of the few constants in his life, his sister had fled court to avoid the marriage Charles had chosen for her. She had crossed the kingdom for the love of the Duc de Bavaria.

All he had left was Bertrada. And now she too was gone. He felt the last tether to his life fall away.

He didn't know how long he sat there. People moved around him. They whispered. They pointed. Mothers ushered their children away from him. It mattered little. Time passed. It started to rain. Pippin didn't care.

"Ye'r scaring the children, Pippin."

Somehow, Gunther, his short, stout lieutenant, had taken up a seat next to him. Pippin didn't have the strength to acknowledge him.

"Lovely weather," Gunther said. "Was just thinkin' how nice it'd be to sit by the rampart 'n watch a cold rain wash the streets. Yes, my Lord Mayor, a grand idea! Glad to see it with you."

Pippin said nothing. Gunther waved at a woman desperately holding her cloak over her children as she passed them. "Evening, Madam, lovely night, isn't it?"

The sky opened and the rain became a deluge. Gunther shook his head as the water cascaded down his face. In the distance, a dark shape climbed the road, gaining substance as it neared. Slowly, it transformed itself into a giant of a man wearing an eye-patch and a brown woolen cloak.

"Childebrand!" Gunther called. "Join us."

"How long has he been like this?" Pippin's uncle asked.

"Ah, tis just a little rest," Gunther said. "We've been takin' in the scenery."

Childebrand peered into Pippin's eyes. "Christ. It's the blackness." He grabbed Pippin by the front of his tunic and hoisted him over his right shoulder. "Get his sword."

Pippin did nothing to react. All his attention turned back towards the abyss. It was there that he at last discovered the peril he had sensed earlier in the day. Too late, he remembered that some dangers arise from within.

* * *

"So, what do we do with him?" Gunther asked.

He and Childebrand stood inside Pippin's command tent on a field just outside Paris. Anger and frustration laced their voices as they debated how to manage the assembly of nobles without him.

Pippin could hear them; he was seated on a cot merely steps away. But the urgency of their argument failed to touch him. He hadn't spoken once in the two days since they had carried him out of Laon. They had cajoled, badgered, and threatened him in an attempt to elicit a response. But where he was, no one could touch him. Nothing mattered. The blackness had him and the howling in the corners of his mind remained at bay.

Nobles had arrived the previous evening, expecting a private audience with him, but Gunther and Childebrand turned each away with a gruff, "Not tonight, maybe tomorrow."

Now it was that tomorrow. Thousands of hooves thudded outside the tent, with the sounds of the morning assembly gathering in the field. Armor clanked; shouts for order and discipline fought to lift above the clamor; and occasionally, an odd horn blared. Soon the time would come, and Pippin would be expected to leave the confines of his tent, mount his horse, and address the nobles who had answered his call.

But he couldn't do it. The way forward was too far.

"I'll address the Assembly," Childebrand offered. "I'm Charles' brother. That should suffice."

Gunther grunted. "I doubt it. This is Pippin's first Assembly since being named mayor. Half of that lot outside has done little but complain about the succession since Charles named his sons mayor. The rest probably wish they had been pledged to Carloman. Gunther waved his hand in Pippin's direction, "He has to show he can lead them, or he won't have an army by the end of the day. Even that may not be enough."

"Christ," Childebrand said.

Pippin felt nothing.

"And that's just half the loaf. Gunther continued. "Ganelon of Mayence is stirring up the nobles. He thinks that Carloman and Pippin are incapable of avoiding civil war. He's calling for a Merovingian to be raised to the throne."

The howling inside Pippin's mind grew louder, but the darkness held.

"And Ganelon's got support. He says that without a king, there can be no peace. He even thinks Hunoald and Waifar of Aquitaine had the right to publicly renounce their oath of fealty."

At the mention of Hunoald and Waifar, Pippin's mind shifted, and he imagined himself at the side of his father's casket. He pictured Waifar desecrating the corpse and the howling became a scream in his mind.

Fury raged in Pippin's throat. "Did Ganelon say that Waifar had a right to spit in the face of my father's corpse?" Pippin stood and seized his sword.

"Pippin!" Gunther nearly tripped trying to stand.

But Pippin was already outside his tent, striding for his horse.

He rode before the Assembly, his fury propelling him

across the front of their formation. There were no more than five hundred nobles, less than half of what Pippin had anticipated. They quieted at his arrival. He searched among the knights for the object of his anger. When he completed his impromptu review, he cantered back to the center to join Childebrand and Gunther, who had taken their places before the Assembly.

"Ganelon of Mayence!" Pippin shouted.

The assembled knights exchanged confused glances with those around them.

"Ganelon!"

"Here, milord."

Heads turned within the assembly. From the rear a warhorse pushed forward, forcing the knights arrayed before it to move to one side. A large knight, his armor dark and dented, rode with grace and confidence. His standard bearer followed behind him, a youngish boy, clearly nervous at the sudden turn of events.

The knight placed himself before Pippin and leaned forward in his saddle. Silence took the field.

Pippin addressed him in a voice that could be heard by the rest of the Assembly.

"I've heard that you support Hunoald's right to renounce his oath."

Ganelon paled at the accusation, but he held himself tall and unbowed. "My lord," he began in a quiet voice.

"You speak before the Assembly!" Pippin shouted. Spittle sprayed from his lips with the outburst.

"Oh, Jesus!" Gunther whispered to Childebrand. "We have to stop him."

Pippin held up a hand to still them.

"My lord," Ganelon began again, raising his voice to the level of Pippin's. "Unlike Duke Hunoald, I am here at your service."

"Yet you support his treason!"

"I suggest that we owe fealty first to the King."

"Fealty is fealty!" Pippin roared, his face contorting. His horse pranced at the outburst. Pippin reined him in. "You placed your hands between mine and pledged fealty to me! Hunoald renounced his oath and named himself my enemy. His son Waifar spat in the face of my father's corpse. Do you still believe Hunoald has a right to renounce his oath?"

"I'm here in your service, milord" the knight replied. "Yet, I suggest that there is a higher-"

Pippin spat in the knight's face. Sputum ran down Ganelon's forehead and into his eyes. Rage took his face, but with an effort, he suppressed it. He quietly removed his gauntlet and found a cloth to wipe away the mucus.

"I am no enemy, my Lord." He replaced his gauntlet.

Pippin spurred forward and backhanded Ganelon across the face.

A deep guttural roar erupted from the knight's throat and the sound of blades being drawn sliced through the air.

Ganelon struck first with an overhand blow. Pippin parried with his sword and Ganelon struck again.

"Christ!" Gunther spurred his horse to intervene. "Pippin, you have no shield or armor."

"Get back!" Pippin never took his eyes off Ganelon.

It was clear that Ganelon also recognized his advantage. As the two knights converged, he stood in his stirrups and rained down blow after blow, forcing Pippin to parry with his sword high above his head. Ganelon punched forward with his shield and nearly knocked Pippin out of his saddle.

Again, Ganelon pressed the attack and again Pippin fell back, parrying ineffectively with his blade. As his arms grew tired, Pippin realized his vulnerability and fear pricked the hide of his anger. Ganelon pressed again. Pippin pulled hard on his reins, forcing his warhorse to rear and slash at Ganelon's mount with its hooves. The knight from Mayence pulled back.

"You, impudent whelp!" Ganelon shouted. "You aren't worthy enough to be a son of Charles."

Pippin's head snapped up at the mention of his father's

name and a subtle change came over him. He pushed aside his anger. His movements quieted; his back straightened and his shoulders dropped. Then he charged. Ganelon countered and the two knights raised their blades in unison. As the distance closed between them, Ganelon's sword arced high overhead, hacking down in a killing blow meant for Pippin's skull.

Checking his mount, Pippin pulled to the side and ducked Ganelon's blade. The knight's momentum carried him far over his horse's head and left him exposed and off-balance. Pippin struck him in the ear with the pommel of his sword. Ganelon sat back in his saddle stunned. Pippin grabbed the collar of the man's armor and spurred his own horse forward, dragging Ganelon backward off his mount.

Pippin scissored his legs over his saddle to dismount and sprinted to the fallen knight. Encumbered by his armor, Ganelon struggled to regain his feet. He was still struggling when Pippin kicked him in the head. The knight of Mayence crumpled. Pippin planted his broadsword in the ground, grabbed Ganelon by the hair and pulled him into a kneeling position.

Raising his fist high above Ganelon's head, Pippin let his fury have its way. He struck Ganelon on the jaw and the knight went down. Pippin pulled him to his knees and began to pummel his face. Ineffectively, Ganelon tried to ward off his attacker. Blow followed blow until Ganelon's cheek split apart and then Pippin's fist produced gouts of blood with each clout. Still Pippin's rage howled as Ganelon's blood splashed over his face, chest and arms until the structure of knight's cheek shattered and the left side of his face seemed to liquefy.

Only then did the demon leave Pippin. He looked down at the barely conscious knight and let him go.

Pippin turned to find his horse and pulled a water skin from his saddle. Returning, he emptied the entire contents over the fallen knight's head. Ganelon sputtered through misshapen lips. Pippin dragged him again into a kneeling position, this time before the sword he had planted in the ground.

He took Ganelon's hands between his and placed them on the pommel.

"I demand fealty!"

Ganelon nodded.

"You will honor my commands and prohibitions," Pippin's voice lifted to the entire assembly.

"I will honor them." Blood and saliva sprayed from Ganelon's lips.

"You acknowledge my right to punish the transgression of my commands and prohibitions."

Ganelon nodded.

"You commit yourself and your vassals to my military service."

Again, he nodded.

"You pledge tribute."

"I pledge."

"You pledge fidelity..."

"Yes..."

"You will not place my life in peril.

Ganelon shook his head.

"You will do nothing to endanger me."

Again, Ganelon shook his head

"On your life, you pledge."

Ganelon nodded.

"Say it!" Pippin barked.

"I pledge."

"So, help you, God."

"So, help me, God."

"Rise, vassal and retake your place."

Ganelon attempted to rise, and then collapsed at Pippin's feet.

Pippin turned to face the assembled knights.

"Commendation – the placing of one's hands between those of his lord – is an ancient rite, the symbol of knighthood, and the ultimate gesture of submission and honor. Without it, there would be no law. Without it there would be no government, no trade, no wealth, and no honor. Without it, there would be no peace. Fealty binds us together. It is our bond, our trust, and our conviction. I will accept nothing less from each of you. "

Pippin stared at the knights in full control of himself.

"In two days, we march south to reclaim Hunoald's oath and Waifar's head. Those who support Hunoald's treason, name themselves my enemy. Who among you supports his treason?"

Silence greeted him.

Pippin raised his sword and his voice. "Who are with me?"

"Hu-yah!" shouted a voice from the ranks.

"Hu-Yahh!" echoed the Assembly.

Pippin turned to Childebrand. "Give them their orders."

Without another word he left the field.

# CHAPTER TWO

*South of the Loire*

Three weeks later, twenty armed men ran towards Castle Loches as quietly as twenty armed men with a ladder and a grappling hook could move, their breath billowing into ragged wisps of white in the cool night air.

They stopped behind a short hedgerow to rest. It was the last of their cover. A fresh set of hands took the ladder while Pippin stole a look at the terrain ahead. The moon cast a ghostly-blue light over the landscape, draining it of color. It made the vast empty fields before them glow ominously and the castle loom black against the horizon.

They were still three hundred paces from the wall. Pippin waited for their breathing to slow.

He was doing the only thing he knew how to do: fight. It was his only way forward. When the men were ready, Pippin gave a nod and again they ran.

A hundred paces farther he stopped them again, this time huddled out in the open. Breathing deeply, he listened for the alarm. *Where was the diversion?*

Pippin had arrayed Gunther and Childebrand on the other side of the castle with the bulk of the army deployed in two large phalanxes. All day they had made a great show of moving the men and rock throwers into position. Pippin had waited until his full army was aligned before signaling to the castle for parley. He had made the Compte de Loches ride out to meet him surrounded by the full might of his assembled army.

The Compte was a small, aging man who had shown no concern for Pippin's battalions. He carried himself with great confidence and surety. After the briefest of salutations, Pippin had had the feeling that he, not the Compte, was the more vulnerable of the two.

"You didn't answer my call to arms," Pippin said. "You didn't pay your taxes. Have you renounced your vows?"

"My vow is to Lord Hunoald of Aquitaine."

"Lord Hunoald also pledged fealty."

"He renounced it on Charles's death."

"You are either loyal to your oath or you are not."

"Don't lecture me, boy. Your brother violated the succession himself by imprisoning your half-brother Gripho." The Compte spat on the ground at Pippin's feet. "My family pledges its loyalty to kings, and the mayors who serve them. So far, I don't see a king for you to serve."

Although rage lanced white within him, Pippin nodded coolly in response. It was a common refrain. At the end of his life, Charles had become so powerful that when the last Merovingian king had died, he refused to raise another to the throne. He had intended to seize it for himself. Only one thing stopped him. He had died.

None of the nobles dared rebuke Charles when he was alive. But now? Raising a Merovingian to the throne was on every rebel's lips. Even some of their allies were calling for it.

After the Compte de Loches returned to the city, Pippin gave Gunther and Childebrand his orders. "We attack tonight."

*What good was all that pageantry,* Pippin thought, *if we get caught out here in open country?* Pippin's hair was damp with sweat. A great shout suddenly erupted from the castle. Flaming arrows lofted high into the night above the wall, and the dull thud of rocks impacting stone rumbled through the ground beneath their feet.

"They're late." Pippin said to Arnot. The thin, disheveled scout smiled in response, his teeth flashing white in the moonlight. With the diversion underway Pippin and his men ran until they were at the wall.

It was so dark near the castle that Pippin could barely see. His men bent over the ladder and lifted the wooden behemoth over their heads. With a muffled groan they pushed it upright to lean against the wall. Once he was convinced that it was secure, Pippin nodded to Arnot and the man raced up the ladder and out of sight. Within moments he was back.

"Too short."

One of his men stepped forward with the grappling hook attached to a coil of rope. Taking it, Arnot again disappeared into the darkness above.

They heard a grunt, and then the clank of metal against stone, and then a scrape.

No one moved, waiting for the cry of alarm. Pippin looked up. Arnot was already pulling up the hook for another throw. Again, he grunted. Again, they heard the clank and scrape. Arnot scrambled back down the ladder and signaled for the men to follow. Pippin was first behind him.

When he reached the top of the wall, Pippin heard a shout. He climbed over the rampart to find Arnot kneeling above an inert body, wiping the blood off his knife onto the man's tunic.

"Must have heard the hook." Arnot's eyes searched the rampart for any further sign of alarm. Pippin motioned for the next man over the wall to guard their left flank. Pippin took the right. From his vantage point, he could see the bulk of the castle defenders running for the rampart on the far side of the fortress. They were shooting arrows and throwing debris down over it to fend off the main attack. Pippin frowned. The longer he took, the more men would die.

When all twenty knights were on the wall, Pippin signaled for the men to use knives and led them along the rampart towards the side gate to find stairs leading downward. Twice, they encountered guards. Each time, blades flashed in the moonlight and the guards drowned in their own blood. Pippin found a narrow stairway leading down and they descended.

The tower itself was well lit and protected by a huge oak door. Two guards stood out front, spears in hand. Huddled in the shadows, Pippin signaled to Arnot. The tall, lanky scout nodded, adjusted his clothing and walked out of the darkness. With a shortened gait and his hand clutching his buttocks Arnot ambled into the light with a pained look on his face. His path took him close to the tower door. The guards stiffened at his approach.

"One hell of a time to shit!" Arnot shook his head. His voice carried the thick nasal twang of the region. One of the men smiled in amusement. Arnot shuffled closer. "God, I'm in pain!"

With a speed that made Pippin blink, Arnot pulled a knife from his pantaloons and slashed it across the throat of the guard to his left. With his other hand, he pinned the second guard to the door and brought the point of his newly bloodied knife beneath the man's eye.

"Not a sound," Arnot hissed, all traces of his accent gone. He waited until Pippin and the men had moved into place, and then whispered in the guard's ear. "Get them to open the door." The knife point touched the man's eye.

"Etienne, Jean-Paul!" the guard screeched, banging his glove on the door. They heard sounds from behind the door and waited for the latch to pull and the door to swing inward.

Pippin was inside first, shouldering the door and planting his knife into the neck of the first man to appear. He shoved him back through the doorway.

The guards inside scrambled to meet the attack. Pippin spun right, towards his blind side, slashing with his knife. His blade sank into the chest of a large burly guard wielding a knife of his own. Without breaking stride, Pippin sprinted past him into the swarm of soldiers drawing swords. Knowing that he would soon be at a disadvantage, Pippin lowered his right shoulder and charged. He caught the nearest guard square in the chest. Together, they crashed into the two men behind him and all four went down on the floor.

Pippin tried to get up, but one of the guards had pinned his head to the floor with an elbow. Pippin jabbed his blade into the man's abdomen repeatedly, until the force behind the arm went limp. Blood oozed over Pippin's body. Someone began kicking his head. Pippin tried to roll to his left but was trapped by the legs of the other guards who fought above him. He stabbed upwards at their groins blindly.

Someone bit his leg and Pippin howled with rage. He kicked down trying to break free. Someone fell on top of him, then another. Pippin managed to loosen his legs and struggled to shove his way free. He pushed his way out of the pile and climbed to his feet, his knife sweeping to find its next target.

The fighting was over.

"Very graceful, milord." Arnot smiled. "Was that a new school of knife fighting? I've never seen anything quite like that."

Pippin grunted and searched the dead until he found a heavy key ring looped into one of the guard's belts. Signaling for his men to follow, Pippin headed through the guardroom and up into the tower. They mounted circular stairs until Pippin found a small door on the gate-side of the tower. He attempted several keys before one caught. With his knife drawn, he opened the door.

It opened onto an empty catwalk leading out over the gate. He and Arnot climbed out onto it and found the huge bar holding the gate closed. It took four men to drag the bar out of its latch.

Grinning widely, Arnot pulled out a small horn and blew into it three times. They heard a muffled shout from outside the side gate and watched as the huge doors of the castle pushed inward. Several hundred men, who had been waiting outside in the darkness, poured through the open space. They had breached the castle.

Defenders quickly rushed to stop the incursion, but they were too late and too few. Pippin's men slashed their way through them, cutting a bloody swath through the court-yard inside the gate. They flooded up the ramparts and onto the wall. Pippin and his men rushed outside and watched the army make short work of taking the castle. Soon, the defenders were yielding in large numbers and the castle was his.

Pippin climbed down to the courtyard just inside the gates and waited. It was Childebrand who brought the Compte to him. In the meager torchlight, the man looked like a dwarf, especially standing next to Pippin's tall uncle.

The Compte de Loches, however, seemed undeterred by his new circumstances. He approached Pippin with a swagger and a sneer that Pippin found amazing.

"I expect you to honor the vow Lord Hunoald swore, first to my father and then to me," Pippin said.

"I will honor nothing," the Compte de Loches replied.

"Offer me your hands and I will withdraw, leaving you your castle, your treasure and your dignity. You'll be held only to the same taxes and fealty due in past years. Your people will be unmolested and unharmed."

The Compte looked at the blood that covered Pippin's armor. After a long moment, he shook his head. "You are no king." The noble's eyes did not waver.

Without relinquishing the Compte's gaze. Pippin called out his orders. "Destroy the gate. Find his treasure. Take his wife and children hostage." After a moment's thought, he added, "Burn the castle."

Childebrand raised an eyebrow. Pippin understood his concern. Castles were assets not easily replaced.

"I want Hunoald, and those who support him, to know that I'm coming," Pippin glanced back at the Compte and added, "And every noble in Aquitaine should know the current price for breaking his vow.

* * *

After burning the Castle at Loches, news preceded Pippin's army on his march south. A week later, it took only a brief parley with the Compte de Vieux-Poitiers before the gates of the city opened wide to escort Pippin and his host inside. Fealty was restored, taxes garnered, and men impressed to serve Pippin's growing, but still meager army.

He had seized a small barracks within the castle and sat alone, wondering how many more castles south of the Loire he would have to take before Hunoald and Waifar left the safety of their stronghold in Toulouse to fight him. He had delayed in Loches hoping to draw them out, but they had ignored the bait. Now he had two castles. How many would be necessary? Five? Six?

After a brief knock, Gunther poked his head in. "Y'eve got guests." He scratched the stubble on his face. "Carloman and twenty knights."

Pippin nodded and Gunther closed the door. He hadn't spoken to Carloman since the siege at Laon. What would bring Carloman here? What was left to say?

Tilting back his chair, he slapped the back of his head against the wall behind him. The dull sound of his skull hitting stone reverberated through the small room and mimicked the sensation he felt inside his head. With an unerring sense of timing, he repeated the motion every few moments, punctuating the raging voices in his mind as he recalled moments from his childhood.

"I can beat you!" Pippin was eight, shouting at a twelve-year-old Carloman. Carloman hit him in the nose so fast Pippin never saw it coming. He lay at Carloman's feet, blood streaming from his nose.

"Don't ever think that again," his brother said. "I don't want to have to kill you."

*"Deus, tu conversus vivificabis nos. Et plebs tua lætabitur in te."* He was nine. Boniface and Carloman were praying above a kneeling knight. Pippin was supposed to be praying with them.

The man's hands were tied to a short post erected before him. He was naked to the waist. A whip snaked across his back, summoning huge welts of white and pink flesh. The sound made Pippin flinch with every crack. Boniface and Carloman never even looked up.

He was ten and dressed in his finest clothes. Childebrand was there. They were saying goodbye to father and mother. He was being sent away. Charles stood with his hand on Carloman's shoulder. Pippin struggled to fight back his tears. Carloman's eyes were gloating.

Suddenly, a knock on the door brought him back to the present.

"Come."

Gunther opened the door and Carloman strode into the room. Boniface was with him. Carloman seemed surprised by the small confines of the space.

Pippin sat behind a table facing Carloman. Only an uneaten plate of food and his broadsword separated them. The latter lay at an angle across the table, its pommel to Pippin's right, and a short distance from his hand. He briefly pondered the significance of his brother's presence.

Gunther left the room, but still Pippin didn't speak.

"You do not welcome us, brother?" Carloman looked to Boniface as if surprised. Carloman crossed the room, and as he did, Pippin sat up and covered the pommel of his sword with his hand. Only then did Pippin's gaze lift to meet Carloman's.

Carloman sighed. "Is that really necessary, Pippin?"

"I don't know. The last time I saw you, you had your sword at Gripho's throat."

"He assaulted a priest!"

"Who was trying to murder him. He is our brother, Carloman"

"Half-brother."

"Still, you seem entirely too comfortable killing off members of our family."

"I haven't killed anyone in our family."

"Can you honestly say that if I hadn't interceded, Gripho would still be alive?"

Now it was Carloman's turn to be silent. He moved to Pippin's left. Pippin's hand tightened on the sword. Carloman paused, and then reached down and took a piece of chicken off the uneaten plate. He lifted it to his lips and took a bite.

"Why are you here, Pippin?"

"I should ask you that."

"Our battles are in the east, not in the west."

"Have you forgotten that Waifar spat in the face of father's corpse? Have you forgotten how Hunoald renounced his oath of fealty? I can think of no more important battle to fight."

"The Gascones don't fight the way we do." Carloman sat on the corner of the table and took another bite. "They hide in their castles and force you to expend all our resources in siege. How many castles can you take this spring? It will take years – three, maybe four – to best Hunoald and all his castles, if you have the men and resources. He wants you to attack. He wants us to split our armies. He knows that Odilo is building an army in Bavaria to mount a rebellion. And," Carloman paused for effect, "He knows Theudebald is back in Alemannia."

Pippin's eyes narrowed at the name. Theudebald was a monster Charles had banished years ago.

"We can't let him stay." Carloman put down the chicken bones.

"I want Hunoald." A vein throbbed at Pippin's temple.

Carloman nodded. "So do I." He pulled a map from his coat and spread it lengthwise across the table. "But our spies tell us Odilo is raising an army to rival ours. He's using Sunni and Gripho's arrest as a rallying cry for Bavaria."

"What did you think would happen when you arrested

her? She's a Bavarian princess."

Carloman was clearly ignoring him. "You don't have to be a Byzantine empress to recognize our vulnerability. The Saxons are encroaching here in the northeast. Odilo is here." He pointed to the southeast. "Theudebald is between them in Alemannia, amassing an army to cross the Rhine. If he does, it will be a dagger at the throat of Burgundy. And, as I recall," Carloman said. "Burgundy is yours to protect."

Pippin continued to regard him coolly. Carloman continued. "If we're to survive this, you and I must be united. If not, the kingdom will be torn apart."

Again, Carloman waited for a response. But Pippin said nothing. "Don't be naïve. You don't have the treasure to sustain this." Carloman said. "The bulk of our funds still come from the Church and the bishops have little time for your vengeance."

Pippin leaned forward over the table and traced his fingers along the colored lines drawn across the map. "The world without Gripho."

Carloman frowned. "You and I split the kingdom. You rule the south and west - Neustria, Burgundy, Provence and if we take it back, Aquitaine. I'll take the north and east - Austrasia, Thuringia, Alemannia, and Bavaria."

"Now I can see why you want me to fight in the east."

"Don't be childish. All you have to do is look at the map to know I'm right."

Pippin didn't look at the map. He held Carloman's gaze, his eyes furious. When he spoke, his voice was a cold whisper.

"You're not right, Carloman. You haven't been right for a while. You had no right to attack Gripho. You have no right to keep him imprisoned. You had no right to send Sunnichild – our stepmother – to a nunnery. You made those decisions alone without so much as a token effort to obtain my consent. We could have avoided this civil war. *I* would have avoided it."

Pippin sat forward. "You've condemned me to a lifetime of bloodshed and now you are here to ask my help in fighting your battles?"

Carloman flashed with anger. He pounded the table. "Gripho is pagan! He burned a church! That couldn't be tolerated. Surely you understand that! He is a sin against God."

"You are not the Pope."

"I am a warrior in Christ!" Carloman raised his fist as if to strike the table again, but with some visible effort, held himself in check. "I didn't come to argue. You must know that this kingdom will never tolerate a pagan state. It's been Christian since the time of Clovis. Even the eastern duchies have officially accepted Christianity."

"Only because we forced them to swear on the cross."

Carloman began to pace. "We can't tolerate heresy. It will divide the kingdom."

Carloman looked to Boniface for support. The bishop nodded but said nothing. "And now Theudebald has returned to renew the threat. I don't need to remind you of what he is capable."

"I shouldn't have to remind you of father's funeral." Pippin said.

"At least, I was there."

Pippin threw the table aside and stormed towards Carloman. Carloman caught Pippin's punch and pulled his brother in close to prevent a second blow. "Stop it, Pippin! I didn't come to fight."

Pippin punched with his left fist, catching Carloman on the ear. Carloman roared in anger.

"Enough!" Boniface was between them, pulling them apart.

Carloman released Pippin and turned away. When he spoke, his voice was laced with regret. "I'm sorry Pippin. I spoke in haste. You couldn't have known that he was going to die. None of us did."

Pippin had retreated to the darkest part of the room. When he spoke, his voice was almost a whisper, hollow and distant.

"I failed him long before that."

Boniface put his hand on Carloman's shoulder and nodded towards the door. Carloman left and closed the door behind him.

"What do you want, Boniface?" Although Pippin held no anger towards the bishop, he was suspicious of the man's motives. He had always been at Charles right hand – and now he was at Carloman's.

"I don't care how the two of you split the kingdom," Boniface said. "I came for another purpose."

"Beware, Bishop. I am not my brother. I am no Knight in Christ."

"No. I suppose, in that, you are more like your father." Boniface chuckled. "Your father was a man of faith, Pippin, but his religion was Francia. Where the Church's needs matched his own, he was our strongest advocate. Where not…" he shrugged.

"Why are you here?"

"Carloman wasn't entirely truthful with you."

Pippin's head came up, but Boniface held up his palm, urging patience.

"I knew Charles was dying. He kept it from everyone else – even his wife and his children – in the hopes of preventing civil war. He was consumed by the succession. No detail was overlooked, no decision made without debate. Charles kept himself alive until he was sure the kingdom had passed safely into your hands and those of your two brothers. Once that task was complete, he felt he could leave this life for the next. Unfortunately, he didn't foresee the possibility that Sunni and Gripho would renounce their faith to form a pagan state."

Pippin said nothing.

"Had I known that you and Trudi were taking your leave the night before he died, I would have stopped you. Unfortunately, I didn't, and neither of you were present to receive his blessing."

"Why did he favor Gripho?" Pippin couldn't keep the pain from his voice.

Boniface seemed to puzzle over the question until he guessed its source. "Neustria," he said. "You want to know why he gave Gripho Paris and a bigger portion of the kingdom?"

Pippin nodded. "At least I had helped Charles conquer the kingdom. Gripho barely saw a battle."

Boniface sighed. "You know Charles's history. You know he was a bastard who usurped the Agilolfings. Charles knew they would challenge the succession. Since Sunnichild is related to them, he gave part of Neustria to Gripho in hopes of preventing a civil war. Essentially, he was bribing them."

"He could have told me."

"He did ask for you. But you and Trudi were already gone."

Silence permeated the room.

"Was he in pain?"

Boniface nodded. "Charles's death was very painful."

Again, there was silence. Pippin's eyes looked away from the bishop. When he spoke, his voice was little more than a whisper.

"Why did he send me away?"

Boniface looked confused.

"To Rome," Pippin turned, his jaw set. "Why did he send me to Rome?"

"When you were ten?" Boniface harrumphed. "The same reason he wanted Trudi to marry Aistulf the Lombard. He wanted an alliance on the Roman peninsula to secure the southern border."

"Why didn't he send Carloman?"

"Carloman was older. Charles wanted him here."

"But not me."

"Carloman was already a knight. You were still a boy."

"I never saw her again. She died while I was away."

Boniface frowned. "Your mother didn't want you to see her suffer."

"She knew she was dying?"

Boniface nodded. "She didn't want that to be your memory of her."

Silence recaptured the room.

"Why are you here, Boniface?"

"Your father asked a favor of me. Boniface put his hand on Pippin's shoulder. "He asked me to give you his blessing."

Pippin looked up, his eyes pained.

"That's my only purpose here." Boniface took him by the arms. "Will you accept it from me?"

Slowly, Pippin nodded. Boniface rested his hand on Pippin's head. He made the sign of the cross and when he spoke, emotion filled his voice.

"I give you this blessing as asked, by Charles, son of Pippin, son of Ansegisil." Boniface paused. "'My son, in sight our Father in Heaven, I give you my blessing and the blessings of my father and of his father. I give you my word to uphold, our name to defend, our blood to protect, and our will to be victorious. Our line is sworn to preserve the might of Francia and to champion the will of God. I leave this solemn task in your hands and in the hands of your children and your children's children. Be fearless in the face of our enemies and humble in the hands of the Father. Be true, my son. And may the blessing of God the Father, the Son, and the Holy Ghost come upon you and remain with you forever and ever. Amen."

Boniface stopped for a brief moment and laid his hand on Pippin's shoulder. "I have known no man who loved his children more."

The tears streaming down his face surprised Pippin. He tried to curtail his emotions, but they welled up inside until silent sobs shook his frame. His father's death had left a hole in his life; one he did not know how to fill. The bishop opened his arms wide and Pippin fell into them, weeping.

❋ ❋ ❋

"Excommunicate her."

Boniface scowled. Not only had Bishop of Auxerres interrupted his morning meal, the man hadn't even bothered to say, "good morning." And as a legate to the Holy See, Boniface deserved, at the very least, a "Your Grace." Nevertheless, Aidolf *had* detoured from Tours to meet him, spending the better part of a day on horseback to reach Vieux-Poitiers, so Boniface ignored the discourtesy, wiped his mouth on a napkin, and pushed away his food.

There could be only one "her" to whom he was referring: Charles's daughter, Hiltrude. "We have no grounds to excommunicate."

"She's pagan."

"A malicious rumor, nothing more."

Boniface picked up his cup and plate and moved past Aidolf to place them on the counter.

"How long are you going to ignore the fact that these Bavarians genuflect when you're with them and worship trees when you're not?"

"Trudi is not Bavarian," Boniface said. "I baptized her myself and taught her the liturgy. She has done nothing against the church. Leaving her father's house to escape an arranged marriage might be embarrassing, but it is no crime against God."

"It's an insult to her two brothers. As mayors, they should denounce her."

"That's up to Carloman and Pippin."

"She must be with child."

At this, Boniface raised an eyebrow. "Then at least she had enough sense to marry the man. Perhaps you take this incident too seriously."

"Odilo's leading the revolt!" The bishop fumed. "Marrying Trudi legitimizes the rebellion. If Carloman and Pippin don't crush them soon, there will be two recognized religions in the land.

A small spray of spittle accompanied Aidolf's words.

"If they have a son, he'll be the grandson of Charles Martel, rivaled only by Carloman's son, Drogo. What if Trudi raises the boy to be pagan? If he makes a claim to be mayor, it may be the Bavarians who elevate the next king to the throne, not you or me. And if they raise a pagan, it will set back the church for a hundred years.

"I know you have a soft spot in your heart for this girl, Boniface, but this marriage is a disaster. We must act now to stop it."

Boniface frowned. Although arrogant, the bishop had a point. If Trudi were pregnant, the child would have a legitimate claim to Charles's legacy as mayor of the palace.

"I won't excommunicate her," Boniface said. "She has violated none of God's laws."

"Then we should condemn her from the pulpit. We should bring down the weight of the church against her legitimacy and that of her offspring."

"We're not even sure she is with child!"

"What else would send her halfway across the world?"

Boniface put his arm on the shorter bishop's shoulder. "Don't condemn her yet from the pulpit. Raise questions about her sudden scandalous behavior. Express concern for what her marriage to Odilo might mean. If she is with child and delivers her babe too soon, you'll have your answer and can rightly condemn her. Her child must never be in a position to contest Carloman's son, Drogo."

Seeing the surprise on Aidolf's face at this sudden capitulation, Boniface smiled. "Although I have a certain fondness for the girl, the Church has already chosen its champion, Bishop. And, without question, it is Carloman."

Aidolf frowned. "What of his younger brother?

"Pippin is a force...and will be a powerful mayor, but our interests align with Carloman. He is a true man of God. It's quite fortunate that he's the only one with a male heir."

Aidolf looked as if he was about to say something further but was distracted by the appearance of a young monk who arrived to clean the dishes. The boy was comely with brown curly hair and a strong chin. Aidolf's eyes seemed to rest on the monk far longer than was necessary.

Boniface coughed to regain Aidolf's attention and dismissed the boy.

"Let's turn to our more discreet endeavor." Boniface waited for the boy to leave. "I called you here because I've had a change of heart. Although, I once had harbored hopes that Charles would claim the Merovingian throne as his own, the opportunity was lost with his demise.

"Half of Francia will soon be in rebellion. Raising a Merovingian to the throne will help resolve questions about the succession and hopefully quell the rebellions in the east and in the south. If we're blessed by heaven above, it may even restore some of the Church lands Charles confiscated.

"Will the mayors agree?"

Boniface belched. "Carloman will see the logic of it. I don't yet know about Pippin."

"You better bring the younger brother in line. Without a king, all Francia will be at war."

"The question is moot until we find someone of the royal blood."

They both secretly had searched in vain for months trying to find a surviving member of the royal family. The Merovingian line was on the verge of extinction. The once great line of Frankish Kings had waned across the centuries as their military power shifted into the hands of regional mayors. And when Charles Martel subjected every mayor within the kingdom, he assumed their authority and ruled as if he were king. When the last Merovingian died, Charles left the throne vacant for the last four years of his life. Now that Charles was dead, the question of royal succession was once again in play.

"Then my news is quite timely." Aidolf grinned.

"You found someone?"

"Childeric, son of King Chilperic III,

"I didn't know Chilperic had a son."

"With Charles Martel's ambitions for the throne, you can imagine why that knowledge might have been suppressed."

"Where did you find him?"

"He was sent to be raised by a rich, noble, Neustrian family with an estate outside of Narbonne. He appears to have been waiting for just this moment to make his presence known"

"Which noble family?"

"Ragomfred."

Boniface frowned. Ragomfred was no friend. He had allied with the Agilolfings and challenged Carloman's right to succession.

Aidolf laughed, apparently enjoying the discomfort this caused. "Yes, that Ragomfred. His estate in the south is quite large."

"I doubt that Carloman and Pippin will support him."

Aidolf spread his arms wide. "You and I know that the king's power is mostly ceremonial, but it gives the mayors legitimacy. Once Childeric gets to Paris, we announce that the Church supports him. That will give the rebellions the fig leaf they need to drop their swords. The boy mayors will have to accept it. Besides, Childeric's the only one left. The bloodline is at an end. All the civil wars over the last fifty years have decimated their progeny."

"Is Childeric lucid?"

"Yes."

"His hair and beard are long?"

"As are his fingernails," Aidolf waved his own. "He's a real Merovingian."

Boniface frowned. The Merovingian line of kings was rumored to have mystical powers. They wore their hair, beards and fingernails long and were rumored to be conjurors and enchanters. They claimed they were descendants of Mary Magdalene and could see the future. The few Boniface had met years ago were a strange lot, touched by a madness that afflicted their line.

"Is he willing?" Boniface said.

"He seemed almost impatient. It was as if he were waiting for me."

"How quickly can he be in Paris?"

"They're already making their way. He should arrive within the month. He'll stay with Lord and Lady Ragomfred until you can talk our two young mayors into elevating him."

That, Boniface thought, might take some time.

"Oh," Aidolf said, "I nearly forgot. He asked me to relay a message to you."

"Childeric?" No one was supposed to know that he and Aidolf were talking, let alone laying the groundwork for a new king.

Aidolf put his hands in the air. "I didn't tell him. He just seemed to know."

"What's the message?"

"He said, 'Tell Boniface, his Bible will not save him.'"

Suppressing a shiver, Boniface made the sign of the cross.

# CHAPTER THREE

*Regensburg, Bavaria*

T rudi sank into the bath's near-scalding water, allowing the heat to permeate her aches and pains. Sliding down the brass tub until her nose was just above the water-line, she watched little tendrils of vapor lift off the water and curl before her eyes. Here, in Odilo's elegant suite of rooms with its rich tapestries and ornate furnishings, she was safe.

She began to cry. No more running. No more fighting. No more hiding. Soon sobs shook her whole frame and she let them come. After all she had been through, she was here in Regensburg and Odilo still loved her. She held onto that truth despite the lies she was going to tell him.

It had taken her three months to reach him. Three months! It should have taken three weeks. But, in that time her entire world had changed.

She had fallen in love with Odilo at her father's court during last year's Fall Assembly. Although he was older than Trudi, she had been taken by Odilo's tousled looks and boyish charm. It didn't take long for her to share his bed. She had counted on Sunnichild to bring her father around, but Charles surprised them all by promising Trudi's hand to Prince Aistulf of the Lombards. Furious, Trudi had fled Charles's court in the middle of the night with the help of her brother Pippin.

How was she to know that her father would die that very night? Charles might have relented in time, but not Carloman. He and Aistulf chased her across the kingdom. They ambushed and killed the guard Odilo had sent to meet her and forced her into hiding as she made her way from Quierzy to Regensburg.

If it hadn't been for Bradius, she would have never made it.

Bradius. Just thinking his name, produced more tears. An outlaw pagan knight, he was nothing like the men she knew. He was noble, devout, fierce-and damaged. For someone who had suffered a life of violence, he had been so tender that it made Trudi's heart ache. It was Bradius's child she was carrying. It was Bradius who had helped her avoid capture.

Aistulf had killed him without ever even knowing his name.

With the help of Tobias, one of Bradius's lieutenants, she again had avoided capture and made it all the way to the banks of the Danube where they were attacked by one of Carloman's knights. They barely survived. When she arrived at the gates of Regensburg, she was wounded and dressed in men's clothes, leading a horse with Tobias draped across the saddle. The guards had laughed at her. They laughed all the harder when she announced she was there to wed Duc Odilo.

But Odilo had swept her into his arms, dirt, blood and all, and carried her across the fort to his palace and his suite of elegant rooms, shouting for assistance. He sent guards to care for Tobias and ordered his household servants to prepare a hot bath for Trudi and fresh dressings for her wounds,

Trudi let him indulge her.

When she emerged from the bath, an attendant – a large, stout middle-aged woman named Eta – applied a fresh poultice to her shoulder and bound her wounds with all the rough competence of a surgeon. She then presented Trudi with a clean shift and a modest dress that, although snug around the waist, fit her quite comfortably. With the brisk pull of a comb,

Eta freed the knots from Trudi's hair and gave her a short grunt of approval before sending her downstairs for dinner.

Word of Trudi's arrival had spread through the city and half of the Bavarian nobility had already joined Odilo in attendance. After some prompting, Trudi regaled them with the tale of her perilous, three-month journey from Quierzy to Regensburg–omitting, of course, any mention of Bradius.

The nobles chuckled at her ability to elude Aistulf and grew furious at Carloman's ambush of her Bavarian guards. As Trudi warmed to her audience, she imbued her story with colorful details and not a little embellishment.

She caught Odilo's eyes and watched as they sparkled with delight. He was as she remembered him, rugged, handsome, and a bit disheveled. And he looked at her as if he wanted to take her right there with all his court in attendance. It gave her confidence, and her story grew with its telling.

She was near the end of her journey, describing the attack within sight of their fortress, when one of Odilo's knights laughed.

"It's already a good story, milady. No need to lie."

"I'm not." Trudi said, taken aback. "He attacked just before we reached the fort."

"And you killed him yourself?"

"Yes."

"Not your man Tobias?"

No amount of insisting would convince them. They laughed and told her how lucky she was to be alive.

Blood rushed to her cheeks. Despite her exhaustion, Trudi stepped forward to challenge the bellicose knight, but a look from Odilo brought her up short.

"I can assure you, gentlemen, she is every bit the warrior she claims to be," Odilo stood with his hands up to stop further quarrel. "She was even trained by Fulrad, Charles's captain of the guard. She used to spar with Charles's knights. I've seen it myself!"

Although Trudi was grateful for his intervention, she had the feeling that no one believed him either.

* * *

To Trudi's relief, Odilo asked for her hand in marriage that evening. In her condition, every day counted. By her calculations, she would already deliver at least a month early, if not sooner. If Odilo had delayed the wedding, it would be unlikely that she could carry off the ruse that the babe was his. Just to be sure, she went to his bed that very night.

His rooms were dark, with just a sliver of moonlight illuminating the chamber. He leapt out of bed and she was in his arms before he had taken two steps. His embrace was as she remembered it, gentle but urgent in his need. He pulled her face to his and kissed her and bent to carry her like a bride to his bed.

She stopped him. "Careful. I'm wounded." To go through with this, Trudi needed to be in control. She needed to keep her emotions at bay and concentrate what had to be done.

With grim determination, she took Odilo's hand, led him to his bed and untied his shift. He stood naked before her, already half-aroused. She pushed him down onto the bed and took off her own shift, wincing with the effort.

She stood before him, watching him watch her. She took a step towards the bed but as she did, a mental image of Bradius assaulted her. Her breath caught in her throat. Grief and self-loathing filled her but still she crawled into the bed, straddled Odilo's body, and took hold of his erection.

His hips thrust upward in response and she caressed him, slowly making a circular motion with her hand. When he groaned, she leaned forward to kiss him on the mouth and guided him, sitting back to take the length of him inside her.

In the darkness, Trudi could hide her tears. It filled her

with remorse to be so cruel. Yet, she could not abort Bradius's child and she wouldn't raise it as a bastard. This was the only way forward.

She had loved Odilo, once. She tried to remember herself in love with him as her hips rocked back and forth, undulating above him. Unlike other men, he had celebrated her strength. He had enjoyed her for who she was. They soon fell into a familiar rhythm that, with time, grew more rapid and Trudi surprised herself by groaning with pleasure.

She stopped, embarrassed by her body's betrayal.

Odilo looked up at her, his eyes arched in a question.

"Shh." She put her finger on his lips, feeling guilty for what she was doing to him. *I will love Odilo*, she promised herself. *I will find a way back to him. Bradius is dead and Odilo deserves more than a shadow marriage.*

She shook her head to clear it of her doubts and grief. Odilo looked up at her like a love-besotted youth and she smiled back at him. She leaned down to kiss him as her hips rolled beneath her. He moaned in response and she let herself give into the moment, her passion mounting with his.

He climaxed before she could and she slid off of him, nestling herself beneath the crook of his shoulder. She felt warm and safe and content to be with him.

For now, that would have to suffice. At least, she was safe.

❉ ❉ ❉

They decided on two ceremonies, one in the church, to protect Trudi's reputation with her brothers and Boniface, and the other under the ash for Odilo and his pagan brethren.

The church ceremony was private, with only a small wedding party. Led by the Bishop of Regensburg, it was a perfunctory affair. The Bishop, a small man with rodent-like features, lorded over the ceremony facing the altar and running through the Latin mass as if it were for his own purposes. Odilo knelt when he was supposed to and stood when it was required. Beyond that, Trudi marveled at his ignorance of the church ceremony. At home in Quierzy, everyone attended mass.

Tobias stood for her at the wedding, giving her hand to Odilo and tying the marriage bond around their joined hands. He dutifully played the role of the indignant father, preventing the wedding party from following Odilo when the newly married couple retired to bed.

This time when they made love, Bradius failed to haunt her thoughts and it allowed Trudi to rediscover the passion she had once known for Odilo.

In contrast to the Christian wedding, the pagan ceremony was a lavish affair attended by most of the nobles at court. Back home in Quierzy, Trudi had received instruction in the pagan religion by her stepmother, Sunnichild. Her training hadn't progressed very far, but Trudi had fully embraced the spiritual and physical facets of the religion, even celebrating the rite of fertility with Odilo. It had awakened in her a profound sense of physical and spiritual power.

Even so, she knew enough about the upcoming rite to be somewhat intimidated. It was well beyond anything a woman from the west normally would experience.

Conducted in the countryside at dusk, the evening had an almost mystical feel to it from the time they arrived. Light from the bonfires and torches danced across the faces of celebrants while pulses quickened to the rhythm of drums.

The early parts of the ceremony involved a ritual where the women and men danced in separate circles. As the music progressed, the circles intertwined becoming a figure eight that then broke into a spiral that spun around Trudi and Odilo. Trudi lost count of the horns of ale she was given to imbibe and, although she didn't know the words, she tried to join in on most of the singing.

A sibyl presided over the final bonding before a large ash

tree. A grid of nine stones lay before it with a small fire on the center stone. Trudi watched as the sibyl threw dried herbs into the fire and inhaled the smoke from it deep into her lungs.

The sibyl was a short woman, with dark hair, and tattoo-covered arms. She had bones in her hair that clacked together as she walked. She held herself regally as if she, not Trudi, were the Duchesse.

Odilo and Trudi approached the fire. "This ceremony is sacred to us," Odilo warned. "It's every bit as holy as your ceremony."

"Yes, I know," Trudi said. "I just hope I have the courage to go through with it."

"It will be disastrous if you don't."

Trudi squeezed his hand in reassurance. Despite her reservations, a part of her was, in fact, excited.

When they reached the center stone, the sibyl disrobed and stood naked by the fire. Tattoos wound their way up her torso, surrounding her breasts and ending at her neckline. She turned her back and approached the ash. From the center of its trunk, she opened a door, cleverly carved into the wood so that it wasn't discernable to the eye. Behind the doors were two wooden figures; one was clearly male with a pronounced phallus, and the other female with an equally abundant belly. The sibyl handed the female to Trudi and the male to Odilo.

The sibyl turned to the crowd. "From the beginning of the world the Fates have lived among the Aesir, spinning the thread of our lives. Living here in the middle realm, we cannot see their purpose, nor know its value. All we can do is accept the brief time they afford us to live, to love, and to create. Creation is the highest form of communion and those who marry before the ash bring from the earth new life and power for us all to witness."

Standing so close to the fire, Trudi was inhaling a good deal of the smoke from the burning herbs. As the ceremony progressed, she felt as if time was slowing down for her. She watched the sibyl speak and her words seemed to surround

Trudi's body. A warm glow flowed through her and the world became only the fire, the ash, the sibyl, and the nine stones.

"We're supposed to exchange the symbols of Freya and Freyer," Odilo said, handing her the male figure. Trudi dutifully handed him the female.

The sibyl stepped to them. "We are of the earth. What is here, is everywhere. All that is in the earth is within us, and all that we become returns to the earth. The spark that gives us life is from the gods. You have come to be united under the ash?"

She looked expectantly to Odilo and Trudi.

"Yes," they both replied at the same time.

"The right of creation is sacred," The sibyl intoned. "Enter it with reverence."

As Odilo had instructed her, Trudi discarded her robe. With that act, the intimacy of the fire disappeared, and she felt the eyes of the crowd upon her. Her skin prickled in the cold air. At first, she felt panic, but seeing Odilo's eyes sparkle gave her renewed confidence. An unexpected thrill suffused her, and she stood confidently before him in the firelight. Odilo followed her lead and soon the two stood naked by the fire. Silence took the nobles in the clearing.

Trudi placed her wooden figurine next to the fire and lay down beside it, a subtle thrill creeping up her frame. Odilo followed, placing his figure next to hers. He knelt and then covered her body with his.

At this point, according to the ritual, they were supposed to copulate, but all that happened was Odilo started thrusting against her leg. Trudi waited, but nothing more happened.

"What is it?" Trudi whispered. "What's wrong?"

Odilo looked sheepish. "I don't know."

Trudi reached down with her hand to find his erection. It was soft as a wet rag. Trudi couldn't help herself; she giggled.

"This isn't at all laughable." Odilo said. "We must consummate our union."

"Consummate?" She laughed and rolled him over. "I don't want you to consummate, I want to – " and she whispered the rest in his ear.

She began to kiss her way down his torso, and it didn't take Odilo long at all to recover.

\* \* \*

Since the wedding, Trudi could count on one hand the number of days she had seen her new husband. He was so busy lining up allies for the expected war with Carloman, he was rarely, if ever, in Regensburg.

Thanks to his efforts, the fields west of the city swarmed with knights and foot soldiers encamping for the spring campaign. Thousands of tents were aligned in precise rows and, much to Trudi's dismay, more arrived every day. She longed to find a way to avoid the impending war, but there was no broaching the subject with Odilo. All her entreaties on that subject were ignored.

With the armies, of course, came merchants, moneylenders and artisans hoping to enrich themselves off the army's needs. Trudi, however, drew a line at the complementary influx of prostitutes. Using her newfound authority as Duc Odilo's bride, she forbade them from entering the fortress. As a result, a temporary city of sorts had grown up outside their walls, adjacent to the military encampment.

She had waited a month before announcing her condition. She was already getting thick about the waist and feared any further delay. Odilo had been ecstatic, as had the rest of Regensburg. She was feted from one end of the city to the other and showered with gifts for her babe. Wagers were being made on the sex of the child and it was clear that the early betting favored a boy.

When Trudi asked Odilo about the obsession with her

pregnancy, he explained that the Bavarian royalty had been devastated a generation earlier by family infighting. With Trudi's child, the nobility saw the chance for a fresh start... a new beginning for the royal family in Bavaria. It also didn't hurt that Trudi's father was Charles Martel. As the grandson of the mayor, the child would have a strong and legitimate claim to power throughout Francia.

Early on, Trudi had been careful to dress herself in a way that hid her advancing condition to preserve the illusion that the baby was Odilo's. Despite this caution, Tobias had heard gossip in the inns and taverns, speculating about the timing of her pregnancy.

"It is nothing to fear, milady," he had said. "Such talk is sport among the common folk. Most shout it down. People want their heir. And you are giving them one."

The nobles weren't so generous. She caught whispers of conversations not intended for her ears. There was speculation, to be sure. At least, no one had dared to comment about it in her presence.

* * *

Having put on a set of riding clothes, Trudi went down to the stables to pick out a horse. The stable master, however, refused to saddle a mare for her, saying something about it not being allowed.

"Who told you that?"

The man's response, of course, was a mystery to her. The accent that she had found so endearing in Odilo's speech back at court was much harsher and unintelligible among his subjects here in Bavaria. She caught no more than every third word. Getting nowhere with the stable master, she went to search for her husband on foot.

It was because of her pregnancy, she suspected. Ever since they had announced it, she had been treated as if she were made of glass.

Trudi had just about given up her search for her husband when she found him at the Northern gate greeting a small troop of men on horseback. They were covered in dust and their horses were lathered. As she drew closer, it was clear that their leader was related to Odilo. Although much larger and stronger than her spouse, there could be little doubt that the man was his kin. He had the same dark hair, the same tousled look, the same eyes, nose and mouth.

Up close, however, she began to notice differences. A deep scar twisted the man's face into a permanent smile that showed several teeth were missing. One of his eyes had a vacant look to it and his hands and forearms were heavily tattooed. He was also quite grey. Older, and more battle worn, Trudi thought as the man dismounted. But instead of embracing, he merely clasped Odilo's forearm. Something had come between them, Trudi surmised. She strode purposefully into the gathering.

At her sudden appearance, Odilo gave a start and looked to his guest. No words passed between them, but Trudi had the feeling that much was said.

She stepped forward and greeted Odilo. "Husband." Turning to the newcomer, her eyebrows arched. "Your guest looks familiar."

For just the slightest moment Odilo hesitated. "May I present my half-brother, Theudebald."

Trudi's breath caught at the name. One of Godefred of Alemannia's oldest sons, Theudebald had ruled in Alemannia when Trudi had been a little girl. His short reign had been so violent that the priests back home still used his name to scare misbehaving children into obedience. One of the stories they told had been so effective that it had troubled Trudi's sleep for years. It was said that if Theudebald deigned to sleep in a man's house, he took "the pleasure" of his host's wife in return for the honor.

Theudebald had been banished by Charles more than

a decade earlier for persecuting a bishop. A gentle man of God sent by Boniface to minister in Alemannia, Bishop Eto had arrived at the Reichenau monastery only to be seized by Theudebald and stripped naked. Saying that he "wished to send Charles a message," Theudebald had marched the poor man through the streets of Constance, whipping him in a pathetic imitation of the Passion.

Charles arrived several months later with a massive army; he forcibly removed Theudebald from office, and, to send a message of his own, stripped Theudebald naked and had him whipped him down the same streets as he had tortured poor Eto.

Trudi struggled to keep her composure. "I've heard so much about you," was all she could think to say.

Theudebald stared right through her. He made no move to respond. Trudi struggled to hold his gaze, the vacant eye disorienting her. Finally, she looked away.

Theudebald turned to Odilo. "A lovely girl." A smile took his face. "Thank you, for having me as a guest in your home."

\* \* \*

"We can't push our armies that far," Odilo complained for the third time in as many minutes. "You'll stretch our supply lines too far and leave us vulnerable to being split by Carloman and Pippin. We need to stay in the east and let them extend their lines."

"We won't need a supply line," Theudebald said. "All of Alemannia will rise to our call. If you join us, we can defeat them in one blow. We'll be fighting from our homeland. Or have you forgotten who you are now that you have your little throne here in Bavaria?"

"I am Godefred's son as much as you, Theo." Odilo leaned across the table. "But you've been gone a long time. The

Church has made great gains in Alemannia and the Hessians may not be as unified in their hatred as you think. But if we can lure Carloman and Pippin to march this far east with an invading army?" Odilo's hand slapped the table. "Then everyone will join our fight and we will best Charles's sons far from their home."

They were at dinner. The duck was cold, and Trudi was tired. The two half-brothers had talked in circles for nearly three hours and neither had yielded a point. She wondered if all of Odilo's relations were so bull-headed. She picked at the breastbone, hunting for an additional shred of meat and shifted uncomfortably on the long wooden bench they used to sit at the table.

She found it difficult to listen to her husband plotting a war against her brothers. Unfortunately, there was little she could do about it. From what she had gathered since arriving in Bavaria, it was Carloman who was provoking war with the east. By violating Charles's succession and imprisoning Sunni and Gripho, Carloman had left little choice to Odilo. Sunni was his niece and a princess of Bavaria. They had to support Gripho's claim. And by using the excuse that he was combating a "pagan uprising" Carloman was in fact instigating the very thing he sought to oppose.

The passions surrounding the conflict ran deep, far deeper than anyone in her family understood. Bradius had shown her what her family history looked like from a pagan perspective and it wasn't a flattering portrait. Her brothers were walking into a hornets' nest. She wished she knew where Pippin stood.

"And what does our little spy think?" Odilo was smiling. He must have sensed she was uncomfortable with the conversation. "What should we be, bride of mine, a lion or a snake?"

"Women are only good for two things," Theudebald barked, "and giving war counsel isn't one of them." He glared at Odilo and then turned his attention to the duck on his plate.

Silence greeted him. He ripped what was left of the bird into pieces and sucked on its bones.

Trudi ignored the rebuke. "I would suggest that you try talking with them."

"I did," Odilo said, "just after your father died. Carloman knew the consequences. I begged him not to attack Sunni and Gripho."

"What about Pippin? Has he taken the field with Carloman?"

"From the stories I've heard, he did try to intercede at Laon."

"Then he doesn't support Carloman," Trudi said. "At least not yet. If you can appeal to him, he may be able to intercede. I wouldn't want to fight a war against the two of them."

"Maybe *I* would." The anger in Theudebald's voice stunned Trudi to silence. "Maybe I want a war against both of them. Maybe I've had enough of your family meddling in the affairs of Alemannia. Maybe I want to send them a message."

His glazed eye bore into Trudi. She turned away from it to look down at her plate, blushing with anger. "Like that bishop you whipped through the streets?"

Theudebald's face went white with rage. "Your father was a liar and a murderer. Your brother is a fiend of the church who butchers women and children even as they pray before the ash. Your family is the scourge of my homeland. The fact that my half-brother married Charles's little cunt doesn't change any of that."

Trudi hissed and rose from the table. Odilo was faster. "Enough!"

Theudebald spat between them. "Send this one back to her brothers, Odilo. How do you know she wasn't sent here to betray us?"

Odilo was shaking with anger. "She tied the marriage knot before the ash and carries my child."

"So, she tells you. But you have to admit, her timing seems somewhat convenient."

Enough, she thought. Before Odilo could move, Trudi seized the knife from her plate, put her right foot on the bench and vaulted across the table. Theudebald pushed backwards off his bench, toppling to the floor and rolled to his right, away from her. He came up into a crouch on the balls of his feet.

Seeing her standing before him, knife in hand, with her day-dress billowing around her, Odilo's brother started to laugh.

"I told you, we shouldn't trust her, brother. One night, you'll wake up with that knife sticking out of your throat." Theudebald waved at Trudi's blade. "Did you really think you could have gotten close enough to cut me with that, little girl?"

Trudi slashed down diagonally across his body. Theudebald slapped aside the knife, his face snarling with contempt at her feeble effort.

Trudi, however, never meant for the blade to touch him. Her upper body followed the path of the knife, using it to build momentum as she bent double. Pivoting on her left foot, she whipped her body around, threw open her hips and kicked high with her right heel. It caught Theudebald squarely on the jaw and knocked him to the floor. Trudi stepped over him, her blade slashing downward. She slammed it into the floor next to Theudebald's face.

"You are right." Trudi seethed as she stood above him. "I am Charles's daughter. If I were you, I'd never forget that."

She walked to the doorway and turned back to face her husband. "I know what my brothers are capable of. So, should you. Talk to Pippin! See if he's willing to intervene. War is a hard thing to stop once it has started." She walked out of the hall.

* * *

Tobias was Trudi's lifeline. Her one-time guide had

stood by her, ensuring that she survived her arrival in Regensburg. Now he was her only refuge from the politics of the city. He was both her confidant and her eyes and ears in the court.

"Let's go for a walk outside the gates. You should get to know the city outside of court."

"I would love to," she said, with a gleam in her eye. "But let me change into something less grandiose. If I'm to see the city, I'd like to see it like everyone else. I don't want the attention that comes from being a Duchesse."

When she returned in a simple robe, Tobias was holding out a scarf to improve her disguise. She wrapped it around her head and covered the lower portion of her face. Tobias offered his arm and together walked out of the palace and strolled towards the arched gateway on the eastern side of the city.

The city originally had been built as a fortress by the Romans back in the fourth century after Christ. Large thirty-foot walls made of salt block faced each of the four winds and housed the entire city on over one hundred hectares of land. Over time, markets and neighborhoods had developed around the main features of the fortress: the palace, the church, the barracks, and the armory. The palace stood in the northeast corner of the fortress and shared two of its walls. It towered three floors above a small courtyard and was intended to be a fortress of its own. Noble families who had grown rich farming the surrounding countryside had built their own houses inside the fortress walls. The most prestigious of these, of course, were those closest to the palace. The same was true for the merchants and the inns operating inside the city walls. Proximity to the palace came with a price.

Once outside the fortress walls, Tobias showed Trudi the makeshift marketplace just outside the gate. She had heard that it had tripled in size since her arrival, but the sheer magnitude of it still startled her.

Brothels, ale halls and gambling dens were housed in large tent-like structures on dirt "avenues" adjacent to the soldier's camp. And, to Trudi's astonishment, whores, cutpurses, and worse plied their trade out in the open air.

Almost as overwhelming as the size of the bazaar was its smell. Without any attempt at sanitation, the odor of urine, vomit and manure was ubiquitous and overpowering.

"The prostitutes have dubbed it 'Trudiville,'" Tobias said, "in retaliation for your decision to banish them from the city."

It wasn't lost on Trudi that the whores had used the western term "ville" rather than the eastern "burg" to highlight her Frankish origins.

"Lovely. How do they stand the smell?" She held the scarf up to her nose.

"A soldier's life." Tobias said. "You should be thankful you didn't become a knight."

Trudi shook her head. "Carloman would never allow this. Black humors grow in places like this. They'll spread disease to the men in camp."

After a quick tour of the grounds, Trudi was glad she had banished the market inside the city walls. It was a violent place. On more than one occasion, Tobias had to steer them clear of a fight. When he suggested they should return to the gate, Trudi was more than ready to comply, but then she heard Theudebald's voice.

Raising her hand in signal to Tobias, she led him towards the sound while adjusting the scarf over her face. They found Theudebald outside an ale tent with two of his men. And from the slur of his voice, she was certain the man was drunk.

"We should have exposed him as an infant." Theudebald spat. "Did you see Odilo prancing with those silly mustache soldiers? You would never know he was Godefred's son. The man never left his mother's teat and now he suckles off Charles's daughter!"

Furious, Trudi moved to confront him, but Tobias pulled her aside.

"None of that, now," he whispered. "Think of the baby. If you confront him, you'll only make it worse."

No one was restraining Theudebald. "I'll make them pay. All of them! Especially Carloman and his cross-bearers."

As if springing from Theudebald's words, a lone priest strode into the marketplace across from them, holding aloft a large book.

"Shame!" The priest shouted at the throng of patrons. He was tall and lanky with dark hair and an impossibly large nose.

A Frank thought Trudi.

When the priest spoke again, the soft consonants in his speech proved it. "Shame! Shame on you sinners! Behold the Bible. Behold the book of God!"

Trudi had seen a number of bibles in her lifetime, but she was certain that few of the residents of Trudiville had ever been given the opportunity. Copied by hand in monasteries, the books were rare, and rumored to be powerful instruments of magic.

The priest singled out a prostitute who was enticing customers. A fervent flush spread across the priest's face. "Fornicator!" His voice carried through the marketplace piercing the din of its trade.

"This shall be your salvation." He held the bible aloft. "This is His word!! Pray with me for your sins to be forgiven. Pray with me that your soul may be saved from the eternal fires of Hell. Pray with me to follow the true path and I will lead you to salvation."

A small crowd gathered around the lanky priest. "I am the way, the truth, and the light,' sayeth the Lord. 'No man cometh to the Father but through me.'"

Some of the onlookers stretched out their hands to touch the big book.

"Kneel," the priest said and several of his newfound flock obeyed. He raised his hand and many of them bowed their heads. He waved the book over their heads.

"In the name of the Father, the Son and the Holy Ghost," he began.

"Fuck your ghost." Theudebald sauntered into the crowd.

"We should leave," Tobias whispered.

Trudi shook her head.

The priest turned as Theudebald came towards him. Holding the bible in front of him like a shield, he said, "The Word of God cannot be silenced by men."

Without breaking stride, Theudebald hit the priest in the face. The man went down, and the bible flew from his hands. Spinning through the air, it landed face up in the mud. Its black and red lettering looked crisp and colorful against the brown sludge of the street.

The priest tried to stand, but Theudebald kicked him in the head and again the man went down, blood covering his face. The crowd stood frozen, stunned by the sudden violence.

Theudebald spat on the priest.

"I am the way and the light," he mocked. "I'll show you the way!"

Theudebald strode to the fallen bible and stood over it, fumbling with his breeches. He pulled out his penis.

"No," the priest screamed.

"This is what I think of your book, cross bearer." A thick stream of yellow piss poured from Theudebald onto the open pages. The priest scrambled through the mud on his hands and knees and threw his body over the book to protect it. Theudebald laughed and redirected his stream to the priest's head. He pissed directly into the man's ear.

The priest took it, refusing to relinquish his grasp on the book. Steam rose from his newly drenched robe as the urine cooled in the afternoon air. Some of those who had gathered to hear the priest started to laugh and taunt the man. Finally, Theudebald's stream ran out. He smiled at the crowd and shook off the last drops.

"You don't belong here, priest. Your bible doesn't belong here. Go back where you came from or next time we'll do more than just piss on your book."

The crowd cheered as Theudebald walked away, his arms held wide as if accepting accolades for winning a tournament.

Someone in the crowd threw mud at the priest. Another stepped forward and kicked him back to the ground. Within moments a circle of four men had surrounded him, taunting and shoving him as he tried to escape. A crowd gathered and cheered as a particularly large brute hit the priest in the face with his fist. The priest crumpled to the ground.

"Enough!" Trudi was among them, using her body to shield the priest. "Stop this at once!"

At her sudden appearance, the group hesitated.

The brute sneered. "Get out of our way, little girl. Or we'll have fun with you, too." He took a threatening step towards her holding his crotch.

"Duchesse!" Tobias stepped forward to take her arm. "I'm sure these men mean no harm."

The brute stopped short, a skeptical look crossing his face.

Trudi took off the scarf that had covered her hair and stared defiantly at him. "You will leave this man alone or I will have you lashed."

The three other attackers scurried away into the crowd. Only the brute remained. He looked torn between fear and fury. Trudi had seen that look before and shifted her feet, anticipating his attack.

"Shall I call the guard, or are we finished here?" Tobias asked.

With a low growl, the brute spat on the ground. "Frankish whore." He too, bolted into the crowd.

Trudi turned to help the priest to his feet. "You were very brave, Father. You saved the book."

He brushed at the mud clinging to the cover. "I should have known not to bring it among this rabble."

"I will send guards to protect you and your bible."

The priest scowled before staring in the direction the brute had taken. "If there is war milady, I fear you will need them more than me."

"War or no war, Odilo will protect me."

The priest frowned. "Then you must pray that he survives it."

# CHAPTER FOUR

*Laon*

It was early morning, the air thick and cold and wet from the night rains. Sunlight crept over the horizon, splashing brilliantly over the sodden landscape. A small party of armed men rode south from the city on the road to Soissons. They looked small and impotent against the broad plain they crossed. Moving at a measured pace towards the horizon, their horses kicked up huge clumps of red and black mud behind them as they slogged through the swollen road.

High above them on a balcony overlooking the southern gate, Bertrada stood watching. It had been six weeks since Pippin had taken the same road south. She had stood on the same spot and prayed for him to turn his head – to look for her one last time – before he left her and Laon behind.

Bertrada had watched him ride out of sight, her heart sinking with every stride of his warhorse. Pippin's back had not wavered. When the certainty of his absence finally struck her, she had collapsed on her balcony. It had taken three days for her tears to run their course, and still she was not over him.

To bury her pain, she had thrown herself into rebuilding Laon. As the daughter of the Compte, Bertrada had much to do and was welcomed doing it. She rose with the sun to tend those who had been wounded in battle at the temporary hospital her father had constructed on the eastern side of the city. She changed bandages and bed sheets and chamber pots in a never-ending attempt to honor the service of the wounded. At lunchtime, she took food out to the workmen repairing the city walls. In the afternoon, she helped the church organize charity for the women newly widowed by the war. Before dinner, she met with her father to discuss reinvigorating trade relations with Soissons and Reims. She didn't have time to think of Pippin. And she preferred it that way.

But as she watched these new riders' progress across the plain, her features softened for just a moment and a single tear ran unchecked down her cheek.

*Why did I let him go?* She shook her head to dispel the thought and swiped at the tear with the back of her hand before turning away from the view. *Stop being a silly* cow! she scolded herself. Tilting her head back, she shook her hair out behind her and wrestled it up into a workmanlike bun.

There was a hammering on her door.

"Please, Bertie let me in!" It was her younger sister, Aude. "I've brought you some cakes and tea."

Bertrada threw on the white smock she wore for her work at the hospital and opened the door.

"Thank God." Aude blew into the room. She was a smaller version of Bertrada, though with brown hair instead of blond. "I was catching my death out there in the hall." She carried a tray with the promised tea and cakes and set it down on the table in Bertrada's drawing room.

"I have the most wonderful news!" Aude squeaked. "You will assuredly pee when I tell you!"

"You'll have to hurry, Aude," Bertrada pushed past her younger sister. "I've got to get over to the hospital."

"Oh, you'll wait for this," Aude grabbed Bertrada's hands and spun her around. Bertrada tried to hide the desolation in her eyes.

"Oh, Bertie!" Disappointment laced Aude's words. "Not again. You do recognize that he's only a man."

Bertrada tried to turn away but Aude held on tight and pulled her onto the bed. "He's not even that good looking! And all that brooding?" She made a scowling face to mimic Pippin and shuddered. "He'd never be able to have a conversation if you didn't supply him with half the words."

"You do him injustice."

"I think not. The man's a stone! If he wasn't the son of Charles Martel, Father would never have let you see him."

"I'm a grown woman, Aude. I choose who I will see."

"My point exactly! You're nearly twenty. Most men won't even look at a woman past seventeen. Why are you wasting your time on Pippin? Mayors don't marry for love. They marry for treaties."

Bertrada sighed. "I'm beginning to think you're right."

"Hah!" Aude got up to pour them tea. "I knew you'd see it my way. Now I have just the man for you."

Bertrada felt the blood drain from her face. "Oh Aude. I can't even begin to think about another man."

"Oh, you don't need to think, Bertie." A coy smile took her sister's face. "Most of them like it better if you don't."

Bertrada laughed in spite of herself. "I'm serious, Aude. I'm not yet done with Pippin. It's too soon for me to consider another."

Aude poured tea for the two of them. "That man is gone. And it's time for you to stop hiding yourself in the rebuilding effort. Oh, yes, I know that's what you're doing. You aren't that generous a soul. Fortunately, I have wonderful news."

Aude set aside her cup. "Next week, Father is taking us to Paris!" She squealed with excitement. "He's hoping to open trade discussions to help us rebuild. He and the Compte de Soissons are throwing a dinner party and you and I will be the hostesses!"

"I don't know, Aude. It's just too soon."

Aude's eyes flared and then, her mouth pouted. "Don't do this, Bertie. I'm sixteen, already past marrying age. If you don't go, Father won't let me. You must go."

Bertrada looked down at her hands. She had to admit that it wouldn't be right for her to stand in Aude's way.

Almost casually, Aude said, "Tedbalt will be there."

Tedbalt? Blood rushed to Bertrada's face. So this wasn't about Aude after all. The son of the Compte de Soissons, Tedbalt was born the same year as Bertrada and, from their earliest years, it was commonly believed that the two would marry. As children, they had played together. As adolescents, they had secretly kissed and groped their way through the awkwardness of youth. When they had turned sixteen, their fathers had even negotiated a dowry.

But that was before Pippin. All talk of dowries ended when Bertrada took to Pippin's bed. She had been so sure of herself then, and so sure of him. Her father had been furious, and Tedbalt devastated.

"What are you plotting?" Bertrada eyed her sister. "Tedbalt is married."

"Alas, the poor man is a widower," Aude corrected, her eyes alive with implication.

The news stunned Bertrada. "When?"

"Christmastime. Annette died of dysentery."

Tears sprung to Bertrada's eyes. "She was never well, was she?" She made the sign of the cross and paused to honor the dead woman with her silence. With only the slightest look of vexation, Aude bowed her head as well.

Bertrada again made the sign of the cross to close the prayer and dabbed at the corner of her eyes. "How is Tedbalt?"

"He mourned. But of late he has been seen about Soissons. They say he's returning to himself."

"That's good."

"She was never his true love."

"Stop it, Aude, I know what you're about. I won't go."

Aude patted her older sister's hand. "Then do it for me and for Father. He says it's time for you to stop thinking about Pippin. And he's right. That man will be the death of you."

Bertrada's eyes welled again. "But he loves me so."

For the first time since she entered the room, Aude expressed some sympathy. "Of course, he does." She tucked an errant lock of Bertrada's hair behind an ear and wiped away a tear with the palm of her hand. "The man's no fool. But loving a man like Pippin is never easy. You must be very sure of yourself or you'll drown."

Bertrada nodded her head, thinking for once she agreed with her sister. She was not sure of herself at all.

❊ ❊ ❊

Miette smoothed her skirts to make them more elegant, and then fluffed them out to make them look fresh. As the newly married wife of Lord Ragomfred, she had an impression to make and she planned to make it. She paced across her Paris living quarters scowling at any servants who crossed her path. At a sound from the street, she leapt to the window. Peering out discreetly, she groaned in disappointment. Would the king never arrive?

Her right hand strayed to her face as she watched the elegant and distinctive coaches rumble by on the street outside. She began playing with her eyebrow. Her fingers isolated the longest hair and instinctively plucked it.

The sharp pain brought a tear to her eye. Miette looked down on the curly black hair ruefully. When she was a child, she had picked up the strange habit and plucked all of the hair from her right eyebrow. It had taken half a year for it to grow back. *A lady of the court shouldn't act so childishly,* she scolded herself.

Born the daughter of a commoner, Miette had always known that she would marry into a noble family. Her father, Maurice, was a Paris merchant and extraordinarily wealthy. And with half of the Neustrian nobles being land-poor, there was little doubt that her dowry alone would bring a long list of suitors.

She thanked heaven that she didn't need to rely solely on her father's wealth to attract offers from the leading families of Paris. She was proud of her waif-like beauty that drew men to her in droves. She cultivated this look of vulnerability, using powders to make her skin pale against her dark features and rouging her lips and cheeks for contrast.

She also had a practiced ability to appear frail and demure. She used this on occasion to protect herself from suitors she thought inappropriate. When she was attracted to a man, however, there was nothing like a bold, provocative stare to make him weak in the knees. If she wanted to, she could drive a man wild with desire and she loved the power this gave her.

That was, of course, before her father had made *his* decision. Why he picked Lord Ragomfred to be her spouse, she would never understand. More than twice her age, the man didn't have an ounce of sexual desire left in his body. She shuddered, thinking of their wedding night. He had forced her to strip naked and to kneel before him on all fours like a dog in heat while he stroked himself. He was never able to consummate the marriage even though she had tried to help with her hand. In the end, he had blamed her for his impotence and stormed out of her room. They had been married a year and he had never once returned.

The tension this created within her was overwhelming. All through her courtship she had kept herself pure, waiting for the promised mysteries of the marriage bed. Now she would never know them. She would never know what it was like to be with a man or discover what lay behind the sly smiles of those who had. And the frustration of never being touched was unrelenting!

As if his sexual incompetence wasn't enough of a burden to her, Ragomfred loved to gamble – not in the gaming rooms, like most men – but in the politics of court. He regularly challenged the mayors of the realm, even backing one of Carloman's rivals during the succession.

For Miette, the impact of that decision had been immediate. It was as if she suddenly had contracted a catching disease. She was snubbed across Paris from one salon to another. She could understand being shunned by Carloman's wife, Greta, but what cause had Lady Hervet, Lady Dricot and Lady Trinon? No amount of civility mattered. She had been more accepted in court before she got married.

And now, her husband was upping the stakes.

A commotion in the hallway disturbed her reverie. Shouts came from the lower floors. "He's here! Yes, hurry. The king is here!"

Miette checked the window and indeed her husband's beautiful black and gold coach had pulled up to the gate of their villa. Her heart slammed inside her chest. Desperately, she tried to calm herself and restore the confident demeanor she had practiced for the occasion. She walked down the staircase leading to the front hallway, but arriving at the bottom, she couldn't help herself; she broke into a run.

Technically, Childeric, son of King Chilperic III was not yet a king. That would require Carloman or Pippin raising him to the throne through acclamation. So far, the two mayors had been reluctant to discuss the matter. In fact, they even disputed the existence of a Merovingian heir within the kingdom. Childeric's sudden appearance in Paris, however, resolved the question of "if a Merovingian would be found" to "when he would be raised to the throne." How her husband became involved in the king's political resurrection, Miette would never know. She knew he was ambitious, but this was beyond her understanding.

Miette took her place inside the receiving room. A smile of excitement took the corner of her mouth and she bowed her head to hide it. The outer door to the room began to open and Miette tried to remember what Lady Hélène had told her. "Head tilts forward, hands wide on the skirt. Right foot behind left and bow from the waist as the knees fold smoothly."

Miette folded gracefully into the formal bow she had been shown. She tried to slow her breathing to regain her composure. She wanted this moment to be perfect. She held herself still, resisting the urge to look up at their guest. Footsteps approached from her left and then, stopped in front of her. A trickle of sweat ran down the back of her spine. All she could see was a small patch of the wooden floor before her. An elegant pair of black shoes lined with gold embroidery entered her vision.

"Milord, may I present the Lady Ragomfred?" her husband offered.

"Milady." The king's deep masculine voice resonated within her.

She looked up tentatively and his eyes embraced her. Deep pools of black, they penetrated hers like a lover's, discarding her practiced layers of decorum. She began to panic at the frankness of his stare, but his smile reassured her. She didn't look away. It was mesmerizing. She felt herself opening to him, as if she were offering him her innermost secrets. He smiled and his eyes twinkled in amusement. A tremor rolled through her.

"My king."

Childeric laughed. "Not as yet, my dear. But soon." He extended his hand to her. "Join us."

"Thank you milord." She rose to take his hand and caught her husband's eye.

Clearly, he hadn't envisioned the invitation and was alarmed by the development. But what else could she do, but accept? Childeric swept her through the foyer.

Now that the future king's eyes had released her, Miette had time to assess him. What struck her first was his hair. A symbol of Merovingian power, it fell nearly to his waist in long black tresses. Cinched behind his head with a simple gold band. It was, to Miette's surprise, clean and combed – much like a woman's. His beard too, was long, but it was parted into two long braids and laced with pearls and jade. It accentuated a hawk-like nose and two sensuous lips that smirked with a lifetime of indulgence.

He was not a tall man. Surely, her husband was at least a hand taller. Nor was he physically strong in the way of the court's warriors. He had none of the upper-body strength necessary to wield a long sword. Instead, he was lithe and graceful, almost like a dancer. To suggest, however, that he was not powerful would be to lie. The man exuded power. Every step he took was confidant, every gesture assured. A king, she thought.

As they walked, her eyes strayed to his long and painted fingernails. Most were bejeweled and colorful. Several on his left hand had been allowed to curl under. The sight made her shudder. When she looked up, she found him watching her with an amused grin.

Lord Ragomfred led them into a small vestibule off the grand hall. He stopped there and signaled to several servants who came forward to offer the future king wine and an assortment of cheeses. When he accepted, Miette copied her husband's bow and the two stepped back to remove themselves from his presence while he ate.

When he was finished, they returned to the vestibule. "Before showing you to your rooms, milord," her husband said, "I hoped to introduce you to our household as well as to a few close friends in a welcome to your temporary home. I hope that you'll not think the gesture too forward."

Childeric's dark eyes turned on her husband and Miette's breath caught in her throat.

"I am not a pony for you to put on display, Lord Ragomfred."

Silence fell on the small party. Miette's husband made a feeble attempt to bow, but Childeric waved him off.

"For the moment, however, I suppose I am in your debt - that and your lovely wife has enchanted me with her presence. Lady Ragomfred, would you accompany me?"

Her husband looked torn between relief and shock. Miette bowed her acceptance to Childeric. "I would be grateful."

The future king offered his right arm. Miette rested her

left hand on it, and they turned to the portal leading into the grand hall. A servant scurried to push the door. It swung open, revealing over a hundred guests lined against the walls. Each of them bowed deeply in place. A number of servants knelt off to the left of the hall.

A few guests? Miette thought. Her husband must be crazed to take such a risk.

"Thank you for making this ordeal somewhat bearable," Childeric whispered to her. She nodded her head and looked up to meet his dark eyes. Again, she fell into their depths. She was so disoriented she nearly stumbled.

"You will, of course, be my lover," he said.

The shock of his bold assertion was muted by the distinct thrill that swept through her body. She imagined him kissing her beside his royal bed as he slowly undressed her and felt a tremor roll through her body. She groaned inwardly and fought to compose herself by focusing on their guests.

The bulk of the court's nobility stretched across the hall. At some unseen signal, probably from her husband, the nobles knelt, almost in unison. In that moment, the value of Ragomfred's bold gamble became apparent. Assembled before them were most of the leading families of Neustria. On her left were Lady Hervet and Lady Trinon. On her right, Lady Hélène knelt next to at least a dozen of the women who had taken great delight in snubbing Miette. She smiled grandly at each of them. By taking her arm, Childeric had transformed her status at the court. Everyone in the room would now curry her favor and seek her support. She was more important than all of them. A warm languor suffused her body. Her long wait was over.

"Lovers, my king?" She gave Childeric her most penetrating stare. "I am yours to command."

❖ ❖ ❖

Bertrada checked her reflection in the darkened window one last time before going downstairs. They were holding a private dinner at the inn with the Compte de Soissons and his family. She had tied her hair into two long braids that folded together just past her shoulders and hung down half the length of her back. She liked the effect. It looked how she felt, both youthful and sophisticated at the same time. The dress she wore was light blue and had simple lines that showed her figure well.

She had to admit that Aude was right. Paris was good for her. She hadn't felt this happy in a very long time. They had spent two wonderful days in Paris shopping. Her sister had a passion for the hunt. She had rousted the dressmakers, shoemakers and jewelers in the main markets and harassed those strange merchants from the orient who sold creams and lotions for hands and faces. Her father had turned pale when they brought him the bills.

Descending the stairs, Bertrada felt all eyes in the room turn her way. She almost laughed at the looks from the men in the room. She paused to savor the moment before gliding down to the lobby. She felt beautiful.

She joined and embraced her father and the Compte and Comptesse de Soissons as well as their daughters Mary and Catherine. The Compte was a tall man, thin and graceful. His nose was a long projection that defined his face and gave his voice a tinny sound. His wife was a stout woman with great breasts who used them as weapons on those around her. Bertrada remembered being crushed into them as a child and thinking she would suffocate beneath them.

Both daughters were lovely girls, although Bertrada could tell that as they grew older, Mary was destined to look like her father and Catherine, her mother. They were fifteen and fourteen respectively and their parents were appropriately ensuring that they were seen at court. Bertrada accepted a small glass of white wine from the innkeeper and waited for Aude to descend.

Tedbalt's arrival in Paris had been delayed for another two days and the relief Bertrada felt could not have been more profound. She didn't know what to say to him. Although she was fond of the boy, their feelings had never matured to romance. She was still confused over Pippin and didn't want to build up the poor boy's hopes. He had been so hurt.

At the Compte de Soisson's gasp, Bertrada nearly spilled her drink. Looking up, she found most of their party staring at the top of the staircase.

It was Aude. Bertrada had always thought of her sister as "pretty" in an innocent and unassuming way. Now, seeing her on the stairs, Bertrada was forced to revise her appraisal. Aude's hair was pulled tightly into a bun that accentuated her dark features and set off the white lace of a dress that just barely covered the nakedness of her shoulders and the top of her breasts. Her waist was so thin Pippin could have circled it with his two hands. Her eyelids sparkled with a soft green color that proved a worthy counterpoint to the rouge on her lips. The girl radiated beauty. For the first time in her life, Bertrada had to admit she was a touch envious of her sister's youth. She gratefully accepted another glass of wine.

Before Aude could descend a stair, the door to the inn flew open and Tedbalt was there. He was windblown and ruddy and covered in a great coat that emphasized his height. His hair was longer than the last time Bertrada had seen him and although he had his father's nose, he had grown into it in a way that made it appealing. He took one step into the room and followed the eyes of everyone to the top of the stairs. The shock on his face was palpable. He watched Aude take every step down. By the time she reached the floor he looked like a man in love.

Bertrada drank her wine in a gulp.

Tedbalt greeted his parents and his sisters in workmanlike fashion. Bertrada's father gave the young man a warm embrace and a short cuff to the back of the head. Everyone laughed. Eventually he finished exchanging the requisite pleasantries and turned to find her.

He smiled. It was an easy smile. One filled with warmth and confidence. He was no longer the besotted youth who fumbled through his courtship with her.

He's turned into a man, she thought. And a good-looking one at that.

"Hello, Bertie."

"Hello, Ted." Bertrada couldn't help but notice how hot the room felt.

"You look wonderful."

"You've grown into quite a man." She was sure she was smiling like an idiot. Then she remembered. "I am so sorry about Annette."

He sobered, his eyes welling before he could get them under control. "Thank you for remembering."

An awkward silence ensued. Bertrada snagged another glass of wine.

"May I sit with you at dinner?" he asked.

"Of course, you great oaf!" Aude swept into their presence and took Tedbalt by the arm. Bertrada noticed that she fit nicely there. "That's the whole idea!" Her radiant smile lifted their mood and they all laughed.

The innkeeper rang chimes to signal dinner and they allowed themselves to be ushered into the dining room. Tedbalt never let go of Aude's arm.

More wine was poured, this time, red. Bertrada suggested to the server that he bank the fire to reduce the heat in the room. He looked so puzzled at the request that she decided he must be part idiot. When the glasses were filled, Tedbalt's father toasted their health. Bertrada's father toasted their trade mission, and Bertrada toasted Paris. Everyone laughed, glasses clinked, and Bertrada again felt euphoric.

"How goes the rebuilding effort?" Tedbalt asked.

Bertrada told him about the nightmare of rebuilding a wall in winter and the devastation to the people in the city. She was about to describe her work at the hospital, when Aude cut in.

"He doesn't want to hear about that! We're in Paris! We have to be able to come up with better conversation than that!!"

"What would you suggest?" Tedbalt seemed thoroughly taken by her.

"Let's," she whispered, "talk about the King!"

"He's not King yet."

Aude waved off Bertrada's objection with the back of her hand. "It's only a matter of time. I've heard his hair is longer than mine!"

"I thought that was just a rumor," Tedbalt said.

"And his fingernails!" Aude held her hands nearly a foot apart. "They're covered with jewels."

She wove a spell over the table with her stories of the Merovingian. At first Bertrada listened with the others as she sipped her wine. She remembered something Pippin had said about the strange line of kings but couldn't quite remember what. She tried to join the conversation but couldn't seem to find a way in. Either she spoke too slowly or out of turn. She began to feel foolish. Her euphoria dissipated.

Aude was whispering of dark black magic and evil enchantment and telling stories of the King's ability to see the future. She had Tedbalt's complete attention.

Bertrada looked down at her glass, disoriented. How many had she had?

They started serving dinner. It was a healthy slab of roasted beef.

"It's just a matter of time before Carloman and Pippin elevate him," Aude said.

"Really?" Tedbalt turned his attention to Bertrada. "What does Pippin say about him?"

"Oh, she's no longer with Pippin," Aude laughed. "That's over."

The server set down Bertrada's plate of beef. It was red and bloody. The smell of it wafted up towards her.

"You're no longer with Pippin?" Tedbalt asked.

Bertrada had just enough time to shake her head no, and then she vomited on her plate.

# CHAPTER FIVE

*South of the Loire*

Pippin groaned awake and found himself lying spread-eagled on a mat inside his tent, still fully clothed, his head thundering from the drink he had consumed the night before. It took him a moment to remember where he was. When he did, he groaned even louder. He and his army were marching with Carloman and Boniface back to Paris.

This is the way of it, thought Pippin. He was always deferring to Carloman. Despite his anger over Hunoald and Waifar, Pippin had agreed to fight in the east. Carloman's logic had won the day. If they split their forces, they risked losing control of Francia, so vengeance would have to wait.

What bothered Pippin were his doubts about Carloman's motives. All his life, he had always trusted Carloman, but after Laon he didn't know what to think.

He rolled off the mat and stood up. As with most mornings, his body refused to straighten. His joints ached, especially the spot just above his left shoulder blade where he had taken an arrow in Saxony and his left knee where his warhorse had fallen on him in Narbonne. The latter injury forced him to limp until he could loosen the joint. Making matters worse, his eyes had also crusted shut during the night and now refused all attempts to open them. He stumbled his way outside.

There was a water bucket outside his tent and, whispering a word of thanks, Pippin dipped both hands into the cold liquid and splashed it on his face to try and rub some life into it. Displeased with the results, he lifted the bucket and upended it over his head, shouting at the cold shock of it.

"Milord?" It was Gunther.

Pippin groaned. Gunther only used such titles when Carloman was around. Pain pounded behind Pippin's eyes at the thought. He wiped the water from his face and straightened. Carloman, however, was nowhere to be seen. Instead, Gunther stood beside a middle-aged woman and two children. Pippin guessed the boy was six and the girl ten. He didn't recognize them and couldn't understand why Gunther was being so deferential.

"What do you want?" Pippin threw the bucket aside, cleared his throat and spat a thick mass of phlegm on the ground between them.

"Milord, the Comptesse de Loches?"

The hostages. Pippin had asked Gunther to bring them around at first light. Now, he wished he had said noon. He made a half-hearted attempt to bow.

"Milady," he said. "I-"

With a look of disdain that would wither a nun, the Comptesse swept past Pippin and disappeared into his tent. Bewildered, Pippin turned to Gunther. The eyes on his short lieutenant were each as big as a gold solidus. Gunther shook his head in warning.

The Comptesse reappeared from Pippin's tent carrying a small towel. She thrust the cloth into Pippin's hands.

"You are not an animal, young man. Go make yourself presentable. I am a noblewoman whose family dates back to Roman times and, if I'm not mistaken, you are mayor of the palace. Go get yourself cleaned up. Your father would be ashamed to see you behaving like this."

Pippin was dumbfounded. "You knew my father?"

"Of course, I knew your father." She grabbed Pippin by the arm and turned him around to face his tent. "And he would be appalled to have you greet me in such fashion. Now, go!" She pushed him. "I'll wait for you out here. And please." She sniffed the air. "Change your chemise. It smells as if you've slept in it since you took our castle."

Much to his surprise, Pippin found himself back in his tent dispensing with his doublet and changing his chemise. His mind raced. Who was this woman? He couldn't recall his father ever mentioning the Comptesse de Loches. He dried his hair and used the towel to wipe his armpits.

Not that it should matter, he thought; she's a hostage. He donned a new chemise and used his fingers to comb his short hair. Anger gripped him and he shook his head. The Comptesse was every bit as arrogant as her diminutive husband.

He stormed out of his tent to find the Comptesse directing Gunther. The poor man was trying to erect a small table and two chairs for her. Pippin couldn't imagine where Gunther had found them.

"Comptesse," Pippin said.

She turned to face him and held up her hand for silence. She examined him, first up one side, and then down the other. Finally, she released him with an audible sigh.

"I suppose that will have to do for now. Please sit," she said. "I've asked your man to find us tea."

Pippin looked up for Gunther and found that he was already gone.

"I don't think you understand your situation," Pippin said, trying to regain control of the conversation.

"Don't be silly," the Comptesse snapped. "Of course, I understand my situation. It is you, milord Mayor, who has not bothered to comprehend yours. And please." She waved the back of her hand at him. "Close your mouth when you're not speaking. You look like a buffoon. Didn't King Liutbrand teach you anything while you were on the Roman Peninsula?"

Pippin was so shocked that he closed his mouth. He had indeed spent much of his youth with the Lombards. Liutbrand even had adopted him as a son.

"That's better." She sat and gestured to the seat across from her. "Since I am not a servant or a family member and I haven't given you permission to use my Christian name, you, Milord Mayor, will address me as Comptesse or as Milady. Anything else would be disrespectful."

Pippin sat down. The hammering in his head hindered all attempts to recall his childhood lessons in civility.

"Milady-" he started. The Comptesse nodded in acknowledgement. "Please, forgive me for having failed to greet you properly. You are free to make yourself welcome here in our camp so long as I have your word that you recognize your status as a hostage and that you agree you won't try to escape."

Again, the Comptesse nodded. She seemed to expect more.

"Ah-" Pippin searched for words. "Allow me to introduce myself. I am Pippin, son of Charles, son of Pippin of Herstal. I am pleased to make milady's acquaintance."

The Comptesse beamed.

"Well met, Pippin, son of Charles. I am Catherine, Comptesse de Loches, daughter of Henri, son of Guy. May I present my daughter Charlene and my son Henri," she said pointing to her two children.

Pippin nodded to them and turned back to the Comptesse. "You may, of course, call me Pippin."

The Comptesse smiled in response but didn't return the courtesy.

Pippin sat back to reevaluate this woman. Tall and elegant, she had graying brown hair gathered into a bun at the nape of her neck. She sat on the edge of her seat, her back straight and her posture perfect. She had sharp angular features that on another woman would have looked manly. The Comptesse, however, radiated such confidence that she was, in a strange way, compelling and beautiful. Her eyes demanded attention. They were a cool, piercing blue, so sharp they could penetrate armor. Her smile had a confident smirk that suggested that she knew what kind of personal power she wielded. A big-boned woman, she had kept herself slim, despite the fact that she had given birth to the two children standing beside her. Pippin couldn't put an age to her.

"Comptesse, how did you know my father?"

"Everyone knew Charles, milord."

"But you knew him personally."

The Comptesse smiled almost to herself and nodded only once.

"How did you meet him?"

Her eyes flickered away from him as if her thoughts took substance across the horizon. For the briefest moment, the Comptesse smiled before masking her thoughts. The corners of her mouth tilted downward, and she turned back on Pippin. Again, her eyes pierced right through him.

"One needn't bother with ancient history." She cleared her throat. "I have come to bargain."

"Forgive me, milady, with what could you possibly bargain?"

"My treasure."

"I already have your husband's treasure."

"What you have is perhaps one part in ten of the whole. The rest is hidden."

Pippin's breath caught in his throat. He braved the throbbing in his head to calculate the value of the holdings she described and found it worth the effort. It was a staggering amount, assuming she was telling the truth.

"Why would you tell me this? Your husband could have bought your release with a quarter of such a fortune. And if I find it, I can merely take it as a fortune of war."

"If you can find it. Without my help, you would likely search for the better part of a lifetime and never uncover a single denarius." Catherine held up her hand before Pippin could respond. She turned to her children. "Charlene, would you and Henri please stand over there by that tree? The mayor and I have some matters to discuss."

Charlene curtsied, Henri bowed, and Catherine rewarded them with a radiant smile. Turning back to Pippin, Catherine's eyes took on a measure of heat. "As to my husband, I doubt he would put such a price on my freedom. In fact, he is probably somewhat relieved to find me in your care."

"Once you give me the location, why should I uphold my end of the bargain?"

"Because you are Charles's son. You will not be false with me."

Pippin, again, was puzzled. She continued to invoke his father's name as if he were a close friend.

"What do you want in return?"

"I wish to start a new life. I am finished waiting for my husband to gain any sense and as long as he remains the Lord of Loches, I have little use for my family's treasure. You, on the other hand, have need of treasure and can protect me from the wiles of my husband's more juvenile inclinations. I, and my children, will remain in your household and under your protection, but will have the freedom to come and go as we please. Think of us more as members of your household than as guests. In addition, you will grant me an annual stipend of," she pursed her lips, "four hundred gold solidi so that I may raise my children appropriately to their station. You will educate them in your household and enroll Henri in knight training. Is Fulrad still your weapons master?"

*Who was this woman?* Pippin had never met anyone like her. "Fulrad still teaches the young knights, although his age impairs him. Tell me, why you would do this to your husband?"

"The man's a fool and an arrogant one at that. He's the third son of a minor noble family and has done little to distinguish himself other than to become a hunting companion of Duc Hunoald." She shrugged her shoulders angrily. "My father must have been very anxious about my prospects to agree to such a marriage."

Her face reddened and she looked away. "At twenty-five, I was quite old when the betrothal took place. My father saw the union as an opportunity to tie our family more closely to Duc Hunoald, and as I have no brothers..." she let the thought hang in the air. "Of course, whatever political advantage there was in such an arrangement, my husband quickly squandered it. His arrogance trebled when he inherited the title of Compte from my father. He dismissed those knights loyal to our household and in a drunken stupor he insulted Duc Hunoald, himself."

The Comptesse paused to look up at Pippin. "You might have found taking the castle considerably more difficult had you come when my father was alive."

Pippin grunted. Taking the castle had been easier than expected. For reasons he couldn't articulate, Pippin decided that he liked this blunt-speaking woman. "I'll give you two hundred gold solidi annually," he declared.

Her eyes squinted. "Three," she said.

"Done. Assuming the treasure is as large as you say, you will be treated as a guest within my household and your children will be raised there as if they were my kin."

"I believe Charles would find that appropriate."

Gunther appeared carrying a pot of boiling water and two cups. He set them on the table and rolled his eyes at Pippin. He was clearly frightened by the woman.

Pippin was beginning to understand why.

❊ ❊ ❊

"It could be a trap," Childebrand said.

"That it could." Pippin chuckled, thinking of his conversation with the Comptesse. "She is certainly capable of it."

They had taken ten trusted knights and left under the cover of darkness to hunt down the Comptesse's hidden treasury outside Loches. Given the size of the horde, Pippin was taking every precaution to limit knowledge of the treasure to all but a chosen few. Wealth that large could tempt many a man and Pippin still lacked confidence in the loyalty of many of his knights.

Loches lay within a two-hour hard ride of the army's route north. Traveling at night, however, their progress was impeded, and Pippin began to worry that they wouldn't return until after first light. Wheeling heavily laden carts into camp in full daylight would arouse significant attention.

Pippin looked down at the small map drawn in the Comptesse's sure hand. "For some reason, I trust her. She has more confidence in me than many of my knights."

"I wouldn't trust her," Childebrand said.

"It's odd. She seems almost happy to be going with us to Paris."

"Who else but a spy would want to be a hostage?"

"She seems to know quite a lot about my father."

"Everyone knew Charles," Childebrand said.

That Childebrand's words echoed those of the Comptesse so closely troubled Pippin. "She seems to have known him rather well. Did you ever meet her before?"

Childebrand looked away. "I'm just saying we should be careful. We're out here in the dead of night with only ten men, hunting a treasure that may not exist, at the bidding of a woman who's married to a man whose castle you just burned to the ground."

Arnot rode back to their position and pulled up alongside Pippin.

"Huh-yah," Pippin called as the man approached.

"Huh-yah," came the response. "Milord, the graveyard is up ahead to our left."

"Any sign of ambush?"

"No, milord. We've scouted in every direction. There's no one here but ghosts."

Pippin smiled at Childebrand and spurred his horse

forward. Just to be sure, he kept Arnot and the scouts circling their position while Childebrand assigned men picks and shovels. Pippin walked among the headstones tracking the Comptesse's family backward in time.

"She wasn't lying," he called to Childebrand. "Her family does date back to the Romans."

Pippin found the headstone he was looking for and ordered two of his men to dig. The knights knelt before the burial mound and offered a fervent prayer asking forgiveness. They made the sign of the cross and raised their picks high against the moonlit sky and sank them deep into the earth. The gravesite was soft and the work quick; within two hours the men were shoulder level deep in the earth and covered in mud.

"Nothing, milord," one of them reported.

Pippin replaced them with two fresh hands. It was already two bells; they were running out of time. The shovels hit something solid and the men below scurried to unearth a small wooden coffin, the size used for a child. Ropes were lowered and the coffin lifted out of the grave. As soon as it was free, the two men resumed their positions and began to dig again.

By three bells, they had uncovered three more coffins, each full-sized and heavier than the last. It took all ten of his men to lift them out of the ground with ropes. Pippin laid them side-by-side and ordered the men to open them. Again, hands lifted to foreheads to make the sign of the cross. When the lids were open, Pippin was faced with one dead child and three very large treasures.

The Comptesse had told the truth.

Childebrand whistled. "I had no idea she was that wealthy."

Pippin eyed his uncle. "Where would she get this kind of treasure?"

# CHAPTER SIX

*Regensburg*

T rudi followed Tobias back to the castle in silence. It was a formidable building, built by the Romans three centuries earlier. The southern gate, overlooking the roiling Danube, was typically the busiest entrance for merchants, farmers and visiting nobility. It opened to an interior courtyard that served as the primary marketplace for the city where only favored merchants were allowed to sell their wares. All else had to content themselves outside in Trudiville.

After the confrontation with Theudebald and the priest, Trudi pointed them towards the northern entrance to avoid further notice. She had had enough controversy for one day. Before they reached the gate, however, Trudi had a sudden thought.

"Do you think he's right?"

"Who?" Tobias said.

"The priest. Do you think I need protection?"

Tobias stroked his chin, a habit he had picked up since starting to grow facial hair. "It wouldn't hurt to have a guard or two with you. As much as you are being celebrated at court, there are many who despise the Franks' rule and still associate you with your father."

"But am I in danger?"

"No. As long as Odilo is alive no one in Bavaria will threaten you."

"And if Odilo dies? It took less than three months after Charles's death for Carloman to send Sunnichild to the Abbey at Chelles. Who will protect me?"

Tobias shook his head. "The baby will succeed Odilo. They'll need you to act as regent until he is of age…assuming it's a boy."

"And assuming he lives," Trudi whispered. "And Theudebald." Trudi shuddered. "He's a threat. He is already calling me a traitor."

"But he's not Bavarian." Tobias assured her. "Our people trust Odilo. His half-brother is Alemannian. And we don't like Alemannians."

"Have you heard any more rumors suggesting Odilo isn't the baby's father?"

Tobias nodded. "I'm afraid that one will always be with you. You announced your condition so quickly after the marriage it almost begged the suggestion. It will get worse when you deliver the babe early."

The thought hung in the air between them. Trudi swore under her breath, furious with herself for falling into such a trap. Thank God she could trust Tobias. Without him, she would have no one in which to confide. He was the only one who knew the babe wasn't Odilo's.

She tried not to burden him with such talk. If they were overheard, it could mean the death of both of them. But he was the only one who shared her grief over Bradius. Her sorrow was still like an open wound that wouldn't heal. Her hand strayed to her stomach as a sudden wave of sadness swelled in her. "Do you still think of him?"

Tobias nodded, clearly knowing of whom she spoke. "Bradius was my general. I owed him my life. At least now, I can honor him in service to you and his child."

Trudi grimaced. "Sometimes I think how simple my life

would be, had I never met him. I left home to be with Odilo. I thought he was the love of my life. If I hadn't known Bradius, I could have been so happy being Duchesse of Bavaria."

"And now?"

"I'm deathly afraid that I will be found out – that my child and I will be cast out."

Tobias put his arm around her shoulder. "I will keep your secrets, milady."

"My marriage to Odilo is based on a lie."

Tobias chuckled. "Aren't most noble marriages?"

Trudi grunted. "I suppose you have the right of that. I just miss him! Bradius changed me. He took me outside of myself – outside of the life I had known. Before Bradius, I never once thought about what my father did, or what Carloman did for the sake of the kingdom. I never questioned their decisions. I just assumed they were right. How could I not? The Church was behind them. They always were successful in getting what they wanted. I couldn't understand why people opposed them! I imagined all pagans as savages – as people who didn't understand the true nature of faith or the divine right of kings."

"People can do despicable things in the name of their gods," Tobias said.

Trudi nodded. "But Bradius had no ambitions. He just wanted to stop Carloman. Carloman desecrated their sacred tree and forced people to choose between their faith and their lives. I'll never see Carloman again in the same light."

Tobias nodded. "The Fates spin their wheel with the thread of our lives. They don't ask our permission. You changed Bradius as well. He was a broken man, intent on a violent end to a life filled with violence. He didn't expect to fall in love with the sister of his enemy."

A tear escaped from one of her eyes and Trudi wiped it away with the back of her hand. "God help me, I loved him! He made me feel so alive. I never hungered for anyone the way I hungered for him."

Tobias put a comforting hand on her arm. "You must let him go, Duchesse. As much as you loved him, your life is here now. There is no going back. Bradius is dead. You must think of this child as Odilo's. If you think of it as Odilo's, it will be Odilo's."

Trudi nodded, trying to steel her resolve. "I know. There's only one path forward. And Odilo deserves better from me. None of this is his fault. He was my first love and now he is my only love.

"I just wish I could talk him out of this war with Carloman. He doesn't understand how ruthless Carloman can be."

* * *

Odilo provided more grist for the mill when she arrived home.

"I can't believe you would ask this of me," Trudi said. "That man called me a cunt in my own home. He said you should have been abandoned as an infant."

Odilo tried to reach out for her. Trudi batted his hands away. "I want him out of our home."

"I need him, Trudi. I need Alemannia in this war."

"From the sounds of it, he doesn't need your encouragement. He's ready to fight Carloman with or without you."

"But if we don't fight in concert, Carloman will take us one at a time. There is only one hope I have in defending Gripho's claim, and it's with Theudebald."

"Why must you defend it? I know for a fact that Gripho wouldn't come to your aid if the situation were reversed. You're using Gripho as an excuse to war on Carloman."

Odilo didn't answer her.

"Theudebald is a beast, Odilo. You're less of a man for allying yourself with him. He holds no interests other than his own and will betray you without a second thought."

"It's a risk I have to take."

"It's a risk you want to take." Trudi paused, evaluating her husband. "I want Theudebald out of our home. I want him out of Regensburg."

"He's leaving in the morning."

"That's not soon enough."

"It will have to suffice. I won't throw him out."

"I will not abide him staying here."

"What harm can come from one more night?"

"Do not do this, Odilo."

"It's already done."

The bluntness of his answer shocked Trudi. She could feel her face flush with anger.

"I will not debate this. He's my older brother. We carry my father's legacy to rule and I will uphold that legacy. Gripho had rights to his succession and Carloman took away those rights. I warned Carloman. I told him of the consequences. I spoke to him as if he were my brother. Don't make this my fault, Trudi. Carloman is seeking to impose his religion and rule over both Alemannia and Bavaria. I cannot let him."

"Gripho isn't worth fighting for," Trudi said.

"It's not just about Gripho. Our child has rights to protect as well. Other than Carloman's son, Drogo, he is the only grandson of Charles Martel. He has his own rights to succession. Carloman won't want Drogo to have a rival, especially one that has an army behind him."

"Carloman would never harm my child."

"Perhaps not, but he'll do whatever he can to keep our son weak and politically powerless."

"Promise me that you'll parley with Pippin. He isn't like Carloman. He may be open to reason."

"Then, promise me that you'll let me handle my brother in my own way. I'll keep him in check as long as he's under our roof."

Trudi shook her head. "I don't want to see him. He gives me nightmares."

Odilo smiled a broad and guileless smile and kissed his

wife on the forehead. "Don't worry," he said. "I'll save you from them."

\* \* \*

The wind shifted, lifting Trudi effortlessly, hoisting her above Regensburg where the air swirled with abandon among the high wisps of white cloud. She yielded to its currents and let herself ride the turbulent updrafts; her body moved in a series of arcs as she moved from one to the next.

Beneath her, the city's stone fortress stood black and impenetrable next to the churning blue waters of the Danube. The river rumbled east beneath her as the wind blew her west across the fertile green valley. Small villages marked the shoreline and tiny fishing boats dotted the river. She passed the willow that marked Bradius's grave and the pier from which she made her escape. In the distance, a tributary flowed into the Danube from the mountains to the south. She had seen it before. It was the River Leche. The winds took her there.

On the west bank of the river, a battle raged. She saw Odilo's blue banner, with its charging black boar. His back was against the river. Pippin's white eagle on a field of green rose from the south and Carloman's red and white Lion of St. Mark held the North. While she watched, her brothers chopped and hewed their way methodically towards the river. No one could withstand them and nothing but carnage lay in their wake. It was as if Death himself preceded them in battle. If they reached the river, her husband would die.

"Stop," she called from the clouds. "Stop!" she screamed. But no one could hear her.

\* \* \*

She awoke shivering. The night was brisk and the bed

warmers the servants had placed beneath her blankets no longer offered much heat. Trudi drew her knees to her chest, cursing the nightmares that plagued her. She climbed out of bed and padded into the anteroom where the chamber pot sat in the corner. She hoisted her nightdress, squatted over the bucket, and let her urine flow. For the hundredth time that day, she relived the argument that pushed her to attack Theudebald and for the hundredth time, felt that she was in the right. The man had insulted her in her own home.

She supposed that her husband was still down in the hall drinking with "the beast" as she now called Theudebald. She was sure they would drink all night. She had seen men drink before at her home in Francia, but it was nothing like the practice in the east. Here, they consumed great horns of ale in enormous quantities and held competitions to see how quickly one could down the dark liquid in one draught. As the night wore on, more often than not, they vomited to make room for more ale. Trudi had learned that, once the drinking had started, it wouldn't end until morning when the revelers fell asleep in their places.

She braved the cold stone floor to go in search of her husband.

As expected, Trudi found him in the great hall. What was left of a large fire dwindled in the corner. Odilo and his brother were alone, seated opposite each other, their torsos draped across the table between them. Both were unconscious. Odilo snored.

Trudi grunted in disgust and began to circle the table to rouse her husband. As she passed Theudebald, she saw a knife. It was like the one she had planted by his head the day before. It stood point down in the table between the two men, sharp and lethal. Trudi stared at the blade. Theudebald lay next to it, his neck exposed and vulnerable. A swift blow would do it. She could put an end to the threat he posed in that moment. Odilo would never know who did it. No one would. She thought about the lives it might save. Her hand reached out for the blade. Her fingers touched its hilt, caressing the smoothness of it.

But for all her boldness the previous day, she couldn't do it. She wasn't that cold hearted. With a sigh, she withdrew her hand and finished circling the table to waken Odilo.

"You should have done it," Theudebald's voice cut through the quiet. Trudi froze in mid-stride. Theudebald sat up, his sightless eye staring at her as he pulled the knife from the table. His good eye followed the edge of the blade as he held it up to the light of the dwindling fire. "Charles would have. Maybe you are not your father's daughter after all."

Trudi glared at her husband's half-brother. "There's already been enough bloodshed."

"Oh no," Theudebald's eye still held the knife, "we've only just begun to shed blood." He stood and walked around the table. Trudi backed away, putting the unconscious Odilo between them. Her heart slammed inside her chest.

"Your brothers will come from the west." Theudebald's voice was distant and cold. "They'll think I'm weak and unprepared as I was when I was young and faced Charles." He chuckled and turned his gaze to Trudi. "And I'll let them believe it. I will retreat before them, leading them into the valley near Canstatt. Their arrogance will spur them forward for the kill. They'll imagine themselves crushing the rebellion just as their father did so many years ago. Only they'll be wrong. When their line is stretched, all of Hesse and Alemannia will descend on their flank and we will crush them between us."

"My brothers wouldn't be so careless." Trudi silently prayed for Odilo to waken.

"Oh, but they will." Theudebald's good eye strayed over Trudi's nightshift. "They will. Especially when they find out what I've done to their sister."

Trudi shoved Odilo. She shouted his name, but he didn't move. She hit him with her fists, but he didn't stir.

"Oh, he won't wake. He never could hold his drink."

Theudebald closed the two steps between them. Without room to kick, Trudi punched up at his face – two quick jabs and tried to circle past him. Theudebald's backhand caught her on the cheek and she instinctively gave way with the blow to lessen its impact. And then Theudebald was on her using his weight to force her back against the table. She clouted his ear trying to back him away, but he grabbed her hair. Furious, she tried to kick his groin, but he blocked the blow with his knee. When she felt the point of his knife at her throat, however, she went still with fear.

He lifted the blade, forcing her chin up until she was staring into his good eye. There was nothing there but malice. He pulled her down onto the table next to her husband.

"Not a sound." Theudebald drew the point of the knife down her neck to the tie that held her nightdress closed. With a flick of his wrist, he severed the tie and brushed aside the fabric that covered her. His knife descended to the nipple of her breast, blood welling in its wake. Trudi began to cry.

"Tell the truth, now, whore." The knife etched a line down her belly. "Whose child lies in your womb?"

Fear, as she had never known before, surged through Trudi.

"Is it truly Odilo's child, you carry?"

"Yes," she whimpered.

"Liar!" He raised the blade high above her and used its hilt to clout the side of her head. She lost consciousness. When she awoke, Theudebald had his breeches open and was attempting to push himself between her parted legs.

"No!" She twisted away from him. He hit her again and grabbed her hips with both hands to push past her dryness.

She howled at the ceiling and beat her fists against his face and chest. Ignoring her, Theudebald plunged himself into her with long deliberate strokes as if savoring the humiliation each delivered. As the degradation sank into her, Trudi began to sob. She turned to her husband, his face mere inches from her.

A sharp pain seized her and her abdomen clenched in reaction. Fear for her baby gripped her and with it came renewed fury. She spat at him and gouged at his good eye with her fingers. He slapped her across the face. She spat again. This time, his hand closed on her throat and he started to squeeze. The light in the room began to fade. His thrusting grew more rapid. Just as the blackness surrounded her, she felt his body heave. His semen poured inside her.

"Cunt!" he said, and all went dark.

# CHAPTER SEVEN

*Tours*

After their armies arrived in Tours, Pippin checked to see that his newfound cargo was still hidden within their supply train. Satisfied that they had carried off recovering the Comptesse's treasure in secret, Pippin went to look for Carloman. He found his brother where he expected him to be, kneeling before the altar of the local monastery. It was a holy site, one that held the remains of Carloman's guardian saint, Saint Martin of Tours.

Carloman was deep in prayer. His right hand clasped a small wooden canister hanging from his neck that held a finger bone of the good saint. Boniface had given it to Carloman on the morning of his elevation to knighthood. Carloman never took it off.

Pippin's brother had his left hand extending towards the altar, palm up in supplication. His eyes were crinkled in concentration. Candlelight from the altar flickered before him and wove odd shadows across the damaged side of his face. Boniface stood beside Carloman, hands folded in prayer.

*"Gloria Patri et Filio et Spiritui Sancto."* Boniface's solemn voice resonated through the chamber followed by Carloman's as the two worked their way through the ritual responses as priest and server. *"Sicut erat in principio et nunc et semper at in*

*saecula saeculorum. Amen."*

"*Kyrie eleison*," Boniface intoned.

"*Kyrie eleison*," Carloman replied.

"*Christe eleison.*"

"*Christe eleison.*"

"*Christe eleison. Kyrie eleison.*"

"*Kyrie eleison.*"

"*Kyrie eleison.*"

Boniface raised his arms and looked heavenward.

"*Gloria in excelsis Deo.*"

Pippin found himself responding with Carloman, albeit under his breath, just as he had during every mass he had attended since he was seven years old.

"*Et in terra pax hominibus bonae voluntatis. Laudamus te, benedicimus te, adoramus te, glorificamus te, gratias agimus tibi propter magnam gloriam tuam.*"

The Latin came so readily to his lips that Pippin couldn't help but wonder at the true power of the church. The mass was so embedded in him that any priest in the land could recall such words from him at will. What did that say about the hold the church had over him and his brother? How deeply could they sway his family's purpose?

Carloman's face flushed with religious fervor and he brought his extended left hand back to join his right, holding the holy relic of St. Martin. His passionate voice filled the monastery.

"*Domine Deus, Rex caelestis, Deus Pater omnipotens. Domine Fili unigenite,*" Although Pippin refused to voice the words, they came unbidden to his mind, nonetheless.

"*Jesu Christe; Domine Deus, Agnus Dei, Filius Patris.*

Boniface raised his right hand and drew the sign of the cross in the air. Automatically, both Carloman and Pippin mirrored the sign on their foreheads, chests, and shoulders.

"*In gloria Dei Patris. Amen.*"

Pippin decided to wait for them outside.

As he left the chapel, Pippin found the Comptesse de

Loches outside the monastery giving alms to the poor who had gathered there. As he watched from a distance, it became clear to him that it was no empty gesture. The woman was clearly moved by those who touched her hands for charity. Her children were with her, carrying bread, water, and oils. The Comptesse dispensed these gifts as needed, kneeling to speak to those who could not stand and clasping the hands of those afflicted with disease. From the efficient way the trio moved through the small crowd of beggars, it was clear that this wasn't their first time.

When they had finished conferring all they had brought to the poor, the Comptesse gathered her children and turned to enter the monastery. She seemed surprised to find Pippin waiting on the steps. She came to him, a broad and genuine grin adorning her face.

"Did you find the small token left by my ancestors?"

"Yes, milady. I hope I didn't overly disturb their sleep."

"All for a good cause, young man."

"Would you care to walk with me, Comptesse? I would ask you a few questions."

The Comptesse adjusted the light blue shawl that covered her shoulders. "I'm at your service, milord."

Pippin led her back through the beggars, who shrank away from his broadsword, and headed towards a park that stood before the monastery. The Comptesse's children followed at a polite distance, as if used to giving their mother such space.

When they reached the park, the Comptesse took Pippin's right arm as one would a close friend. He found the gesture comforting. He rested his hand on hers and together they strolled without speaking. Pippin noticed for the first time that the day was exceptionally beautiful. The sky was blue, the air crisp and the park green and bursting with spring flowers.

"How did you know my father?" Pippin felt awkward asking the question.

The Comptesse laughed and tugged at Pippin's arm. "Some things are best left to the past, Pippin. It's better to know that I was an ally of sorts, and that I held his trust."

"But when was this? Except for my time in Rome, I was at his side and I don't recall ever hearing your name."

"I'm not sure that your father would have told you about me, even if you had been with him at the time."

Pippin eyed her. Although her words could suggest an intimate relationship with his father, her tone did not. He wanted to ask her directly, but somehow felt that such a question would offend her, especially with her children so near. He was stymied as to how to proceed.

As they walked, two Knights in Christ in their distinctive red and white doublets, headed towards them from the other side of the park. Having failed to pay adequate attention to his brother's knightly religious order, Pippin couldn't determine the men's rank. He was about to ask the Comptesse another question when the two knights barred their way.

"Such public displays of intimacy are forbidden," one of the knights, said. "They are an affront to the Lord our God."

More curious than offended, Pippin kept his tone polite. "Who are you?"

"I am an acolyte of the Knights in Christ," the same knight responded. There was more than a hint of pride in the man's voice.

"And who forbids such innocent displays?"

The knight's face turned red with anger. He clearly didn't like being questioned. "By order of the Knights, women are to walk three steps behind their men and their head and shoulders are to be covered." The knight grabbed for the Comptesse's shawl to force the issue.

Pippin caught the man's wrist with his left hand and moved to usher the Comptesse behind him. She took her children and moved several steps away.

The second knight advanced, circling to Pippin's right, his hand moving to the pommel of his sword.

Pippin let go of the first knight's arm and backed away one step, shifting as he did so to the balls of his feet.

"You had best comply or suffer judgment." The first knight drew his sword.

Pippin's hands dropped to his sides near the hilts of his two knives, a calm descended upon him.

"Pippin, please don't," the Comptesse begged.

The two knights froze in place. A worried look was exchanged between them.

"He shouldn't have touched you." Pippin kept his eyes on the first knight.

"Pippin, please!"

A look of panic stole across the second knight's face. "Pippin," he whispered. "The son of Charles?"

Pippin's voice was cold. "You shouldn't be touching anyone."

"It's forbidden!" The first knight insisted.

The second knight began to pray under his breath even as his hand began to pull the sword from his scabbard. *"Our Father, who art in heaven..."*

"Oh, this is asinine!" The Comptesse strode between Pippin and the two knights. "Put away your weapon!" she scolded. "Put it away." She waved at the second knight. The man straightened and slid the blade back to its hilt. The first knight only lowered his blade.

The Comptesse bent to retrieve her shawl from where it had fallen from the first knight's grasp. All three men looked at her, astounded. She folded her arms and addressed the two Knights in Christ.

"Do you know who this is?"

Both knights nodded. "Then you know if you persist with this ridiculous charade, he will kill you where you stand. And if he doesn't, you will likely hang for murdering the mayor." She glanced over her shoulder at Pippin. "I'm betting he kills you. Now, you have two choices. You can apologize to me and answer a few questions from the mayor, or you can persist in this silly confrontation that will ultimately cost you your lives."

She stepped aside so that they faced Pippin directly once more. "Which will it be?"

The second knight didn't hesitate. "I beg your forgiveness, Madame."

The first knight was sweating profusely. His eyes were angry and kept moving from the Comptesse to Pippin. He shifted his weight from foot to foot. "It's an affront to the Lord our God."

"It's an affront to no one. Who is your commander?" Pippin asked, his voice low and lethal.

"Commander Raymond de Beauville," the second knight replied. The first knight's face grew redder by the second.

"Do you believe that his rule supersedes mine?" Again, Pippin directed his question to the first knight the only one who still posed a danger.

"This is a religious matter. The Knights are advocates of the Church," the second knight replied.

"Have the Bishops issued an edict on this subject which has failed to come to my attention?" Pippin watched the first knight's eyes. They would give him away if he attacked.

"We are the keepers of the faith!" The first knight was insistent. "We confront evil. We confront faithlessness."

"Not here, knight."

"God's word is law!"

Pippin harrumphed. "I am the law."

The first knight raised his sword and rushed at Pippin. It was a move based in anger rather than skill and Pippin's knife caught the man just below the rib cage. Pippin could have killed him. The knight's armpit had been vulnerable. He let the knight slip to the ground and turned to face the second knight.

The man didn't go for his sword. Instead, he made the sign of the cross.

Pippin pointed to the first knight, now covered in blood. "Take your man here back to de Beauville. Tell him I expect his presence at my command tent by the eighth bell tonight. In the meantime, no subject of mine is to be harassed by his men on penalty of death. Is that clear?"

The knight nodded and bent to retrieve the fallen knight.

Pippin turned back to the Comptesse. She stood facing him, her two children pressed to her sides. The boy was crying. The girl looked up at him dispassionately. The Comptesse clearly was furious.

"You have a lot to learn, boy."

"I just saved your life!"

"There was no need for violence. You baited him. You almost begged that knight to attack you. It was an adolescent display. How will you rule Francia when you can't even rule yourself?"

"He attacked me."

"Only because you didn't tell him what else he could do."

"I would think you would be grateful."

"Obviously, you haven't thought much at all." She turned to her son and daughter. "Come children. Our audience with Lord Pippin is over."

Stunned, Pippin watched them leave.

# CHAPTER EIGHT

*Paris*

**M**iette offered a gloved hand, allowing it to hang in the air with just the slightest bend to her wrist. The elderly Duc de Tricot captured it and swiftly brought it to his lips. The speed of this gesture didn't go unnoticed by his wife. Smiling to herself, Miette embraced the Duchesse next, kissing the air near both cheeks as one would a familiar. The woman stiffened in her arms. Again, Miette smiled. She was sure that the Duchesse hated seeing a commoner like her marry into nobility, but it had to be an affront to the woman's sensibilities to have her serve as hostess to the future king.

"We should arrange to have tea one day soon," Miette offered.

"Yes. Yes, of course." The Duchesse de Tricot reddened. Miette knew full well that the older woman would never have tea with her. Based on the way the Duke's eyes lingered on her chest, however, Miette was sure he held no such reservations.

"As the future King has yet to be elevated to the throne, there's no need to kneel in his presence." Miette's voice brooked no objection. "A simple bow and a curtsy will do. He is to be addressed as 'Your Grace' and shouldn't not be touched under any circumstances. Wait until he addresses you before speaking, and I will advise you when the audience is over. At that time, you should bow again and walk backwards three paces, before turning towards the door. Do you have any questions?"

Miette was delighted that the redness of the Duchesse's face was turning a shade of purple.

"Perfect." Miette turned to lead the couple into what had recently been the grand salon of her husband's villa. Since Childeric's arrival she had redecorated the hall to accommodate the endless stream of nobility come to extend their respects to the future King of Francia.

Two knights stood guard over Childeric, one by the door to the hall through which they entered, and one directly beside his chair. Both, according to her husband, were absolutely loyal to the future King. Salau, the one by the throne, was his champion. He was a brute of a man with a pockmarked face and one misshapen ear.

Her father had once taught her to look to a man's eyes to judge his worth. He said they always defined a man far better than the clothes he wore. When Miette first looked into Salau's eyes, she saw nothing but cruelty. The man valued nothing. Worse, when Miette saw herself in Salau's eyes, she was nothing. She couldn't stand the sight of him.

Even today, when she walked into a room, Salau's eyes mocked her. A shiver ran up her spine. She refused to look at him, concentrating all her attention upon her future king.

He was seated casually at the end of the hall on a chair that had once belonged to her husband's late father, Ragomfred the Elder. As happened every time Miette saw Childeric, all other thoughts disappeared.

Somehow, his eyes owned her, absorbing her into their depth. Her breathing became short and labored, her heart pounded and her skin blushed. His magnetism drew her across the room, and she had to strain to keep her stride stately as she led the Duc and Duchesse to him. By the time she reached his presence, her undergarments were wet through. She folded herself into a curtsey and waited for Childeric to nod. When he did, she stood and announced her guests.

"Your Grace, may I present the Duc and Duchesse de Tricot." Miette turned and was pleased to find the couple trying to bow as she had instructed them.

"I'm delighted to make your acquaintance," Childeric said and Miette stopped listening. She had stood through dozens of audiences and knew that nothing but banal pleasantries would be exchanged. Their value to her was the status she received throughout Paris as the hostess of the future king – that and the frustrated looks she caught from the condescending likes of the Duchesse de Tricot.

To occupy herself during their audience, Miette watched Childeric's hands. She imagined his long, bejeweled fingernails slowly raking down the length of her body.

It had been three weeks since Childeric had uttered the words, "You will, of course, be my mistress." But, as yet, he had failed to act upon his bold assertion. There was no question that he continued to want her. Daily, he devoured her with his eyes. Yet, he never again mentioned his intention. And there had been ample opportunity. She couldn't understand his hesitation.

Miette was more than willing; she was in fact desperate for him. She spent hours in her room, imagining his hands exploring her. And, in their absence, she had begun to use her own. She imagined him slowly removing each article of her clothing until she was naked before him. She imagined long passionate kisses on her lips, her neck, and shoulders. And when he disrobed, he was always ready for her.

Each morning, she blushed with shame when she saw him; he had to know how eager she was. Endlessly, she played hostess to his audiences with the Frankish nobles and waited for a wink, a nod, a touch, a kiss – anything that would trigger the romance she so desired. *Why did he make her wait?*

Childeric was beginning to tire of the Duc and Duchesse de Tricot. His hands always wandered when he was bored.

Miette let the Duchesse babble until the old woman took a breath, and then stepped forward.

"Milord and Lady, his Grace thanks you for your visit today. He asks for the Lord's blessing upon you and your children."

The Duke and Duchess looked up confused. Their eyes went first to her and then to Childeric and then they shuffled to comply with her directions. They bowed and backed away three steps, bowed again, and backed up three more. Still uncertain, they bowed yet a third time and then turned hurriedly to leave the room.

Miette nearly laughed out loud. The knight at the door escorted them out and closed the door behind him. She was still smiling when she turned back to face Childeric. His eyes caught hers and he motioned for her to approach. One corner of his mouth curled provocatively. She stepped forward cautiously, keeping her eyes averted from the hated Salau. *Please let it be now!*

Childeric leaned back into her father-in-law's chair and with both hands pulled open his robe to the waist. He was naked beneath it. His erection rose above creamy white thighs and a thick, black tuft of hair. It was just as she had imagined it would be. Miette couldn't breathe.

"Do you know how to use your mouth?"

Miette's stomach clenched with the shock of his question. She was both thrilled and repulsed by it. She wanted to touch him, to hold him, yet she was horrified at the bluntness of his proposal. And with Salau standing beside him! She pried her eyes away from Childeric's erection to look up at his champion. The knight's eyes were alive with amusement.

"Salau never leaves my presence." Childeric answered her unasked question. "It's an unfortunate consequence of being a Merovingian. There are so few of us left among the living."

Miette looked at him imploringly. *Not like this*, she silently begged.

He held out his hand, his eyes reassuring.

"Do you know what to do or shall I instruct you?"

Although a virgin, Miette had had girlfriends who took great delight in informing her about the ways of the marriage bed. And there had been a young boy once when she was thirteen; she knew enough of what to do. She looked down at him, thrilled that he wanted her. But not here. Not like this. Not with Salau watching.

Her heart pounded in her ears. She knew intuitively that if she refused, he would not ask her again. And, she knew that she would never again serve as his hostess. Her place at court would be lost cast aside as if it never existed.

This knowledge, however, paled before a new compulsion that gripped her. She couldn't take her eyes off his nakedness. She wanted him. Her face flushed. A deep need within her urged her forward and overwhelmed her hesitation. She wanted him even if it was under the hateful eyes of Salau. She knew she would comply, whatever he asked of her; her need was that great. Miette stepped forward, her knees weak and her head light, to kneel before her future sovereign.

"Good girl," Childeric whispered.

Salau chuckled.

Miette bowed her head.

* * *

Tedbalt brought her lilies. They were so beautiful Bertrada almost wept.

It was the third morning since she had spewed the contents of her stomach onto her plate and destroyed what had been, up to that point, a perfectly wonderful dinner.

It was Aude who had come to her rescue. While the rest of their guests sat stunned at Bertrada's regurgitation, her younger sister was at her side spreading a napkin over the former contents of her stomach. Aude wiped the residue off

Bertrada's face and cooed into her ear.

"Everything will be alright, Bertie. Don't you worry about a thing!"

Aude instructed Tedbalt to carry Bertrada to her room and then turned to the innkeeper and signaled for him to clean up the vomit left behind on the table. The man adroitly whisked away the tablecloth and quickly spread a new one. It was all over in seconds.

Except for the humiliation. Bertrada had never been so ashamed in her life. She had wept most of the night, cursing the wine she drank and her own inability to handle it. Never before had it affected her so. She had even vomited the next morning.

By the third day, Bertrada began to feel somewhat more stable. Only a touch of nausea remained. The shame of the incident, however, lingered with her. When Aude announced that Tedbalt was downstairs waiting to see them, Bertrada shook her head no.

"You have to see him," Aude scolded. "He comes by every morning."

Reluctantly, Bertrada consented.

She fidgeted in her drawing room while Aude went to retrieve him. Within moments Aude was back ushering Tedbalt into the room. The two were laughing gaily and Aude hung from his arm. Bertrada wasn't sure why this bothered her as much as it did. It was perfectly acceptable behavior. It was just that Aude seemed to enjoy it so much.

Bertrada's eyes, however, were drawn to Tedbalt; whose presence in her room was having the same impact on her as it had at the inn. She found herself, once again, stunned by how handsome he had grown during their years apart.

And he carried an armful of lilies.

Blinking back unexpected tears, Bertrada took the flowers into her arms. "They're beautiful," was all she could manage to say.

The lilies' scent, however, billowed around her, making

her lightheaded. She wondered when she last had eaten solid food. Tedbalt towered over her. Looking up into his face, Bertrada suddenly felt quite dizzy.

"Here, let me have them." Aude took the lilies from Bertrada's grasp. "I'll fetch some water. Why don't you two sit down?" It seemed more of an order than a suggestion.

But Bertrada barely heard her. Without the flowers in her arms, she felt naked. She wasn't sure of what to do with her hands and could think of nothing to say. She stood looking up at Tedbalt, her cheeks blushing.

"I hope you are feeling better," Tedbalt said.

"Yes, yes, forgive me." Bertrada recovered herself and laughed. "I am much better, thank you. Although I'm still terribly embarrassed about-"

"Please, don't be. There is no reason to – "

"It was just so awful." Bertrada turned away from him. "I don't know how it happened."

"I'm only glad that you feel better."

"She's fine, now." Aude reentered the room with the lilies in a vase. She placed them on a table across the room from Bertrada. "A touch of tainted food, that's all."

Before Bertrada could venture an opinion, Aude had turned and grabbed Tedbalt again by the arm. A huge smile adorned her face. "Tedbalt has a surprise for us!" she announced, standing on her tiptoes.

"Yes." He smiled in turn. He cleared his throat and took on a more formal air. "I hope the two of you will consent to be my guests at a ball at the home of Lord and Lady Ragomfred next Saturday evening."

"The King will be there!" Aude squeaked.

Bertrada smiled at Aude's enthusiasm. The girl was so excited by anything that had to do with the Merovingian. Bertrada, however, was wary. She wondered what Pippin might say if he knew she was going to a ball where the would-be heir was in attendance. People still associated her with Pippin - and he was mayor. She wasn't sure of the politics. But then again, she was done with him, so why should she care?

While her inner musings ran on unabated, Bertrada couldn't help but notice that Aude had yet to let go of Tedbalt's arm. Frowning, she also noticed that he didn't seem to mind.

"We'd love to go," Bertrada said. "I think it would be wonderful."

Aude clapped her hands like a little girl. Tedbalt laughed at her exuberance.

"We will of course," Bertrada said, taking her sister's hand, "need to buy new gowns for the occasion."

"Of course!" Aude laughed. "What would a ball be without new gowns?"

"A room full of lonely men?" Bertrada offered.

All three of them laughed.

"We've little time," Bertrada said. "M. Le Compte de Soissons, you will have to excuse us." She looked to Aude. "We have some shopping to do."

Aude's face, however, fell at the suggestion. Her cheeks were burning. She looked to Tedbalt and then to Bertrada.

Tedbalt too, looked uncomfortable.

"Yes, of course," Aude said looking at her hands. "It's just that–"

"We had planned…" Tedbalt cut in.

Neither of them could finish the sentence. Bertrada looked from one to the other as understanding bloomed within her.

"You've made plans to do something else." Her heart felt like it had collapsed inside her chest.

Tedbalt looked aghast. "We didn't expect that you would recover so quickly."

Bertrada looked to Aude, disappointment dripping from her eyes.

"It's just a boat ride." Aude was pleading for forgiveness. "I didn't think your stomach could handle it."

"You can still join us, of course," Tedbalt said.

Bertrada held up her hand to stop the conversation. "That won't be necessary. You both are right. I'm still a little too queasy to be riding in a boat on the Seine. You two go ahead. If my strength returns, Aude, I'll shop for the two of us. You go. Have fun."

Relief flooded their faces.

"Are you sure?" Tedbalt queried.

"It's quite alright," Bertrada took his hands and walked him to the door. She smiled and looked past his long straight nose into his eyes. Something in them stirred, a memory, something. A barrier seemed to fall away and Bertrada thought for a moment she could see into his soul. She saw him hesitate. He felt it, too. Again, she felt lightheaded and had to look away.

Laughing at her weakness, she took his arm. "Enjoy yourselves. I'll join you next time." They stopped at the door. Bertrada turned her cheek to accept Tedbalt's kiss. He leaned forward and she felt his body brush up against hers. She leaned into it ever so slightly until her breasts lingered against his chest. Surprised, his eyes recaptured hers.

Aude took Tedbalt's arm, but Bertrada held his eyes. She released him and then turned to kiss her sister.

"Thank you so much for understanding." Aude was hurrying her through the goodbyes.

"Not at all," Bertrada said. As Aude turned to go, Tedbalt's eyes continued to follow her and Bertrada liked the fact that they did. "I'll do the shopping. Don't worry, sister, I'll make sure you have the perfect gown."

Aude looked back over her shoulder suspiciously as the door shut behind them.

❊ ❊ ❊

Miette watched Childeric from her position beside his makeshift throne. She had to will herself to do this discreetly, as it would be unseemly for her to stare. Yet everything in her body begged her to keep her eyes to him. Every once in a while, he turned to look at her and she trembled within his deep black eyes. She ached to have his hands on her body. *I am enamored of him,* she thought. She bowed her head slightly, worried that an observant noble might notice the redness of her cheeks or the shortness of her breath.

Her future king was meeting with the last group of subjects to visit that day. If he wanted to have her, it would be after they were dismissed. She prayed that he wouldn't send her away, again. She couldn't stand to wait until tomorrow. Why did he torture her so?

It had been just weeks since her first intimacy with Childeric and yet in that short time her life had been made anew. She could almost laugh at the naïve, virginal girl she had been if that girl hadn't been so pathetic. She had been a dull, dry husk of a girl. Now her body knew and craved the delicious sensuality of Childeric's touch. How had she lived without such passion? The need for it fermented inside her. It took over her whole being, haunting her days and nights until she again could be with him. She shuddered with both the pleasure and the humiliation of it.

 And it was humiliating. From the time she was a little girl, Miette had always been in control of the men in her life, but she was powerless before Childeric. She had tried to assert herself. She had tried to take control. But every effort was rebuffed. He commanded her and she rushed to obey.

It was nothing like she had envisioned. Childeric never kissed her or showed her the slightest tenderness. She was forbidden to approach him or touch him, unless, of course, he instructed her to do so. When he wanted her, he took her and for the most part, he used her body callously. God help her, it only seemed to add to her desire for him. Childeric had but to raise a bejeweled fingernail and she grew wet with anticipation.

She had progressed from satisfying him with her mouth to lifting her skirts for him. Of late, he had taken to bending her over the arm of his makeshift throne to enter her from behind. It was an awkward position, with her face pushed down into the rough wooden seat and her abdomen pressed hard against the arm of the chair. Yet she quivered with pleasure and matched his passion with her own. She was overwhelmed by her need for him.

*At last!* Childeric signaled for her to dismiss his subjects. She excused them from his presence and escorted them to the door. Childeric's subjects whispered their appreciation for her hospitality and she bade them a pleasant good-bye. After they left, she held the door ajar and turned to face Childeric. If he wanted her, he would signal it now. She held her breath in anticipation. It took all her self-control not to beg him.

With the smallest of gestures, Childeric waved her back into the room. Miette nearly fainted with relief. A tiny tremor descended her body as she closed the door to the great hall and re-crossed the room. She nearly skipped to his throne. When she drew within six paces of him, however, Childeric held up his hand for her to stop.

"Lift your skirts."

Miette's face flushed. He had done this before. He knew she hated Salau and enjoyed seeing her embarrassed in front of him.

But she wasn't such an easy mark. With only the slightest glance at Childeric's champion, Miette bent to pinch the fabric of her dress just above the knee and lifted it to her chest. With a look of defiance on her face, she turned to afford Childeric - and Salau - a better view. She wore nothing beneath her skirts.

The boldness of her act had its desired effect. Both Childeric and Salau's eyes were locked onto her nakedness and the thick triangular patch of hair between her legs.

Childeric recovered first. Chuckling at her ingenuity, he upped his price by waving vaguely at her sex. "Now, touch yourself."

With a frank look in her eyes, again Miette complied.

She parted her legs and probed herself while the two men looked on. She understood the sexual power behind this game. Her youthful appearance and innocent features belied the brazen behavior and made it all the more provocative. Their eyes followed her fingers and she thrilled with the knowledge that she could affect them so. A vein throbbed in Salau's forehead and Childeric had already parted his robe. Miette closed her eyes and moaned.

"Ah." Childeric's voice thickened. "Show them to me."

She extended her hand as if waiting for a gentleman's kiss. It glistened with the wetness of her sex. Childeric rose to take it. *I have him,* she thought.

Stepping towards her, he hesitated. "No. Taste them yourself."

She raised her fingers to her lips and she sucked on them, one at a time, her eyes radiant with the spell she had woven over him.

Childeric slapped her. She reeled beneath the blow. The shock of it coursed through her body. He slapped her again. She fell to the floor.

"You think you have power over me?" There was menace in his voice. Fear flooded through her. She struggled to her feet. He was on her then, bending her over double and lifting the back of her skirt. As he pushed himself into her, she convulsed around him. She was drunk with him, unsure if it was from her passion or from the pain of his blows. She only knew that he, once again, had mastered her.

Her head snapped up in pain as Childeric pulled her upright by her hair. Salau stood directly before her in his place next to the throne. She tried to look away, but her head was held by Childeric's hand. She couldn't hide from Salau the passion that was coursing through her as Childeric thrust himself into her from behind.

"How should I punish you for your arrogance?" he whispered.

She whimpered in response.

"Undo your blouse," he commanded. "Show Salau your breasts."

She did as he asked, untying the fasteners that held up her blouse. Within moments her breasts lay bare for Salau and his hateful eyes to take her in.

"Touch her," Childeric commanded and his champion stepped forward. The triumph in Salau's eyes was unmistakable; he grabbed her nipples hard between each thumb and forefinger and Miette recoiled at his touch. His rough pull, however, reverberated through her, forcing her to arch her back. The pain of it echoed the pleasure of Childeric's thrusts. She grew weak with its intensity.

"You will deny me nothing," Childeric said.

"No," she whimpered.

"Say it!"

"I will deny you nothing." The pain in her nipples was excruciating.

"I don't believe you."

"Anything," she pleaded.

"Take him in your mouth," Childeric commanded. Miette realized that Childeric would always be like this, bending her will to do his bidding. With trembling hands Miette bent to untie Salau's pantaloons and pulled aside his undergarments.

"Yes," Childeric whispered and Miette nearly wept at his praise.

When she left them, Miette checked to be sure that her outer appearance was restored to a demeanor more appropriate of the Lady Ragomfred. Her blouse was re-fastened and her skirts were aligned. She nodded politely to those she passed in the hallway, but secretly she reveled in the semen still smeared on her thighs and the memory of its taste on her lips.

# CHAPTER NINE

*Paris*

"Do you think his claim legitimate?" Carloman asked Boniface as they stood upon a hill near Gentilly where the combined armies had encamped. Carloman had delayed their march east upon receiving reports that a Merovingian "heir" had appeared in Paris and taken up residence at the home of Ragomfred the Younger. Carloman had always known that raising a Merovingian might become a necessity, but he had also assumed that he could do it on his own terms and according to his schedule.

The appearance of this "heir" just as he was marching east was suspicious and the fact that he was residing with a noble who had a long history of opposing his family was alarming.

He raced through the potential objectives Ragomfred might have for making such a move and found none of them good. He swore under his breath. A trickle of mucous escaped from his nose on the damaged side of his face and he searched for a handkerchief to staunch it. The liquid made it halfway down his chin before he could arrest its progress.

"My sources say the legitimacy of his claim is well documented," Boniface said. "I've asked Bishop Aidolf of Auxerres to review evidence of his lineage, but from the reports I've received, Childeric is next in line for the throne. I think it's time we consider the potential benefits of elevating him as king."

Carloman grunted in response.

Below them on an open expanse of grass, roughly twenty knights participated in a mêlée tournament. Carloman had organized the contest as a means of keeping the men occupied during their unexpected encampment.

The ultimate measure of a soldier's fighting skill, the mêlée pit every man against all others. Much as in real combat, attacks came from all sides suddenly and lethally. A fighter's ability to move quickly and effectively and to anticipate attacks was sorely tested. Mêlée tournaments were bloody affairs. The only way off the field was to win, yield, or die. And many a knight's pride prevented the second choice from being made in a timely manner.

A large crowd of soldiers surrounded the combat, cheering and hooting as knights were either dragged or humbled off the field. To add some spice to the encounter, Carloman had promised a large purse to the victor. And when the cheers had subsided, he offered to double it if one of Pippin's knights emerged victorious. The idea prompted a wave of betting that was rumored to include half the men in the combined armies...with most betting on Carloman's champion, Hamar.

An elegant swordsman, Hamar appeared to be making good on their bets. He advanced through the field like a dancer, leaving a trail of knights either ashamed or wounded in his wake. He carried two weapons; a stout Frankish sword and the short, flat blade made famous by the Roman legions. The two blades flowed from one blow to the next in a horrid choreography of pierced shoulders and arms. His speed made opponents look clumsy by comparison. Wiser knights yielded before his mastery to the hoots of the watching throng. Foolish knights paid for their arrogance by being carried from the field.

"Raising a Merovingian to the throne won't stop the civil war," Carloman said.

"No." Boniface nodded. "But it will quell the growing opposition to your waging it. You need the nobles' support in this. Without a king, you'll be constantly defending your claim to rule as mayor."

"That's why Ragomfred is such a danger. With a king's support he could raise a formidable army to do just that. While I'm in the east, he could cause quite a bit of trouble back here in Paris."

Below them, the field of knights thinned rapidly as nobles yielded rather than being gutted or sliced in two. Carloman's knights now far outnumbered Pippin's men. Carloman knew his extra purse was safe. With Hamar moving mercilessly through those who remained, it would be short work for him to finish the contest. Knights in Pippin's camp were already groaning as the outcome had become obvious.

Suddenly, a commotion stirred from Pippin's side of the field as a short stout knight entered the fray, banging his sword against his chest plate and bellowing, "AUSTRASIA!"

Carloman groaned. It was Gunther. Known far and wide for his temper, Pippin's commander was clearly furious that the fight would be lost. He had joined the fray in a pitiable display of loyalty. Although Gunther had been a courageous fighter in his day, his victories were mostly behind him. And Carloman knew that, even in Gunther's prime, Hamar would have humiliated him.

"I've heard that Lord Ragomfred is hosting a ball at his residence," Boniface said. "He's fêting the arrival of the Merovingian as heir to the throne."

Another trickle of mucous escaped Carloman's nostril; this time, his handkerchief was at the ready. "Trying to force my hand. He's pushing me to acknowledge his legitimacy." Carloman looked up. "I'm not ready to do that yet."

"It's hard to unmake the fact that an heir is here. Sooner or later you'll have to acknowledge him. The longer you wait, the more time Lord Ragomfred will have to exploit him. If you elevate him to king, Childeric will owe his allegiance to you, not Ragomfred."

"We don't have time enough for a coronation," Carloman said. "This business with Pippin in Aquitaine has allowed Odilo and Theudebald time to mobilize. My spies tell me that Theudebald is planning to attack a city on this side the Rhine. The longer I delay here, the greater their threat will be."

"It's only one night. You needn't stay long."

"I won't give Childeric any hint at legitimacy until I'm ready. If I go, the entire room will wait to see if I kiss his ring. If I do, his elevation will be as good as done. If I don't, Ragomfred will have more fuel to spread his fire." Carloman searched for another handkerchief. "Going to that ball is the last thing I should do."

Shouts below them stole away their attention. Gunther had organized the few remaining knights Pippin had in the field and created a wedge of sorts that pressed into the center of the makeshift arena. As Carloman and Boniface watched, one side of the wedge pushed forward in a coordinated movement, like a door on a hinge, and slammed into the knights on Hamar's left flank.

"Clever," Carloman said. Gunther was using battlefield tactics to organize Pippin's men. Although the mêlée hadn't been structured as a contest of sides, Carloman couldn't fault Gunther's instinct to bend the rules. He himself had opened the door to such tactics when he offered to double the prize for one of Pippin's knights. Carloman had always thought of Gunther as a bit of a buffoon. Now he was reevaluating his opinion.

From where they stood on the hill, it was clear that Hamar saw the hinge movement and understood Gunther's strategy. He began issuing orders to Carloman's knights and a counterattack leapt to oppose Gunther's closing door.

"What about Pippin?" Boniface asked. "Will he accept the Merovingian?

"I don't think it will matter." Carloman enjoyed seeing the surprise on Boniface's face. "Pippin has half an army and no treasure. He suffers from the blackness. Worse, he combats it with drink. You saw him in Poitiers, he was banging his head against the wall."

"I think you underestimate him," Boniface said. "He is more like Charles than you think."

"He will fail. He only has a small following of knights who are truly loyal to him and no mind for political strategy. That's why I wanted him in the east with me. I need to be there to pick up the pieces. It would be a disaster if Hunoald and Waifar defeated him. I'll let Pippin oversee Neustria or Burgundy or Bretagne, but in the end there will be only one mayor. And it will be me."

Below them, Hamar had successfully countered Gunther's strategy and once again the weight of numbers appeared to doom Pippin's men. Hamar pressed forward, slicing through his opposition until he confronted Gunther directly. Within seconds, it was clear that the older man's speed was no match for Carloman's champion. After a flurry of blows Gunther lost his shield. After another, his left shoulder had been cut. After a third, Gunther was bleeding from his left side. Hamar stepped back to allow the shorter knight time to yield

"AUSTRASIA!" Gunther raised his sword high over his head. "AUSTRASIA!!"

He launched an attack with such fury that Hamar had to retreat to parry effectively.

As the two combatants circled, Gunther's cry was echoed among Pippin's ranks. "AUSTRASIA! AUSTRASIA!!"

Hamar looked up for a sign from Carloman and Carloman nodded his permission. Hamar's blades flashed in the afternoon sun and Gunther fell to one knee under the weight of his blows. Silence took the field at the sudden turn of events. Hamar again fell back to let the older knight yield.

Carloman knew that Gunther wouldn't yield. He said a silent prayer for the man's soul.

A new knight joined the mêlée and for the second time that day, Carloman groaned. This time it was Pippin. Carloman's brother had borrowed a sword and shield and hadn't even bothered to put on armor. His crowd erupted. "AUSTRASIA! AUSTRASIA!!"

"There!" Carloman said to Boniface, shaking his head. "He dooms himself. He lowers himself to their level. How can you lead men if you act like one of them? And when Hamar defeats him, as he most assuredly will, Pippin will lose all credibility."

"I think you underestimate him," Boniface said. "He's more comfortable in that mêlée than you are at court."

Gunther had seized the diversion to retreat to the opposite side of the field and was shouting instructions to Pippin's knights to press Hamar's right flank anew. Pippin slammed into the line nearest him like a battering ram. His speed matched that of Hamar, but Pippin's strength lent an ominous brutality to his fighting that few could withstand. He waded into the knights on Hamar's left flank, using his shield as a weapon as effectively as his sword. Many of those left in his wake were either knocked unconscious or embarrassed at how quickly they were forced to yield.

To meet the threat posed by Gunther's flanking maneuver, Hamar quickly shouted instructions for his knights to protect him while he turned to face the onslaught from Pippin.

"NO!" Carloman shouted. From his vantage point on the hill, Carloman could see Hamar's mistake before his champion made it. Gunther's move was a feint designed to leave Hamar vulnerable to Pippin. The few men remaining on Hamar's left flank were no matches for his brother. Pippin would reach Hamar in minutes.

"As I said," Boniface repeated. "He's more like your father than you suspect."

Pippin swept the legs out from under the knight facing him with the flat of his sword and quickly placed the point of his sword against the soft flesh of the man's neck.

"Yield!" the man cried and the crowd hooted. Pippin,

however, was already on to his next opponent.

It was Hamar. Both sides of the contest roared in anticipation. The fighting by all the other combatants melted away as each of the remaining knights offered truces to witness the contest. Hamar and Pippin circled each other, their breath billowing in the morning air.

Hamar was the first to attack. With incredible speed he launched a series of blows that had the crowd cheering and Pippin in full retreat. Pippin fell back desperately, using both sword and shield to deflect Hamar's blows. Frustrated, Hamar paused to assess his opponent and, again, the two men circled.

Hamar feinted, hoping to draw Pippin out, but Pippin chose caution. When Hamar struck again, his attack was as fast as it was unrelenting. Again, Pippin retreated before him. One of Hamar's thrusts caught Pippin's right arm, but the young mayor continued on, countering each blow with grim concentration.

Carloman stood high on the hill wondering what held his brother back. Pippin made no attempt to counterattack.

A third time, Pippin retreated before the speed of Hamar. Many in the crowd began to boo. Hamar could no longer hide his anger and frustration. His face was red with fury and he banged his chest plate with his sword, unconsciously, mimicking Gunther's earlier challenge.

Pippin, by contrast, was expressionless. His eyes looked dead as he faced Carloman's champion. Hamar roared and attacked again. Pippin again fell back before the barrage, but never left an opening for Hamar to exploit. They circled. Hamar's chest heaved as he sought to regain his wind. Pippin raised his shield and closed.

From atop his hill, Carloman noticed that Pippin held his sword awkwardly. The wound Hamar dealt must have done more damage than he had thought.

It was obvious that Hamar saw it too. Before Pippin could raise his arm, Hamar thrust for Pippin's shoulder.

Pippin was no longer there. He stood to one side of

Hamar and punched forward with his shield, catching Carloman's champion in the face. Hamar stepped back, stunned. Pippin's followers roared.

Growling, Hamar attacked. Again, Pippin fell back before him and deflected the onslaught. This time, however, several of Hamar's blows went wild. One such blow left Hamar off-balance and Pippin quickly took advantage by again stepping forward and to punch Hamar with his shield. Hamar stumbled backwards but stood his ground.

Pippin waited for Hamar to compose himself. When Hamar attacked next, Pippin was a blur, spinning lithely beside him and kicking the side of Hamar's knee and then banging the side of his head with the sword's pommel. Hamar fell back. This time, when he began to circle, Hamar was limping.

The soldiers surrounding the battle began to bang their swords on their shields. They sensed Hamar's vulnerability. Pippin lowered his shield and saluted Carloman's champion, raising the pommel of his sword to his forehead. It was a gesture to acknowledge the honor of one beaten in battle. Hamar screamed his outrage and charged.

Pippin stepped aside and slammed Hamar once more with his shield. Hamar went down to one knee, his blade punching into the earth to stop his fall. Pippin's sword flashed in the afternoon light. The crowd hushed to silence as the blade fell in a deadly arc above Hamar's head.

"No," Carloman said under his breath.

At the last second, Pippin stepped to his left and swept his sword so that it struck Hamar's blade just under the pommel. The blow lifted Hamar's weapon into the sunlight, flipping it far from its owner. Hamar, still on one knee, closed his eyes. Pippin waited.

"I wished you had delivered the blow," Hamar said.

"No honor was at stake," Pippin said. "And we need your sword in the east." He offered Hamar his hand.

The crowd erupted. Somewhere in the back a chant began. It quickly gained momentum and it soon took over the collective voice of the crowd.

"CARLOMAN! CARLOMAN! CARLOMAN!" Everyone looked up the hill to where he stood.

"They want their purse." Boniface chuckled.

"Yes, of course, they do." Bowing to his mentor, Carloman collected the two purses and strode down the hill. The cheering rose in volume with each step he made. He soon found himself standing next to Pippin and Hamar, the crowd delirious. He signaled for quiet.

"The day is yours, brother." He handed Pippin the two purses.

Pippin lifted them over his head and then, with a bow, gave one to Hamar and held the man's hand aloft. The crowd roared anew. Pippin's men rushed into the arena and carried him around the makeshift field.

Carloman looked around to find Boniface. He was where he had left him, standing alone at the top of the hill. His friend and mentor had been right. There might be more to Pippin than Carloman had thought. And it could change everything. Carloman nodded his head in acknowledgement of his godfather's wisdom. He hated it when the bishop was right.

\* \* \*

Pippin winced as Childebrand poured salt into the hole in his shoulder. The wound had surprised him. Hamar was faster than he had expected. Childebrand squeezed together the two edges of the wound with his fingers and shoved a needle and string through them until the knot in the string took hold. His face was a mask of concentration, his tongue flicking across his lips as he sewed. Gunther sat next to Pippin, waiting his turn under Childebrand's needle.

"Don't know why you took the field," the short knight was saying, "I could have bested 'im."

Pippin grunted as Childebrand pulled tight the thread.

"Oh, he's good," Gunther admitted. "Fast as a fox. But no match for the likes of me. You shouldn't've stepped in. You don't need all the glory, Pippin."

Pippin winced. Childebrand sank the needle in again, this time more roughly.

"Easy," Pippin chided. "I'm on your side."

As he spoke, the Comptesse de Loches made her way across the field where the mêlée had taken place. Her pace faltered as she passed the first of many large swaths of blood-stained grass. By the time she reached the last, her pace had slowed. She lingered at the edge of the field, bowed her head in prayer and made the sign of the cross.

When she turned in his direction, Pippin stood and made his way to her, brushing off Childebrand's needle and his protest.

"Comptesse." Pippin bowed. Her eyes took in his half-sewn shoulder. She grumbled her disapproval before speaking. "Milord Pippin."

"Milady-"

The Comptesse held up her hand to cut him off. Her eyes warned him to silence. Pippin closed his mouth.

"I have yet to forgive you for your disturbing behavior in Tours," she began. "But we are finally near Paris and I am in need of an escort."

"I'll have four of my men take you into the city."

"That's not what I meant," the Comptesse snapped. "The Lady Ragomfred is holding a ball in honor of the expected heir." She paused. "I'd like you to escort me there."

Pippin's face colored at the suggestion. "I just spoke to Carloman. He doesn't think we should attend. He said it would only fuel the Merovingian's fire."

"What do you think?" The Comptesse's eyes narrowed.

"I can't see how it would help. It either forces a confrontation, which plays into the hands of our detractors, or it builds momentum for his elevation. What purpose would be served?"

"What would your father have said?"

Pippin thought before answering. "He wouldn't have cared. He would have gone just to see how the court would react."

The Comptesse waited for more.

"And he would have enjoyed their discomfort." Pippin smiled at the thought. "He wouldn't have let anyone think for a moment that he wasn't in charge."

Now, the Comptesse was smiling. Pippin chuckled at his own naïveté. He bowed to the Comptesse and offered her his arm.

"Milady, would you do me the honor of accompanying me to the Ragomfred ball?"

"Why, I would be delighted, milord Mayor." She took his arm. "I'll send a tailor to provide you with some proper clothes. I daresay he'll do a better job of sewing than your lieutenant."

"But-"

The Comptesse held up her hand to stop his protest.

"If you are to escort me, you will dress appropriately."

Pippin decided that, perhaps, discretion was in order. He bowed again to her and began to escort her from the field.

"I still haven't forgiven you for your behavior at Tours."

"Comptesse," Pippin protested. "I've apologized several times for that."

"Yes." She looked over her shoulder at the bloodstained field behind her. "But your tendency to violence is disturbing."

"I didn't kill him," Pippin said.

The Comptesse de Loches grunted.

# CHAPTER TEN

*Regensburg*

One of Trudi's eyes opened before she came awake. She was cold, terribly cold, and her face hurt. Odilo was snoring softly next to her and the fire in the corner was nearly out. For some reason, the bed was hard.

She struggled to sit up and found herself on the table in the great hall. Looking down at herself, she discovered that her robe was torn open and her nakedness was on display for all to see. Confused, she pulled at the corners of the garment to cover herself and saw the ugly line of dried blood that descended her belly and the blood on her thighs.

She remembered.

She reeled backward onto the table with revulsion as the memory of Theudebald's rape revisited itself upon her. Again, she felt Theudebald's knife on her skin. Again, he struck her face and head. Again, his flesh penetrated her flesh.

His ravaging cascaded over her. She tried to ward against it, batting at the air above her, but her defenses were as useless as they had been the night before. Unchecked, the memories assaulted her and Trudi wept with humiliation.

She struggled to sit up, her hands fumbling to cover her nakedness. Odilo's soft snore broke through her confusion and the paradox of his presence gripped her. Anger surged through her. How could he sleep?

In a rage she turned to strike him, to demand why he had failed to awaken, why he failed to protect her, but a sharp pain lanced across her abdomen and her anger turned to fear. She flung open her robe. Grabbing a corner of the fabric, she wiped away the fluids that smeared her. When she was finished, she thrust a hand between her legs. She lifted her fingers up to the firelight. They were streaked with blood.

Panic seized her. She gathered the bottom of her robe and stuffed it between her legs. Holding the ball of fabric tight against her, she edged off the table and tried to stand. She was so lightheaded she nearly fainted. She put a hand out to steady herself, and after a couple of deep breaths, made for the door and shuffled her way across the room.

The hallway leading to the stairs was empty. Trudi offered a quick prayer of thanks and crept through the darkness. She peered up past the curve of the staircase and seeing no one, advanced up it. She stopped again to peer past the next curve and again moved on. She just had to make it to her apartment unseen. Then she could decide what to do.

Unbidden, an old wives's tale leapt to Trudi's mind and struck her like a rock. "Ravaged women share the blame; their bodies be forever stained."

She began to sob. She covered her mouth to mute the sound. Her feet stopped their ascent and she sat on the stairway, curling herself into a ball. She rocked herself back and forth.

Harsh voices on the stairs above frightened her into silence. Soldiers were descending the steps towards her. Scurrying, Trudi retraced her steps down the stairs to the main hallway and looked for places to hide. She found no furniture or draperies to shield her. Her only option was to return to the great hall. She shuddered. She couldn't go back there. The soldiers' steps were now directly above her. Within seconds they would find her. She stepped into the shadow of the stairwell, hoping its darkness would keep her out of sight.

Their accents were too harsh for Trudi to understand, but the progress of the soldiers' voices allowed her to mark their descent down the circular staircase. They were above and behind her - alongside her - before her. She held her breath. She prayed. They passed within several feet of her and walked on to the great hall.

The moment they were out of sight, Trudi was again on the stairs, making her way to the second floor. She was desperate now, all her attention on reaching her rooms. She made the second landing. No more than fifty feet separated her from her apartment. She cautiously peered around the corner to look down the hall. There was someone there. A large form patrolled near her doorway and seemed to be walking away from her. She waited.

Shouts came from downstairs and Trudi heard footsteps coming up the staircase. They must have seen her blood on the table. She had to risk getting to her room. Holding the ball of cloth between her legs, she sprinted down the hallway towards her door. The dark figure, a guard, at the end of the hall turned and called out to her.

Trudi reached her door first and struggled to open it. The latch wouldn't cooperate and slipped in her hand.

"Duchesse!" The guard ran towards her.

The latch lifted and she was inside. She slammed the door and locked it from the inside as the guard banged on her door.

"Duchesse! Your robe! Are you well?"

Trudi rested her cheek against the door; silently thanking it for the temporary safety it afforded her. She tried to compose herself.

"Duchesse!"

"It's the baby. Send for a doctor." Trudi started to cry.

"Please let me in."

She pounded on the door. "Send for the doctor!"

After a moment's hesitation, she heard the man's footsteps running down the hallway. Relieved that he had gone,

Trudi slid down the length of the door to sit on the floor. She longed to crawl to her bed but knew she could not.

*"Ravaged women share the blame; their bodies be forever stained."*

She had to get control of herself. She stood and found the mirror on the wall across the room. A beaten and very frightened, pregnant young woman stared back at her.

Anger coursed through her. They must never know.

She took off what was left of her bloody robe, hurriedly stuffed it beneath her bed, and returned naked to the wash-basin.

With a clean towel, she washed the remaining evidence of the rape from her thighs and then hid the towel under the bed with her robe. She rolled a second towel into a pad and placed it between her legs to staunch the bleeding. Next, she washed her face, tentatively probing the swollen and bruised parts of her cheek and lips.

She donned a new nightdress and began to brush her hair.

There was pounding at her door. It was Odilo.

"Trudi! What's happened?"

Her anger spiked at the sound of his voice. How could he sleep through it?

Furiously, Trudi fought to choke back her tears. "Get the doctor. I'm bleeding!"

"Trudi?"

"I fell down the stairs. I think my cheek is broken." *Why didn't he protect me?*

"Open the door!"

Trudi cleaned away every trace of her hurried toilet and climbed into her bed. The pounding on the door continued. She pulled the blankets over her.

Odilo, with the help of a guard, kicked in the door. He ran to the bed to take Trudi into his arms.

She recoiled. "Don't touch me!"

Odilo retreated, stunned.

"I'm bleeding," Trudi said. "I need a doctor."

Odilo took her into her arms and searched the bruising on her face. "You fell?"

"I'm losing the baby!" she shouted.

Odilo grabbed the guard and began barking instructions. Trudi waved her hand to interrupt them. "Post a guard," she said in a faint voice.

With a frightened look on his face, Odilo nodded. "I'll be right back."

Much to Trudi's relief, the two left her room. She rolled over, drew the blankets around her, and cradled her belly in her arms. She tried not to think about the growing wetness between her legs.

*  *  *

Eta arrived with two Bavarian midwives in tow, dressed in crisp, white smocks and grey skirts. With a wave of authority, she took complete control of Trudi's chambers. She brusquely dismissed all the men from her quarters, hung temporary drapes to cordon off her bed from the rest of the apartment and ordered workman to replace the door. Banks of candles were produced to push back the night. New bed linens and blankets replaced those she had soiled and the furniture that served no utilitarian purpose was removed while supplies of linens, bandages, soaps, sponges and washbasins were brought in and placed in perfectly aligned rows on the table next to her bed.

The two midwives, large and buxom with broad hands, ignored the panic and passion of Trudi's protests and gently removed her robe. They washed her methodically and thoroughly from foot to scalp.

There was no question that the women knew she had been raped. They found and disposed of the ripped and bloody clothing Trudi had hidden beneath her bed. And they had

129

watched as Eta examined her. Trudi saw their eyes hardened with recognition when her loins were inspected. She watched as their mouths pulled into frowns when Eta probed her scalp and dressed the wounds to her breast and belly. No words were exchanged between them. But they knew.

Trudi wept in humiliation. The midwives with their big hands replaced the bloody pad between her legs and lifted her again to settle a new night robe around her shoulders. They laid her back onto a deep soft pillow and tucked her in between two stiff, white bed linens. Trudi turned her face into the pillow to hide her tears. One by one, she heard the midwives leave. Only one remained. When her tears had been spent, Trudi turned from the soft haven of her pillow to find Eta sitting next to her.

Eta was much older than the other midwives and had a jaw that had been set by decades of responsibility. Her hair had lost most of its color and was tied tightly into a bun at the base of her neck. The skin on her face was so bloodless and thin that she appeared almost translucent. It reminded Trudi of the way Charles had looked just before he died. Grayness clung to her like a shroud.

Eta's eyes, however, sparkled with strength. They exuded knowledge and a fierce resolve that Trudi found intimidating. She wanted to look away, but the older woman's gaze held her with an urgency that Trudi couldn't resist. She abandoned herself within Eta's eyes and discovered an empathy that touched her deeply.

"Did your husband do this?" Eta asked.

Trudi shook her head. She couldn't seem to bring herself to speak.

"Do you know who did?"

Trudi nodded, the memory of his face blotting out her sight. Anger and humiliation coursed through her. Tears stung her face again. "Theudebald," she whispered.

A hissing sound emanated from Eta's lips as she spat a curse and drew runes furiously in the air. "I should have strangled that boy in his crib. Does the Duc know?"

Panic seized Trudi. "No!" Then in a quieter voice she said, "Odilo must never know."

As the older woman weighed the choices before her, Trudi saw the hardness return to Eta' eyes. They flashed with possibilities. When she came to a decision, however, Eta's eyes returned to their previous warmth.

"We won't speak of it," Eta's voice was soft but firm. "None of us. You have my word."

Trudi believed her. She fell back onto the bed, exhausted.

"It's unjust that you bear this, alone." The older woman's voice carried a wave of weariness. She stroked Trudi's hair. "But I will honor your desire for privacy. I had hoped that you would be the harbinger of a new day in Regensburg with your new customs from the west. Instead, it's you who have fallen victim to the darkness of ours."

Eta paused for a moment.

"We are an ancient people. Such violence is deep in our race. What happened to you has happened countless times before to countless women within these walls. Oh, I've have seen the faces of women..." Her voice seemed to drift off into nothingness. Eta laid a hand gently on Trudi's stomach. "I regret that now you too, know of our sorrow."

Trudi grabbed Eta's hand before she could leave. "I can't live with this."

Eta's eyes returned to her, resolute and angry. Trudi saw the conflict buried deep within them. Eta understood her suffering. She understood the humiliation. She had faced such demons herself and withstood them.

"Yes, you can," Eta said. "You will." But she didn't offer how. "You and I will see your little Duc born right here on this very bed. And we will rejoice in his coming." The passion in Eta's eyes accepted no dissent. She grabbed Trudi by her arms and lifted her. Her face drew close to Trudi's and her voice lowered to a whisper. Her words came hard and urgent.

"I have known such men," Eta's eyes were dangerous. Trudi felt small before them. "They revel in your pain and humiliation. You will defy him. You will not weaken! You will not fail."

"How can you be so sure?"

"Because I won't let you." Eta held her then. She rocked Trudi in her arms like a baby. Trudi lost her sense of time and didn't remember falling to sleep. When she awoke, she was still tucked within two crisp white sheets. The door to her chamber had been repaired and one of the midwives sat by her bed.

Every six hours, the midwives came and went in shifts of three. Their voices had a lilting quality to them. They fed her, bathed her, and combed her hair as if she were a child. It gave Trudi a measure of serenity. She noticed too, that guards had been posted outside her door. That too was comforting. She refused all visitors.

After three days, the color on the bruised side of her face had softened to a darkish purple and yellow and one of her back teeth had jarred loose. More importantly, however, the bleeding had stopped. For that, she was grateful.

Still, Trudi refused to get out of bed, save to relieve herself. She wasn't sure that she could explain why. She told Odilo that she was afraid for the baby. But the truth was embedded in a fear far deeper than she could explore. She couldn't imagine leaving the safety of her room with her bevy of midwives. Just the thought of it made her weak.

After another six days, Eta returned to her bedside.

"Your body is healing," the gray midwife said.

Trudi nodded.

"The bleeding has stopped."

Again, Trudi nodded. The woman's erect posture was a tower of strength and she found herself shrinking from it.

"Yet, you stay in bed."

"I...I'm afraid for the baby."

Eta's eyes bore into her. "And your husband?" Eta's voice

was unrelenting. "You recoil from his hand?"

Trudi's face bloomed with embarrassment. How could she know that? Trudi indeed had withdrawn from Odilo. The thought of his touch only made her nauseous.

"I can't," she said. "It sickens me."

To Trudi's surprise, Eta nodded knowingly. "The stain of it remains with you," she said. "It isn't easily washed cleaned. "

Trudi shook her head resignedly.

"And you blame your husband?"

Trudi was awash in humiliation. She couldn't speak the words. She nodded her head.

"You must forgive him – for the sake of the child." She laid her hand on Trudi's shoulder compassionately. "And you cannot remain in bed." Eta swept aside Trudi's sheets. "Out with you!"

"I can't," Trudi stammered in surprise.

Eta waved away her protests and leaned close to Trudi's face. The hardness in the woman's eyes was back. She would accept no compromise. "It's time to get up."

Unconsciously, Trudi moved to obey. The instinct to survive compelled her forward. But, as her feet moved, panic gripped her. She looked helplessly up into Eta's face, begging for mercy.

She found none.

Eta stood over her like a sentinel, refusing anything but complete obedience.

Trudi's will seemed to collapse in on itself and she sank back into the safety of her pillows. She turned away from Eta, ashamed of her weakness. She wept quietly until the midwife left her room.

# CHAPTER ELEVEN

*Paris*

**M**iette swirled into the great hall, her dress flowing behind her in a great circle of fabric. She had her arms up, dancing in her mind with her lover, much to the obvious amusement of her servants. They were busy putting the finishing touches on the ball room, pushing tables and chairs into place and hanging wide purple banners from the ceiling to create a more festive air. Purple had been her idea. It was the color of kings and she wanted her guests to know that there was no disputing the vaunted stature of her guest.

The past six weeks at court had been good for Miette. She had become a force with which to contend. As hostess to the future king, she was one of the most sought-after guests in Paris. *Commoner indeed!* Never again would the noble ladies snub her as they had when she was newly married. Invitations swamped her doorstep in wave after wave of affirmation for her newfound popularity. She took great delight in deciding whose home she would grace and whose invitation she would refuse. *It's like a dance,* she thought. *One had to be seen, yet appear unattainable, and then when the music started only an elite few would be granted a step onto the floor.*

Her presence at a Paris salon immediately caused a stir.

At first, there would be hushed stares and discreet whispering. Then as guests became accustomed to her, the gathering would become more boisterous; the host would serve better wine; the musicians would become livelier, and the dancing would start in earnest. It was almost as if the king himself had arrived. Lesser nobles invited her, knowing that if she accepted, their status at court would improve. And if she snubbed the house of a great lord, rumors would follow to speculate about the cause. It was delicious!

Her dance among the salons of Paris, however, had a greater purpose than satisfying her vanity. For the most part, she accepted invitations where it might serve Childeric's purpose. It was surprising how much one could learn at a dinner party and how much more at a ladies' tea. She had become quite adept at flattery and the art of pretending to know more than she did. She found it would entice others to speak more freely. After a while, she didn't have to pretend much at all.

She also used her appearances as vehicles to dispense information. She was amazed at how damning a well-placed word could be. Each evening upon returning home, she carefully catalogued each new item of gossip for her husband and together, they sifted through what they thought was useful and true and what was not.

In an odd way, her role as hostess to the Merovingian had brought about a form of truce with her husband. While Lord Ragomfred raised money and private arms for the future king, she sowed distrust for the mayors and hope for the king's ascendancy. While Ragomfred counseled Childeric on building financial and military support for his elevation, Miette acted as their eyes and ears at court. Ragomfred even had asked her advice before contacting a noble to gauge his best approach and then expressed respect for her counsel. As well he should, she thought. It was good advice.

Ragomfred no longer avoided her presence at home and even had accompanied her out to an occasional evening function. Once, to her great surprise, he had deigned to dance with her in public.

Not that he ever visited her bed at night. No, thank God. That would never change. After Childeric, she was happy that her husband avoided her chambers. She would never like the man but was tired of being angry with him.

As if summoned by her thoughts, her husband strode into the hall. Miette leapt into his arms and twirled him onto the dance floor. As usual, Lord Ragomfred didn't share her buoyant mood.

"I have news." He took Miette's hands from his shoulders. With a nod of his head, he dismissed the servants. When they were alone, he said, "Pippin is coming." His face was creased with lines of distress. "He's coming to the ball!"

For the life of her Miette couldn't understand his anxiety. "That is wonderful. Just as you planned it! Pippin will be forced to pay homage to Childeric and if he doesn't, you will have more evidence to turn the remaining nobles against him."

Her answer didn't seem to satisfy him. "What is it?"

Ragomfred began to pace.

"Husband?"

"I expected Carloman," Ragomfred sputtered.

"I don't see what difference it makes, which brother comes. They're both mayors."

"Pippin is unpredictable." Ragomfred was clearly nervous. "The man is a beast. Who knows what he'll do? At his Assembly, he personally beat Lord Ganelon of Mayence until the man's face was unrecognizable."

"I'm sure you're exaggerating."

"I saw the man. His face was crushed."

"Pippin wouldn't dare do something like that here."

Ragomfred grunted.

"Are you afraid of him, husband?" Miette couldn't help letting some of her scorn seep into her voice.

"Of course, I am! Only a fool would fail to take a son of Charles seriously."

"I've heard he's weak," Miette sniffed. "Half of Paris thinks he will fail. He's taken to drink and has no treasure. Most of the alliances we've made for Childeric have been with nobles who lack confidence in Pippin. I think you overestimate him."

"Well, perhaps that is because Pippin doesn't count you among his enemies."

Miette was taken aback by the rebuke. She never imagined that Ragomfred was such a coward. She watched her husband pace across the room. *Look at the fear in him!* The disdain she harbored for him grew by the minute. *He delights in plotting behind the scenes but can't stand to be center stage.* She thought about Pippin's potential to disrupt the ball and shrugged. "We'll double the guards. I'm sure Childeric will handle him."

"Childeric has never lifted a sword in his life."

Miette's reaction to the slight was immediate. Anger flooded through her veins and her face flushed with it. She turned on her husband.

"At least he's a man!" She spat. "He wouldn't quiver in his boots like a boy on his wedding night."

Blood drained from Ragomfred's face and Miette instantly regretted the jibe. The sword fell too close to the man's heart.

"How dare you say that to me." Ragomfred's voice was cold and lethal. "You were nothing before I wed you. You were a commoner."

Miette's body shook with frustration. "That didn't stop you from taking my father's dowry."

"Had I known what a witch he raised I would have doubled the price."

Rage flashed through her. With a crude phallic gesture used by commoners, she cocked her forearm before his face. Then, with her eyebrows arching, she dramatically let it wilt.

"Remind you of anything, husband?"

Ragomfred slapped her.

The shock of it made her think of Childeric. "Would that you were such a man."

"I will see you destitute."

"You arrogant fool! You're not the only man in my life."

Ragomfred spun back to her, his face contorted with rage. He seized Miette by the arm and drew her to him.

"Oh yes," she plunged on. "You've been cuckolded! I found a man who can fill the void you left between my legs."

Ragomfred hit her again. "Who?" His voice choked with rage.

She relished his fury. It gave her power over him. She couldn't wait to tell him and see the shock on his face.

"Childeric," she gloated. "Your king." Ragomfred lowered his hand, stunned. "And I can assure you that he has no problem lifting his sword."

Her husband's eyes turned away as if to search the room for understanding. When they returned to her, they were alight with irony.

The look confused Miette. She wanted him wounded. "He took me right here. In this room, on your father's chair."

Ragomfred's eyes, however, didn't change.

"I've been his lover," Miette crowed, "ever since he entered this house."

Ragomfred let go of her arm and laughed. "As have I," he said. "As have I."

❋ ❋ ❋

While Pippin dressed for the Ragomfred ball, Carloman was ducking into a cave deep within the forest of Boulogne. He was dressed in a dark robe with the mask of a demon covering his face. Hamar stood beside him. He too, was dressed in black, but wore the mask of a rodent.

Before them, two members of the Knights in Christ First Order led a line of aspirants deep into the cave. To a man, the initiates were naked, blindfolded, and exhausted.

Since the days of Rome, secretive pagan religious orders were common to military men of the ranks. Often made up of slaves or impressed soldiers from conquered lands with different languages, religions and customs, soldiers found cohesion and trust through arcane religious cabals and brotherhood. The initiation rites typically were grueling, exhaustive affairs with gruesome displays of butchery to prepare the initiates for the gore they would witness on the battlefield.

Most Frankish nobles who knew of these practices refused to acknowledge their existence, preferring to turn a blind eye to them rather than challenge the deep roots of their custom.

Until Carloman. The son of Charles Martel had usurped the pagan practice to form a religious brotherhood based on Christian values of faith, loyalty and service. Called the Knights in Christ, it was intended to produce a cadre of zealous holy warriors devoted to the Christian faith. The men joined voluntarily, each being tested and initiated regardless of rank or station. Those initiated would be placed in the Seventh Order to advance through the next six degrees of piety based on their deeds and loyalty.

The resulting religious order had succeeded far beyond Carloman's expectations. The brotherhood had by-passed the traditional oaths of fealty by commission and provided him with a command of his army that was absolute. It also provided influence over every noble family in Francia.

Carloman and Hamar took positions before the entrance to a large chamber within the cavern. At Carloman's signal, the chanting began. It was an ominous sound, the low-throated growl of fifty men.

*"Ware, knight, ware! Walk this path and walk as one. May god show mercy, for we have none!"*

Carloman led the first aspirant into the chamber. It was his son Drogo. Carloman had ensured that the young man would join his Knights in Christ. Together they would lead the

Knights across the kingdom from one generation to the next.

Until now, Carloman had shielded Drogo in battle, keeping him well outside the deadliest fray. This year would be different. Carloman planned to give Drogo great visibility putting down the rebellion. His son would be one of his lieutenants and would lead a division of cavalry. Eventually, Carloman would raise Drogo to the rank of mayor. He had yet to decide where and when his son would rule and, more importantly, how to convince Pippin that the time was right for such a move.

It was a delicate subject. Pippin had no children and so couldn't hand down his post through succession. With Drogo being the sole male heir, he ultimately would inherit the whole kingdom. The only threats to this plan were Gripho, whom Carloman had imprisoned, and Trudi's expected offspring. If she gave Odilo a son, he too would have a claim. By crushing the rebellion, Carloman hoped to remove that possibility from the table as well.

As Drogo was led across the threshold, Hamar clouted him on the head with the butt of his sword and removed the boy's blindfold. Drogo stumbled into the center of the hall, squinting in a futile effort to see through the flaming torches that surrounded him.

The fifty knights of the First Order sat on rows of benches on all four sides of the room.

*"Ware, knight, ware! Walk this path and walk as one. May god show mercy, for we have none!"*

Carloman gestured for Drogo to kneel. Before him stood an arch made of two posts bisected by two crossbeams. Between the crossbeams hung a live goat, muzzled and struggling against its restraints. A short Roman sword lay beneath the animal on the ground.

The First fell silent. Carloman drew his sword and stood next to his kneeling son.

"You have finished the tests of faith and loyalty. You kneel before the Gate of Passage. Through this gate is a life of service. Do you vow to serve our Lord through the Brotherhood?"

"I so vow," Drogo said.

*"Your vow is sacred,"* chanted the First.

"Do you vow to obey the covenants of the Brotherhood?"

"I so vow."

*"Your vow is eternal."*

"Before you is a symbol of the false gods. Slay it. Devour its heart. Then you may take your place among us."

Drogo stumbled to his feet and picked up the short Roman sword below the struggling animal. After only the briefest hesitation, he plunged it into the belly of the struggling goat and drew it up towards the beast's chest.

*"I am the lord your God,"* chanted the First.

Blood and entrails poured from the writhing, suspended animal, covering Carloman's son in viscera.

*"Who brought you out of the land of Egypt, out of the house of bondage."*

Drogo thrust his right hand into the wound and shoved it up inside the animal's ribcage. Steam rose from the cascade of blood covering his body. After several attempts, he ripped his arm free and triumphantly held its heart aloft for the First to see.

*"You shall have no other gods before me!"*

Clearly, choking back a wave of nausea, Drogo bent his lips to the still-beating organ and, sank his teeth into the flesh. Carloman swung his blade in a wide overhand arc and severed the goat in two. Blood sprayed the floor. The First Order stood.

*"Those who walk this path, walk as one. Rejoice now, brother, for we are one!"*

Two of the First seized Drogo and forced him to his knees. A smoldering brand in the shape of a cross was pressed into his flesh, just above his right breast. Drogo screamed and began to pass out. A bucket of water was used to revive him, and he was escorted through an exit at the far side of the hall.

A new goat was led into the room and tied to the cross-beams of the arch. Hamar accompanied Carloman back to the entrance to bring a new aspirant into the hall. The voices of the First rose behind him.

*"Ware, knight, ware! Walk this path and walk as one. May god show mercy, for we have none!"*

Hamar clouted the man on the head and removed his blindfold.

Carloman gestured for him to kneel.

# CHAPTER TWELVE

*Paris*

"Damn these seamstresses!" Bertrada fumbled with the neckline of her gown. She had failed in her mission to secure new ball gowns for Aude and herself. Not only was every seamstress in Paris already employed sewing gowns for the ball, they laughed at the audacity of a lady wanting two made in such a short time.

This forced Bertrada and her sister into the uncomfortable position of choosing between the gowns they had worn the night Tedbalt had arrived in Paris or wearing older gowns they had brought from Laon. As all of the older gowns were woefully out of fashion, Aude chose the newer one. Bertrada's gown had been damaged, so she had been forced to use an older one. Tedbalt would have to forgive them.

Again, Bertrada fussed with her neckline. Aude must have fastened her dress too tightly. At least she had her favorite earrings. They were jade stones set in circlets of gold. Pippin had given them to her after his campaign in Navarre.

Tedbalt arrived on time to escort the two sisters to the home of Ragomfred the Younger. The man lived across the Seine in an ancient neighborhood that overlooked the water from the southwest. Tedbalt had rented an expensive carriage, that Bertrada was sure was more expensive than he could afford, and the three made their way over the wooden bridge to the lower bank of the river. As they did, they were assaulted by the odor of offal and human waste that was shoveled daily into its expanse.

Tedbalt pulled down the shade covering the carriage window. It did little to suppress the stench.

Aude, as usual, was maintaining the conversation for all three of them. She comically batted away at the awful smell, which drew a laugh from Tedbalt, and then returned the conversation back to the ball. Her excitement over meeting the Merovingian could barely be contained.

"What if he talks to me?" she gushed. "Do you think we'll be introduced?" Then her mood became more sober. "How does one address a king who isn't yet a king?"

Bertrada stopped listening. Tedbalt was clearly captivated by the girl and Bertrada had other things on her mind. She wasn't sure about the politics of going to this ball. Ragomfred had been a known enemy of Charles. And no one knew that she was no longer Pippin's lover. She wasn't sure how her attendance would look to the nobles at court. She wished she could ask Pippin.

A wave of longing swept over her. She was glad of the darkness inside the carriage; no one could see her face flush. She let her thoughts stray to the place in her mind where she kept her memories of him. She let them flood through her in waves. She saw him standing naked, high on the rocks near their pond at Quierzy, bold as a Spartan and foolish as an apprentice, casually flipping himself into the water far below.

She saw his eyes as they were just before he entered her. Smiling but reverent, they held her fast beneath him as her body opened to take him inside.

Bertrada shook her head. *Enough of that!* Instead, she watched Tedbalt and Aude banter and laugh in the darkness of the carriage. They seemed so happy and comfortable with each other. *Why does it upset me so?* she wondered. She had never wanted Tedbalt as a boy. But as soon as Aude desired him, so had she. Was she so frivolous?

Tedbalt had grown into a fine-looking man. She could do worse than to marry him. But did she love him or was she merely jealous of the attention he showed Aude? She didn't know.

She also didn't know if she could forget Pippin. Or forgive him.

The carriage trundled forward, jostling its inhabitants with every bump in the dirt road. As her weight shifted, Bertrada's hand went again to adjust the line of her gown. Damned seamstresses!

\* \* \*

The ball did little to improve Bertrada's mood. The affair was so crowded that their carriage was forced to wait in line out on the street before letting them off at the villa. They queued again to leave their cloaks at the door and yet again when they were announced. By the time all three got inside the great hall, the throng was so pronounced they struggled to find a spot to congregate.

Tedbalt ushered them next to a large column near the doors to a broad patio, overlooking the Seine. As soon as they were settled, he disappeared to find them wine.

Much to Bertrada's irritation, she immediately became a focal point in the room. Her relationship with Pippin had given her a degree of celebrity and a stream of nobles made their way to her place by the column to pay their respects. No one knew that her association with him was over. Most expressed surprise at seeing her at the ball and asked about Pippin. Bertrada decided to forgo explaining their recent break.

"Thank you so much! Yes, he's out on campaign... You are so kind! I will be happy to tell him...that is such a lovely gown! May I introduce my younger sister Aude?"

After an interminable absence, Tedbalt reappeared

bearing three half-filled glasses of red wine. Bertrada finished hers in less than a minute. She began to wonder why she'd come. Despite being in a room full of people, she felt inexorably alone.

By contrast, Aude's excitement grew with each passing minute. She could barely restrain her enthusiasm. She smiled and curtsied to the nobles Bertrada introduced and commented on the gowns of all the women present. One would think it was the first time the girl had seen jewelry! She was hanging onto Tedbalt's arm as if tethered. Worse, Bertrada was forced to introduce them together as if they were a couple.

She saw Boniface at the food table. The Bishop apparently couldn't get enough of the duck meat. As was his custom on ostentatious occasions such as this, Boniface wore a plain brown robe to contrast himself with the excessive couture of the invited nobles. He was making a great show of harrumphing at the low necklines of the noble women in attendance. Bertrada decided to keep Aude clear of the man.

Bishop Aidolf of Auxerres was also present. After making his rounds to greet the hosts and the more notable nobles in the room, the small wiry man had joined Boniface by the food table.

Bertrada fanned herself, feeling closed in by the crowd. So many were in attendance that the doors to the patio had to be opened to make room. She wondered which of the nobles were there to show their support for elevating the Merovingian to the throne and which had come out of curiosity. Many were knights currently out on campaign with Carloman and Pippin. Hedging their bets, she thought.

Lady Ragomfred had done an excellent job as hostess, providing an abundant amount of entertainment, food and drink. Bertrada was stunned that such a young girl could move so competently through the room. She stopped at each cluster of nobles, greeted each person by name and made sure that their needs were being met by her host of servants. It was an excellent performance. Just a wisp of a girl – rather pale –

but she lorded over the room like a queen.

Bertrada watched as Boniface dribbled some of his duck meat down the front of his robe. He casually brushed it away, leaving small oil stains in its wake. Aidolf was not eating. He seemed too excited. The graying bishop was busy greeting every young nobleman who passed them by.

Across the room two young trumpeters marched through a side entrance and took up positions on either side of the door. The long instruments they carried were nearly as tall as the boys themselves. Acting as one, they lifted the horns to their respective lips.

They stood absolutely still, waiting for silence. It took some time and a great deal of "shushing" for the crowd to quiet. Still, the boys waited, their arms trembling from the weight of the trumpets. When the last murmur had faded away and the last glass had finished clinking, their chests rose in unison. As one, their cheeks ballooned outward and the horns trilled. It was a high and hesitant sound, the notes muted and confused. It was almost as if the boys were rehearsing. Guests looked about the room in surprise. Then the randomness of the notes evolved into a playful pattern where one coyly echoed the other as the two experimented with and rejected themes until at last, the hint of a fanfare emerged. It grew in complexity and force until the boys embraced it in a final triumphal progression. Its crescendo and strength filled the room. The last note was so high and clear it was an expression of hope and joy.

The doors opened. Childeric stood behind them, relaxed, confident and regal. He was dressed in a white chemise, white pantaloons and an elegant purple doublet trimmed in gold. He stepped into the room with a flourish.

The nobles erupted with applause. Childeric waved his hand and bejeweled fingernails in acknowledgement. The gesture brought cheers and Childeric smiled at them.

He is, Bertrada thought, "comfortable" in his role as king. She was at once surprised by the support he received in the room and concerned over its import. Pippin should be careful with this man.

Aude was begging Tedbalt to join her in line to meet the king. He looked hesitant to leave her alone, but Aude smiled so coyly and pulled on his arms so playfully that he had a hard time resisting her. Aude even found ways to "accidentally" press her body against him. *My God, she was a flirt.*

Bertrada had had enough. "You two go ahead. I'm going out to the patio. I need some fresh air." Without waiting for acknowledgement, she headed for the door. It took every ounce of her will not to run. She couldn't wait for this ball to be over.

She burst out onto the patio and into the safety of the night air. To her surprise, she found herself crying. She bolted for the darkest corner and tried to wipe her eyes with the palms of her hands.

"Bertrada!" a voice called from behind her. Not another noble! She struggled to compose herself. Not now!

"Bertrada!"

She took a deep breath and turned.

It was Tedbalt. Bertrada burst into tears. He rushed to her and she collapsed in his arms, sobbing into his shoulder. He rocked her as he would a child and waited for her to calm down.

"I've been such a fool." She looked up into his eyes.

Then, to her surprise, she kissed him.

\* \* \*

"We will wait," the Comptesse said, "until we're announced."

Although Pippin thought such pomp utter foolishness, he had agreed to follow the Comptesse's lead during the ball. They stood waiting on a small landing at the entrance while a plump little man in an impossibly ornate costume barred them from descending the staircase down to the revelers. Pippin pulled at the neck of his new doublet, trying to loosen its vise-like grip across his chest. Without looking at him, the Comptesse brutally pinched the inside of his arm. Pippin decided it might be prudent to stop.

Her tailor had fitted him with a white chemise, black pantaloons and a dark green doublet with a matching green cloak. It was the most elegant clothing he had worn since leaving Rome.

What had surprised him more, however, was the Comptesse. Already an attractive woman, she had transformed herself into an arresting beauty. She wore a stunning red gown that displayed her shoulders in the latest Paris fashion, but she covered them discreetly with a thin, almost transparent, lace shawl. It was risqué and conservative at the same time. Although clearly age had touched her, Pippin was hardpressed to imagine that a woman could look more stunning.

The plump little man at the head of the stairs finally turned to attend them. He held them in a haughty regard as if no one on the guest list could ever hope to impress him. When he recognized Pippin's name, however, his eyes grew wide with surprise. The little man bowed, and then turned to a small table where an array of punch drinks was aligned. He offered each of them a glass while they waited. Frowning, the Comptesse refused. Pippin by contrast, accepted both, and downed each in a single draught. He grabbed a third to carry into the hall. There were still two more couples to be announced ahead of them.

When it came their turn, Pippin was sure that no one would hear anything over the great din in the room.

"*The Lord Mayor, Pippin,*" boomed the little man's voice, "son of Charles, son of Pippin of Herstal and his guest, the Comptesse de Loches!"

The hall hushed to silence. Everyone in attendance turned to find them and the air thickened with tension. Pippin felt a sudden, giddying sense of power.

"Do they feel guilt or fear?" Pippin asked under his

breath.

"A little of both, I'd say."

"I'm betting on fear." Pippin surveyed the room. "What do you suggest we do now?"

"I think a smile might be in order."

Pippin chuckled and lifted his head to give the room his best smile. In a wave of relief, the nobles began to applaud. Pippin raised his drink in recognition and the room thundered its approval. It took every ounce of self-control not to laugh out loud. He could see why his father enjoyed stirring the political stew. He felt as if Charles was there beside him. He downed his drink and grabbed another from a passing waiter.

"The heir is across the room on your right," the Comptesse said.

Pippin spied the man out of the corner of his eye. Childeric was sitting in a throne-like chair that was flanked on either side by the Lord and Lady Ragomfred. There was no mistaking him as a Merovingian. He had the long hair and bizarre fingernails made famous by the line. Behind Childeric stood two knights: one tall, bald and youthful, the other older, scarred and lethal. Pippin made a note of his face. There was something very dangerous about him.

"Boniface," the Comptesse said, "is directly across the room at the food table."

Again, Pippin felt the urge to laugh. "Now, that is a surprise."

"Hush. I suggest you make your way to him first, and then to the Merovingian. Remember, no politics! No acknowledgements. No challenges. No vows. Don't engage the Merovingian. Simply demur, bow gracefully and move on. Your presence here, alone, will create enough of a stir. Let them wonder at its meaning."

Pippin took another moment to bask in his applause. He even waved smugly to a few nobles who had always hated his family. The Comptesse took his arm and led him down the short staircase into the room. Immediately, a swarm of well-wishing nobles strove to clasp his hand or clap his back. Pippin took his time to indulge them so that he could remember their names.

The Comptesse guided Pippin across the room until they arrived at the food table. Boniface opened his arms in welcome.

"Well met, Pippin!"

"Bishop," Pippin pointed to the stains on the man's robe, "you look elegant in duck."

"You know, of course, Bishop Aidolf of Auxerres."

Pippin nodded and pulled the Comptesse forward. "May I present the Comptesse de Loches?"

Boniface's face froze. The Comptesse, by contrast, beamed.

"So good to see you again, Wynnfred," she said.

Pippin was stunned. He had never heard anyone beside his father use Boniface's given name.

"Catherine," Boniface acknowledged, his face reddening. Now everyone was looking. Before Pippin could recover his composure, the Lady Hélène leapt into the Comptesse's arms and kissed both her cheeks.

"Sister," she said. "I had no idea you were in Paris."

"Ah, that is because I'm Mayor Pippin's hostage," the Comptesse replied, smiling. "He brought me to Paris after burning my husband's castle."

"Take care, my lord Mayor," her sister said. "Make sure you know who is captor and who is hostage."

"Milord Pippin," the Comptesse said, "may I present my sister, the Lady Hélène."

"We've met." Pippin bowed in acknowledgement and then looked to Boniface for an explanation, but the good bishop was looking anywhere but at the two women. Pippin wondered what he had gotten himself into.

The Comptesse returned her attention to her sister. "You've cut your hair short! It suits you. You look lovely tonight. That green scarf brings out the color of your eyes."

Lady Hélène looked bemused. "You were always the flatterer, sister."

The Bishop of Auxerres looked like a predator awaiting his kill. With a cough, he leaned in and asked, "Comptesse, how do you know...Wynnfred?"

But the Comptesse had already moved to take Pippin from the circle. "So nice to see you all again," she was saying, "but you must forgive me. Milord Mayor must pay his respects to our host." The Comptesse pulled Pippin in the direction of Childeric and he dutifully followed her. This time, as they made their way across the room, the crowd parted before them and Pippin found himself quickly before Childeric's makeshift throne. The crowd hushed in anticipation. Pippin's only thought was how small the Merovingian looked sitting on Ragomfred's chair. He had to suppress an urge to laugh. Again, silence took the room.

With practiced elegance, the Comptesse stepped into the breach.

"Milord and Lady Ragomfred, may I present to you the Lord Mayor, Pippin, son of Charles, son of Pippin of Herstal."

"Milord Pippin," Ragomfred bowed. Pippin returned the gesture. "May I in turn present Childeric, son of his Highness Chilperic III?"

"Childeric," Pippin acknowledged, nodding politely with a slight smile on his face.

Childeric offered his ring for Pippin to kiss. The room seemed to pivot on the gesture. All eyes focused on the outstretched hand with its bejeweled fingernails and proffered ring.

Pippin started to chuckle, and then laughed out loud. "Do not rush things, Childeric," Pippin's voice carried the room. "You haven't been anointed by the holy oil and the dove has yet to fly. You are not yet a king."

"My day will come, Mayor."

"Should your claim be true."

"Oh, it's true, Mayor. Have no doubt. It's true."

There was no hint of deception in the small man's eyes. He was telling the truth. A wave a doubt assailed Pippin. The Comptesse stepped forward, reattached herself to Pippin's arm and bowed politely to the heir and to their hosts. "I am grateful to make your-"

"Do you believe it is right for a king to rule who has no power?" Pippin asked.

The Comptesse glared at Pippin and again pinched the inside of his arm. He ignored her.

The Merovingian's eyes, however, were twinkling with delight. "The Romans used to say that power is fleeting. You, of all people, should understand that."

"Yet the Romans ruled for a thousand years."

"Ah yes, Rome ruled," the Merovingian said. "But their generals came and went like customers at a house of courtesans." Titters from the crowd punctuated his point. "The power behind Rome was that her citizens believed in Rome itself. In Francia, we believe in the divine right of our kings. We have since the heavenly dove brought the holy oil to anoint Clovis. The question that should be asked, Milord Mayor, is who believes in you?"

In the hushed silence that followed Childeric's question, Pippin recognized that this was a mistake. A trickle of sweat rolled down his back.

Childeric's eyes continued to bore into him. "Let me see if I understand the power you claim to have. You have half an army. You have no treasure with which to wage war. Without a king or the church's support, you have no financial or moral authority to rule Francia and your brother drew your right of succession into question by imprisoning your half-brother Gripho and seizing his territory. Do I have this right, or am I missing something?"

It had been naive to bait him. Pippin had never felt more foolish.

The tension in the room blossomed in the ensuing quiet. Childeric's eyes remained locked on Pippin.

"You, of all people," Childeric stood, "know that you're not meant to rule." His voice softened. "I see the suffering within you. I see the blackness coiling in the corners of your eyes. I see your doubt."

Pippin looked away.

"I asked you once before, Mayor," Childeric said, almost as if he addressed a child. "Who believes in you?" He waited for Pippin's response. "Did your father?" His last words were almost a whisper. "Do you?"

Childeric had touched upon the one place Pippin was always vulnerable. Pippin could see the wave of blackness rise above him.

Childeric leaned towards Pippin. "Pledge me your sword. Rule in my name and all of Francia will be united behind you. Defy me and Francia will be divided until the very end of your days. But know this, Mayor, either way, I will be king."

Pippin's strength seemed to crumple before the onslaught of Childeric's words. His hands reached down to detach his sword and scabbard from his belt.

"Milord, Mayor-" Again the Comptesse tried to interrupt.

But Childeric raised his hand to silence her.

Pippin lifted the sword and scabbard aloft before Childeric.

A smile crept onto the heir's face and he sat back in his oversized chair to await Pippin's vow.

"Oh Pippin!" a small voice cried from across the room. Pippin's head snapped to find it. It was Bertrada. She was standing in the doorway to the patio. She had been crying. A tall young man stood next to her, with his arm around her shoulders. She leaned into him for support.

Fury swept over Pippin and his eyes leapt back to his sword. His body began to shake. His lungs pumped air in and out through his teeth in rapid succession and his body coiled for combat. When he looked back to Childeric, his eyes were filled with rage.

Childeric's bodyguards stepped forward, their hands reaching for their swords, but Childeric held them back with a gesture.

Pippin drew his sword and held it high over his head. With both hands he slammed its point into the floor at his feet. The blade stood erect, embedded in the soft wood.

"I am the son of Charles, the son of Pippin." He turned to address the room filled with nobles. He pointed to his sword. "THIS is my power. With THIS, I have fought and bled with the sons of Francia since the time I was seven...just as my father fought before me and his father fought before him. And tomorrow, I will take this sword with many in this room to fight again for Francia against the evil of Theudebald and the treason of Odilo."

Pippin stopped for a deep breath.

"Power isn't my purpose." He turned back to Childeric. "Though it, too, is a weapon. Know that when I wield that weapon it is for the might and glory of Francia. I wield it for the safety of our people and the wealth of our noblemen. I wield it so that our sons and our daughters aren't threatened by Saxons or Saracens.

Pippin stared defiantly at the intent faces of the nobles.

"I refuse to wield it for a man who has never lifted a sword in defense of his realm, and yet has the nerve to ask me to kiss his ring. Those who have served and given sons in combat know me."

"Huh-yah," several voices in the crowd echoed.

"I will not fail. Francia will not fail." Menace was heavy in his voice.

"Huh-yah," more voices agreed.

"And while some stay behind to play chess with puppet kings, I will lead men into battle in defense of our land."

"Huh-yah!" shouted his chorus.

"I will double the usual treasure of all those who join with me on my campaign in Alemannia and Bavaria."

It was a princely sum and the room hushed in a stunned silence.

He turned to face Childeric. "Do not speak to me of Rome or your divine right of kings. The first Merovingians were warriors. Clovis united Francia by the power of his sword. Your line has become weak. You ask for my sword? Tell me, Childeric, where is yours?"

Pippin grabbed the pommel of his sword with one hand and wrenched his blade from the floor. He braved one last look over his shoulder at Bertrada by the patio. She was still standing in the doorway, her young man beside her, but he no longer had his arm around her. Pippin shook his head in disgust and headed for the stairs

# CHAPTER THIRTEEN

*Paris*

T he Comptesse did not follow Pippin from the room. She held back to study the girl who had broken Childeric's spell. Although young and beautiful, a tremendous sadness held her captive. That Pippin loved her was obvious. And from the look of the girl, she loved him too. But something held her back, something important, something noble. She had made the decision to end their relationship. This was a sacrifice for her.

Satisfied with her assessment, Catherine was about to follow Pippin's footsteps out of the hall when something else about the girl caught her eye. It was a small thing, the girl tugged at the breast line of her gown, but it caused the Comptesse to consider the girl anew.

When she released her gaze, she found that she wasn't alone in studying Pippin's deliverer. Childeric's eyes studied the girl as well. And as if sensing her gaze, Childeric looked up from the girl directly into the Comptesse's eyes. Surprised by the frankness of his gaze, she dipped into a curtsey and turned to leave.

On her way to the door, she drew alongside her sister.

"Do you still honor the dark path, Hélène?" Catherine asked.

"Yes, of course, sister."

"Then I require your services."

"I've always been in your service, Catherine."

"The girl, the one who spoke out just now, to break Childeric's spell?"

"Bertrada, a beautiful girl. Until the siege of Laon, she was Pippin's lover. Then, something happened that ended their relationship. Few know of this. But, because of my oaths..."

"Watch after her. No harm must come to her. Start this instant. No one," the Comptesse turned as they walked to be sure her sister understood the importance, "no one under any circumstances is to harm her. Do you understand?"

"Yes, of course, Catherine. Consider it done. But may I ask why?"

The Comptesse looked again at Bertrada, testing her instincts and knew them to be true. "She may not know it yet," the Comptesse said, "but that girl is with child. I'd swear by our mother's grave that I'm right. And if she is, then Pippin is the father."

"My vow is my life." Lady Hélène bowed solemnly.

"And make sure you tell—" the Comptesse turned back to her sister, but Hélène was gone. Catherine searched the crowd, but her short-haired sibling was nowhere to be found. Neither was Pippin. She would have to ask Wynnfred to escort her home. Despite the gravity of the night's events, that made her smile.

* * *

Miette was furious at, yet impressed by, Pippin's challenge to Childeric. Ragomfred was right; Pippin was a force. His courage in the face of Childeric's withering verbal assault had stunned the room. Oddly, she discovered a small part of her rooting for him. She wondered at this, replaying the confrontation over in her mind. Somehow, Pippin had seemed been both vulnerable and powerful at the same time. She had detected no deception to him, no court artifice to cater to the nobles in the room. He was as he appeared to be. Miette worried that Childeric had lost in the exchange.

Her future king, however, calmly studied the jewels that studded his long fingernails while the mayor made his exit. When Pippin was gone, the room's attention turned back to him. Silence settled around the Merovingian like a gaoler's noose. Miette held her breath.

Someone coughed. The collective gaze of the evening's revelers turned to the Merovingian. He indulged himself with a yawn. Lifting his gaze from his fingers to the stunned and blank faces in the room, he stood with practiced majesty and let the room absorb the strength of his confidence. He smiled and cocked his head slightly to the left.

"I had imagined him to be somewhat...taller," he offered.

Miette nearly wept with relief. A chuckle answered from off to his right and Childeric played off it with a chortle of his own.

"One would think that a son of Charles, son of Pippin, son of...well, whoever sired the other Pippin," he waved dismissively, "...would be so much more imposing." He was rewarded with more chuckling. A palliative relief began filtering through the crowd.

"I am thankful, however, that at least he has a big sword..." There was outright laughter. "I'm also delighted that he's finally off to protect Francia with it!" The laughter grew. "Isn't that why we have short mayors with such big swords?"

He let the laughter roll past him and waited for it to ease. He let his face fall into mock seriousness. "I just wish he hadn't damaged Lord Ragomfred's floor."

This time he rode the laughter like a wave. With a wink, he bellowed, "I propose a toast!" He gestured for a cup and raised it high above him. The room jumped to mirror his movement.

"To our beloved Mayor Pippin!" he shouted, "Pippin the Short!"

The room burst into laughter and then, upon reflection, applause. Childeric smiled and bowed deeply in response.

As the room returned to its prior frivolity, Childeric turned to Miette. "I thought you said that he had little treasure?"

"From everything I've heard he has none."

"Then find out if his boast is the truth or lie."

"Yes, my Lord."

"And that woman who called out to Pippin," he whispered. "Who is she?"

"Bertrada," Miette replied, "daughter of the Compte de Laon. I had thought that she was Pippin's mistress, but she came in the company of the son of the Compte de Soissons."

Childeric nodded and signaled to the younger of his two bodyguards, Calleau. The huge, bald, young man approached. He stood at least six hands tall and his shoulders looked as if they could carry a warhorse into battle. His face was broad and plain but accented by a fierce block of a jaw that seemed at odds with the rest of his small, round head.

Childeric tilted his head to whisper.

"Yes, Excellency." The brute nodded, his eyes darting towards Bertrada and the Compte's son, who were making their way to the door.

* * *

"I should have guessed as much," Bertrada said. "It's as if a host of demons have been loosed on the night to torment me." Their coach was not in its designated spot so Bertrada had sent Tedbalt off to search for it.

Her feet hurt, she was lightheaded and one step short of bursting into tears. She was afraid for Pippin. She had seen the darkness in his eyes and the doubt on his face. She was sure that if she hadn't called out, he never would have come to his senses.

*And why should I care?* Bertrada chastised herself. But she knew in her heart, that she did care. After Pippin's departure, Bertrada had been stunned by the mocking words of the Merovingian. They had infuriated her. And she had been more infuriated by the crowd's fawning response. Despite Aude's protests, Bertrada had insisted that they leave immediately. She couldn't wait to get away from them.

She also needed to get away from Tedbalt and Aude. *Why did I kiss him?* Her stomach squeezed into a knot. What do I want from him? She could see that Tedbalt still had affection for her. But she also knew her sister was besotted with the man. Bile gathered at the back of her throat.

"It's no longer here." Tedbalt returned from his search for the coach. "I checked with every coachman waiting and no one has seen it."

Bertrada's alarm grew.

"How will we get home?" She could hear the panic in her voice. "We have to get away from here."

"I don't know what to say," Tedbalt said. "I'm terribly embarrassed. "Perhaps I can prey upon the graces of good bishop Boniface to take us back to the-"

"Can I be of assistance?" A woman in a nearby coach called out. "Bertrada? Is that you?"

The door of the coach opened, and the coachman scrambled to place a step down so the woman could descend. She was dressed in a green cloak with a hood that obscured her face. Still, Bertrada was sure she knew the voice. The woman drew closer.

"Lady Hélène!" Bertrada sighed with relief. The woman had been a friend of her father and was now a close confidant of Carloman's wife, Greta. Hélène had lost her husband years ago and had never remarried. She was one of the court's more celebrated hostesses.

"Yes, we could use some help. Our coach has mysteriously disappeared. and we're desperate in our need of a ride back across the river."

"Please." Lady Hélène held the door to her coach open for them, "I think we can all fit."

Bertrada nearly wept with gratitude. She kissed the woman on both cheeks and climbed into the cab. After a moment's hesitation, so did Tedbalt and Aude.

"I am forever in your debt."

"It's my pleasure. Please, Bertrada, why don't you sit next to this fine-looking young man, so you can face forward? You look a little peaked."

"I am a little out of sorts."

Lady Hélène took the seat opposite Bertrada on the street side of the coach and closed the window shade, leaving only a small crack. Bertrada introduced her fellow passengers as the coach pulled out into the street. They traveled several blocks before Bertrada realized she was babbling girlishly out of relief. Lady Hélène, however, seemed not to notice. She was focused on the small slit in the window's curtain.

"I'm sorry," Bertrada said. "I'm such the fool of late."

"It's perfectly all right, dear." Lady Hélène patted her knee and then returned her gaze to the slit in the window curtain. The cab's occupants fell into an awkward silence as the coach steered through ever-darkening streets. Riders occasionally overtook them and each time, Lady Hélène peered out into the darkness.

"Is something wrong, Lady Hélène?" Bertrada asked. "You seem worried."

"Hopefully, it's nothing. I've heard rumors that highwayman roam this road. Tedbalt, do you know how to use a sword?"

"Of course. But I didn't bring one."

Bertrada frowned. "Surely the danger is slight."

Lady Hélène fumbled in the darkness. Bertrada heard something like a latch open. "There. I thought my late husband kept a weapon in here." She handed Tedbalt a short Roman sword. "Will this suffice? Just as a precaution?"

"Yes," Tedbalt said. "But I can't imagine that we'll actually need it."

"Hopefully not." Hélène turned her gaze to the window.

They traveled again in silence. The cab jostled and bounced its way down the streets along the southern bank of the river. Bertrada had the distinct impression that Lady Hélène was discretely analyzing her appearance. It made her self-conscious.

"I'm am no longer Pippin's consort," she blurted.

"Yes, I'm aware of that. How long has it been since you've seen him?"

"Before tonight, two months or so." Again, Lady Hélène's eyes swept over her. "I didn't expect to see him tonight."

"From the look of it, he didn't expect to see you, either."

Again, they rode in silence. There was something about the woman that put Bertrada on edge, but for the life of her, Bertrada couldn't identify what it was.

Suddenly, the coachman pulled hard on the reins and the coach came violently to a stop. Harsh voices rumbled in the night and the coachman started to protest. Bertrada heard a grunt, and then all was silent.

The four waited inside the cab for some indication. The door flew open and the face of a huge bald man peered inside. A massive arm thrust inside the cab and latched onto Lady Hélène. With an ease Bertrada couldn't fathom, he picked up her up like a doll and tossed her out into the darkness.

Tedbalt lunged. His sword thrust through the open door at their assailant. Bertrada heard a grunt outside the coach. Then a hand grabbed Tedbalt by the arm of his cloak and he, too, was pulled from the cab. Aude began to scream. More hands reached into the cab and Bertrada found herself lying in the mud next to her companions. Only Lady Hélène had regained her feet. She looked small in the feeble moonlight. Their captors had their backs to the moon, which made them appear as dark and menacing silhouettes.

There were three highwaymen, the bald man and two others. From what Bertrada could see, they wore rags for clothes. One held the reins of the coach and another had his sword pointed at Tedbalt's throat. The bald man stood before them, gesturing with his sword.

"Purses and jewels," he commanded. All of them rushed to obey.

"Please don't hurt us," Aude whimpered.

In moments, their purses and jewels littered the ground before them.

"On your knees," the bald man said to Bertrada. Her heart pounded within her chest. She could barely breathe.

"Please, no," Aude whispered.

"I said on your knees!" He grabbed Bertrada by the hair and forced her into a kneeling position before him. This put him between Bertrada and the others. The man's private parts swung obscenely beneath his ragged shift and Bertrada could smell the foulness of him. She tried to recoil, but he held her fast. Twisting her hair, the bald man pulled her head to one side. Panic took her. Oh God, no! He raised his sword, its point down, high above her exposed neck.

Aude began to pray.

Bertrada caught a flicker of movement out of the corner of her eye and with a grunt, the man guarding Tedbalt pitched backward into the mud. The highwayman lay face up, unmoving with a knife in his chest. Tedbalt started for the man's sword but the bald brute was faster. He had his sword at Tedbalt's neck. He called to the highwayman still holding the reins of the carriage. "Do you suppose you can keep an eye on this one? Be careful, he's quick with a knife."

He turned back to Bertrada. She looked back up at him, realizing she could have run while he was distracted. The bald man recognized it too and laughed. Again, he seized her hair.

"Bertrada!" It was Lady Hélène. She was running toward them, waving Bertrada away. The brute hit Lady Hélène in the face with the back of his hand. She crumpled beside them. Bertrada stared down at her dumbfounded. Everything seemed to stop.

"Fight," Lady Hélène's voice was insistent.

Humiliation bloomed within Bertrada. *I'm not that strong.* Once again, her captor's crotch stood an inch in front of her face. Once again, he raised his sword high above her neckline. Bertrada saw an opportunity but lacked the courage to act. She felt her captor's body tense.

"BERTRADA!" Lady Hélène screamed.

Bertrada grabbed the man's testicles. His body jerked and his blade sank deep into the ground just behind her. The man doubled over as he tried to pull away, twisting in her grasp, but Bertrada refused to let go. His testicles felt like two bird eggs. She tried to crush them in her hand.

Screaming in agony, he clouted her on the side of the head, and she collapsed into the mud. The bald man stumbled away from her holding his hands between his legs.

Lady Hélène was back on her feet and moving with incredible speed. The noblewoman spun towards the man holding Tedbalt and with a grunt he collapsed to the ground. Then she threw something at the bald man who dropped to one knee. Suddenly she was behind him with a large stone. She brought it down on his head and he collapsed into the mud.

"We must leave, now!" she said.

Bertrada looked down at their attackers. Knives protruded from the chests of two of them, while the bald brute had a knife sticking out of his back.

Tedbalt checked on their coachman, still sitting atop his perch on the cab. He shook his head to indicate the man was dead.

"How? How did you do that?" She looked to Lady Hélène.

"We don't have time for such questions." The left side of Lady Hélène's face was bleeding. She stepped over the dead highwayman and pulled the knife from his neck. She wiped the blade on the man's tunic. She moved next to the bald man and repeated the ritual as if she were dusting off furniture.

"Tedbalt, can you drive a coach?" she asked.

He nodded.

"Take us to my home. I'll give you directions. We have to get out of here at once."

"I want to go back to the inn," Bertrada said.

"No." Lady Hélène's voice brooked no quarter. "I don't think that will be safe."

"I don't understand." Tedbalt came to her defense. "These highwaymen won't be following us. Why wouldn't we be safe at the inn?"

"They aren't highwaymen."

"What do you mean? Who are they?"

"Look at their mounts." Lady Hélène pointed. "Highwaymen don't ride warhorses. These men are knights. They were sent to kill you. And I'm betting if they don't return soon, there will be more."

Tedbalt clearly wasn't convinced. "Why do you think they're after us? Perhaps they're chasing you."

Lady Hélène seemed to assess each of their party in turn. Then she sighed. "I'm not pregnant with Pippin's child." She pointed at Bertrada. "She is."

# CHAPTER FOURTEEN

*Regensburg*

For Trudi, time appeared to slow. Odilo was away buying armaments for the Slavs and she was left alone to mend in a never-ending progression of white linens and clean towels. The evolution of her days was measured by the chamber pots left to replace her food trays and the appearance of a new guard outside her door to replace the old. Nameless midwifes came and went, but Eta wasn't among them.

Over time, the weight of these days dulled the edge of Trudi's panic and dried the bulk of her tears. Every morning, she left her bed to stand by the window, hoping that the dawn of a new day would restore her. When it didn't, she retreated to her sheets and pillows to await the potential of another day.

Three weeks after her confinement Trudi rose again to greet the dawn. As with every other morning, light peered over the eastern horizon, a blend of gold and orange hues spilt above the blue and white roiling Danube. At first, the cloud cover obscured the curvature of the sun, but soon it lifted ever so slowly, asserting its dominance over the world.

And like every other day, Trudi found no sense of renewal, no restoration of her former self. She still felt alone, violated, afraid...and *angry*.

The realization caught her by surprise. She seized this new emotion, exploring the depth and texture of it. Ire welled within her, becoming a torrent of fury that flooded her being. Relieved to feel anything other than humiliation, her pulse raced to keep pace with her exhilaration and she strode back and forth across the span of her chamber, seething in the throes of rage.

When she no longer could contain it, she screamed. It wasn't the scream of a victim but a full-throated howl of wrath, a defiant battle cry, carrying the promise of retribution.

The midwife seated by her bed grew pale and ran for the door. She threw it open to an alarmed guard outside Trudi's room.

"Milady? Are you well?" The guard's eyes searched the room. "What is amiss?"

"Get me Eta." Trudi's voice sounded odd to her. Cold and distant. She had never given an order before; she had always asked for help. She noticed that the guard hadn't moved.

"Now!" She barked and the man obeyed.

The ancient midwife arrived minutes later. She entered the room with a stately calm, her back straight and her hands folded before her. Even in the face of Trudi's rage, the woman radiated power.

"Why did you stop coming to see me?" Trudi resumed her pacing. "I was hurt. I was alone."

"I couldn't give you what you wanted."

"I wanted your help."

"You wanted my pity. And that wouldn't have served you."

"You know what I went through!"

Eta's eyes flashed with an inner anger, but it was gone almost as it appeared. "Such things are never forgotten. The question you must ask of yourself is, will you let it define who you are?"

"I am Hiltrude, Duchesse of Bavaria, daughter of Charles,

son of Pippin of Herstal, mayor of the palace."

A small smile tugged at the corner of Eta's lips. "And so, you are, Duchesse. Now, how may I serve you?"

With Eta's quiet affirmation, Trudi's sense of herself – her worth – surged within her. She wasn't the same young woman who had arrived in Regensburg, but neither was she the humiliated victim she had been for the past few weeks. She was something new.

Trudi looked to the door. "How did you get the guards to watch my door? They were here before Odilo ordered them."

"I've lived here a long time, Duchesse. Such a request from one so old is often granted out of respect."

"I must never be put in such a position again. I need a cadre of knights loyal to me to guard my person."

"Only your husband can authorize such a command."

"They must be loyal to me." Trudi scowled. "Only me."

Eta seemed to weigh her next words. "If Duc Odilo will order it, I'm sure we can find men loyal to you."

Trudi had no time for platitudes. "How?"

"One has been outside your door every night since your...tragedy. He's as steadfast and loyal as any man in Bavaria. He could recruit your cadre of knights."

"What's his name?"

"Hans."

"How do you know him?"

"He's my son."

Trudi blinked away the sudden emotion that sprang to her eyes. "I will speak to my husband."

"Milady." Eta curtsied to leave.

"Eta?"

The midwife turned.

"Thank you. I won't forget this."

❋ ❋ ❋

Hans was a veteran soldier in Odilo's service. He wasn't a knight, but a man at arms, skilled with sword and ax. He had long, brown hair, a bold Roman nose, and moved with the grace of a swordsman. Trudi guessed that he was older than forty years of age but had the athleticism of a much younger man.

Refusing to wait for Odilo's return, Trudi insisted that Eta broach the commission with Hans that very night. She paced about her room while Eta ushered her son inside. He stood in Trudi's chambers as if still on guard. His hand rested on the pommel of his sword and his eyes searched the chamber for hidden dangers. He looked as vulnerable as a mountain.

Eta spoke first. "Milady, may I present my son, Hans, son of Manfred."

Trudi stopped her pacing to stand in front of him. Hans bowed stiffly and Trudi nodded her head.

"Did Eta explain why I wished to speak with you?"

Hans nodded.

"Do you understand the nature of this commission?"

Again, he nodded.

"Is it something you would be willing to accept?"

Another nod.

Trudi needed to hear him say it. "Will you vow to give me your loyalty above all others and to protect my person with your life?"

Hans hesitated and looked to Eta.

"You may speak." Eta rose to stand behind Trudi. "The Duchesse will answer your questions."

Hans frowned. "I don't understand why it's necessary."

"My protection?"

"We already guard your door. Everyone in the Duc's command would protect you with his life."

"But what if the Duc ordered you to arrest me, or confine me, or take my life?"

"We would comply. But, if I may ask, why would he do that?"

"What if it was his brother Theudebald?"

"We are in the service of Duc Odilo."

"What if he wasn't here? What if he died?"

Hans looked confused.

"Who would protect me?" Trudi's voice was rising with urgency. This wasn't progressing as she had imagined. Hans didn't understand. "Who would protect my child?"

"Your station wouldn't be forfeit by such an event. Nor would your child's."

"Who would ensure that?"

"I can conceive of no one who would harm your person."

"Can't you?" Trudi was getting frantic. How could she make him understand? "Who stands to gain if there is no clear succession? Who might benefit by an accidental death of the Duchesse and her child?"

Hans shook his head. "Perhaps I should-"

"I was raped." She had not intended to say that. A horrific silence filled the room. Hans looked to his mother, dread and malice staining his eyes. Eta's face had flushed red and she nodded. Something unspoken passed between them.

He knows, Trudi realized. Hans knows about Eta's rape all those years ago.

Tears leapt to Trudi's eyes. She couldn't stop her words. "I was raped right here in this house by Odilo's own brother." Her face crumpled with the memory. "I...I nearly lost my baby...your future Duc. Who will stand up to such a man? Would Odilo?"

Trudi left the question in the air, suddenly sure that it was the basis of her fear. "I don't need protection by people loyal to my husband, Hans. I need protection by people loyal to me."

The muscles on Hans' body coiled and clenched as if they might explode. His face was furious in indignation. Trudi half expected that he might shout in rage.

Instead, he knelt. "I pledge my sword and my life to your protection. With or without your husband's approval, I will defend you and your child to the limits of my power."

"As strong as your arm is, I will need others to defend us."

"You will have them."

Trudi nodded in appreciation and laid her hand on his shoulder. "Thank you, Hans. You may rise. I will accept your vow publicly once I've secured agreement with my husband. Until then, we'll need to keep your pledge secret. If you have someone who you think might serve me, bring him to me under the guise that my husband is establishing a household guard for the family. I wish to evaluate each candidate before you speak with them of our true purpose."

Hans's impassive face had returned. "Milady," he said, bowing to take his leave.

"Before you leave," Trudi said, "I'm going to need some knives. Small ones that I can hide on my person."

"Of course, milady."

"And Hans?" She waited until his eyes met hers. "Make them sharp."

# CHAPTER FIFTEEN

*Paris*

P regnant? Bertrada's hand explored the outside of her stomach, trying to feel the presence of life within her. She felt nothing. When was her last menses? She couldn't remember. Of late, she had been so distracted.

Although she could hear Lady Hélène barking orders to Tedbalt, the woman seemed so far away that her words barely registered.

"Help me get these bodies off the road. Ladies get back in the carriage. We have to get out of here."

Bertrada had trouble focusing. Aude was still on her knees and there was blood pooling beside the two bodies in the road. Tedbalt too, seemed immobilized, standing over one of the bodies as if he was trying to remember how it had gotten there.

Hélène grabbed Bertrada's arm. "We must go! Help your sister."

That broke the spell. Bertrada bent down to gather the girl in her arms, shushing her like an infant. "Come, Aude, let's get you into the carriage. Let's get away from here."

Tedbalt still hadn't moved. Hélène shoved him, forcing him to look at her. "I need your help!"

After a moment, he nodded and helped Hélène drag the

attackers off the road. One of the bodies left a swath of blood trailing behind it.

"Can you drive this thing?" Hélène's voice was uncompromising.

Tedbalt nodded.

"Good. Take the first road east. We'll head to my estate in the banlieu."

"No." It took Bertrada a moment to realize that she had been the one who spoke. "We have to go to the palace. We have to find Pippin." It was the only place she would be safe; he could protect them.

"Pippin isn't staying at the palace. He's encamped with his army on the other side of the river." The frustration was showing on Hélène's face. "What if the gate is compromised? What if the king's men are waiting for us there? We'd be dead before Pippin could save us. No. We can't chance it. It's far safer to flee until we understand what the threat is."

Tedbalt had yet to climb into the driver's seat. "Why is your house any safer?"

Hélène frowned. "They didn't know I would intercede and so they couldn't have planned for that course of action. But it won't be safe for much longer. Our position is simple. We have too little information to make a sound judgment so we must choose the most conservative path. My sister bade me to protect Bertrada and I intend to, with my life, if necessary. But standing here only increases our danger. We must go, now!"

It took another moment before Tedbalt nodded. Hélène gave him further directions before joining Bertrada and Aude in the carriage. With the crack of a whip, the carriage pulled back onto the road.

As she had before the attack, Hélène kept watch at the window as they rumbled over the rough roads northeast of Paris. This time, however, no one spoke. The only sound they heard was Aude's whimpering. Eventually that too drifted into silence. The carriage lurched at every turn and bounced over every rock, shaking Bertrada's confidence in Tedbalt's driving abilities. At every crossroad, Hélène banged her hand against the carriage and pointed the way for Tedbalt.

After what seemed like an eternity, Hélène announced they had arrived. She leaned out of the window to shout last-minute directions and the carriage pulled through a large iron gate.

It was a cloistered estate surrounded by high walls and thick bushes on all sides. At a sign from Hélène, a servant closed the gate behind them. Hélène ushered her three charges inside, calling for servants as they went.

Bertrada was stunned by the opulence of the estate. Thick tapestries hung from the walls and elegant rugs covered the floors. A servant went to light a fire in her public rooms, but Hélène waved him away. "We won't be staying."

She ushered the three of them into her private rooms on the far side of the house.

"Tedbalt, you and Aude must flee. Although you are not the target tonight, Childeric might try to use Aude as hostage. I'll give you horses. Take Aude back to Soissons or Laon where she can be protected. Avoid the main roads when you can. If you can't get back home – if they are searching the highways for her – find somewhere in the south where you're not known and wait until Pippin returns and can assure you safe passage."

Tedbalt had already assumed the role of Aude's protector and had his arm around her. Although clearly still shaken by the night's events, Aude looked comforted by it and took his hand in hers.

"Aude and Bertrada, there are riding clothes in my closet. Best change now. Tedbalt, there's a coin purse in my desk. Take it and whatever else you need from here." She opened a tall cabinet on the far side of the room filled with swords, knives, and a dozen weapons Bertrada didn't recognize. When the three women were finished changing their clothes, Hélène began arming herself with a number of the blades.

"Tedbalt, if you make good time now, you probably won't have to kill anyone. Every hour you delay, however, increases the likelihood that you will."

"I should go with them." Bertrada trusted Tedbalt more than Hélène

"You're going with me." Hélène's face brooked no argument. "We have to disappear. It's you they're after. Going with Aude only puts her life in danger. You won't be safe anywhere until Pippin returns."

"I don't want to disappear."

"I'm afraid you'll have to trust me. At least until Pippin returns."

To Bertrada, the urgency in Hélène's tone coupled with the distress in her eyes was far more compelling than her words. Hélène was telling the truth – at least as far as she could perceive it. Bertrada decided to trust her. She nodded her agreement.

Hélène led them to the stables and ordered horses saddled for the four of them. It gave Bertrada time to say a hasty goodbye to Aude and Tedbalt. She tried to put a brave face forward for her sister's benefit.

"We will survive this, Aude. We're from a long line of strong people. Be brave. Trust Tedbalt and I will see you when Pippin returns. We'll spend long leisurely days in court together watching our future children play."

"Do you promise?"

"I do." Bertrada kissed Tedbalt on the cheek. "I'm holding you accountable."

"I won't let anything happen to her."

"See that you don't." Bertrada hugged Aude one last time. "Come back to me." And then they were gone.

Hélène turned to Bertrada. "Have you had any bleeding?"

"Bleeding?"

"Spotting. Your pregnancy. Have you bled?"

"No."

"Good. Then you can ride." She instructed one of her stable hands, an elderly man named Javier to drive the carriage east to the edge of the city – enough to be seen – and then once outside of town, to circle back to her estate.

"Where are we going?" Bertrada asked.

"Someplace where no one will ask any questions. Now, wrap this scarf around your head so that your blond hair doesn't show."

The stableman came forward with two more horses. "Bit late for a ride, Milady."

"Yes, I know Javier, but we have to be in St. Denis by morning."

The man knuckled his forehead and helped them mount. Hélène put her heels to horse and led them out of the estate and up the northern road.

"I thought you said we weren't going back to Paris?"

"We aren't." Hélène turned down a side street. "But we have to assume that Javier will be questioned. Now he'll be able to give them an answer."

After five minutes Hélène turned east, heading back into the farmland that surrounded the city. The rolling countryside looked black against the night sky, but there was plenty of light from the moon and the array of stars above them. They settled into a comfortable pace and Bertrada's panic began to recede.

Hélène stopped to give the horses water at a stream bed alongside the road. While Bertrada was glad for the rest, she didn't like being so exposed. She felt as if her attackers could see her from afar. She stayed close to her horse, hoping to blend into the shadows.

They regained the road and again headed north, but after passing a small village, Hélène turned east again, this time on a road that looked well-travelled. The landscape began to change from farm to woodland. Tall trees girdled what was left of the pastures and Hélène rode straight to them. Soon, dark branches towered over them, cutting off the light from above. They could barely make out the outlines of the road and had to slow the pace of their horses.

The sounds of crickets and small animals grew loud around them, as if the relentless beating of their horse's hooves angered them. After an hour, Bertrada called for Hélène to halt.

"It's not safe here." Hélène looked around frantically.

"I have to piss."

"Christ."

"Just for a minute." Bertrada dismounted. Hélène followed and led their mounts into the trees for cover. Bertrada squatted down, leaning her back against a tree. "Where are you taking me?"

"Someplace where I can protect you."

"And where is that?"

"I don't know yet."

"You seem to know what direction to take."

Hélène hesitated. "I have a friend who can keep us for a day or two. But after that?" She shrugged. "We have to – "

They could hear the hoof beats coming up the road behind them. Hélène signaled for quiet. The hoof beats grew louder as the shadow of two horsemen grew large and then passed by them. Bertrada held her breath. The riders disappeared around the bend and silence retook the night. They waited another minute just to be sure.

Hélène shook her head. "They were too close behind us. They must have seen us take the forest road."

"What do we do?"

"We can't go forward or risk overtaking them. And if they realize they've missed us, they'll just lie in wait to ambush us. Our best bet is to wait here, make sure they've gone ahead, and then turn back."

"Turn back? But where will we go?"

"We could ride north. There's a road east."

"A fine plan." A gruff voice called from the road. "But what if they double back on foot to catch you here?"

Hélène spat on the ground.

"Come out and show your face." The voice called. "Only thieves ride this road at night."

Hélène swore under her breath and led her horse out onto the road, signaling for Bertrada to stay behind.

"Both of you." The man ordered, peering into the darkness.

Bertrada captured her horse's reins and followed Hélène onto the road.

A large bearded man stood in the middle of the road. "Now what business would two women have riding this road at night?"

Hélène was closer to him. "You would do well to ride along."

The man laughed. It gave Bertrada a sick feeling inside. He turned his head to shout over his shoulder. "I was wrong, Pierre! Mayhaps something good does ride this road at night." He stepped towards Hélène.

"Stay back." Her right foot stepped backwards.

"Don't you worry, little miss," he came closer, "I won't hurt you. You might even like it."

Hélène called to Bertrada. "Run!"

Bertrada needed no further encouragement. She grabbed the reins and tried to mount her horse. Too late she saw the second man. He was on her so quickly she barely had a chance to react. He pulled her off the horse and threw her to the ground. The impact knocked her breath from her. She grunted, trying to breathe.

With her attacker above her, Bertrada didn't hesitate. With all the strength she could muster Bertrada kicked upward with her foot and caught the man between his legs. A grunt escaped his lips and he doubled over. Bertrada scrambled to her feet.

A quick glimpse behind the man showed Hélène a blur of motion in the darkness, twisting and turning in ways that seemed impossible all while landing blow after blow on her assailant. Bertrada ran to her horse but her attacker had recovered enough to block her way.

She didn't know what to do. She couldn't fight him. Her only option was to run. She had barely taken two steps when a backhanded blow caught the side of her head. She tried to turn her head away from it, but its force jolted her and sent her reeling. The man was on her in seconds, his hand closing around her throat.

She struggled against him trying to hit and kick her way free, but his grip was too strong. As the seconds slipped by her lungs began to burn and her eyes started to bulge from the lack of air. Bertrada's exertions became more frantic. She tried to gouge his eyes and scratch his face. She was weakening and her vision was growing clouded. She tried to pry the hands from her throat knowing the effort was useless.

She was going to die. The thought seemed absurd to her. Not here. Not like this.

She looked for Hélène, praying for her intervention. She found Hélène still trading blows with her own attacker. A quick strike to the man's throat seemed to immobilize him for a moment and then the palm of Hélène's hand shot up into the man's nose. He keeled over onto his back and didn't move.

Although Bertrada felt a moment of celebration, she couldn't help herself from slipping away. It was as if the corners of her sight crowded in on her until there was nothing.

She awoke to Hélène kneeling beside her. "Sorry I took so long. I must be out of practice. Are you okay?"

Relief washed over Bertrada. She sat up and tried to clear her throat. "I thought I was going to die."

"It was close. I wasn't expecting them to be such good fighters. I took too long to get to you."

"I'll be alright." Bertrada said with more confidence than she felt.

"Good. We have to go."

Bertrada gave no argument. She stood and straightened her shift.

"How did you – " She looked down at the body of her attacker. A knife was buried in his ear. "Oh."

They regained their horses and left the two bodies where they lay. Hélène grabbed the reins of their attackers' horses and led them east along the road for a few miles before letting them go.

Bertrada's followed dutifully, no longer questioning where Hélène led. Her thoughts seemed oddly detached from her body, as if the events of the night were but a dream or had happened to someone else. The only thing that kept her mind present was the ache in the left side of her jaw. She realized she didn't care where they were going, as long as Hélène stayed with her.

\* \* \*

As the eastern sky grew pale with the morning's first light, Hélène pulled off the road. Bertrada could see that they now followed a path – not much more than a trail – heading southward. The landscape had changed back to farmland and it seemed to roll away from them to the ends of the earth.

After an hour, Hélène turned east again, but this time Bertrada could discern no path. It was as if Hélène knew her way by heart. They climbed one rolling hill after another. Each one seemed to tap whatever was left of Bertrada's strength. "Just one more," she whispered as they began each climb.

At last, they came to a small farmhouse well back from any road. It had a barn for livestock and a pen for chickens. Hélène led them up to the front porch and dismounted. Bertrada slid down from her horse, quietly thanking God for the respite. At last, she could rest.

A young man with a long wooden staff appeared at the door of the house. "Don't need strangers here."

"Patrice? Is that you?" Hélène strode easily towards him

as if the staff was a welcome bouquet of flowers.

"Who are you? What do you–"

"Put the staff down, Patrice." A comely woman emerged from the house behind him. Bertrada guessed she was the boy's mother. She had a stateliness about her that belied her dress and surroundings. "Don't you recognize nobility when you see them?"

"Agnès." Hélène pronounced the name like a sigh of relief. "*Ahh-nyess.*"

The two women embraced and held each other for a long moment. When they separated, the peasant woman noticed the blood on Hélène's clothes. Her eyes quickly assessed Bertrada in turn.

"You're in trouble." It was a statement rather than a question. Hélène nodded. "Were you followed?"

"No. But they'll come looking. They know we are on this side of the river."

"Who is looking for you?"

"The king's men."

Agnès looked to her son. "Patrice, put these horses up in the barn and see that they're fed and rubbed down. Turning back to her guests, she said, "Let's get you inside." She led them into the small cottage. It had but one large room, a fireplace, a table, a pantry, and two bedrolls placed in the corner. They sat at the wooden table.

Hélène's eyes rested on the two bedrolls. "Jacques?"

"Dead now, three years."

Hélène's voice fell to a whisper. "I'm so sorry."

Although sadness touched her eyes, Agnès chuckled. "Bah! You never liked the man." "But you did."

Hélène was still serious. "That's all that mattered to me."

Bertrada struggled to understand the connection between the two women. Agnès was clearly well below Hélène's station, yet the two spoke and acted as if they were equals. If anything, Hélène appeared to defer to Agnès. It was as if the two were sisters.

Agnès focused on Bertrada. "And who do you bring me under the cloak of night? A young noblewoman in distress?"

"This is Bertrada, daughter of the Compte de Loan."

"And what trouble are you in, child?"

Before Bertrada could protest that she was not a child, Hélène interceded. "She's carrying Pippin's babe and the Merovingian is trying to kill her."

Angès's eyes widened. "That certainly qualifies as trouble. And Pippin?"

"He doesn't know. And we can't reach him directly. His army left today for Regensburg. He won't be back until the fall."

Agnès frowned. "So, you must hide."

"I was hoping you would have some ideas. Given her condition, we can't go too far."

Agnès turned to Bertrada, her eyes assessing her as her lips thinned into a straight hard line. "How far along are you?"

The question caught Bertrada off her guard. "I beg your pardon?"

"How many months have you been with child?"

"I – I don't know."

Agnès nearly growled. "When were you last with Pippin?"

"I don't see how that is your affair –"

Hélène cut her off. "She's asking if you want to keep the babe."

The question shocked Bertrada. "I don't know what you mean. I am not aware that there's a choice in the matter."

"There are always choices." Agnès's eyes were uncompromising. "Some harder than others."

Bertrada shook with the implication of such words. Again, her hand spread across her belly looking for some sign, some reassurance that there was in fact a life growing inside her. Again, she felt nothing. In fact, she still wasn't sure she was with child. She only had Hélène's word for it.

But a choice? She thought she had already made her choice when she left Pippin. She didn't want his life. But could she refuse his child?

She now understood the implications of it. It was not – as she had thought – a moment of celebration that would make her the envy of the court. It was a terrible responsibility. With a child, she was the target of assassins, and forever would be threatened. Her children would be a target; her husband would be a target. What kind of a life was that to live?

If she accepted Agnès's offer she would be once again simply the daughter of a Compte. She would fade from prominence, fade from court. No harm would come to her. She could live the life she wanted, one of comfort and wealth.

But could she sacrifice the child for herself? The thought horrified her. She turned back to Hélène. "Is this why you brought me here? Is this woman – "

"She is many things, Bertrada. As am I. We provide choices to those such as you. Right now, you have to choose who you will be. Will you marry Pippin? Will you bear his child, be his queen?"

"Pippin is the mayor, not a king."

Hélène voice grew quiet. "On my life, Bertrada, Pippin will be king. It's best that you understand that now."

"I don't understand." Her voice sounded frail, against such surety. "What about the Merovingian? What about Carloman?"

Hélène shook her head. "I don't know if they will rule. I only know that Pippin will."

"Most women would sell their soul to be queen." Agnès's voice too was just above a whisper.

"I'm not like most women," Bertrada said.

Agnès nodded. "You can have until tomorrow morning to decide. After that, you won't have another chance. I'm guessing it is already somewhat late for such measures. I will have Patrice bring in water for a bath. Although we're far from the road, it's best that you stay out of sight. I'll go into town to see if anyone is searching for you and be back before sundown."

*  *  *

It was a cold bath, but Bertrada relished the opportunity to wash the stink of the night's attacks from her. Patrice had provided half of a barrel for her to stand in and two large pitchers of water before attending to chores on the farm. Bertrada stood in the barrel and soaped her body with a rough wet cloth until her skin was raw.

Hélène had agreed to help serve as her attendant as long as Bertrada returned the favor. The older woman stood next to her with the pitcher of cold water and tilted it carefully to rinse off the suds without splashing water all over the floor.

As the shock of the cold water hit her, Bertrada's skin prickled. Looking down, she became acutely aware of how naked she was and how close Hélène was standing. It shouldn't have bothered her. Throughout her life, Bertrada had taken countless baths with attendants, but never with another women from court. She lifted an arm to cover her breasts and used her other hand to conceal the hair between her legs.

Hélène caught the movement and raised an eyebrow. Embarrassed, Bertrada smiled sheepishly. Hélène dumped the rest of the pitcher over her head.

Screaming from the shock of the cold water, Bertrada struggled to push the wet hair from her face.

Giggling at her joke, Hélène offered Bertrada a towel. "Out you go, my queen. It's my turn." And without a second thought, she untied her shift.

Bertrada laughed in spite of herself. Why had she been so foolish? She used the towel to rub the water from her hair and turned to watch Hélène step into the bath. Her breath caught at the sight. Hélène's body was vastly different than any woman's she'd ever seen. Every one of her muscles was strongly defined, yet still lithe and proportional. When she moved, she exuded strength, grace, and surety. Two jagged white scars marred the skin on the right side of her back. Bertrada had seen the like on Pippin. They were knife wounds.

Hélène caught her eye and Bertrada realized she'd been staring. Again, the woman's eyebrow arched and this time it was Bertrada who giggled.

"Don't just stand there, staring. Help me with the pitcher!" Hélène turned her back and waited. On impulse, Bertrada dumped the entire bucket of water over the older woman's head.

# CHAPTER SIXTEEN

*Paris*

Pippin's rooms at the palace on the Isle de la Cité were never luxurious. Most of those who visited him would describe them as stark or at best Spartan. To Pippin, they were temporary quarters – a place to stay when he couldn't return to their villa at Quierzy. And the few comforts he did have – a rug, a sofa and a bathtub – had all been due to Bertrada's influence.

Now, it looked even less livable. Maps covered the walls of his salon and bedroom and half-filled mugs of ale covered nearly every table in the room. Servants had tried to clear away the detritus, but Pippin shooed them out of the way.

A soldier entered his eyes grim. "Sector five is clear."

"Noted." Pippin dismissed the man with a wave and drew a diagonal line over a small section of countryside surrounding Paris on his map. When he was done, he gently put the pen down, picked up his chair and threw it across the room.

He hated being powerless. Bertrada's rejection had crushed him like an empty suit of armor, but his impotence in the face of her danger –and his child's danger – was crippling him.

After the ball, Catherine had informed him in no uncertain terms that Bertrada was with child. And early the next morning, Bertrada's father had come to the palace to announce that she hadn't returned to the inn with her sister Aude or the young man she had accompanied to the ball. Pippin had put his army's departure on hold in order to search for them. Two days had passed, and he had little to show for it.

An image of her with the young man on her arm – Tedbalt –flooded his mind. Pippin tried to push the thought away. Was the child even his? She had refused to see him again and again. And if it were his, would it bring Bertrada back? Could they be a family? Given the way she had left him, he had his doubts.

None of that mattered now. He had to find her. It didn't matter that she wouldn't be with him. Charles's blessing turned over and over in Pippin's mind. "Our name to defend; our blood to protect." It had become a litany for him, a distant light as a guide from the darkness that crowded around him. If the child was his, he had a duty that left no room for weakness.

Within an hour, two more soldiers reported. Two more sections of the map were clear. Teams of men had searched every inn and tavern within ten miles of Paris and rousted anyone acquainted with the two women. Other than a confused account by Lady Hélène's stable master, they had little information to guide them. Pippin had even searched the Ragomfred's mansion, much to the amusement of the Merovingian. Everywhere the result was the same: no sign of Bertrada.

Reason told him to stop. Either Hélène had found Bertrada some sanctuary or Childeric had taken her. Either way, one of them would send for him. He accomplished little searching door to door through every neighborhood. Plus, there was a war to fight.

But "our blood to protect" wasn't a vague challenge. Pippin vowed to not fail his father again.

A cough brought him out of his reverie. Childebrand stood in his doorway, a frown as deep as the catacombs scarred his face. Pippin waved him in.

"Any progress?" Childebrand looked over Pippin's maps.

"Nothing's changed. Her carriage was spotted heading east. But another stableman swore she took horses, heading for St. Denis. We have nothing to direct us one way or the other."

The big man frowned. "We don't have time for this, Pippin. You need to make some decisions." Childebrand picked up Pippin's chair and put it back in its place by the desk. "Carloman won't win this war without you."

Pippin's gaze moved from his uncle's face to the maps and back again. His voice fell to a whisper. "What if she's carrying my son?"

"Your son won't have much to inherit if Carloman loses. Half our combined forces are sitting idle while you search for Bertrada. Leave me here with a battalion to search for her, if you must, but take the army south. Carloman will need every man."

Pippin sat down at his desk and used the palms of his hands to massage his eyes. He knew Childebrand was right. It was a bitter choice, but one that must be made.

"I agree. But you take the army – save one battalion – and ride for Regensburg." He waved off Childebrand's protest. "I'll follow in a week. I need to ensure we aren't leaving the city vulnerable to insurrection while our armies are away on campaign. On your way through Austrasia and Burgundy I want you to gather more men. We'll need more than the token number who attended the Spring Assembly."

"And if they claim they've already met their commitment?"

Pippin went to a cabinet and lifted out two sacks of gold. He put them onto the table. "Thanks to the Comptesse de Loches we have enough coin to entice an emperor."

Childebrand lifted one of the bags, weighing it. "This should help."

"I'll keep Gunther here with the battalion. Whether I

find Bertrada or not, I'll ride south with Arnot to overtake the army before you reach Regensburg."

"Gunther won't like missing all the fun. He gets surly when he's left out of a good fight."

"I don't have much choice. With the Merovingian here, I can't afford to take all our troops out of Paris. If Childeric and Ragomfred try to seize the city, I want someone who'll defend the palace without getting confused by politics."

"Then Gunther's your man. He never met a Merovingian that he didn't want to gut. I'll give orders to break camp in the morning." Childebrand picked up the sacks of gold and turned to take his leave. "Don't be late, Pippin. We can't afford to lose."

\* \* \*

Bertrada's father, the Compte, was next through Pippin's door. Not wanting to face him alone, Pippin requested that Catherine join them at her earliest convenience.

By the haggard look of the man, Pippin guessed the Compte hadn't slept since his daughter went missing.

"Anything?" Bertrada's father asked.

Pippin shook his head.

"St. Denis?"

"No sign of her."

"I received a message that Aude is alive and on her way to Soissons with Tedbalt. They were attacked by knights dressed as outlaws. As you suspected, Bertrada is with Lady Hélène."

Pippin tried to put a reassuring hand on the man's shoulder but the moment it made contact the Compte rounded on Pippin.

"This is your fault! You did this. Why couldn't you listen? She told you she didn't want this life. She hated the politics, hated the killing, and hated who you've become." His voice choked. "And now you've put a target on her back."

"I can protect her."

"Protect her? You can't even find her."

Pippin set aside his anger and tried a different tack. "Why didn't she tell me about the child?"

"Are you deaf as well? She doesn't want this life!" The Compte slammed the palm of his hand on Pippin's desk. Oddly enough, the violence of the blow seemed to restore a sense of humility to the man. "In truth, I didn't know she was with child, either. Maybe she didn't know of it."

"I will find her." Pippin said.

The Compte sighed. "If she's alive to be found."

"Perhaps I can be of assistance." Catherine stood at Pippin's door. Relief flooded through him.

The Compte looked doubtful.

Pippin hurried to bring her into the room. "The Comptesse de Loches was the first to recognize the danger to your daughters."

"Your daughters left the ball in my sister's care. I can assure you that they're safe."

The Compte looked back to Pippin. "Is that supposed to comfort me? How can a lone woman stand against the king's men?"

The Comptesse shrugged. "If she were dead or in the Merovingian's custody, we would already know."

"Phah!" The Compte waved a dismissive hand.

"I can assure you that your daughters are alive and safe."

"Are you the one who claimed Bertrada is with child?" Catherine nodded.

"Just how did you decide that?"

The Comptesse crossed her arms. "Swollen breasts, shiny skin, raw emotions. It doesn't require a physician to assess such things."

The Compte frowned. "She did have the nausea. We thought it was a catching disease." The admission seemed to leech the anger from him and he sat down. "If your sister has them, why hasn't she contacted you?"

"Perhaps she has no safe means of reaching us. She will when she can."

The Compte turned to Pippin. "What will Childeric do if he finds her first?"

Pippin frowned. "Hold her as hostage to ensure my loyalty."

The Comptesse shook her head. "Childeric isn't a reasonable man. He's a dangerous one. You can see it in his eyes. I'm afraid he might kill her."

The Compte again looked to Pippin.

Color flooded the mayor's face. It was the truth. "Yes, I believe he could."

* * *

While his men continued their search for Bertrada and Aude, Pippin began a separate investigation into how vulnerable the city was to insurrection. Many of the Neustrian nobility had openly supported the Merovingian heir. After seeing the numbers that attended the Ragomfred ball, Pippin was having doubts about the strength of the court's support.

He tapped Arnot to help him. The young blond nobleman was quite popular with the ladies at court and just as welcome in many of the city's inns and taverns. If anyone could ferret out information about the noble families supporting Childeric, it would be Arnot.

What the young man learned, however, wasn't encouraging. By most accounts, the Merovingian had made considerable inroads among Neustrian families, primarily through the good graces of Lord Ragomfred. It was also rumored that Ragomfred had amassed a sizable cache of treasure and arms to bolster the heir's claim.

Pippin developed three lists: one delineated noble houses loyal to him, a second, the houses loyal to Carloman and the third, those loyal to the Merovingian. A fourth list catalogued those who could be bought. When the lists were complete, Pippin sat back to study the political landscape. There was only one conclusion he could draw: he and Carloman were vulnerable. Carloman had men but no treasure. Pippin had treasure but fewer men. And with the Church's support for elevation, the Neustrian families could conceivably corner them into raising the Merovingian.

Eyeing the list of nobles supporting the Merovingian, Pippin was glad he had kept a battalion with him in Paris. He was beginning to think he should have kept two.

"Pippin?" Arnot stood at the entrance to his room a curious look on his face. "There's a lady outside asking to see you."

"Catherine?"

Arnot shook his head. "The Lady Ragomfred."

The shock brought Pippin to his feet, dread sweeping through him. She could only be a messenger – a messenger with bad news. "Did you show her in?"

"She's in your outer salon. Shall I send for a servant?"

Pippin was already out the door. "Yes. Yes, that's good."

He tried to remember what he could about her. A merchant's daughter with a sizable dowry, she had married a much older titled man. It was likely her dowry that had given Ragomfred the means to support the Merovingian's claim. A small wisp of a woman, she had impressed Pippin with the ease by which she had managed the court at her ball for Childeric. But why would Ragomfred send his wife?

He found her standing at the entrance of his salon. She was even smaller than he recalled with skin so pale it seemed absent of color. Her dark hair contributed to this effect, making her look hauntingly beautiful.

"Lady Ragomfred." Pippin made a short bow in greeting.

"My Lord Mayor." She curtsied and offered her hand. Pippin bent over it, ceremonially kissing the air above her fingers and caught the scent of her perfume. It had a delicate hint of lavender that lingered with him.

Looking up into her eyes, however, Pippin forgot what he planned to say. They were as brazen as they were arresting. Alive with passion and sensuality, they looked at him with the intimacy of a lover ready to abandon her clothes. Too late, he realized he was still holding her hand and that it had been far longer than was appropriate. Flushing with embarrassment, he let it go.

"Lady Ragomfred," he said again, and then felt even more foolish for repeating himself.

She laughed and took his arm as if they were old friends. "Miette." Her smile crinkled the corners of her eyes. "You must call me Miette. Shall we sit, my lord?"

"Yes, of course." Thinking he had magically been turned into a buffoon, he directed her to a sitting area across the room. He had to remove some maps to make room for her. He saw a servant waiting by the door. "May I offer you some wine?"

"That would be lovely." She settled into her chair and smoothed out the folds in her dress.

Pippin told the servant to bring wine and to clean up the mugs and rubbish in the room before sitting down across from her. He felt like a giant next to such a delicate woman. He struggled to regain some composure. "I must admit to being surprised by your visit, my lady. How may I be of service?"

"I'm here at the behest of the king." She leaned forward to whisper. "Although, you aren't supposed to know that."

"I'm not?"

"I'm supposed to play the role of a naïve young woman, new to the court, whose impotent husband is recklessly betting her endowment on the elevation of the king."

Pippin smiled despite himself. "And how does that differ from the truth?"

"It doesn't." She grinned. "Except that I'm far from naïve. I'm supposed to tell you that my husband is swimming beyond his depth when it comes to Childeric and that I'd be willing to help you."

"What would you expect in return?"

"Enough to live without my husband. That is ridiculous, of course. You don't have that kind of treasure, do you?"

Again, her eyes held him again, and again he felt as if it was a prelude to something intimate. He coughed. "And if I did?"

"It would still be ridiculous. You and I both know that once Childeric is crowned, I'll have social standing nearly equal to yours. Why would I give that up to be an impoverished court pariah? To be rid of a husband?" She waved her hand in dismissal. "You would never fall for something that stupid."

Pippin wasn't so sure. "What does Childeric want to know?"

"How much longer you'll remain in Paris."

"Why wouldn't he just ask me?"

"He doesn't believe you'd tell him. You made it very clear at the ball that you two are rivals. He thinks you'll be far more willing to share information if I trick you into thinking I'm disloyal."

"And he believes I would tell you?"

"Well, yes...after I seduce you. Pillow talk, that sort of thing."

She said it with such confidence, as if she was sure he would succumb. Pippin felt his face flush, suddenly unsure that he wouldn't. Her eyes found his again. This time there was a challenge in them, almost as if she was baiting him to try.

Pippin knew she was toying with him, but even so it was having its intended effect. He had never known a woman who spoke of such intimate matters so openly. He wondered what she would look like naked. He shook his head in an effort to control his thoughts. "Is your husband really impotent?"

Miette smiled and leaned forward, showing him just a hint of her décolletage. "Yes. At least with me." Again, her eyes challenged him.

"I'm surprised you told me that."

She smiled. "I'm drawn to powerful men, Pippin. I was impressed with you at the ball. Very few men could stand up to Childeric. And my husband? You terrify him. I find that strangely compelling. But don't worry. I won't seduce you."

"You won't?" Despite his amusement, Pippin felt a stab of disappointment.

"I won't have to. I think you'll tell me everything I want to know."

"And why would I do that?"

"Because I can return the favor." Her finger traced a fold line down her dress and she studied him watching her. "What do you want to know? How many families are allied with the king? Which ones?"

"Maybe I already know."

She smiled, letting the boast lie. Her face grew serious. "The two of us are pragmatic people, not ideologues like my husband or your brother Carloman. Rather than waste good Neustrian blood over this matter of elevation, I suggest there are more mutually beneficial ways for the two of us to proceed – even if we don't want the same things."

Although wary, Pippin nodded for her to continue.

"I suggest a secret correspondence between us."

"I thought you said this was Childeric's idea."

She smiled. "Seducing you was his idea. I'm talking about a much more delicate level of cooperation."

The servant returned with two glasses of rosé. Miette raised her glass with a sly grin. "To the future king!"

Pippin's grin became a smirk. "Whoever he may be." The rosé was crisp and cool on his tongue. He was enjoying the banter. The woman was a mystery. "Why would you do such a thing to your husband?"

"My husband is a political ally. She put down her glass, suddenly earnest. "I'm here in service of my king." Her cheeks flushed at this and it looked as if she was about to say more, but she waved away her emotions with a sweep of her hand. "This is the easiest way. He gets what he wants, and you get what you want."

Pippin had an inspiration. "You share his bed."

The blush returned but she maintained her composure. She sat back, assessing him and then smiled. "How dare you, sir. I'm a married woman." Her tone suggested quite the opposite.

She was so close, so available. "He's a dangerous man, my lady. I doubt he'd approve of such betrayal."

"Betrayal?" She knelt before him and ran a finger up his leg. "This is his idea. And what I'm proposing would be better described as diplomacy."

He felt a thrill go up his leg at her touch and a voice far away in his head screamed that he should show her the door, but Pippin ignored it. "I thought you weren't going to seduce me."

"Have I?" With a self-satisfied smile, she sat back in her chair and rearranged the folds of her dress and placed her hands demurely in her lap. "So? How much longer will you be in Paris?"

He told her. He convinced himself that it was no state secret and intelligence of no real value.

"Will your army remain behind?"

Pippin hesitated, assessing how much more he should divulge and then nodded. "A battalion. Childeric may have assurances from Neustrian nobles, but they won't take the field against my men. Not when I can return with an entire army."

"And what if, after the war, there's little left of your army?"

Pippin frowned. It was a good point.

Lady Ragomfred stood. "Fair is fair. Show me a list of the nobles you fear are with the king."

He walked her to his room, but when she entered it, she bypassed his desk and went straight to his bed, assessing it and the room with a studied gaze. "A bit small for someone of your stature."

"I need little by way of comfort."

"Do you?"

Pippin felt his face flush. "Not all men are the same."

She gave a sardonic laugh. "To that I can vouch."

She studied his lists, her hands moving quickly through the names. "These two have allied with Childeric. These three are still neutral. And this one," she pointed to a name on the bribe list, "is a liar. He could be in either camp."

Pippin frowned. It was worse than he had thought.

"Now, was that so difficult?" Her voice was mocking and playful, but she was standing dangerously close to him and he felt disoriented. She turned to face him, her body mere inches from his. She looked up into his face, and Pippin knew she wanted him to kiss her.

He took her by the arm, and they returned to the salon. "I look forward to our next meeting, my lady."

He watched her go, mesmerized by her confidence. As she exited, she stopped to examine the maps on his wall. When she turned back, her face showed no trace of her smile or their previous banter.

"Now that our friendship is sealed, Pippin. Beware of reports sighting Bertrada in the banlieu south of Paris. If you decide you must investigate, take plenty of men with you."

And then she was gone.

\* \* \*

Raising the hood of her cloak as she left Pippin's palace, Miette couldn't miss the fact that her hands were trembling. She scurried across the bridge that connected the Île de la Cité to the northern bank and ducked between two homes into a side alley. If she followed it for two blocks it would lead to where her carriage waited. Once hidden from view, however, Miette stopped to lean against the wall to compose herself.

It was then she discovered that her whole body was shaking with fright.

What was she thinking? Warning Pippin about the trap at the banlieu had been as foolish as it was suicidal. If Childeric ever discovered her betrayal, he would beat her to death. No emotional bond would protect her from his wrath. When the trap failed – and surely it would fail – he would suspect duplicity and she would be his primary suspect.

Yet some instinct had goaded her to warn Pippin.

Her mind raced at her folly and she tried to calm herself by closing her eyes and taking deep breaths. Her panic seemed to redouble with her effort. She had an overwhelming desire to flee even though she had nowhere to run.

The longer she tried to contain her fear, however, the more she realized her anxiety was not something new; it was something that had grown over time. The euphoria she had once felt for Childeric and her newfound role at court had been slowly replaced by a growing sense of apprehension. Where she had once reveled in his game of dominating wills and sexual exploration, she now found their trysts simply violent and degrading. And no matter how many times Miette's husband had explained "succession in the game of kings" it seemed cowardly to attack a woman pregnant with child.

Her disillusionment had spiked when Childeric commanded her to sleep with Pippin. It was humiliating. He had mollified her, of course, explaining that she was a trusted weapon in his defense, and that the intelligence she gained would protect him and his dynasty.

But who would protect her when Childeric cast her aside? Not her husband. No. He was weak in the face of Childeric. He had already shouted her down when she complained about Childeric's growing violence, telling her not to destroy all that they had worked to achieve.

Only Pippin had stood up to the future king.

And therein lay her answer. She had spared Pippin on

the chance that one day he might return the favor.

Miette felt her breath slow and her trembling hands calm. She straightened her back and squared her shoulders. She didn't know if she would survive her betrayal, but at least she now understood why she did it. By the time she reached her awaiting carriage, she strode to it with confidence.

# CHAPTER SEVENTEEN

*Outside Paris*

T hey slept most of the morning away but awoke when Patrice brought in vegetables from the garden. Hélène took the cue and started chopping them into the stewpot that hung in the fireplace. Its aroma filled the house and for the moment, Bertrada felt safe. Hélène's presence plus the warmth and quiet of the house, somehow reassured her that Childeric's men wouldn't find them there.

Agnès arrived at dusk, carrying bread and cheese in a wrap slung over her shoulder. Her face was grim. "There are armed men about town. They were asking for two women, one of them blond."

Bertrada's moment of safety vanished. "What did they look like?"

"Ruffians, save they ride war horses."

Hélène nodded. "Those are the men chasing us. I suppose they knew we couldn't go back to the palace and there's little safety to the north. I'm not surprised they're here. They had to guess we'd head south and east."

Bertrada tried to sound calm. "Can we get away?"

"Maybe it's best that you stay here for a few days. They

may move on."

"What if they start searching houses?"

"If they do, we'll have to move. It will take them some time to reach here and news like that travels quickly. We should be able to avoid them.

The four of them ate much of their meal in silence. Bertrada asked questions to fill the void.

"How do you two know each other?"

Patrice looked up at the question while Hélène seemed to focus on her stew. It was Agnès who answered. "I'm from the mountains. My family raised us in the ways of the Church. But, in the mountains, the journey of the devout is ... different. There are many paths to faith. I chose the most difficult one. I chose the dark path."

Hélène seized the story. "When I was young, I left my father's house. Unlike my sister Catherine, I refused to be sold to the highest male bidder. I swore that if I ever got married – and many years later I did – it would be a match of my own choosing. I fled to the mountains and sought refuge in a monastery. It was there I met Agnès. She showed me her path and I chose to take it up as well."

It sounded like heresy to Bertrada. "I don't understand. Doesn't the dark path lead to Satan?"

"You know of the seven virtues?"

"Of course. Temperance, Justice, Prudence, Fortitude, Faith, Hope and Charity."

"The monastery asks each of the faithful to adhere to all the virtues but to dedicate their lives to the pursuit and fulfillment of one. That pursuit becomes our life's work and is called a "path." The wooden path is the path to Temperance, The iron path – the path to Prudence. Our path – the dark path – is the path to Justice."

"It's a difficult road." Agnès dipped some of her bread into the stew. "I'm not as righteous as Hélène."

Hélène smiled. "She means she met a man who led her astray...a good man and a good father." She rubbed Patrice's head. "It was the right choice."

"But you never did like him." Agnès teased and the two women smiled.

It was a sweet moment. Bertrada could sense the bond between the two women. It was old and weathered and had lived through the pain of life. Despite that, the affection between them was clearly still strong. "Did you have such a choice, Hélène?"

The women's faces faltered at the question.

"Would you like some more stew?" Agnès moved to pick up her bowl, but Hélène stayed her with a hand.

"We always have choices." Her eyes were fierce and her voice a whisper. "That doesn't mean there are always good choices. I came to such a moment in my life, much like Agnès. Yet, all my choices led to the ruin of everyone I loved."

"How did you choose?"

"The truth is always present to the righteous eye." Hélène's eyes filled with emotion. She tried to speak again but couldn't.

"Sometimes the path requires sacrifice." Agnès took Hélène's hand in her own. "To protect those she loved, she chose her own ruin."

When the meal had ended, they washed their dishes and moved the table aside to make room for their bedrolls. Agnès sent Patrice to sleep in the barn and produced a spare bedroll. She left Bertrada and Hélène by the fire and moved her bedroll to the other side of the room.

Although exhausted, Bertrada had trouble falling asleep. The haunted look in Hélène's eyes disturbed her. What had she sacrificed? And for whom? The fire dwindled down to a narrow flame, giving only the barest crimson finger of light to the room. She drifted in and out of a fitful sleep and awoke to see Agnès kneeling beside Hélène. Hélène turned her face up in the flickering light. She was crying. Agnès brushed away her tears and then, leaning forward, kissed Hélène on the mouth. It was the gentlest embrace Bertrada had ever seen. Agnès stood and held out her hand. Hélène took it. Picking up her bedroll she followed Agnès to the other side of the room.

From her place by the fire, Bertrada could hear every sound they made, every sigh, every moan, and every cry. She thought about her own choices and wondered if they would lead to such a desolate place. She went to sleep listening to Hélène weep softly in Agnès's arms.

✻ ✻ ✻

Bertrada woke up to an empty house. Sunlight streamed through the two front windows and she found milk and bread on the table. She ripped off a piece from the loaf and washed it down, wondering where everyone had gone. Stepping outside in her shift, she saw Patrice in the pen feeding the chickens. She waved and he pointed to the back of the house. Bertrada walked tentatively around the back so as not to surprise the two women.

She found them standing next to each other, dressed in what looked like loose petticoats and a pair of men's pantaloons, going through the motions of what looked like a very slow dance. Their movements flowed from pose to pose in unison. Sometimes they bent at the waist and their legs arced high over their heads, at others their arms swept up in a dancer's pose, trailing their hands in a delicate weaving pattern. It was oddly beautiful.

"Join us." Hélène had not turned her head or missed a step. "It's one of the rituals of our path. It focuses the mind and spirit."

Bertrada stood next to them and tried to mimic their movements.

"Don't forget to breathe." Hélène whispered. "Let each pose flow in with your breath and release it on the way out."

Bertrada was already behind and skipped a pose to catch up. "Let the rhythm find you. Be open to its flow."

Bertrada only felt awkward. She tired quickly and some of the poses were too difficult for her to hold. By the end of their "ritual" her limbs were shaking, and she was covered in sweat. They knelt, facing the sun, and bowed down to touch their foreheads to the ground.

Agnès took them over to the well and drew out a bucket of water. All three of them drank deeply.

"As long as you're here," Agnès grinned. "I've got a fence to mend and could use a few extra hands with the planting."

Bertrada was so tired she could barely move. "I'm happy to help, but first you might need to carry me back to the house. I'm exhausted!"

The two older women laughed and together they helped Bertrada return to the house.

Bertrada sat down at the table and took another handful of the bread. She watched the two women banter back and forth as they cut up more vegetables. Bertrada found it odd that Hélène was so comfortable here. As a noble woman, she was used to servants and luxury, yet here she was in this one-room house acting like she belonged in the kitchen chopping tomatoes with Agnès.

She liked these women. They were strong, resolute, compassionate – qualities Bertrada had always claimed for herself. Yet, next to Hélène and Agnès, she felt little more than a spoiled child.

Agnès noticed her watching them. "Have you made your choice, milady?"

Bertrada blushed at the woman's use of the title. "Please, there's no need to use such a formal address."

"It is, however, a formal question." Agnès had stopped chopping, so had Hélène. They were waiting for her answer. The significance of the choice filled her with dread. On one side was a child, Pippin, and all the horror that came with his family's power. On the other was a life of ease, comfort and peace. At first it seemed an easy choice. But try as she might, she couldn't imagine the second side. Her life looked empty, devoid of love. It wasn't really a choice at all. What was it that Hélène had said? "Truth is always present to the righteous eye."

"I will keep the babe."

The moment the words left her mouth, she knew they were just. All the tension in the room evaporated. Hélène and Agnès went back to chopping their vegetables and trading affectionate insults.

Bertrada got up to help them. She grabbed a knife and some asparagus. "What do I do now?"

Hélène was smiling. "We stay here until we can come up with a place to hide. And then we try to figure out how to get there unnoticed."

# CHAPTER EIGHTEEN

*The Reichswald Forest*

Although snow still clung to the north side of the sibyl's mountain home, a haze of green had begun to infiltrate the forest canopy. Sunlight sparkled off surging streams that splashed their way down into the valley and the earth smelled of loam and life. The sibyl savored the morning air on her tongue. Cool, crisp and wet, it tasted of possibilities.

As ritual required, she had waited for her moon's blood to flow before her descent into the valley with her two attendants. The villagers there would expect her. They wouldn't plant before she blessed their fields; they would not marry until she kissed the bellies of their brides and they wouldn't name their children before she marked their babies' foreheads with the gods-rune. She relished the stature this gave her and the awe she could evoke.

Although the villagers called her "sibyl," the term was far too short for all that she had become. She was a healer, a truthsayer and a seer. Runes denoting her station and knowledge tattooed her skin, snaking up her arms and shoulders and curling around her breasts. Small bones from her sacrifices to the Sisters of Fate adorned her hair and clacked when she moved, announcing her as a seer and devotee of the lore.

But it was the gift that defined her. Entranced by sacred herbs, the past and future spread out before her and unspoken truths leapt to her attention. The villagers said she had "visions." She preferred to call it "sight."

At the outskirts of the first village, she smiled. She liked this place. Large farms surrounded the town on all sides. The roads were well kept, and the houses well built. Men already were turning the soil in preparation for spring planting and she could hear laughter and women's voices calling out to one another as they tended animals, repaired clothes, and watched their children at play.

The people here would be generous, sharing their tables and giving her a warm, comfortable bed for the night. And there were none of the cross-bearers who called her "witch" or "demon" or worse.

She and her two acolytes dismounted before entering the town. They took off their cloaks and dropped their shifts to lay bare their God runes. Together, they led the horses in a stately procession, allowing the villagers time to recognize who they were and the nature of their calling.

It didn't take long for people to gather alongside the road. Men doffed their hats and knuckled their foreheads and women lowered their eyes. As she passed, children were sent ahead to spread word of her arrival. The adults fell in line behind her. With her head high and her eyes distant, she led them into town. As she approached, villagers began arriving from all directions. She continued at her measured pace and all gave way before her.

The stones were where she remembered them. They lay in a grid of nine at the heart of the village. The townspeople spread around the square at a respectful distance while her attendants built a small fire next to the center stone.

She stood in her place on the stone, her head held back, her eyes closed, and her hair with its myriad of bones, dangling around her shoulders. One of her attendants stood beside her, and with open arms, announced her presence.

"From the day the gods first found the runes and shared them with man, we have had the power to touch the three realms of the world. But the power to behold the pattern that the Three Sisters weave is rare."

Her attendant stepped aside and bowed.

"It is both a gift and a curse to those who see. Prize and ware the knowledge it brings."

Her attendants drew dried leaves and herbs from their reticules and spread them over the small fire. The sibyl's nostrils flared as the first tendrils of smoke drifted up to her and she recognized the unique scents of her burning plants. She inhaled deeply and often. Soon, colors swirled inside her closed eyelids and an inner warmth coursed through her veins. She spread her arms and the crowd hushed to silence.

Her attendants took off the last of her garments leaving her clothed only in the ephemeral grey-blue veil of smoke. They removed the small towel from between her legs and silence took the square. Her moon's blood drained down her thighs, past her knees and her ankles. When it reached the stone beneath her feet, her attendants took up their instruments. Their drumbeat filled the silence, and the acolytes began to chant, slowly at first, and then with an insistence that matched the beating of the drums.

Abruptly, they paused. And when they began again, the villagers joined them, echoing the chant, line for line.

The sibyl swayed her hips to the punctuated beat of the drums and as the strength of the chant swept over her in irresistible waves, she lifted her arms in supplication, letting herself be carried away by the sound. She flushed with the momentum of the chant and was lost in its current. She opened her eyes.

It was as if she were in two places at once. She could still feel the blood trickling down her legs and the cold stone beneath her feet, and yet, somehow, she was not inside her body. She was high above the square looking down on the villagers gathered below.

The scene tilted. She tried to hold it upright in her mind, but the village, and all of its people, toppled over and flattened out into a single vast thin line. It shimmered before her. As she watched, it began to unfold, cascading before her like the folds of an opening fan. She no longer saw one village square filled with people; she saw a thousand village squares filled with people. They moved so fast her mind couldn't hold onto one. She reeled before the images, trying to clear her head. Her hand reached out to stop it.

The images froze and she found herself again in the square surrounded by the villagers. But they and the square had changed. It was a smoldering ruin, an endless landscape of ash and blackened tree stumps. The people stood frozen in place as if time itself had stopped. Like a ghost, she floated among them unnoticed and invisible.

The faces of the women had grown drawn and haggard. The children were thin, and dirty, their eyes sunken and hollow. She tried to reach out and touch their faces, but her hand had no substance.

Something was wrong, she thought. Something afflicts them. They are aged but no older.

She turned in every direction and found only women and children. Confused, she moved back to the center of the square. Where were the men?

She looked down and wished she hadn't found them. They lay in rows, head to toe and toe to head, in barely covered graves. They stared up at her through sightless eyes, their features contorted and their limbs little more than bone. Leeches, slugs and roaches moved through nostril holes and eye sockets. She wanted to wail but had no voice. So many. She knelt among them and the gravity of the loss overwhelmed her.

Abruptly, her vision ended, and she was back on the center stone. Her knees buckled beneath her. One of her attendants caught her by the arm and struggled to hold her upright. The drums stopped and the chanting died. The sibyl had to fight to stand. Straightening, she took a deep breath and looked up.

Their faces were normal. They looked healthy and happy. She nearly wept at the concern she saw on every villager's face. But the haunting image of the men lingered, and she had to avert her eyes from its memory. Scolding herself for her weakness, she tried to meet their collective gaze and again could not.

"I need to speak with the women alone." She focused on the ground. "Only to them."

At first, no one moved, and she cursed her impotence. They expected more, but more she could not give. It was all she could do to keep from weeping. Some of the men grumbled and still she refused to look up. With an oath, one of them turned away. Others followed until a growing exodus of men and their children left the square.

When the last had gone, the sibyl raised her eyes. Her hands and lips trembled. Nothing in her training had prepared her for this. All her well-practiced queenly demeanor had shattered.

"What is it?" A woman called, clutching her shawl around her chest. Silence and fear held the square.

The sibyl looked into their expectant faces and mustered all the strength she had within her. "Death comes."

Looks of confusion spread among the villagers and the sibyl drew a deep breath. A frightened sob pierced the air. "Death comes," she said. "For the men.

"It will take them all as assuredly as I am standing here." Tears escaped her. She fought them back. "Most of you and the children will be spared."

She tried to approach her audience, but they backed away in horror. "You don't have much time." She looked again to the ground. "This year, maybe next, but it will be."

"What can we do?" a voice called out.

"We can leave," another stated.

The sibyl shook her head. "It cannot be avoided."

"Then what can we do?" a woman hissed directly in front of her.

"Prepare," the sibyl's voice was hollow.

With an angry cry, one of the women bent and picked up a stone. "Witch!" She threw the stone, hitting the sibyl on the scalp and cutting her. Blood began to ooze from the wound and trickle down over her cheek.

Strangely, the blow strengthened her. She raised her head with all the majesty that remained within her and faced the woman.

"The Sisters have spoken. Death comes. Nothing will change what will be. You can only savor what is. Tend to them. Cherish them for the time they have left."

The anger began to drain from her. "And prepare. Prepare for life without them." She turned toward the horses. Her two attendants stood behind her, stunned and pale. At a nod they accompanied her as she walked away.

The women of the village remained where she had left them. But one young girl, no more than fourteen, followed her to the road. She was pretty, even with tears streaming down her face.

"My Otto." Her voice broke. "Surely, not my Otto. He's so young."

The sibyl shook her head. "Death comes." She touched the girl's cheek. "Take him to your bed. Have his babe. It will be your memory of him."

The sibyl reclaimed her robe, turned away from the town, and rode past the well-built homes and well-kept farms. She rode with her back erect and her head held high until she knew she could no longer be seen in the distance. Only then did she allow the sobs to take her.

# CHAPTER NINETEEN

*Worms*

A crow, perched high in the trees above them, flapped its wings and cawed mockingly at the army passing below. Carloman scowled at the black beast. He didn't believe in omens – no good Christian did – but he was beginning to worry that in the short two weeks since he left Paris his campaign had been cursed.

First, Pippin refused to join him on the march, offering only vague, last minute assurances that he would eventually bring his army into the fray. Then, a catching disease had swept through the ranks, devastating the readiness of his men. Those who caught it retched and shat for three days and became so weak they couldn't march. Although it didn't deplete their numbers, the symptoms slowed their progress to a mule's pace. The smell of puke and excrement hung over the army like a cloud. Those who hadn't yet caught the disease knew it was but a matter of time before they did.

Last, he had received troubling reports that Theudebald had crossed the Rhine to sack Worms, killing dozens including the Duc and his son. The Alemannian was last seen taking his army east.

Carloman, who had planned to cross the Rhine at Strasbourg, altered course at Metz to capture the old Roman highway to the northern city of Worms.

Carloman cursed under his breath. If he hadn't had to chase down Pippin in Poitiers, the sack of Worms would never have happened.

As they approached the city, smoke still clung to its skyline. Carloman had his men camp alongside a lake near the city while he, Drogo and Boniface took a small contingent of men in to assess the damage.

They entered through the Western gate and the sickly-sweet smell of rot assaulted Carloman. The city walls were lined with carts overflowing with bloated corpses, grotesque in decomposition. A third of the city had burned, mostly the buildings along the river. All that remained were charcoaled two-storied skeletons of what had once been the nicest homes in Worms. The air was still thick with soot and ash that clung to building walls and stones in the street.

People fled at the sight of their warhorses. They reached the city's center before anyone confronted them. A lone woman stepped forward in the middle of the street. It took Carloman a moment to recognize her.

"Lady Hilda." He bowed from his saddle. When he last saw the Duchesse, she was a tall and elegant woman of great wit and grace. Now, she looked stooped and forlorn with a pall clouding her eyes.

"My greetings, Carloman, although I doubt that you'll find your visit here welcoming."

Carloman dismounted and took her hands in his. "I am sorry for the loss of Duc Robert and your son. I pledge to you that I will see them avenged."

Her eyes didn't seem to register his words. She turned to lead him through the city as if he was on tour. When she spoke, her voice was distant. "We were no match for such numbers. After he took the city, Theudebald gathered what was left of our garrison and sent them into the barracks." She waved vaguely in the direction of a charred, husk of a building. "He burned them alive. Then they came for the women and children."

"Hilda, you don't need to–"

"They raped us." Her words were flat, devoid of emotion. "They made great sport of trapping us and ripping off our clothes. We begged them, pleading for the children. Some of the husbands and fathers tried to stop it. They, too, were bent over barrels in the town square and sodomized, right in front of their wives and children. There was no one to stop it. It never seemed to end."

For the first time, the Duchess looked up at Carloman. The emptiness of her gaze unnerved him. "They took our souls."

As much as the city's plight pained Carloman, it didn't surprise him. Taking the spoils of war was common, even among the Franks. Charles had tried to rein in the practice to stop the endless cycle of retribution it caused. He would say, "A vanquished foe can be an ally. A ravaged foe will always be an enemy."

The Duchesse led Carloman to a garden at the center of the city. A large oak tree stood at the northeast corner. From its limbs hung the bodies of Duc Robert and his son Hilfred. Their genitals had been cut off and tied around their necks. Vultures and insects picked at their bloated bodies. "Theudebald said not to cut them down until you arrived. He said it's an offering to their gods."

While Boniface ministered to the Lady Hilda, Carloman himself cut down the bodies of Duc Robert and Hilfred. Drogo oversaw the digging of massive graves for the dead and began the task of rebuilding the barracks and the church. A count of the survivors showed over two hundred had been killed. Although the men comprised the greatest number of those slain, the toll among the women and children was also high. Many had died from wounds suffered during the rape. Others simply had been beaten to death.

Carloman reluctantly replaced the city's garrison with two hundred of his men to guard the city. He would need every man to defeat Odilo's rebellion. Given the circumstances, however, he had little choice. He couldn't leave the city undefended.

It took four days to bury the bodies and clear the remnants of the buildings devastated by fire. What crops needed planting were planted. What cattle that needed tending were tended to. The markets were reopened, and Carloman sent word to Metz requesting artisans and laborers to come and help rebuild the city.

On the Sabbath, Boniface held mass in the courtyard before the edifice being constructed for the new church. While Carloman was happy to see that a large crowd gathered to attend, he was concerned that they still looked stunned as if they had received a collective blow to the head.

As the mass got underway, the congregation seemed to revive, albeit slowly. They knelt at the appropriate places and gave the correct responses prescribed by the ritual of the mass. *It's a start*, Carloman thought.

When it came time for the homily, Boniface walked down into the courtyard to stand among the survivors. "Brothers and sisters in Christ, we've lost many in the past few weeks. Wives. Husbands. Sons. Daughters. We grieve for them. And we grieve for the innocence that's been taken from us and for the cruelty you all have had to suffer. It's a harsh world and you have been treated harshly by it. I won't speak today of forgiveness, for looking into your eyes, I see little room for a concept so noble. And I won't speak of vengeance because the Lord has said that vengeance is His province alone."

Boniface paused for effect.

"But know this: justice will be served. The army outside these gates will not falter in its pursuit of those who have brought such harm. The wicked shall be brought low as they are an offense to God."

Heads nodded and murmurs of assent rippled through the crowd. *Good*, Carloman thought, noting the signs of life. But something felt out of place to him. Something was missing.

"For those we bury today," Boniface continued, "I take great solace in the knowledge that they now stand before God and the gates of Heaven to receive His judgment. Their journey on this earth has ended. Our journey, however, continues. Your journey continues. You survived. You remain. It is time to bury our dead and turn our eyes to the living. There are mouths to feed. Wounds to heal. Crops to grow. And lives to live."

Boniface's face lit up with his message of hope.

"We are people of faith. We have faith that life is worth living. We have faith that our lives have purpose. We have faith that love will bloom anew and that children will be born to our families. You survived the attack of the Allemanni. You are living proof that God's plans for you are not finished. Tomorrow this army will march east to seek justice, peace and security. Your work is here. Rebuild your lives and this city. Only then will your enemies truly be vanquished for they will have failed to crush your spirit."

It was then that Carloman realized what was missing. It was Lady Hilda.

During the Eucharist, when his departure wouldn't be noticed, Carloman slipped away. Drogo, ever watchful, followed and the two ran to check her residence. They never made it that far. They found her at the northeast corner of the garden at the city's center. She was hanging from a limb of the large oak tree.

# CHAPTER TWENTY

*Regensburg*

T rudi was welcomed back to court with a tremendous round of applause. According to Tobias, fear for her and her baby had spiked during her confinement, with many speculating that she would lose the child. Her reappearance did much to quell, but not stop, the gossip.

Given the military preparations that surrounded the city, few gave much thought to the quiet process she and Hans had developed for vetting potential candidates for her household guard. Hans would invite potential candidates to the training grounds where Trudi could evaluate their skills with a sword. Having been trained by Fulrad, Trudi felt more than qualified in her ability to judge a candidate's ability with a sword. What concerned her more was something one couldn't see on a training ground. She wanted loyalty. And that would require some discussion.

Her interviews were always short. Those who expressed ambition were dismissed outright. A similar fate fell to those whose eyes wandered below her neck. She asked the candidates about their families, their service, and their faith. She preferred married men to those who were single, men who had grown up with a sword in hand versus a pike or cudgel, and pagans over Christians. Having watched Carloman subvert hundreds to his Knights in Christ through their faith, she wanted no such vulnerability in her guard. Fanatical worship of either faith was a cause for disqualification.

By the time Odilo had returned, Trudi identified more than five score who qualified for the guard, including seventy-five swordsmen, twenty pike men, and ten proficient at the two-handed staff. Although pleased with her success, she recognized that convincing Odilo would be her real challenge.

Her husband arrived like a summer storm, sudden and teaming with emotion.

"Carloman has left Paris and is heading east."

"What about Pippin?"

Odilo turned back to her. "He doesn't ride with Carloman. He remains in Paris."

Trudi's relief was palatable. "Induce him to intercede. With Pippin's aid, you won't have to fight Carloman."

"We're well beyond suing for peace, Trudi. Theudebald has sacked Worms."

Trudi couldn't hide her exasperation. "You have yet to engage!"

"Why don't you trust me in this? We're going to win, Trudi. Carloman is not your father."

Trudi's fear spiked at the boast. Odilo did not – could not – understand. "Carloman was my father's right hand. He was raised on the battlefield. He's ruthless and cunning." Tears sprang to her eyes as she thought of the consequences. "He never loses. If Pippin joins him against you there'll be nothing you and your armies can do to stop them. Please, Odilo, please send word to Pippin. I'm begging you on the life of our child. Stop this before it's too late."

Odilo's face was furious. "You doubt me? Me?" He pointed to the window. "Look at the army outside our walls. It is every bit as large as those your brothers can field. Bavarians, Slavs, and Alemannians. This is our land! And we will defend it with our lives. I asked your brother to avoid this war and he ignored me. I won't ask again."

"Please – "

"Stop this. Your place is here, beside me. Do not take their side!"

Trudi threw her arms around him. "It's your life I'm trying to protect. Yours and our child's."

At her touch, Odilo's tension abated. He put his arms around her and hugged her to him. "You've recovered from your injury?"

Trudi stiffened, but held on to her husband. "I am better. The baby will survive."

"You must be more careful. You gave us all a scare."

She let go of him. In a soft voice she said, "I was very afraid. I still am. You were gone so long, and I'm a woman alone."

"You are my wife. You're hardly alone."

"I'm vulnerable here in a way I never was at home."

"No one would dare touch you."

Trudi stifled a shudder but lifted her eyes to his. "How can you be sure? I am Charles's daughter and Carloman's sister. They have many enemies and not everyone celebrated our marriage."

Taking Odilo's silence as agreement, she pressed on. "I must ask a boon."

"A household guard?"

"You know?"

"It's hard to keep something like that a secret." He smiled at her. "Of course, I understand. It will be done."

"I have one caveat," she whispered. "It must be loyal to me. Only me."

"Sedition, my love?"

"Peace of mind, should something happen to you..." Her eyes welled with tears. "Your child and I will become pawns in a much larger game."

"Then be at peace, my love. I will assign you men in the morning."

"I've already chosen those to serve. All you need do is

make the announcement."

Odilo looked surprised but nodded his head. "It will be as you say."

* * *

Trudi's next task was to organize her men into a fighting force. She needed her own Fulrad to train them into a cohesive unit. Having spent so many days in the practice yard looking for candidates, she had the chance to size up most of Odilo's top swordsmen. One, an Avar named Kovrat, was nearly as good as Carloman's champion, Hamar. Fast, lithe, and confident, Kovrat fought with such grace and ease that Trudi had trouble remembering that his movements were meant to be lethal. She sent for him.

Up close, Kovrat was shorter than she expected. He had dark hair, dark eyes, and dark skin and a chest as wide around as a barrel. He wore his hair long with a short beard to frame his face. Everything about him, from the way he stood to the slight smile on his face exuded confidence. He bowed upon meeting her. "Milady."

"You're quite a swordsman, Kovrat."

He nodded, accepting the compliment.

"Have you ever led men in battle?"

The look on his face suggested he found the question amusing. "It is why I am here, Milady. I'm a gift to the Kagan."

"Kagan?"

"My...lord," he said.

"Do you give this gift to others?"

He shook his head. "Only the Kagan."

"My husband fights with the Kagan."

He nodded.

"If he asked you to train my guard, would you?"

Kovrat shook his head. "I am for the Kagan."

"I can offer you gold."

"I have all the coin I need, milady."

Trudi frowned. "Is there nothing I can offer you?"

"No, milady."

She found another swordsman, but the difference in caliber was substantial, especially on the practice yard. This man belittled the men more than he taught them and pranced around the practice field like he was a prince. Trudi dismissed him after the first day.

Frustrated, she coaxed Odilo into asking the Avar's Kagan to attend a dinner he was hosting for some of the leaders of the rebellion. Clearly delighted to be invited, the Kagan overdressed for the occasion, wearing the traditional formal attire of the Avars. His hat was conical, and his red robe festooned with great medallions celebrating his many victories in battle. His skin wasn't as dark as Kovrat's but his eyes had the permanent squint of easterners.

If he recognized his error in overdress, the Kagan didn't show it. In fact, he seemed to feel he was entitled to be in such august company despite being a minor chieftain among the great armies of the rebellion. Trudi bade him to sit next to her.

She flattered him throughout the evening, extolling the Avars as great fighters and swordsman. She worked the conversation around to Kovrat and tested the idea of loaning his services to train her guard. The Kagan cut her short.

"He is a gift."

"Kovrat said that. It's a strange thing to call allegiance a gift."

The Kagan waved away the assertion. "There was a great war among the Avars. Many claimed to be first among the Kagans and were willing to shed blood to settle the question. The war lasted for years and thousands died. Avar became weak with the loss of our youth. In the end, all but one Kagan fell before my army. Although the last was a lesser Kagan, his general, Kovrat, had a reputation so great that none wished to fight him.

When at last I took the field against him, I had him

outnumbered and surrounded. Rather than spill the blood of another Avar, I sued for peace and suggested "a gift" of the general's service in exchange for their lives. His Kagan agreed and we withdrew the next day. I can't offer Kovrat's service to you. He serves a debt for his people. I won't dishonor that debt by having him train your guard."

* * *

The next day Trudi arrived at the practice yard in her armor. She had had to adjust her leathers and remove a plate to make way for her growing belly, but it felt good to be wearing them again. When she entered through the gate, however, Hans stepped forward. "You can't do this, Milady. You'll dishonor the men sworn to serve you."

"I can train them better than that last idiot I picked."

"That may be, but still they will be humiliated when others discover that they're being trained by a woman."

"I was trained by Fulrad, himself. I can best any man here. You pick one. Anyone." She grabbed the nearest man, a young Slav she had selected on the first day. "Draw your weapon."

The man looked at her stupidly. He didn't touch his sword.

"You." She pushed Hans. "Come on." She traced eights with her sword. "I order you to draw your weapon." Hans didn't move.

"Milady?"

Trudi turned to find Kovrat standing behind her, sword in hand.

"Will I suffice?"

She had no chance against the Avar and she knew it. Nothing would be gained by fighting him; he would humiliate her. He was humiliating her just by asking. She raised her blade to her forehead and extended it to the side, a gesture of submission. "I yield to your sword, sir. I am no match for you."

Kovrat nodded. "You are right to yield. Although I'm surprised you did. You're wiser than I had thought. Why do you challenge these men? Do you really think you could best them?"

"I've seen them fight."

Kovrat laughed. "Indulge me." He brought his sword up to his ear in the ox position, his left leg forward.

Instinctively, Trudi drew back her right leg, lowering her weapon's point to the ground, the fool's position. She turned her hand so that her left hand was on top. Kovrat attacked, a feinting stab followed by a cutting blow to her midsection. Trudi ignored the feint and raised her blade to block the first blow. Spinning, away from his sword arm, she counterattacked, slashing downward to attack his knee. Kovrat's blade was there to block it and he spun with her to come face to face.

His second attack was more forceful, using the roof position to rain blows down on her from above. Trudi parried each as they came but was forced to retreat before them while waiting for an opening to counterstrike. She saw her chance, a small opening to his midsection. It had to be a ruse. He was too good a swordsman to leave himself so vulnerable. She began to stab forward from the plow position and waited for his blade to parry. Spinning with it to move behind him, she again slashed downward and again, his sword trailed behind to catch it. He spun towards her and lifted his blade so quickly that Trudi hadn't time to parry. The point found the soft part of her throat.

Trudi froze. "As I said, sir. I am no match for you."

Kovrat lowered his blade and returned it to its sheath. "I've heard of Fulrad. You say he trained you?"

Trudi nodded.

He took the sword from her hand, hefted it, admiring the curve of its blade. "A Moor's blade. Light. Deadly." He turned back to her. "You are well trained. Most would have fallen for that opening. You anticipated it. Perhaps you could best these men." Kovrat swung Trudi's blade, testing its feel. "But not when I'm finished with them."

Trudi was stunned. "I thought you were prohibited."

"I'm my Kagan's gift, to be sure. And I won't forsake my duty. But I can give gifts of my own making."

He handed Trudi back her sword. "Your men wouldn't attack you because you're a woman and carry their Duc's child in your womb. It gives them no honor to fight you and might cost them much if they lose. You are not the one to train them. I am."

"Why change your mind?"

He turned to look at her as if evaluating her worth. "I'm not sure. Perhaps it is because I never before met a woman in armor. I certainly have never met one who could use a sword, let alone train men in its use. You are a surprise, Duchesse, to a man who is rarely surprised. If your brother is half as formidable, we'll have a long, hard battle before us."

# CHAPTER
# TWENTY-ONE

*Hesse*

I t took nearly three days to ferry his army across the Rhine. Although he was relieved to have finished the arduous task, Carloman was more than a little anxious to be on the east side of the river. After years of campaigns with his father in Alemannia, Frisia, and Hesse, he had come to realize that he was a man of the west where century-old roads and highways connected one province to the next, where cities with great churches and markets gave way to towns and villages, and where people worked the land and plied their trades. In the west, the language was common, the Church was ubiquitous and the power of the mayors, unquestioned.

East of the river, chaos reigned. A Babel of tribal chieftains waged incessant war that left their people scarred, desperate, and violent. Dark and endless forests covered the landscape where huge wolves often held dominion over mankind. Even the mountains were made to intimidate, towering over their counterparts in the west with peaks so close to heaven that trees no longer grew.

In such a place it was easy to understand the pagan worship of nature deities. The gods of such a wild and untamed land would have to be terrible gods, indeed.

To Carloman's amusement, crossing the Rhine had the opposite effect on Boniface.

"This is the way the earth looked when God created it." Boniface swept his hand across the horizon where the flat marshland gradually gave way to undulating green hills reckless with wildflowers. "It's as if we are present on the fifth day of Genesis and only the beasts and plants inhabit the world."

Having made this journey with Boniface in the past, Carloman wasn't surprised by the bishop's enthusiasm. The east roused a wild nature in the man that one rarely saw at court in Paris. Crossing the river changed him.

Carloman decided to tease his godfather. "I disagree, Boniface. One side of the river looks much like the other."

"Then you, Carloman, are a blind man. Do you see any roads, or towns, or cities to mar the countryside? Are there monuments here to man's self-glorification as there are in the west? Here, the people are *of* the land. They don't deform it for their purposes. Life lived here is as our Lord intended it should be lived."

"You are hardly objective, Boniface."

The bishop harrumphed. "I suppose you have a point. Though not my native land, Hesse is the land of my making. It was here that I first came under the tutelage of Willibord. It was here that I first ministered to the pagans and here that the fires of my spiritual passion took hold. My work east of the Rhine made me a missionary and ultimately a Bishop. Everywhere I look, the land conjures up such memories that I feel like laughing at the sheer joy of it."

Carloman had agreed to honor a request from the bishop to escort him to the Hessian monastery at Fritzlar and then a few days march south to Fulda where Boniface planned to found a new monastery. It was intended to be the central seat of three new dioceses. Carloman had gifted an old royal fort that long ago had been sacked and burned. He suspected that the bishop's request involved more than just safe travel.

Arriving with an army at his back would send a powerful message to the local chieftains.

Carloman also hoped to use the northern detour to enlist the support of the local Hessian chieftains in his war against Odilo and Theudebald. Even their neutrality would be a benefit to his campaign. Although the Hessians lacked the military order and discipline of armies in the west, they were fierce fighters and not to be taken lightly. It would be difficult enough to fight the Bavarians and the Allemanians. He didn't relish the idea of adding Hessians into the mix.

As they marched inland, the thin line of the horizon slowly swelled into an immense forest of pine and fir trees that towered over the army. The farthest reaches of the forested expanse exceeded the limits of their vision and made Carloman feel puny, even with an army at his side.

There were no roads into the forest, only footpaths. And they were too few and small to be an adequate passage of an army such as his.

Hamar hurried from the rear to ride alongside Carloman. "You're committed to going in there?"

"It is the way forward."

"We'll be vulnerable. This forest can hide many sins and we only have one army."

"It's a big army." Carloman smiled for the benefit of his champion. "And we don't have time to go around. Send scouts ahead and keep patrols on our flanks to provide us some warning. I don't expect too much trouble until we're further east."

"As you wish, milord." Hamar raced back along the line to relay the instructions.

Within moments, riders galloped forward in a semicircular formation to lead Carloman's army into the perpetual dusk of the forest's interior. The men had to halve their columns to cross the tree line, marching five abreast instead of ten. Still, their passage cut a path through the forest that could accommodate an oliphant.

As day followed day, Hamar's caution appeared to be

unfounded. They advanced unchallenged by man, or boar or wolf. The only thing to harass their progress was the cawing of unseen crows.

After another week, the terrain grew more mountainous and their march more labored. As they climbed, however, the forest thinned and Carloman saw evidence of humanity. They passed farms and villages nestled in the valleys along their path. Unlike their counterparts in the west, however, these villagers ran from the sight of Carloman's army, shooing their children before them and drawing pagan runes in the air.

He sent for Boniface. "I thought you had converted the pagans in these parts."

Boniface frowned. "Conversion is a complicated affair, especially in a world where the forest defines one's existence. There's a great tendency to embrace the false gods of the land rather than to aspire to an afterlife in the Kingdom of Heaven. It can take decades to convert the pagan to true Christian belief. And, of course, not all the tribal leaders bent their knee when I was last here."

From their elevated vantage point, Boniface pointed to three great hills rising from the forest floor next to a sliver of blue water. "There lies Fritzlar. With your permission, I'll ride ahead and pay my respects to Father Sturm and bring word of your arrival. I'm sure that his welcome of your officers will be most generous."

"I'd like to camp there for a few days. Can we expect the good father to extend us his hospitality?"

"I should think so." Boniface paused. "Although pushing on to Fulda might be a better choice. The fortifications of your old fort there will provide a much better defensible position."

Carloman frowned. "I imagine that Theudebald is well south of here."

Boniface shook his head. "I was referring of the local Hessian chieftains. Although most formally acknowledge their vassalage to you– and to our Lord – some can be as difficult as the Gascons."

"How much of a threat are they?"

"They're too few to affect a direct attack. But they can certainly provide a frustrating level of harassment as we continue east. Like wolves, they prey on strays and attack vulnerable points in the line. In the forest, they can inflict significant damage. You will never see them, but they'll be there the moment you let your guard down."

"Then we should root out the rebellious chieftains while we're here."

"That's something your father would have said." Boniface again shook his head. "It only would rebound against you. We already have won the war. Most of the tribes accept Christianity, even if not embraced wholeheartedly. Those who refused aren't critical to the cause, but they're all Hessians. Attacking one will rally the others, pagan and Christian, to their defense.

"The Church has forged a fragile truce. The pagan chieftains leave us alone. A few priests on a mountain top aren't much to tolerate," Boniface said. "But an army of Christians camping among them for days?" Boniface let the thought hang. "It may bring out the worst in them."

"Let Father Sturm know that we'll push on to Fulda in the morning," Carloman said, "but before we leave, I'd like to see the stump of your tree."

"Ah!" Boniface grinned. "It wasn't my tree, it was Thor's."

❖ ❖ ❖

Carloman's reference to the tree touched Boniface deeply. Many years had passed, and few remembered his feat, especially in the west. He suspected that with the passing of another generation, no one would recall it at all.

With a bow to acknowledge the compliment, Boniface kicked the flanks of his horse and left the road to skirt the ranks of Carloman's army.

As he overtook the lead units, he said a short prayer of thanks and pressed on towards the three hills in the distance. To his joy, he soon was surrounded by oak and elm on the Forrest Road and gave his mare her head. As he plunged deeper into the forest, massive trees towered over him, filtering out the grey clouds above and leaving the woodland below in a soft orange light.

He thundered through it, delighting in the recognition of the trees and rocks and flowers that spread through the undergrowth. Familiar landmarks leapt out at him and he veered to the right of a boulder nestled at the apex of a fork in the road, and taking a smaller, less-traveled path, he rose high above the main road. His mare slowed as the path grew steep. He urged it forward, digging his heels into her flank. Rocks skittered down the path at his intrusion and soon it was difficult to navigate. In places Boniface had to dismount to continue up the slope.

It was farther than he had remembered, but he was determined to reach the summit. When at last he topped the hill, the forest around him opened onto a plateau of tall grass. Boniface led his horse to the far end of field where the world fell away, offering a view of over a hundred miles. It was his favorite spot in all of Hesse. Two great hilltops stood to the south of him, flanked by a ribbon of water. The furthest was Büraburg where the monastery stood. He could just make out the outlines of the chapel and the monastery's dormitories. Across the Eder lay Fritzlar to the southeast. As much as any place in the world, this was home to him. His eyes moistened at the sight.

Although Fritzlar was primarily a small farming town, its position adjacent to the Eder made it a waystation for those who traded along the river. Merchants and craftsman from many different tribal clans gave the town the feel of a much larger city. On the rare occasions that tribal leaders from the northern regions gathered, they met at Fritzlar.

Boniface suspected that originally this was due to Thor's Oak. He hoped that by now, his monastery had replaced the pagan site as a place of worship.

Boniface led his horse to a small pond at the east end of the field and let her drink. Looking out over the horizon, he pulled from his pack a piece of bread and cheese and sat against a rock that faced the outlook. He had plenty of time to reach the monastery, so he ate and drank slowly, savoring the view. It had been too long since his last visit.

He was far from young when he came to Hesse, but looking back on that time, he had been quite naïve. His years in the Church had been that of a pampered cleric. Having devoted his life to the Rule of St. Benedict, he had studied long and traveled far, but his true calling wasn't revealed until his tutelage with Willibord whom the Pope called "the Apostle of the Frisians."

Willibord had taken him out to proselytize among the tribes. The chieftains had accepted them as holy men and listened respectfully to their news about the one true God. Although the Hessian chieftains welcomed the new god, they laughed at the claim that he was the only one - the true God. To Boniface's horror, they merely added the cross to their panoply of idols, vowing to serve Him along with the likes of Freyer and Odin. No amount of assurance would move them to understand that they worshipped falsely.

"We give no offense to your god," they would say. "Give no offense to ours."

Several months later, Charles came east with his army to demand an oath of fealty from Radbod of Frisia and the Hessian chieftains. With an army of ten thousand camped across the Eder River, the tribal leaders gathered in blot, an ancient pagan ritual to augur the chances of military victory. The rite was held in a clearing just outside Fritzlar before their sacred tree, an oak dedicated to the pagan god, Thor.

With divine inspiration, Boniface led a procession of priests and acolytes into the clearing and interrupted the rite.

Holding the cross aloft before him, Boniface circled the elders and stopped before Thor's oak. There, he produced an ax and shaking his fist at the heavens, challenged Thor to strike him dead with a thunderbolt if the pagan gods were superior to the one true God. Then he cut down the tree.

When the magnificent oak crashed to the earth, a great wind blew across the clearing and Boniface raised his arms as if in holy embrace of his Savior. The tribal leaders fell to their knees and Boniface converted them where they knelt. The next day Charles accepted their hands in fealty and helped Boniface haul the tree across the Eder to a tall hill overlooking the town. There, Boniface ordained that the oak be used to build the Büraburg monastery. Nothing in his life, including his first visit with Pope Gregory, had brought him closer to God.

❋ ❋ ❋

Boniface awoke to a hand shaking his shoulder. He tried batting it away, but something hard poked his chest. He opened his eyes to find an iron pike two inches from his heart. Boniface pushed it away and did his best to get to his feet. "Who dares assault a bishop of the one true God?"

A thick hand shoved him backwards and Boniface sat hard on the ground, his robe hiking up to display his legs. Spindly and pale, they spread out before him, making Boniface feel vulnerable and old. He squinted into the sunlight to see his attacker.

"Mistake to come back, tree-killer," a gruff voice said. "Some don't forget."

The voice was familiar. If only he could see the man's face...

"I fear no man," Boniface said.

"Should." His captor knelt before him. It was clear that the man expected Boniface to recognize him, but Boniface could see only the silhouette of a head with long gray hair framing a balding pate. Two men with pikes stood behind him. It wasn't until the man's acrid odor assaulted Boniface that he knew who was delaying him.

"Immelt." Boniface filled the name with all the distaste he held for the man. A minor tribal leader who refused to convert, Immelt was a mystic who held to the pagan beliefs honoring Vaettir, the spirits of the rocks, rivers and trees. His sharp odor derived from rituals that burned brimstone to "release the breath" of the Vaettir living in the stone.

"Da, priest!" Immelt smiled and motioned for his men to pull Boniface to his feet. They lifted him by the armpits and bound his wrists together behind his back. "Come to pay for sins?" Immelt asked. "What do cross bearers call it?"

Now that Boniface could see Immelt, he found his captor a ghost of the man he had known twenty years earlier. The man's eyes were sunken deep in dark sockets that shrank from the light. A thin beard covered the pale skin of his face and yellow stains covered his hands. He was too thin, as if he was wasting away from something that burned within him. Immelt was tall, but Boniface would be surprised if the man weighed ten stone, His captor wore a large animal pelt over his shoulders that made Boniface shudder. It was wargskin, the hide of a great wolf of the forest. According to pagan lore, a warg guarded the Hall of Hel. Its pelt was considered to be magic of the darkest kind.

"It's called atonement," Boniface said. "And no, I have nothing to regret. You detain me at your peril, Immelt. I'm not alone."

"Saw army." The tribal leader folded his arms. "One god no longer protects you?"

"Do not mock the power of the Almighty. It is His hand that guides this army. You were witness to the felling of Thor's oak. The time of the pagan gods is drawing to a close. One day soon, you will witness their end."

Immelt moved so fast, Boniface barely saw the knife at

his throat. Boniface could feel the man's breath on his lips. "You destroy our sacred tree and have stones to come back? You're a fool, priest."

It wasn't the first time Boniface had been threatened. He held himself erect, refusing to grovel before the man who held him. "Beware of what you do here, Immelt. There's a special place in Hell for those who murder priests."

"Save sermon for pigeons," Immelt said. "I don't fear one god. Fates bring you here. Bring you to our gods. Bring you to me."

Furious to be at the mercy of such a vile man, Boniface briefly strained against his captors. "There are no Fates, Immelt. But there is justice. I was brought here by Carloman, son of Charles, now mayor of the palace and leader of the Franks. You would
do well to remember it."

"Da, priest," Immelt threw his knife into the ground. "I have a message for him."

Boniface didn't bother to hide his surprise. "You? What could you possibly have to say to Carloman?"

"Do you think of us as children?" Immelt sputtered, his face blotching red. "Charles is dead. War comes. Chieftains gather in blot. Choose allies. Bring son of Charles to Fritzlar on Thor's day. He will sit on the High Seat."

Again, Boniface was surprised. Very likely, the tribal chieftains were being recruited as allies by the rebellion and were gathering to decide which side to join. Carloman's sudden appearance might be taken as an omen. Inviting him to sit on the High Seat was both an honor and potentially an offer. To Boniface's relief, it also was a reprieve from Immelt's declared oath of vengeance.

"I'll take him the message."

Immelt motioned for the guards to untie his hands. "Next time, tree-killer, you pay for sins. Next time."

# CHAPTER
# TWENTY-TWO

*East of Paris*

I n the end, they decided to walk. It was Agnès's idea. "They're looking for two noble women on horseback. We'll be three peasant women afoot. We'll walk right past them."

Bertrada's week working the farm helped perfect the look. Her fingernails were cracked and underlined with dirt and her skin had darkened under the noonday sun. Agnès had also insisted on another change; she had dyed Bertrada's hair black and cut it short.

"I'll have you looking like a peasant yet," she said, admiring her work.

Once they had decided on a destination, all three were anxious to be on their way. Patrice would manage the farm while Agnès journeyed with them. They left at first light and headed up the north road into town.

It was a good walk. Bertrada was already tired when they reached the crossroads that served as the area's center of commerce. It offered an inn, a stable, a store selling sundries, and an open-air market for food from nearby farms. Agnès stopped at the market and bought bread and fruit for their journey. She introduced Hélène to the woman who owned the market as her sister and Bertrada as her niece.

Bertrada marveled at the ease and intimacy of the women's conversation.

"You tell that Giselle to keep her husband off her," Agnès was saying. "She's had six babes already and the last two were trouble. She'll not live through another."

"She won't listen." The woman waved her hand. "She's worried he'll bed down with the shepherd's daughter."

"Better that than bear another child."

"Unless you're the shepherd's daughter. Won't be long before Patrice is ready."

"Aye, he's already spilling seed."

"Whom have you got your eye on?"

"Well, it's not the shepherd's daughter!"

The two women laughed.

They carried the food bundled in sacks over their shoulders and walked past the inn. The armed men were there, Bertrada recognized none of them from the attack after the ball. Agnès dropped her eyes and dipped into a half curtsy on their way past and Hélène and Bertrada followed her lead. The men barely looked at them.

"Don't hurry," Agnès whispered as she led them out of town. She kept their pace to a slow and steady walk. After a mile Bertrada offered a small cheer of celebration. The two older women laughed.

"We've got a long way to go," Hélène cautioned.

And she was right. The downside of walking is that it takes a long time to get where you're going. It took an entire day to reach the next village, especially with Bertrada having to stop so frequently. Although, embarrassed to be so weak in the presence of such strong women, there was little she could do about it. She didn't have the stamina to keep up.

They stayed with the sister of a woman from Agnès's village and left in the morning at first light. Bertrada groaned at the blisters on her feet and the aches in her legs. Hélène and Agnès ignored these outbursts and marched on at a steady pace. At midday, they stopped at the side of the road for a bite. Three armed men rode by them, the same men from the inn. Again, they paid little attention to the women on the road.

But they were waiting in the next town, sitting in front of the inn, eyeing all those who passed and asking questions of the villagers.

A spike of fear shot down Bertrada's spine. She wanted to run. "They saw us in the last town and again on the road. They'll stop us this time."

Hélène frowned. "Our only way is forward. We should stay at the inn tonight."

Bertrada had trouble breathing. "Why would we do that?"

Agnès nodded in agreement. "It's a good plan. If we were fleeing them, we wouldn't spend the night at their inn."

"But they'll question us. They'll know."

They were drawing close to the inn. Hélène whispered. "Three women, not two, and none are blond."

Bertrada repeated this to herself a dozen times.

The king's men eyed them as they approached.

"What's your business here?" One had a thick mustache. He barred their way with an outstretched arm.

Agnès stepped forward. "I am Agnès. You know us. At least, you saw us in the last village and on the road here. This is my sister and her daughter. We're travelling to Meaux."

"And what business do you have there?"

"I'm Meldois. It's my home. My husband took me from my family. He died last month of the fever. So now I go home."

"And you?"

Hélène's face was made of stone. "I came to watch the bastard die." She spat on the ground.

Surprise took the man's face. After a moment, he turned to his companions and laughed. "Remind me to be wary of women from Meaux."

He waved them inside and Agnès took a small room by

the stables for the three of them. It was clean but had only one bed for the three of them.

Bertrada frowned. "You could have asked for a bigger room."

"That's what a noblewoman would do." Hélène patted her shoulder. "For the duration of this trip, we're common folk. Besides, the Meldois are known to be a frugal people."

"I'm glad I was born in Laon."

\* \* \*

They took their dinner in the inn's great room. It held no more than fifteen tables and only half of them had patrons. The evening's stew was rabbit and Bertrada was glad for anything other than their road staple of cheese and bread. Agnès ordered a pint of ale and the three of them shared it,

The king's men came in and took a table. Bertrada paid a great deal of attention to her bowl of stew to avoid staring at them.

"You shouldn't have ordered the ale." Hélène scolded. "It suggests we're wanton."

"Hush," Agnès laughed. "I'm a widow, celebrating."

"They're staring at us." Hélène whispered. "We should have taken our meal in the room."

The three men were indeed staring at them. They had bathed and so looked less like ruffians. They were talking among themselves and laughing. The mustached man, in particular, seemed overly interested in the women's table. Agnès looked over to the three men and lifted her glass in salute.

"What're you doing?" Bertrada's whisper was urgent. "They'll come over here!"

And the mustached man did. He stopped at the bar and brought a new pint with him. He had piercing hazel eyes and placed the pint before Agnès. "My pardon, my good woman, but after such a long day on the road, I thought you might like another pint of ale."

"From a handsome man like you, how could I resist?" Agnès' smile was as broad as her shoulders. They clinked beakers and she slopped some on the table. "Oh my!" She giggled.

Bertrada didn't know what to do. She was afraid to look at the man directly, but not looking at him would draw his attention. *What was Agnès doing?*

"Did you find who you were looking for?" Agnès asked him.

The man shook his head. "Two, maybe three women and a young man, were travelling this way." His hand seemed to wave over their table by explanation. Bertrada felt like she had to pee.

Agnès's eyes never left his face. "What did they do?"

He shrugged. "It doesn't matter. We serve at the pleasure of the Merovingian." His chest puffed out at this. "I assume they're a threat to his person."

"Two or three women? That seems unlikely."

"They escaped once already." He frowned. "They are... more than they seem."

"What will you do to them, if you find them?"

The man shrugged. "They're a threat."

"Well, I'm sure you'll find them." Agnès clinked his glass again. "A king! Oh my!" Agnès blushed and then giggled.

"Will there be a coronation?" Hélène asked.

"When the mayors return from campaign in the fall."

"How wonderful!"

Bertrada couldn't bring herself to speak. Why the two women would banter with these men she couldn't fathom.

"Will your search take you to Meaux?" Agnès looked as if she was going to invite the man to dinner.

"Perhaps." He looked hopeful. "But, if not, maybe later in the year when our business is complete."

"Something I would look forward to." Agnès all but batted her eyes at the man.

"You're are welcome to join our table," he offered.

Hélène stiffened. "Agnès, we are good Christian women!"

Agnès frowned and then looked up at the man, shrugging as if she were helpless. She smiled. "Perhaps when you come to Meaux."

The mustache man gave a sly smile to Agnès, bowed, and returned to his table.

"Have you lost your sanity?" Bertrada whispered.

Agnès still seemed preoccupied by the other table. "Now they're all focused on me – the widow. They don't even see the two of you." She smiled, her cheeks blushing.

Hélène stood. "We should go before she gets any other ideas."

* * *

When the three women came down to the main room in the morning, there were three more armed men at the inn. One was a bearded man with an angry scowl, who seemed surprised by the women's presence. He began to question the man with the mustache who was waving away his concerns, but after some argument they turned towards Agnès.

"Who are you and where are you going?"

"I am Agnès. This is my sister and her daughter and we're going to Meaux."

"Where are you coming from?"

"My husband's farm outside of Paris."

"Where is he?"

Agnès spit. "Dead. I'm going home to my family."

"And you? He looked at Bertrada.

Hélène answered. "We came when the pig grew sick. Now we go home."

"The girl can't speak?" He grabbed her face. "Where did you get those bruises?"

Hélène slapped his hand away. "We are Christian women

and she is unmarried. The pig did that. He liked to hit women."

Again, Agnès spit on the ground.

The mustached man interceded. "They aren't the ones. I've seen them before. You haven't."

"But three women on the road?"

"Do they look like nobility to you?" He grabbed Agnès's hands and turned them over. Dirt caked her nails and callouses lined her fingers.

Agnès straightened her back and held a pinky aloft. "I beg your pardon, kind sir?" Her voice lilted in a mocking tone. "Will you fetch my carriage?"

Hélène barked a laugh and then they all laughed. The bearded man finally nodded. "It's been nearly a week and we have nothing to show for it."

"We'll find them." The mustached man seemed confident.

"We should be on our way." Agnès touched his arm. "I hope you find your way to Meaux."

"Milady." He bowed and they all laughed again.

* * *

It rained that afternoon, a thin mist of a storm that cooled them after such a long walk. After an hour of it, however, their clothes were wet, and the cold had seeped into their bones.

"We need to find shelter." Bertrada hated being the weakest of the three, but she was miserable. Her shoes were sticking into the mud and it made walking even harder.

Hélène didn't even turn her head. "Almost there."

Another hour passed. They labored up a large hill hampered by their attire, now sodden and clinging to their limbs. "We have to stop."

"Here." Hélène took her by the arm and walked her to the crest of the hill. "This is your new home."

As she looked down into the valley, understanding dawned in Bertrada. "It's the perfect place to hide."

Agnès grunted and started down into the valley. "If they let us in. That will be Hélène's job."

# CHAPTER TWENTY-THREE

*Hesse*

Arriving at Fritzlar, Carloman immediately ordered scavenger teams out to replenish their food stores and asked Father Sturm to assist in purchasing what was available in the marketplace. Hamar and Drogo arranged for their defenses, stationing troops near the river and pickets at intervals around the circumference of the large hill upon which the monastery stood.

Carloman and the nobles in his army were given rooms in the monastic dormitory, which, like the chapel, stood at the top of the hill. As they climbed, the lush green forest landscape stretched out below them for miles, disturbed only by the blue of the Eder River and the brown buildings and mud streets that defined the town of Fritzlar.

The dormitory was a long, one-story building made of stone flooring and plaster walls. A large circular eating hall occupied the east end of the building, a residence, the west. A single corridor ran through the residence wing providing interior access to some twenty rooms. Carloman found them simple and purposeful - a bed, a chamber pot, a cross on the wall, and a mat to kneel on - more than enough for him and his officers.

The chapel, by comparison, was relatively small. Wood from Thor's oak was featured prominently in the archway over the door and on the altar. The pulpit, too, was made from the tree. Boniface had used half of a section of the great trunk to fashion it as a constant reminder of the Lord's dominance over the nature deities.

Father Sturm proved to be a pleasant man whose generosity was as large as his considerable girth. A short, bearded priest with a stomach that extended well out over the rope cinching his brown cassock, he greeted them with enthusiasm, sending acolytes and priests scrambling to accommodate their presence.

Boniface in particular was treated as a conquering hero. Sturm and the priests fawned over the bishop, providing him the best rooms, and assigning him a priest to act as his clerk. Sturm also announced that dinner would feature roasted duck and Bavarian Ale. This selection appeared to be widely valued among the priests of the monastery.

Father Sturm led them in a prayer of thanksgiving and left them alone until vespers. Carloman asked Boniface to show him the stump of Thor's oak and they descended into Fritzlar.

Carloman couldn't help but whistle at the size of its trunk. Boniface hadn't been young when he felled the tree. And it would have been a challenge for a man at any age to do it alone. Boniface seemed to revel in the memory of it. He showed Carloman a great pine tree that had been planted nearby as a symbol of Christianity. It was a spruce and was already towering over the clearing.

"I have a message for you," Boniface said, with a serious look. As he related the invitation from Immelt, Carloman grew furious.

"They struck you?"

"It was more like a shove."

"You travel under my protection. No one is to lay a hand

on you."

"Which is why they sought me out. It's likely that Theudebald is recruiting the Hessians. Your invitation to their blot may be your chance to thwart him."

"I will still have Immelt's head."

"There's a time for such gestures," Boniface said, "but perhaps this isn't such a time. Immelt is a minor chieftain and not one to be taken too seriously. He's one of the few left who adhere to the old ways."

"He was important enough to deliver the message."

"That, I think, was more a personal matter."

"I see no reason for attending. Fealty is sworn and due. I shouldn't need to attend their rite to demand it."

"Yet if allegiance is given willingly, there's no need to lift a sword," Boniface said. "You don't have to spill blood."

It was a practical argument. His men could use the rest and needed to replenish their food stores. But, for once, Carloman wasn't inclined to be practical. He was anxious to take the initiative. And he was surprised that Boniface would encourage him to attend this "blot."

"Isn't it a pagan ceremony?"

"The rituals are empty relics of the past. You need not fear them. To sit in the High Seat asserts your place above the tribal leaders. It's a place of honor."

Carloman recognized the blot's value, of course. Allying with northern tribal chieftains would be a powerful tool in his war against Odilo. In addition to augmenting the army with their numbers, the coalition of tribal chieftains would be a powerful symbol to the rebels. Even an assurance of neutrality by the Hessians would demoralize his enemy. Theudebald's ability to recruit in Alemannia would be impaired and his supply lines through the north would be secure.

Despite his misgivings, Carloman acquiesced. At least they wouldn't have to wait long. Thor's Day was only two days away.

✾ ✾ ✾

"Tell me again how this isn't a sin." Carloman asked Boniface. They had led a retinue of soldiers, including Hamar, down to Fritzlar for the blot. Carloman had left Drogo in charge of the army in his absence. It was dusk and the rapidly descending sun left long shadows across the landscape. The ceremony itself was to be held outside the town on a large hill. Only he, Hamar and Boniface had been invited to attend.

"It's a pagan ceremony at a pagan holy site with pagans in attendance," Carloman said.

"Only two of the chieftains in attendance have not kissed the cross. And while the ceremony is pagan in origin, it is also how the chieftains parley to reach agreement. Think of it as the format for the discussion rather than a pagan rite."

"It will be a rite for the two pagans."

"But not for you."

"You're turning a deaf ear, Boniface."

"Yes and no. The rites themselves are unimportant. You, yourself, have usurped pagan rites for your Knights in Christ."

Carloman looked up in surprise.

"Oh, I have heard a confession or two about them. The point is: the belief in God is what matters. Rituals are a great source of comfort. The church would be foolish to ban them all. When I cut down Thor's Oak, I planted a spruce. To the Hessians, it's a symbol of their new god – the one and only God.

"As long as the chieftains believe in Christ, the rite is irrelevant. It will disappear over time, or the Church will adopt it. This afternoon, you're attending a war council. The rite merely makes the chieftains more comfortable with it."

"I'm more concerned about the numbers," Hamar said. "Each of the six chieftains is bringing one second. That leaves Carloman and I outnumbered six-to-one. What if it's a trap?"

"Violence at a blot is strictly forbidden – punishable by

death," Boniface said. "And a grizzly death at that. You needn't worry. There will be no bloodshed."

Boniface led them to a field outside of town. "Your men will have to wait here. I'll take you and Hamar up to the grove." He pointed to a hill subsumed by oak trees. Hamar lit torches to guide them in the waning light.

Boniface found a path into the oaks and the three of them made their way up the hill. Before they reached the crest of the hill, the path leveled off into a clearing where they were met by the six chieftains and their seconds. To a man, the Hessians were taller than Carloman. Each of them wore great, long beards that reached their waists.

"Hodar, Rasling, Ucher, Ragnar," Boniface greeted four of the men, grasping their forearms. He nodded to two others. "Einbeck, Immelt." Carloman noted them as the two pagans.

Boniface assumed a more formal tone. "May I present, Carloman, son of Charles, son of Pippin, mayor of the palace to the Merovingian kings, conqueror of many kingdoms and keeper of the faith."

Most of the chieftains bowed. Einbeck and Immelt nodded.

"Charles was a mighty general who cast a long shadow." Hodar's eyes appraised Carloman. "Does his son?"

Carloman held the chieftain's gaze. "My father's shadow was long. Only the years can tell how long mine will be. But I am sure of this: my shadow will be long enough to defeat those who ally with Theudebald. On that I vow."

Hodar appeared to consider this and then nodded and motioned for the group towards the crest of the hill. At its top, they entered a circular plateau framed by the oak trees of the grove. Their branches interlaced to form a massive cordon twenty feet off the ground. It was so thick that it blocked what was left of the evening's light and reminded Carloman of a fortress wall. A lone oak stood across the plateau, apart from the forest, but there was too little light to see it clearly. Hodar led them forward to a natural, bowl-like depression in the center of the clearing. Its circumference was shaped by rock, giving it the appearance of a small amphitheater. At its center, a large fire burned.

Carloman had expected there to be an actual "high seat" from which he would preside over the blot. There was nothing so elaborate. They bade him stand on the outcropping of rock and presented him with a band of gold.

Lifting it up, he saw that it had three sharp talons facing inward. Hodar signaled that Carloman should put it on his arm.

"It is worn by the highest chief," Boniface whispered to him. "It goes on your right arm." Carloman pulled back his sleeve and slipped his hand through the ring. He pulled it up his arm until the three talons caught against his bicep. They were sharper than he had imagined and produced a warm sensation down his arm.

At a signal from Hodar all six of the chieftains took places around the fire. Carloman looked to Boniface and the bishop nodded.

Carloman pronounced in a loud voice. "The blot is begun." From somewhere behind him, a lone drum began to beat and a procession of three men carrying statues approached the fire. One man carried the cross, the second the figure of a woman, the third the figure of a man.

Hodar stood, opened his arms and looked skyward. "God of the cross, the Odin of gods, we bow to your strength, to your power." All the chieftains bowed, so Carloman did, too. He didn't like not knowing what was expected of him. The cross was placed facing him on the near side of the fire. The two other statues were placed to his left and right. As night had fallen the fire provided their only light and defined the limits of Carloman's vision.

Hodar began to chant in the Germanic dialect. It was low and guttural but there was a rhythm to it that begged a response every few lines. The other chieftains supplied it, grunting, "Dah!" at every missing beat. Hodar threw scented herbs on the fire and its smoke stung Carloman's eyes.

The longer Hodar chanted the more uncomfortable Carloman became. The night and open air unnerved him. They were vulnerable out here, standing in the shadow of the grove and illuminated by the fire. Any man or beast would find them easy prey. He thought he heard a struggle in the direction of the tall solitary oak, but no one reacted, and he assumed he was imagining dangers that weren't there.

It took him a moment to realize, Hodar had stopped his chant.

One of the other chieftains – Carloman guessed it was Ragnar, – stood, "For what do we blot?"

"War," the chieftains said as one.

From the shadows surrounding the great oak, a man stepped forward into the firelight. He carried a bowl filled with a steaming liquid and, bowing, offered it to Immelt. With equal solemnity, the wiry chieftain accepted it and offered it up to Hodar.

"The blood of sacrifice," he said.

Hodar dipped his fingers in the liquid and painted Immelt's forehead and cheeks. He then moved with Immelt around the fire, streaking each of the chieftains' foreheads and cheeks in turn.

Carloman guessed that they had slaughtered a goat under the large oak just outside the light of the fire. That must have been the struggle that he had heard. He understood the role blood played in pagan ceremonies. It was a measure of the sacrifice offered to gain favor with the gods. The greater the need, the larger the animal would be butchered.

Boniface, however, was not so sanguine. When Hodar approached Carloman to paint his face, Boniface interceded. "No."

Hodar turned, clearly irked by the interruption. "It is custom to wear the blood of sacrifice."

"It is against our beliefs," the bishop explained.

"No." Hodar spat the words, his anger growing. "It is

your custom. Body of Christ. Blood of Christ. You eat. You drink." He held up the bowl. "We wear. "

"But you sacrifice to false gods."

"No false gods. Only gods. Here is your god." He pointed to the cross.

"There is only one God." Boniface pointed to the two other statues. "These are false."

Hodar frowned in apparent confusion. "They are not false. They are like...like...your saints."

Carloman put a reassuring hand on the bishop's shoulder. "It's just a rite." He said, purposely echoing Boniface's words. Carloman turned his face to Hodar to receive the streaks of blood. They were warm.

The chieftain poured the rest of the blood over each of the statues, ending with the male. The air was filled with the newly spilt blood's pungent odor.

"Mighty Thor," Hodar lifted his hands before the fire. "We ask your blessing for war. Give thunder and fire to conquer our enemies..."

At the mention of Thor, Boniface grew even more agitated. Carloman could see his mentor struggling with the turn of the events. It was as if the chieftains were testing the bishop's resolve.

"Something is wrong," Boniface whispered, without taking his eyes off Hodar. "They know better than this. They're trying to provoke us."

More wood was added to the fire as the chieftain spoke, and the blaze leapt to consume it. As the fire grew its blaze pushed back the darkness and painted the grass and the rocks and trees around them in its flickering red light.

The chieftains were chanting again in their Germanic dialect and although Carloman couldn't understand the words, the malice of them was evident, the anger palpable. Immelt caught Carloman's eye and smiled, an odd look of derision on his face. Carloman struggled for comprehension. What was he missing?

The blaze crackled on a wet log and a spark leapt sky-ward. Carloman's eyes followed. In the distance he could see the long branches of the great oak, now illuminated by the red light of the larger fire. It was there that Carloman found the answer to his question.

Ignoring a protest from Boniface he stepped from the circle and made for the tree. It was some fifty strides away from the fire. Hamar grabbed a torch and followed with Boniface close on his heels. The chanting behind them stopped.

Two human corpses hung from the tree by their necks. With each step he took, the blood on Carloman's face grew more appalling to him. A third body, hung upside down by his feet, had a gaping slash cut across his throat, still spilling blood.

"The blood of sacrifice." Carloman spat.

"Sweet Mary." Boniface made the sign of the cross.

The chieftains had followed them to the great oak and formed a semi-circle around them.

Carloman stepped forward. "What's the meaning of this?"

Hodar shrugged. "Offering." Seeing Carloman frown, he added, "Thieves."

"God doesn't ask for such sacrifice." Boniface said.

Hodar looked confused. "Did God not die on his cross?"

"Yes." Carloman said.

"He was sacrifice. Like Odin from tree, he was sacrifice."

"God gave his life for the sins of others." Boniface said.

"This man gave his life for others."

"Not willingly."

Hodar shrugged.

"I've had enough." Carloman took off the gold armband and tossed it to Hodar. A stunned silence took the clearing.

Boniface whispered. "Don't strike a blow, Carloman. I beg you. They mean to provoke us into violating the blot. It will justify their betrayal."

Carloman looked to the bishop and smiled. "Hamar,

give your torch to the Bishop. I'm going to need both of your hands."

"Listen to your priest, Carloman." Immelt's grin had grown triumphant.

Carloman ignored him. "Hodar, you've sworn an oath of fealty and bent your knee to accept the Christian faith. My only question today is, do you honor your oaths?"

"You are not your father. Your shadow is not yet long."

"Fealty is fealty." Carloman said. "Allegiance is owed."

"You are far from your army to make such demands."

"You will kneel or die."

"It is death to violate a blot."

"Kneel or die, so help me, God."

"Fuck your God," Immelt leapt in front of Carloman, his sneering face an inch from Carloman's nose. "Fuck your book. Shit on your–"

Immelt's eyes registered surprise at the knife in his throat. He made a gurgling noise and coughed blood onto Carloman's face. Carloman's mind registered some satisfaction that this blood joined the blood of the blot's "sacrifice."

He pulled his knife out of the man's throat as the chieftains descended upon them.

"*Michaeli Archangelo!*" Carloman drew his sword and spun to his right to avoid the initial charge of the chieftains. He wanted to keep them between him and Hamar. He slashed his blade down on the nearest chieftain, clipping off the man's leg at the knee. Without waiting to watch the man fall, Carloman smashed his elbow into the face of the next attacker and was reassured by the sound of facial bones cracking.

Again, Carloman whirled. It was too dark to see clearly and there were too many of them, but he ducked, parried, stabbed and retreated, always trying to keep Hamar to his left and the enemy between them.

To block an overhanded blow, he crossed both his blade and his knife above his head, but the shock of it overpowered

Carloman, forcing him to kneel. The chieftain howled in triumph and pressed forward to give a finishing blow. The man's sword arced behind him and then high above his head. Carloman stabbed upward with his knife, slicing the man's belly from his groin to his sternum.

The Hessian's blade went wide but still caught Carloman's left shoulder. Carloman shouted and spun away from the pain, stabbed blindly with his sword. He hit nothing. Another blade stabbed forward and Carloman nearly fell trying to parry the thrust. Reeling, he stepped backward to orient himself in the darkness and found himself surrounded by the three corpses hanging from the great oak.

He ducked behind one of them to stave off an attack and began using them as shields in his battle with the Hessians. He darted in and out of the swinging bodies to keep his attackers at bay.

One of the chieftains screamed as his clothing conflagrated. A human torch, he whirled among the Hessians, howling in horror as his skin immolated. It both distracted and illuminated Carloman's attackers. Although he was relieved to have his threats clarified, their numbers dismayed him. They couldn't vanquish so many. He had been foolish to come to this place and to trust these people.

With desperation his only ally, Carloman again shouted, "*Michaeli Archangelo*" and pressed the attack, hoping to catch the distracted chieftains off-guard.

To Carloman's surprise, his battle cry was answered.

"*Michaeli Archangelo!*"

The men Carloman had left in the nearby field had come to their rescue. With a visceral roar, they charged across the field.

The Hessians abandoned Carloman and Hamar and fled for the grove. Carloman's men gave chase but were too late. What was left of the Hessian chieftains disappeared into the darkness of the grove.

Carloman bent over double to catch his breath.

"Hamar?"

"Here, milord." His champion was covered in blood, but little of it was Hamar's.

"Boniface?"

"Here, Carloman." Boniface stepped out from behind the oak. "I'm unharmed. Only Einbeck came searching for me. Like Immelt, he worships the Vaettir and refused to convert. He wished to punish me for cutting down Thor's tree."

"How did you stop him?"

"I had a torch." Boniface smiled wickedly. "Pagans who dabble in brimstone should be more careful around fire."

Carloman chuckled at that. "How many of the chieftains were slain?"

Hamar responded. "Four. Immelt, Einbeck, Ucher, and Ragnar."

"That leaves Hodar and Rasling," Boniface said. "By violating the blot, you've allied them with Theudebald. They'll use it to justify breaking their oaths and unite the tribes between them."

Carloman returned to the hanging corpses. "Do you notice anything about these bodies?"

Boniface made the sign of the cross. "They were killed in ritual, just like the bodies in Worms."

"None of them are wearing animal skins or pelts. Their clothes are woven."

Boniface looked up in surprise. "Franks."

"Franks from Worms," Carloman finished. "That one on the left was a member of the Duc's court. I met him the last time I was there."

"Then the chieftains were already allied with Theudebald." Hamar frowned and looked at the hanging corpses. "This wasn't a ritual. It was an ambush."

"It was both." Carloman said. "We were supposed to join those on the tree."

# CHAPTER TWENTY-FOUR

*Outside Paris*

Pippin was with Arnot and Gunther when news came about the Banlieu brought by one of Pippin's own men, Jean-Pierre, a captain in charge of the search south of Paris.

Pippin feigned surprise. "Did you see her yourself?"

"No. I heard from an innkeeper that she had rented a room. It's on the south side of the Banlieu on the road to Gentilly. I searched her room and found this." It was an earring, a jade stone set in a circlet of gold. Pippin recognized it immediately. Despite his foreknowledge, his heart thudded inside his chest.

As a trap, it was well set. A trusted aide brings an earring that Pippin himself had given Bertrada as proof of her existence nearby. Its presence shook Pippin. Perhaps they had recovered the piece from the attack on her carriage.

He took ten soldiers to investigate the sighting. Jean-Pierre led the column; Arnot and Pippin followed at a discreet distance so they could talk privately.

"If you know it's a trap, why are we going?" Arnot shifted his weight in his saddle as if he was uncomfortable.

Pippin had to think for a minute before answering. "At least we know it's a trap. I'd rather confront an enemy I know is there than wait for their attack. I also want to see if we can trust Miette's information."

"Miette?"

Pippin frowned at the slip. "Lady Ragomfred."

"Yes, I know who she is." Arnot chuckled. "Aren't we just a little familiar after one encounter with this woman?"

"Two. She was the hostess for the Ragomfred ball."

"Two? Well, that's an entirely different situation." Arnot grinned and shook his head. "Watch yourself with that one, Pippin. If she's not a demon herself, then they are certainly in her employ."

"She's quite arresting. I'll give you that."

"Are you sure that bringing ten men is enough? What if they bring twenty?"

Pippin smiled. "I'm sure we'll handle whatever they throw at us."

"What if it's a trap within a trap? What if we're out chasing ghosts through the Banlieu while Ragomfred makes a play for the bridge at the Palace?"

"I already have the better part of a battalion with Gunther to guard the palace. If Ragomfred has enough men to take it, we've already lost."

They had ridden in a two-column march for over an hour before coming to the inn. It was a two-story wooden building facing a small square. Trees lined their approach on both sides of the road, leaving Pippin blind to potential attackers in the square. It was just as he envisioned it.

Jean-Pierre rode ahead to the inn and waved them forward.

"This is where it will be." Pippin frowned. "Ready-up! Right column with me on the right."

"Huh-yah!" came their reply.

"Left column with me on the left." Arnot received as similar chorus in response. All ten of Pippin's men loosed scabbards as they entered the square.

Arnot had underestimated. Pippin counted thirty men in the square.

They were led by Robeson, Dubois and Petit, three of Pippin's nobles that Miette claimed had sided with the Merovingian. They were lined up, fifteen men on each side of Pippin's cohort.

He reined in. "Gentlemen, so good of you to come help with my search for Bertrada."

"Fuck Bertrada." Robeson looked like he was enjoying the moment. "Fuck you, your brother and all your Austrasian allies. Your time as mayor has ended, Pippin. The king sent us to deliver a message. Your service is no longer required."

Pippin grinned. "And you think thirty men will suffice?"

Jean-Pierre spat on the ground and rode to Robeson's side. "Thirty-one."

It might have been dramatic if Pippin hadn't known in advance he was a traitor. Pippin whistled a high trilling note.

Petit pitched off his horse, an arrow through his throat. Robeson's mare shied from the sudden movement and he struggled to rein her in. He searched frantically for the archer.

Dubois was next. The man grunted and looked down, finding a bolt through his chest.

"You should have brought more men." Pippin said.

"Attack!" Robeson waved his men forward. Three more of their number went down to arrows before the melée began.

As Pippin had planned, the archers stationed on the roof of the inn did more than thin the number of attackers; they threw the entire assault into disarray. Two of the three nobles leading the charge already were dead, leaving two thirds of the men without a captain in the field. Only Robeson was able to orchestrate an attack and he jumped to fill in the breach.

"Attack! Attack!" he shouted. "To me! To me!"

But many of his men were slow to respond and others were wheeling to avoid the continued barrage from Pippin's archers. Pippin's men split to face the enemy, forming two inverted wedges, one behind Pippin and the other behind Arnot to advance their attack.

Pippin crashed into the enemy line, stabbing and hacking with his sword in a fury. In combat this close, strategy mattered little. There was no room for orchestrated tactics. The fighting was brutal and savage. Pippin cleaved arms and heads from bodies and cut torsos in two. He stabbed horses and men alike and their blood cascaded onto the quaint garden square, soaking the hedges and flowers red.

When Pippin broke through Robeson's line, the balance of numbers shifted in his favor. The archers kept up their attack, but more carefully so as not to hit Pippin's men.

It was over in minutes. Pippin had lost three men. All thirty of their attackers lay dead or wounded in the square. Pippin went first to find Jean-Pierre. The man was wounded in a flowerbed trying to crawl his way to safety. He stopped when Pippin's shadow fell upon him.

Rolling over he lifted a hand to shade his eyes. "Lord Pippin? Oh, God have mercy! They made me. They threatened my family."

"And yet, you spat at my feet."

"I had to do it."

"And I have to do this." Pippin shoved the blade through the man's neck and watched the light disappear from his eyes.

Arnot stood at Pippin's shoulder. "Robeson's over here."

The man was nearly cut in two. He lay gasping for breath as his blood fled his body. He motioned for Pippin to come closer. Pippin knelt beside him in the man's blood.

Robeson lifted his head to speak. "Fuck you."

Pippin chuckled. "Well said. A brave man to the last."

Robeson's last breath shook with the death rattle and he was gone.

Pippin stood. "Search the inn for Bertrada and then, let's get back to the palace. I want to make sure it isn't under attack."

\* \* \*

A week later Pippin and Gunther were bent over a map of the palace.

"With Carloman and I out on campaign, it's your job to hold the palace. There's a chance that Childeric may not wait for Carloman and I to elevate him. He may try to seize the palace and the throne with the nobles Ragomfred has gathered up for him. Under no circumstances is he to succeed. It would give him the appearance of power and force us to respond with force. That would only serve to destabilize the kingdom. As mayors, only Carloman and I have the right to elevate a king. So, while we're away on campaign, you must protect the palace from attack."

Pippin drew a quick breath before continuing. "All sorties should be at least ten men to prevent an ambush, but I want no more than four sorties at a time." Pippin pointed to the barracks on the west side of the isle. "Keep the bulk of the regiment inside the palace."

Situated as it was on the Isle de la Cité in the middle of the Seine River, the palace was almost impervious to attack. The river's depth and swift current limited any attack on the high stone walls that surrounded the island. And the two bridges connecting the island to the right and left banks of the Seine – the only potential access point – were narrow. Any enemy attacking the palace would be forced into a phalanx of no more than six across, greatly prohibiting their ability to force or scale the front gate.

Pippin pointed to the two bridges. "This is where we're most vulnerable. Should they breech the front gate, set up a barricade here." He pointed to a square just inside the main gate. "And make it a kill zone from here and here." He pointed to two high buildings just inside the gate. "I don't think they will get that far, but if they do, keep forcing them from one kill zone into another."

Gunther chuckled under his breath. "I know all this, Pippin. I taught you most of it when you were fifteen."

"They'll try to draw the main body of our forces out on some pretense to leave the palace thinly guarded. Whatever you do, don't fall for it. It will likely be an uprising just north of the city or a fire at the monastery at St. Germain des Prés."

"Want to show me how to use a sword while you're at it?"

"I just don't want any mistakes when I leave."

"And when exactly is that to be?"

"Soon. I don't know."

Arnot poked his head into the room, interrupting them. "Pippin. You've got a guest."

Pippin looked up, waiting for the name, but Arnot had a troubled look on his face. "Who is it?"

"Your newest acquaintance." Arnot's voice trailed off.

"Oh." Pippin blushed. "Thanks Gunther. I know the palace is in good hands. I'll send word when I'm ready to leave."

Gunther hesitated and Pippin knew the man was surprised at being kept in the dark about his "guest." It made Pippin feel guilty. He was, after all, leaving the palace in Gunther's hands. Why wouldn't he trust him? He told himself that Miette's visits must be kept a secret to avoid scandal, but in his heart, Pippin knew the truth: he was embarrassed by his fascination with the woman.

Pippin had met with Miette twice since she had first presented herself at his door. Each time she had come in secret. If she had been seen it would have been a scandal to rival his sister Trudi's marriage to the rebel Odilo. Miette was, after all, a beautiful woman and the wife of a rival and he was unattached. He'd likely suspect himself too.

Unfortunately, he couldn't help himself. The woman was unlike any he had ever met. Intelligent, brazen, compelling, and amusing, she had a way of keeping him off guard. He had ignored or rebuffed every advance she had made; yet she seemed so certain of his desire for her. And, he had to admit, she was right. She had successfully painted a picture of her in his mind and in it she was always naked.

Pippin knew he was being manipulated. Yet she had given him valuable information about his allies. She had let him know that the Merovingian had not yet found Bertrada. She had warned him about Robeson's trap in the banlieu and she was keeping tabs on the Merovingian in a way no one else could. From a short-term political point of view, she was invaluable. But he was not naïve. He knew that one day there would be a reckoning.

Arnot let Miette into Pippin's salon. With a smirk and a bow, he closed the doors. Pippin crossed the room to greet her. "Miette."

She was wearing a white dress, pinned to accentuate her figure and a green wrap that she had kept over her head to disguise her face. She kissed him on both cheeks as one would a friend, but her body lingered against his for just a moment too long. It sent a thrill through his body. He stepped back. "Would you like some wine?"

She nodded and he crossed the room to fetch them each a goblet.

"You've cleaned up your apartment. I'm flattered."

Pippin hated that he was so transparent. When he brought the wine, she was standing near a window overlooking the Seine. He noticed a bruise on her cheek that she had tried to disguise with powder and wondered about its origin.

"Forgive me, but I was unaware that you were coming to visit."

"You must start paying attention, Pippin. Childeric is expecting me to carry on an affair with you. How am I supposed to do that if we never see each other?"

"We saw each other two days ago."

Her eyes gleamed with inner amusement. "Now you're insulting me. What kind of affair tolerates such infrequency?"

He laughed and changed the subject. "I want to thank

you again for the warning of Robeson's betrayal. It saved me some valuable men. But may I ask why you told me? If it had worked, Childeric would have removed a political rival. And by telling me, he's lost three allies."

"Traitors are traitors, and never as valuable as they think. And I doubt you would have been so easily duped. By defeating Robeson, the king has become more cautious of you and more adamant that I exploit our affair."

"As long as you know we aren't having one."

She smiled. "That is just a matter of perspective. From the king's perspective, we are already lovers. I've even told him how rough you've been with me."

"Rough?"

She looked out the window and nodded. "I like it rough. Not violent, but rough."

The words startled Pippin. She said them as if she were talking about the color of a gown. "I like it in red." He imagined taking her by the window and for a moment he was at a loss for words.

She looked up, her eyes finding his and Pippin realized she wasn't bantering with him - she was telling the truth to gauge his reaction. It was almost a challenge. She stepped closer and despite his defiance, Pippin's body worked against him. His breath grew short and his heart slammed inside his chest.

She had turned her face up to his and whispered. "You can do anything you want."

Pippin prayed that his growing erection wasn't obvious.

Her hand reached up and her fingers traced the line of his jaw. "In the future, you must send for me, so I can show the king I've seduced you. As my lover, you'd want me day and night. There would be no end to our love-making."

Pippin reached for the bottle of wine to refill his glass even though he had barely taken a sip. "You're talking about the king's perspective," he asserted, keeping his back to her.

"Yes, of course. The king's perspective." But she wrapped her arms around him from behind and pressed her body into his. He felt her warmth invade him and allowed himself a moment to enjoy her embrace.

"Miette, it would be madness."

"Ah, but it is too late for such protests." Her hand found his erection and she gently held it, taking her possession of him. "You've have been alone too long." She let him go. He took a moment to compose himself. When he turned, she was back at the window.

"If you leave Paris, Pippin, you'll lose it to Childeric and my husband."

"Gunther can handle anything Ragomfred's men throw at him."

She sipped her wine. "Gunther may hold the palace, but you will lose your hold on the court. After the war, your armies will be weak, your treasury weaker. The church will openly advocate for Childeric and your brother will acquiesce to the elevation. You will stand alone in your opposition."

"And what if I do?"

Her eyes were cold. "Childeric will be crowned without you. In time, your armies will align with Carloman and you'll find yourself alone one night, drinking with men you think are your friends and one will stab you from behind. Your blood will slip away just like your power."

She paused to see what impact she had.

"It doesn't have to be that way." She came to him and kissed him on the mouth. "Whether you stay or go, one day you'll need me. And I will be your salvation."

❋ ❋ ❋

Pippin couldn't find Bertrada. He searched every room of the palace and still couldn't find her. He tore through the kitchens and servants' quarters, the great hall and the back gardens. He even searched the dungeons. She was nowhere. Only one room remained, the throne room. He hesitated before its huge, gilded, double-doors but they swung open of their own volition, beckoning him to enter. A trumpet fanfare played, and a long red carpet led him across the floor. Nobles of every family at court lined his path. He stumbled forward trying to remember why he was there as the crowd cheered him forward. Soldiers shouted his name and beat their swords against their shields in a rhythmic chant. "Pip-pin! Pip-pin! Pip-pin!"

At the far end of the room, he could see Childeric seated on the throne. Miette was draped across the steps in front of him, her head tilted back to her right and one leg cocked casually to her left. She was waiting for him. Her eyes held him with seductive intensity. It was as if she had expected him. She was dressed in a sheer robe that clung to the slight curves of her body. He could see the outline of her nipples against its fabric and the dark shadow of her sex.

As he approached, she moved languidly to sit upright like a royal waiting in judgment. "You may approach," she purred.

The nobles took up the soldiers' chant. "Pip-pin! Pip-pin! Pip-pin!"

The closer he came to her, the wider she spread her legs. Her sex was open to him, glistening beneath the triangle of her pubic hair. Hands propelled him forward. Voices cheered him onward. He came to the steps before the throne and she shrugged her robe aside. He knelt before her.

"Now was that so difficult?" She wrapped her legs around his shoulders.

The crowd roared its approval.

Pippin awoke. He was alone, lying on his bed, his erection pointing stupidly up at him, a pool of semen covering his belly. He lay back in bed exasperated. *I have got to get out of here.*

He went in search of a towel.

# CHAPTER TWENTY-FIVE

*Hesse*

**W**hile the wound to Carloman's shoulder wasn't grievous, it was painful. His doctor applied a poultice and wrapped the injury to ensure that his arm movement would be minimal. This was particularly frustrating because the scratch on his right arm, made by Hodar's bicep ring, had begun to itch furiously and the bind limited his ability to reach it. And when he did succeed in reaching it, the wound in his shoulder broke open.

As much as he wanted to give chase to the Hessians, he delayed breaking camp for three days in order to resupply the army's food and water. One thing he had learned from his years of campaigning with Charles was that armies don't last long without food and water. He also hoped that the extra days would allow his shoulder to heal.

He sent out scouts to track the Hessians, wanting to finish them before turning south to face Theudebald. Unfortunately, the Hessians appeared to have different plans.

"All the scouting reports are the same." Hamar reported. "After the blot, Hodar united the Hessians under his command and they fled south. All of them. Rather than face us separately, it looks like they plan to throw in their lot with Theudebald.

Although surprised by the speed with which Hodar had moved, Carloman couldn't fault the chieftain's logic. It was what he would have done if faced with the same circumstances.

"We'll see Hodar again." Carloman tried to lift his left arm and winced. "And we'll see him kneel."

* * *

On the fourth day, Carloman ordered the army to decamp. It took most of the morning to stow their tents, supplies, and arms in carts for the march south. He led his troops alongside the Eder until the road turned south into the Forest of Bochonia. As before, the path was narrow, and it forced the men to march five across. This doubled the length of their line and left them vulnerable to ambush. Hamar repeated his caution about entering the forest and Carloman reminded him there was no easy way around it.

Carloman again ordered scouting parties to advance to the south, east and west to prevent ambush as they entered the wood.

Despite the narrowness of their path, the army made good time. Unlike their journey to Fritzlar, the trees in this part of the forest were mostly oak, rather than pine and fir. Tall and straight, the trunks of the oaks allowed more sunlight into the wood, giving them greater depth of vision. After the second day in the forest's embrace, the men began to relax.

Carloman, however, had trouble sleeping. At first, he attributed this to the discomfort from his shoulder, but soon he became feverish and, on two successive nights, sweat through his clothes. The itching on his bicep had increased and little streaks of red lanced down his arm from where he had been scratched.

The doctor examined the wound to Carloman's shoulder and appeared perplexed. "The shoulder is healing well."

"Can you stop the itching?"

"A basil and honey poultice should help. I'll grind some and wrap that scratch to see if gives you some relief. I can also give you something to help you sleep. It's often the best cure."

Carloman nodded but was frustrated to be the one delaying to their progress. They already had lost too much time due to Pippin, the catching disease, and the pagan blot. The army could no longer afford such a slow pace.

When the doctor returned that evening, he applied a new poultice to the scratch on Carloman's arm and offered him a steaming cup of liquid that smelled terrible. But Carloman drank every drop.

\* \* \*

"I'll kill you." Trudi twirled the wooden sword about her like a practiced knight. "Expect no quarter." She was still years before womanhood and wearing that preposterous armor that Charles had made for her.

"None expected," he replied.

"I'm serious, Carloman. Stay away from us." She thrust her sword for emphasis.

"Us?"

"Odilo and my baby."

It was dark. He stood outside the great wooden doors to the church at St. Germain des Prés. One stood ajar and he could see a small sliver of light coming from the inside. He shouldered his way through and made his way up the aisle. Hundreds of candles surrounded the altar, bathing it in a golden light. Standing before the tabernacle was a woman dressed in armor. It was Lady Hélène. A child lay in swaddle behind her on the altar.

"The Church or the throne." Lady Hélène leveled her spear at Carloman. "The Church or the throne."

Charles was ranting, just as he always ranted. Three men with long beards stood behind him. "These Hessians are idiots. They can't comprehend having only one god."

Although still a boy, Carloman spoke up to be noticed. "I went to a blot."

Charles turned to focus on him. "Did you sit on the High Seat?"

Carloman nodded.

"Good boy." Charles patted him on the top of the head.

The three men behind Charles attacked. Carloman drew his toy sword, spun to his right. "Michaeli Archangelo!"

Hamar was in his tent, shaking him awake. "Milord, we're under attack."

His champion seemed so far away that Carloman wasn't sure whom he was addressing. He tried to sit up but his body felt like it weighed a hundred stone. He shook his head, forcing himself to wake and tried to ignore the pounding in his head.

"Who?"

"The Hessians."

❊ ❊ ❊

Over the next three days there was an attack each day, each one was more virulent than the last. Never frontal assaults, they were designed to harass and weaken Carloman's army rather than to confront it. They all had the same profile: employ the protective cover of the forest to target an isolated part of the line, strike quickly, and retreat back into the woods to lure defenders into a second ambush away from the protection of their comrades. The latest target was the army's supply train. Carloman went to inspect the damage.

Dozens of soldiers and cattle lay slaughtered in the mud

and the smell of burned salt pork permeated the air. Carloman groaned. Nearly half of the food wagons had been overturned or were burning. Sacks of grain lay open on the ground amidst an ever-growing pool of blood. Cooks and soldiers were scouring the detritus in search of salvageable food.

*We're going to need it,* Carloman thought. Despite the afternoon heat, he shivered and cursed the fever that left him so weak.

The captain of the supply train stepped forward to report. Carloman noted that the captain wasn't one of his Knights in Christ.

"The extra pickets I ordered?"

"They were posted," the captain said.

Carloman waited for an explanation.

"They blackened their skin to avoid discovery. Flaming arrows gave torch to the forward food wagons. When we dispatched men to protect them and put out the fire, our rear guard was attacked in a pincer movement." The captain pointed to a copse of trees on their left and then to a nearby slope on the right. "Those hiding in the trees went after the cattle. When we brought up the rear guard, the second attack came from the slope behind us."

"Did you expect them to form a line and invite you to dance?" He turned to Hamar. "Find me a new captain to guard the supply line." He signaled by hand that it should be a Knight in Christ. "Redouble the pickets and send scouting parties to find the marauders. I want them routed before nightfall."

Hamar hesitated before responding.

"What is it?"

"We won't find them. Not in this forest. This is their home. Even if we could locate them, they'd pick us apart like boiled chicken."

"Are you telling me that an army of six thousand Franks can't defeat a thousand untrained Hessians?"

"Not in these woods. Our cavalry is of little use here. We can't form a shield wall. We can't even see them until they attack."

"We can't just ignore them. They're winnowing our numbers, trying to weaken us before we reach Theudebald and, to date, they're succeeding."

"What do you suggest?"

"I don't have any idea." Carloman's eyes came to rest on the captain he had just replaced. "But in the meantime, provide this man with a decoy supply train. Keep it free of stores and put thirty archers out of sight on his western flank. If the raiders attack again, I want enough men to finish them."

Carloman turned to the captain, who was still at attention beside him. "Detail a unit to butcher the slain cattle for their meat and find a priest to help, while you bury the men."

The captain ran to obey. Carloman dismounted and stood in the mud for a moment surveying the damage.

To his right, a young soldier stared up from the muck with sightless eyes, his face contorted in a death grimace. He wore the white cross of the Knights in Christ on his tunic. Carloman knelt beside him, closed the soldier's eyes and said a prayer to Saint Michael, asking the Archangel to guide the young man to his side.

Too many of his plans had gone awry. And now the army would be on half-rations. A crow cawed in the distance. Carloman stiffened and turned his head to find the animal. Was it the same one? Boniface once had cautioned him not to underestimate those who serve Satan. A trickle of sweat ran down his back. He certainly felt cursed.

Nearby, men began to butcher the oxen and cattle lying in the road. They ignored the dead soldiers who lay among them. Again, the crow cawed. This time it landed on the body of a dead cook. Carloman threw a rock at it.

✳ ✳ ✳

That night, the night sweats assaulted Carloman until

his blanket was soaked. The next the day he struggled to mount his horse and at times grew so lightheaded that he didn't know where he was. Despite the spring's heat, he wore a great cloak to ward off the chill that had settled deep in his bones. His head seared with pain and his arm became so inflamed that it nearly doubled in size. It no longer itched but throbbed.

His perception faltered and he was unsure if what he was seeing was real. After a brief encounter with his dead father, Carloman realized he was becoming delirious. Drogo was talking, but he couldn't focus his thoughts on his son's words.

"- then send for more supplies."

Carloman tilted his head up. "Drogo, we need to stop. I can go no further."

Drogo looked down at him. "We halted the army two days ago. You've been bedridden since then."

"Get me a doctor."

"You already have been seen by the doctors."

Carloman felt like a mace had struck his head but he forced himself to sit upright. "Then, get me a local one, a pagan with herb lore. Sunni made poultices and potions that cured fevers like this. I need someone like her."

Drogo hesitated. "I won't let them practice the dark arts on you, father. It's heresy."

"For now, it's a necessity." A wave of nausea hit him. "This illness was caused by a pagan. It must be cured by a pagan. If we don't do something soon, I may lose my arm, if not more."

Hamar sent scouts to the nearest village to find a pagan healer. It was a small hamlet at the base of a mountain. Large farms had tamed the surrounding landscape and a cluster of buildings near the town's center suggested it was a trade route of sorts.

The healer was an old man with decaying teeth and a bald circle on his head. He was dressed in animal skins with bags of herbs and potions hanging from a belt at his waist. Clearly nervous to be in such company, he knuckled his forehead and bowed repeatedly until Carloman held up his hand.

"No harm will come to you. I'm ill with a fever. I think it comes from my arm."

The old man stepped forward cautiously, taking Carloman's arm in his hands. His face adopted a look of concentration as he examined the wound. He bent forward to sniff the wound and pulled away quickly.

He felt Carloman's forehead and inspected his eyes. Frowning, he muttered what sounded like curses and stalked around the room until he found a bowl.

"Piss." The healer offered Carloman the bowl.

Drogo knocked it from the man's hand. "This is the mayor of the palace, not some horse."

Carloman put a calming hand on his son's shoulder. "It's alright. Sunni used to require that as well." He picked up the bowl, opened his robe, and pissed into the container. He handed it back to the healer.

The man raised it to his face, sniffed the steam as it rose from the liquid and then tilted the bowl to take a taste.

"Sorcery!" Drogo made the sign of the cross.

The healer spat out Carloman's urine. Frowning, he pulled several of the sacks from his belt. "Your wound is corrupt. It must be cleansed." He pulled out a thin rod about the length of a finger. "It's not a pleasant process. Are you prepared?"

Carloman nodded. The healer pressed the rod against the wound on Carloman's bicep. The pain was immediate. Carloman flinched, but the healer held his arm firmly and pushed the rod through the scab into the swollen flesh. Pus spewed down the length of the rod from the wound. The healer squeezed Carloman's arm, forcing his flesh to give up its putrescence until there was none. From his bag he drew a sack which moved beneath his hand.

"What is that?"

"Maggots." He placed them on Carloman's wound, letting them burrow into the injury. He then mixed a poultice from herbs and a potion that smelled like manure mixed with rosemary and spread it over a cloth that he used to bind the wound. "Let them feed for three days to cleanse the wound and then remove them and wash it thoroughly. It should reduce the swelling. The taint is also in your blood. I will make you a tea of ginger and turmeric to help you fight the sickness. You must take it every few hours."

Carloman nodded.

Within two days, Carloman's fever had passed, but he remained weak and discomfited by the burrowing maggots beneath his dressing. With considerable effort he regained his horse and ordered his army southward. As if on cue, the Hessians renewed their attacks.

Although limited in scope, the sporadic battles took their toll on Carloman's men. Their eyes grew haunted and many began to panic at the slightest sound from the forest. By the time they reached the Monastery at Würzburg, his army was limping.

Located on the crest of a large hill overlooking the Main River, the ancient walled city of Würzburg, provided more than adequate defense positions for the army. Carloman set pickets and fortified the wall with his men but doubted the Hessians would pursue their attack against such a strong defensive position. For a few days, at least, they could rest. And from the looks of his men, they needed it. The relentless forest attacks had sapped the men's vitality, exhausting them through lack of sleep and the sheer dread of waiting for an attack by an unseen foe.

Here, they could rest on the banks of the Main, treat their wounded, and make good use of the city's stores to restock their supply train. Like his men, Carloman was buoyed by the respite. His color was returning to normal and the swelling on his arm was down.

As in Fritzlar, the resident monks and clergy treated

Boniface as if he was royalty. Carloman gratefully tolerated being treated as a lesser dignitary in exchange for a clean bed and a well-cooked meal.

The only thing that tempered his relief was the towering presence of the Reichswald Forest to the south of the city. Nearly as large as the western Black Forest, the Reichswald took up much of the horizon even when viewed from the elevated vantage point of the monastery. Although no one discussed the threat, everyone knew that entering the woods would bring about the resumption of the Hessian ambushes.

Carloman heard rumblings from the men, who were grousing about his detour to Fritzlar and Fulda for Boniface. Carloman couldn't blame them. Had they stayed in the west, they could have used the Roman Road that followed the Rhine for much of the journey rather than march through the forests in the east.

On the third day, Carloman ordered his men to break camp. With a collective groan, they headed back into the forest. As before the half-light of the wood canopy reduced visual perception. And, as before, the Hessians attacked.

❊ ❊ ❊

It came on their second night under the Reichswald's canopy. The Franks had made camp for the evening, cutting back some of the forest undergrowth and setting pickets along the perimeter.

Like all their other assaults, the Hessians attack was well planned. They struck just as the Franks were settling in for their evening meal, concentrating on the eastern picket, in an attempt to overwhelm the perimeter with greater numbers.

Hundreds of Hessians poured over the picket, quickly overwhelming the two-dozen men stationed there and drove deep into the Frankish camp where the cook's fires burned.

An alert Frankish captain was able to sound a horn of alarm before a spear punched through his abdomen. The Franks scrambled for their weapons and tried to form a line, but the Hessians were too deep in their midst and the fighting degenerated into a melée.

Carloman followed Hamar from his tent when the alarm was sounded, grabbing his broadsword as he ran. Sending messengers to the north and south along the line he called for reinforcement but was careful to strengthen the forward and rear lines against further attack.

The fighting became fierce as the sun set on the forest. As Frankish reinforcements arrived, Hessian bowmen slowed their progress from the trees. A new horn sounded from the north and Carloman mounted his horse, shouting for Hamar to protect the supply train in the south. He kicked his heels to his warhorse's flanks and galloped toward the forward line, ordering men forward as he passed. "I'll hang the last man to the fight."

Arriving at the forward line, Carloman knew at once that it was the main thrust of the Hessian assault. He crossed himself, thanking God that he had called to reinforce it. A shield wall there had held against the initial assault and with every passing moment Carloman's ranks continued to grow. He called bowmen forward to shoot into the trees to roust any Hessian bowmen and reinforced the line by forming three parts of a box to ensure they couldn't be outflanked.

With their line strengthening and the sunlight fading with every passing moment, Carloman expected the Hessians to break off soon. Their ploy had failed. Why waste men on a failed strategy?

The center of his shield wall suddenly bowed outward into the enemy line. Carloman took his mount forward, trying to see past the front line. The Hessian line was collapsing.

"With me!" he shouted, sending his warhorse into the fray. A hundred men followed, and they burst into the field, splitting the enemy in two. Carloman hacked down on the

Hessian foot soldiers without mercy, letting his anger and frustration rule.

The Hessians, however, were not finished. A new column crashed into the melee from the east, catching Carloman unaware.

"Form a line! Form a line!" He pulled back to make room, directing men to fill in the gaps in the shield wall.

A stab of pain pierced his right leg. Looking down, he found that a bolt had grazed him, but struck his horse. The animal stumbled sideways, began to right itself but then its two hind legs collapsed.

Carloman had no choice but to dismount. Furious over the loss of his mount, he turned to re-engage, but a Hessian horn sounded, and their forward line melted into the darkened woods.

Hamar appeared at his shoulder. "Shall we pursue, my lord?"

Carloman shook his head, too angry to speak.

"We can't stay here. They'll only attack again."

Carloman nodded. "We have to change our strategy. I'm finished playing mouse to their cat."

"What do you have in mind?"

"We take away their advantage."

* * *

For two days Carloman pushed the men hard, looking for the opening to mount his strategy. He found it in a broad clearing bordered by a shallow river, flowing west to east. He ordered his men to prepare to camp on the northern shore. Trees and brush were cut back, pickets ordered, and tents raised.

He then sent crews to the southern side of the river and cut trees and brush fifty yards into the forest to build a huge wall of wooden debris across the face of the forest. Pickets and guard units were deployed to protect the soldiers though Carloman doubted they would be attacked. To have his army dig in here served the Hessians' interests. The longer he took to reach Bavaria, the weaker the army would become. He was counting on creating the impression that they were building a temporary compound to withstand the relentless attacks by the Hessians.

It took the better part of a week, but when the wall was finished, it stood six feet high and ran nearly a a hundred meters in length. Shaped like the head of an arrow, the wall pushed back the forest, leaving an open battleground on the Franks' side of the wall.

Carloman had his men soak the wall in tar and then retreat to the northern side of the river. There, he waited, letting the men replenish their stores and tend to the wounds they had taken during the recent attacks. He too, was relieved for the rest.

On the fourth day after the wall's completion, the Hessians attacked. Carloman was ready.

He ordered the bowman to harass the enemy surmounting the wall. Scattered as they were, the Hessian soldiers died in droves. But Carloman knew the incursion for what it was, a feint. The real attack would come from the east or west where the Hessians would circumvent the wall. He could wait.

A flaming signal arrow signaled from the west. Two minutes later, a second flew from the east. Carloman let them come. The enemy charged along the south side of the river, clearly surprised to find no counterattack. When they met on the shore opposite Carloman's camp, Hodar quickly ordered ladders placed on the wall to speed his reinforcements and then turned to lead a charge across the shallow river.

Carloman gave a signal and a shield wall, carefully hidden by brush and rocks leapt into existence on the northern shore. The Hessians slammed into it, but their own line was ragged from crossing the stream. Lances and swords stabbed through the wall and Hessian foot soldiers began to die. Carloman reinforced his line and the shield wall began to push the Hessians back into the river.

Behind the Hessian line reinforcements continued to pour over the wall and they joined in the effort to stop the Franks' shield wall.

Carloman waited until the southern shore was filled with Hessians before putting his plan into action. He ordered flaming arrows launched over the stream into the tar at the base of the wooden wall. Runnels of flame lanced along the entire length of it, curling upward to devour the fresh wood. Within minutes the wall became a towering blaze. Dozens of Hessian soldiers still on ladders leapt to the ground, screaming as the flames engulfed them. Panic seized the back of the Hessian line as men moved away from the flames.

As the Franks' shield wall pushed the Hessians to the southern shore of the river. Horses stationed near the shoreline lunged forward, dragging long wooden raft-like structures across the stream to the far side. Soldiers streamed across the newly formed bridge to slam stakes in the ground on each side to hold them in place. Reinforcements poured over the bridge forcing the Hessians backward towards the flaming wall.

In desperation, the Hessians hurled themselves at the shields, trying to forge an avenue of escape. It wasn't enough. The shield wall mirrored the arrow shape of the outer wall and pushed forward using a syncopated step to push the Hessians back towards the growing conflagration behind them.

Carloman sent his cavalry over the bridges to contain the enemy, allowing no one to escape using the river. Panic seized the rear of the Hessian army as they were pushed ever closer to the wall. They rushed forward, trying to add their weight to the attack, but instead they destabilized the Hessian line. The Franks waded into their fallen enemies, hacking them to death.

The battle was over in less than an hour. Five hundred Hessians lay dead on the south side of the stream. But the primary purpose for the wall had just begun to bear fruit. Carloman ordered his men to stand down and watched the forest burn. Whatever refuge it once had offered the Hessians would vanish in the conflagration. For the first time in weeks, Carloman smiled.

# CHAPTER TWENTY-SIX

*Paris*

G unther brought Pippin a message that had arrived late during the night.

*My dearest Lord Pippin:*

*In my dreams, I often relive my joyful days with you and your father. All that I have now is the quiet solitude of these desolate walls. God only knows what will become of our family without Charles to guide us. I beseech both you and Carloman to find it in your hearts to free Gripho so he may serve the greater glory of the kingdom. If you must seek guidance, I pray it is from your heart, as Boniface has already hardened his against it.*

*My Blessings,*

*Sunnichild.*

Pippin set the message aside. "It's from Sunni," he told Gunther. "She wants me to free Gripho."

"Doesn't she know that you have a war to manage?"

Pippin nodded. "And I best be off to manage it. I've stayed too long searching for Bertrada. It's time I join up with Carloman. I'll take Arnot and thirty knights with me for the journey. The rest of the battalion will stay here with you in Paris."

"Will you write to Sunnichild before you leave?"

"The road east takes us near the Abbey at Chelles. I'll make time for a short detour. I haven't visited Sunni since Carloman imprisoned her after the siege at Laon. If I can't grant her request, the very least I can do is to ensure her comfort."

He made it clear that Gunther should continue the search for Bertrada until she was found.

Pippin also left a note for Miette, should she inquire, saying, "War beckons. I will consider your offer." He left that afternoon.

* * *

The Abbey itself was a fortress. Great walls surrounded an enormous compound along the River Marne that included a church, a monastery, an abbey, a cloister, a dormitory, an orchard, a tannery, a smith, a barn full of sheep, pigs, chickens and goats, a mill powered by the river, and an enormous garden that provided food for the sisters and the staff that maintained them.

A royal cloister since the time of Clovis, the Abbey at Chelles had housed some of the most notable women in Francian history - some by choice, some by force, and some for their own protection. Sunnichild was merely the latest guest. Although Sunnichild had willingly taken the orders, she was given little choice in the matter. As long as Carloman was mayor, she would be a resident of the abbey.

Pippin arrived that night at Vespers and had to wait outside until the evening's prayers were complete. Afterwards, he was admitted into an office where he awaited a meeting with the Abbess Clemencia.

She was a huge woman, with Germanic features, no eyebrows and a prominent nose. While she clearly knew who Pippin was, she also clearly wished he were somewhere else.

"This is a place for women." Her right fist stamped

downward for emphasis. Her accent was severe making "women" sound like "vimen."

"They are holy women! And these men," she almost spat the word, "these armed men, are a violation of their sanctuary. I will not allow it."

"Forgive me, Abbess, but this is an affair of state. I will see her."

The abbess was clearly someone who was used to having her way. She shook her head. "I refuse."

Pippin scowled at her. "Abbess, I will either go with your permission or go by force."

"You wouldn't dare!"

"Abbess, don't mistake me for my brother, Carloman. He's a much more devout man. He wouldn't dare. I assure you that I have no such hesitation." He stood. "Which will it be?"

She stood as if to block his way, but her eyes showed doubt. After a moment she nodded. "Wait here."

She came back after a few minutes and led him to the inside of a chapel. A lone nun prayed at the altar. The abbess waved him forward and took her leave. Pippin sat in a pew to wait and pulled out Sunni's letter.

*"My Dearest Lord Pippin..."*

It had been written using one of his family codes. The key was in the address. She could have addressed him as "Pippin," or "Lord Pippin," or "My Lord Pippin" or "My Dearest Lord Pippin." By using his name as the fourth word in the address, it told him that only the fourth words of each sentence were relevant.

He reread the message. What it really conveyed was, *"I have what you seek."*

It could only mean one thing. Bertrada was at Chelles.

After a minute Sunnichild crossed herself and turned to face him.

A broad smile took her face. "Pippin!"

He strode down the aisle to meet her. "Am I permitted to embrace a nun?"

She threw her arms around him with a laugh. "I'm so glad you're here."

The emotion welling in him took him by surprise. Despite the events of the past year, they had been a family. They had cared for and protected each other. To Pippin, after so much time alone, just being in her presence was a relief. They sat next to each other in one of the pews.

"You look terrible, Pippin."

"These past few months have been somewhat...difficult."

"And now you are going off to war."

He nodded. "Odilo left us no choice."

"There is always a choice, Pippin."

"Not this time. Theudebald has returned. He's allied with Odilo."

"Odilo should know better. The man is a monster." Sunni's face paled. "Trudi –"

"Can take care of herself. She and Odilo married."

"She's still in grave danger, Pippin. Theudebald will hurt her to harm you."

Her urgency gave Pippin pause. Being of Bavarian nobility, Sunni knew the region's politics better than most. Charles had held her counsel in very high regard.

"What would you have me do?"

Sunni's face was a stark mask as if all humanity had left her. "Kill him."

Pippin raised his eyebrows in surprise. "A surprising thing for a nun to say."

Sunni's tone tolerated no banter. "Do it soon. The man is a demon."

Pippin nodded and showed her the letter. "I received your message."

"I thought that would get your attention. Yes. Bertrada is here. She and the Lady Hélène asked for sanctuary."

"Where is she?"

"I asked Lady Hélène to fetch her. But, before she arrives,

you must promise me that you will hear her out."

Although confused, Pippin nodded. "Of course. Is she well?"

A look of concern took Sunni's face. "You need to speak with her."

"What are you talking about? Where is she?"

"Here." A voice called from the side entrance of the chapel. It was Bertrada. She was dressed as a prelate; her hair black and cut shorter than Pippin's. Lady Hélène stood beside her.

An overwhelming sense of relief flooded through Pippin. All the fear and anxiety, all the doubt and worry about Tedbalt, disappeared in a moment of clarity. Bertrada was alive and well and that was all that mattered. He ran to her, swept her into his arms, and lifted her off the floor. As before, she didn't return his embrace. This time, however, Pippin didn't care. She was alive and well. That was all that mattered.

He set her down. "I've been so worried. I searched nearly every home in Paris looking for you."

"Pippin, we need to talk."

"I know about the baby."

"Please sit down."

"If you want, we can marry. He won't be a bastard."

"Pippin!" It was Sunnichild. "Sit down."

He sat down in the nearest pew. Bertrada sat next to him.

"You may have noticed that I'm wearing the dress of a prelate."

"A good disguise."

"It isn't. I've asked to take the vows."

The words struck Pippin like a blow. "But why?"

"It is my choice."

Anger and despair wrestled within Pippin. "Please, don't."

She laid her hand on his. "You know that I love you. But this is the right thing to do. I can't live the life you live. I can't raise my child in fear. I'm hounded now and we aren't even wed. What will my life be if we marry? How will our children be protected? If I take the vows, these walls will protect me."

"Bertie –"

"Sister," Bertrada interrupted.

"What?"

"You must call me, Sister."

The rebuke wounded him, but he acquiesced. "Sister, I beg you to reconsider."

"I will not."

"What about the child?"

"It will be raised here. There are many women here, like me, with child. It will be raised in an orphanage and told of its parentage when he or she is of age."

Anger shook him. "I could take the babe."

"You would endanger it, just as you have endangered me. I can' stop you. But if you take our child, I will never forgive you. You will never see me again."

He saw the certainty in her face and in that moment, all hope vanished.

"Good-bye, Pippin." Bertrada stood and walked out of the chapel.

Frustration roared within him. He wanted to tear the abbey down block by block. His mind sprinted down the myriad of choices he had, pushing each to their conclusion. None showed any promise of a future with Bertrada or his child. At best he could return for the child, but it would always be a bastard. It would always be without Bertrada and it would always end in misery.

"I tried to talk her out of it." He felt Sunni's hand on his shoulder. "I tried to talk about our days before Charles died, but it only made matters worse. Once the idea of taking vows occurred to her, she embraced it as her salvation. Her hair was shorn the very next day."

"Can she change her mind?"

"Until she takes her vow."

"When will that be?"

"Whenever the abbess decides to let her. Some kneel right away; some take years."

His despair led him back to the same place he had been before she vanished after the ball. She was gone. Truly gone. "Will you watch over her and the babe?"

She smiled. "What else would a grandmother do?"

He nodded, emotion welling within him. "Thank you."

Sunnichild reached out and took his hand. "I have something to ask you. I meant what I said in the letter, Pippin. I'd like you to free Gripho. It's one thing to send me away in my waning years, but Gripho is a young man. Carloman is wrong to put him in prison."

Pippin nodded. "It wasn't among his better decisions."

"Can't you intercede?"

"Not now. And not without force. As angry as I am with Carloman, I won't take up arms against him."

"Then promise me that, after you deal with the rebellion, you will try to gain his freedom."

Pippin looked at the woman before him. Even trapped in her role as a nun, she exuded strength. He could see why Carloman had been afraid to let her establish regency for Gripho. But had Carloman listened to reason, they wouldn't be facing a rebellion at all.

"I'll do what I can."

"There's one more person you need to speak with."

Pippin lifted his head.

"Lady Hélène." Sunnichild gestured for Hélène to approach. "You need to understand who and what she is. For years, I thought your father was having an affair with her, but the truth is far more … useful." She kissed Pippin on the cheek. "Give Trudi my love. And try not to kill her husband."

Pippin barked out a laugh and stood to say goodbye. Sunnichild hugged him and turned to leave the chapel.

Pippin tried to reconcile the woman who stood before him with the Lady Hélène he knew at court. The short-haired woman had been a socialite, a widow who was welcome in almost every home in Paris. Here, standing in the Abbey chapel, Hélène looked as if some warrior demon had stolen her soul.

Catherine had told him that Hélène belonged to a sect of the church devoted to a strict martial code and that she was capable of protecting Bertrada. Seeing her here, with the grace of a swordsman, he began to believe it.

He stood to greet her. "I am indebted to you and your sister for protecting Bertrada."

"It was the Merovingian. He sent soldiers to kill her and make it look like a robbery. We fled the city, thinking you were already out on campaign. We didn't know you were still in Paris until we reached the Abbey. Otherwise, I would have tried to bring her to you."

"For the moment, this might be a better solution. I can't take her with me on campaign – not if she's with child. And with the army gone, Paris may not be safe. Here, at least, she'll be hidden from view."

Hélène nodded and an awkward silence grew between them.

Pippin didn't know where to start. Question upon question thundered inside his head. He picked the most obvious. "How did you know my father?"

She smiled. "I knew him well."

"I'm in no mood to banter, my lady."

"My sister arranged for an introduction."

"Why?"

Her eyes took a far-off look to them, as if they danced within her memories. When she spoke, her voice rang with passion.

"When the Saracen Abd ar-Rahman crossed the mountains with his false god and thirty thousand men, he defeated the Berber Munuza. He defeated Eudo of Aquitaine. He defeated all who stood before him. The River Garonne ran red with Frankish blood as the Saracen plundered Autun and the land of Bordeaux. Flush with victory and treasure, they turned their eyes north to the holy relics at the Abbey of St. Martin of Tours. With less than half of their number, Charles took up the high ground outside Poitiers. For seven days the Saracen cavalry fell upon them and for seven days they were rebuffed. On the last day, a great battle ensued and it appeared that Charles would be overwhelmed.

"In a feint, Charles attacked their rear-guard, threatening the Saracen looted treasure. Their army panicked, scurrying like animals to save the ill-gotten gold. Charles chased them down long into the night. By morning, twenty thousand lay dead on the battlefield and Abd ar-Rahman's head stood atop of a pike."

Hélène's eyes were filled with righteous fury. "Charles was our savior. He gave us justice. I knew then that I would serve him till the last of my breath."

"How exactly did you serve him?"

Her eyes squinted as if she were judging him. "Some have called me his death knight."

For years, there had been rumors of an assassin in Charles's court, but Pippin had never given them much credence. That it could be Lady Hélène struck him as preposterous. Yet here she was with a calm face suggesting she was that killer.

"You are a murderer?"

"He called me 'his Justice.' He even knighted me."

"A woman?"

Her eyes twinkled. "It was our secret."

A cold feeling stole over Pippin. He remembered rumors linking Hélène to the death of one of Charles's rivals. She was telling the truth. The idea both repelled and intrigued him. Sunni had said she was useful. Now he understood what she meant.

"Whom do you serve now?

She met his eyes. "I have yet to find someone worthy."

The rebuke was plain. "Carloman isn't worthy? I'm not worthy?"

"Are you?" She stepped towards him. "Tell me this, Pippin, son of Charles. Will you be king?"

"I – I don't know."

She gave him a crooked smile. "How would your father have answered that question?"

Pippin eyed her suspiciously. It was the same question her sister Catherine had asked him. He closed his eyes and imagined Charles standing in front of this woman. His father would have laughed at her question. "He would have said yes."

Hélène crossed her arms as if that explained everything. "I will honor my sister's request and protect Bertrada until you return from the war. Then her fate will be in your hands."

# CHAPTER TWENTY-SEVEN

*The Reichswald Forest*

C arloman had never seen anything so formidable. With a howl, the blaze swept through the forest in a wave of fire that sent gouts of flame dancing over the forest canopy. Treetops blossomed at their touch, creating a never-ending wall of fire, roaring fifty feet in the air. It was like standing before the gates of hell as they opened onto the world.

Even from his perch across the shallow river the heat was searing. Carloman ordered a general retreat and his men streamed back across the same wooden bridges they had used to mount the attack. A panic ensued among the forward ranks as they pushed to escape the blistering blaze. Order broke down as men crowded onto the bridge. Others forged into river rather than wait.

Like the breath of a dragon, a plume of fire spewed from the forest into their ranks. Screams pierced the air as men became human torches, their torsos erupting in flames.

Carloman ordered the horns to blow to maintain order but his men stampeded into the shallow river. Those who fell were trampled and drowned as hundreds clawed their way to the other side. He dispatched lieutenants to control the shoreline, funneling those who arrived into ranks to provide room for those still to come.

Dozens of his men were burning and Carloman began to fear that the river wouldn't be enough of a barrier to save them. If the fire leapt across to the forest behind them, there would be no escape. He knelt and prayed to God for mercy and he wasn't alone on bended knee.

His prayer ended, Carloman stood to await his fate. The flames towered above him, alive and majestic, taunting him for his impotence. Scorching smoke filled the air, stinging his eyes, throat, and lungs. Rearing its head as if to laugh, the blaze hurled itself towards the forest in the south, and east roaring away from him over the trees until there was nothing but an inferno as far as Carloman could see.

He had summoned a monster, a demon of incredible power, and he thanked God that it hadn't devoured him and his army.

*  *  *

Nothing of the forest lived after the fire. Not a hare, a boar, a raven, or deer. The wind had swept the conflagration across the horizon and all creatures that could have, fled before it. Every village, every farm, every road, every sign of life was gone. In their place were the burnt and broken specters of the forest's giant oak trees. It took days before Carloman could advance his army with any degree of safety, and even then, his men had to cover their faces to stave off the scent of fire, ash and decay.

Although, Carloman had gotten his wish to take away the enemy's cover, the boon came at a staggering cost. There was no land to forage, no farms to seek grain and eggs, and no wells to give them water. Mile after mile, they rode in the wake of the fire. In some places the ground still burned.

Carloman rationed his army's food and water and sent

scouts to search for anyplace untouched by fire. They returned with nothing but growing desperation as no such place appeared to exist.

For two days they advanced through the ghost wood finding no drinkable water as every stream was filled with ash. Their purgatory was endless. Determined to take advantage of an absent enemy, Carloman pressed on. But with each passing day, his men grew weaker. If he didn't find forage soon, his men would starve.

On the fifth day after entering the burnt forest, a scout reported that the Tauber River was just ahead and that it had broken the path of the conflagration. Carloman's army stumbled to its edge, a specter of the robust force that had entered the forest's desolation. Carloman knelt by the water and gave a prayer of thanksgiving.

It went unanswered. After crossing the river, Carloman found desolation of a different kind. Refugees from the fire overwhelmed the far shoreline. Filthy and barely clothed women and children begged the soldiers as they passed. Hunger ravaged their shrunken faces, and their waste littered the shore. The stench of it was everywhere.

Carloman marched his men onward, finally making good time due to an old Roman trading road that allowed for a quickened pace. But every town and village was similarly overwhelmed with refugees. Hundreds of them huddled in makeshift huts at the edges of each town, while the few men who remained patrolled the village centers with clubs, axes, and swords.

It was clear that the human throng of refugees had already consumed what there had been to forage, so Carloman had no choice but to press on. His men stayed hungry and weak, but marched forward, knowing that there was nothing for them to gain by stopping. The shitting disease resurfaced in his ranks and soon thereafter Carloman's daily accounts showed increasing numbers of his men dying.

As if they weren't challenged enough, it began to rain.

The water fell in wide sheets, slapping his ranks in successive blows. The ground beneath their feet became a bog, sucking their boots into the mud with every step. Still, they marched on, pushing southward towards the rebellion. Although their progress slowed, the men seemed to welcome the downpour as the rain diluted the stench of the fire.

When the next morning's sun rose on their encampment, the men discovered they were on the cusp of a broad valley. Although a forest still covered much of the landscape, huge tracts of farmland were visible from their perch. Carloman made the sign of the cross. He knew a gift from the Almighty when he saw one. His army had survived the fire's devastation and now their supplies would be replenished, and their health and spirits restored.

He sent out foraging parties to gather food. When they returned a day later there was a celebration among the men. They had cattle to slaughter, pigs to roast, bread to eat, and wine to drink. Carloman let them enjoy the moment and ordered them to encamp for two days.

Once he was assured that pickets had been set, Carloman afforded himself the luxury of bathing in a nearby stream. A thick sill protruded into the water's edge creating a small cataract and he sat beneath it, letting the water flow over his head and shoulders. Closing his eyes, he let its thrumming cascade drown out the sounds of the camp and gave himself up to the gentle buffeting of the rushing stream. He let the water carry away the stench of the fire and the taint of its ash. He let it wash away the weariness in his bones and the despair he had harbored for days. He let it cleanse him of the doubts that had plagued his journey.

Regaining his tent, he even changed into a clean set if clothes. He felt as if he had been made anew. He took a few moments to say a short prayer of thanks and then he sent for Hamar.

His lieutenant had also bathed and acquired clean clothes. He had not, however, lost his scowl.

"The Hessians are encamped east of us, just over the horizon."

Carloman ordered a servant to bring food and the two sat down for the meal. "What are they doing?"

"Same thing we are, gathering supplies. Our foraging teams ran into each other."

"Bloodshed?"

Hamar shook his head. "They're just as tired as we are."

"Won't stay that way for long. How many men do they have left?"

"They have more men than they used to."

Carloman arched an eyebrow.

"It's the fire. The chieftains are using it to recruit anyone able to carry a spear. We burnt them out of their homes. And the men who have lost everything – their homes and families – they have nowhere else to go. The forest was their life. We likely have created a generation of enemies with that fire."

Carloman nodded. "Yet, they've learned the conse-quence of rebellion. We are the swords of God here on earth. The sooner they understand that the less likely they'll be to revolt."

"We should attack the Hessians now while our numbers give us a clear advantage," Hamar stood to pace inside the tent.

Carloman waved for him to take a seat. Hamar's pacing was always a distraction. "I would rather not lose half our men in combat before we reach Regensburg. That's where the real fight will be."

Hamar shook his head. "But here we face a smaller, poorly trained enemy. If we wait, we risk a two-front battle between Odilo and the Hessians. They'll have us surrounded. If we attack the Hessians now, we eliminate that advantage."

Knowing in his heart that Hamar was right, Carloman nodded. "I suppose waiting for Pippin isn't much of a strategy. Tomorrow we'll break camp, make our way south, and choose our ground. Then all we have to do is wait for the Hessians to arrive."

Carloman sent pigeons meant for Pippin, hoping they would find his brother already on his way.

The next morning, they broke camp and headed south towards the Danube. It wasn't long before their scouts brought word that the Hessian army was mirroring their movement.

Three days later they reached the river valley and Carloman ordered his army to make camp. Regensburg was a seven-day march from their position and his scouts put the Hessians less than a day to the north.

Carloman chose a field where his army would have an advantage and waited for the Hessians to arrive. When they did, they would find themselves fighting up hill and facing into the sun.

Unfortunately, the Hessians had their own plans. Carloman's scouts reported that the Hessians had formed ranks on a nearby field. It wasn't long before a messenger arrived from the enemy camp. Hamar took a scroll from the man and opened it.

"What is it?" Carloman said.

"They want to parley. They ask to meet on neutral ground."

"Where?"

"A bridge just to the north. We passed it on our way here. They asked for no more than five knights apiece."

"When?"

"The day after tomorrow at noon."

"They're delaying – giving Odilo time to arrive. Tell them I'll meet them at noon tomorrow or not at all."

* * *

Carloman waited at the bridge with Drogo and three of his Knights in Christ. The silhouette of five riders crossed the ridge to their north. Even from a distance, Carloman could see they weren't all Hessians. One of the knights carried an Alemannian banner. Carloman swore under his breath.

"What is it, father?" Drogo shifted nervously in his saddle.

"We had planned on fighting poorly trained Hessians. Alemannians are another factor altogether. They're professional soldiers and much more disciplined. It will be a far more difficult and costly battle."

As the riders approached the bridge, Carloman cursed again, this time much louder.

"Father?"

"It's Theudebald."

He was older than Carloman remembered, but the bastard was anything but aged. The Alemannian exuded power and malevolence on a scale that few men could, and the scar on his face did little to belie the effect. He rode his warhorse casually to the end of the bridge and spat.

"Why if it isn't Carloman the Weak."

"I seem to remember that you were banished, Theudebald. Yet here you are – with an army no less."

"Charles is dead. My vow to him is dead. And by this time tomorrow, you will be as well."

Carloman had always thought such banter childish. "Tell your men that I will pardon them if they leave now and go home. Otherwise, I'll destroy your army and hunt them down. You are vastly outnumbered and half your men are farmers and children with sticks in their hands. Why should they be sacrificed for your vanity?"

Theudebald laughed. "Your arrogance is your undoing, Carloman. You thought the Hessians would never ally with Alemannia. Yet here we are. And in such great numbers!"

Theudebald snort with derision.

"They're here because of you, Carloman. You gave me these men. You burned their villages. You destroyed their homes. They have nowhere else to go. Thanks to you we have twice the number of Hessians ready to fight. And they despise you more than anyone alive – more than the Saxons. More than me! And they'll fight you with their bare hands if need be."

Carloman shrugged. "Then they will die."

Theudebald pointed at Drogo. "Who is this? You bring boys to fight your battles?"

"My son Drogo."

"Where's your younger brother, the real warrior? Why isn't he here alongside you? Is there trouble at home? Without him, you won't defeat me let alone Odilo."

"I'm not worried about you, Theudebald. You've always believed you're a better general than you are. Charles knew it and so do I."

"You are not your father, Carloman. Not half the man. And Drogo is half of your half. Charles would have engaged days ago. Weeks! But you? You cower with your army waiting for the perfect ground. I will choose the ground on which we fight and I will have the upper hand. Why? Because I can afford to wait. Time is my ally, not yours. Every hour you delay brings Odilo closer to us and you know you can't afford to fight on two fronts. Time is running out. Attacking me is your best bet. You will have to come to me. And I will be ready."

Carloman smiled. "I doubt that. Hamar is leading the attack as we speak."

Theudebald looked shocked. "You violate parley?"

"Our parley is still unbroken. You are under no personal threat from me. It's your army that's under attack."

# CHAPTER TWENTY-EIGHT

*Regensburg*

Within a week, Kovrat had organized the men into three units of forty men each. Each unit was made up of eight squads with a designated leader. He drilled them first on defensive tactics using spear and shield to hold positions against a superior force. He was ruthless in his assessment of weakness and drilled the men to the point of exhaustion to shore up their vulnerabilities. In the way of good commanders everywhere, he gave them names based on their size, looks and ability and although they complained, Trudi was sure they secretly enjoyed his attention.

Kovrat drilled the men in defending the palace, setting defensive line after defensive line for them to protect as they retreated. He established teams of five to guard her person and set rules for how they were to position themselves and how to enter a room. Trudi insisted on being present during his instructions to learn as much as she could about how the guard was supposed to act. If she had questions, she asked them and, the most part, Kovrat answered.

Satisfied that her guard was being shaped into a lethal force, Trudi turned her attention to stopping the war between her husband and her two brothers. There , she found no easy answers. Odilo had refused to budge on the question and Trudi had no means to reach out to either Carloman or Pippin. After a week spent pondering the dilemma, she sent for Tobias.

The former wine merchant entered her chambers, nervously eyeing the guards outside her door. Even after months in her service, he was still uncomfortable being a commoner surrounded by nobility. She gestured to the chair beside her and took his hand in hers to put him at ease.

"I have one last task for you to undertake."

"Last? Have I failed you, milady?"

His distress touched her deeply. For too long he had been her only friend in Regensburg. "You've more than paid your debt, Tobias. You took care of me when no one else would. But I've kept you from your family far too long."

Her voice caught in her throat. She was sending him home, sending him away. Even a month ago, that would have been inconceivable to her.

Tobias made light, easing her emotion. "I'm not sure my family would see it that way. I think they've enjoyed my time here." His face grew serious. "We didn't come here by accident. The Fates intervened in both our lives and I for one am not sorry they did. You escaped the Prince of the Lombards and I was given a chance to pay my debt to my commander, Bradius. I was glad to make good on it. It had weighed heavily on me for years."

He leaned forward, his voice falling to a conspiratorial whisper. "I am honored to have known you. It's a rare thing to befriend a Duchesse, milady. I begrudge none of my time serving you. I only worry that with me gone, you will be alone amongst the wolves."

Trudi patted his hand, to distract him from the tears crowding her eyes. "I'm no longer alone, Tobias. I have a husband to protect, a newborn to raise, and a guard to defend me. But I will miss you."

"I will always be yours to command, milady."

She nodded in acknowledgement and they stood. "Unfortunately, this assignment will require a further delay in your family's reunion and pose some danger as well."

"Have I yet turned from hazard, milady?"

Trudi smiled and handed him a sealed letter. "This is addressed to Sergio, Legate to the Holy See in Rome. I want you to personally hand it to him and no other."

The color drained from Tobias' face. "It is a Christian city, milady. I'm a pagan. They'll kill me."

She handed Tobias a ring. "This should be enough to protect you and to give you entry to see Sergio. You're there as my messenger. Nothing more or less. I'll send men with you for protection but speak nothing of religion. It will only draw attention to you."

Some of the color returned to Tobias' face. "When am I to leave?"

"Tomorrow morning. Tell anyone who cares that you are going home to be with your family in Donauwörth. In two days, my men will meet you there to take you south to Rome."

Tobias bowed to take his leave. "As milady commands."

"And Tobias? Take this." She tossed him a bag filled with denarii.

He looked at the bag as he weighed it in his hand. "A minor fortune, milady. Far less would be enough for the journey."

"You've earned far more in my service. The rest is yours. You saved my life and put yourself at risk for me. You've kept my secrets. But, most of all, you've been a friend when I sorely needed a friend. I am forever in your debt."

Tobias bowed and took his exit.

\* \* \*

It was late in the afternoon when Trudi with two guards in tow mounted the western wall to watch the sunset. It was a cool evening, and she drew a shawl around her, shuddering at the cold breeze off the Danube.

She used to wait for her father back home at Quierzy on nights like this, standing on the rampart, hoping to catch a glimpse of the army's return. Now she was awaiting Carloman's army. He would come from the west and God help them all if Pippin was with him. She could imagine Odilo strutting before his men, dressed in armor that reflected the sun's light. He would shout out commands and the army would advance, confident in their numbers and their passion to protect their homeland.

But they would be mistaken. Carloman's army was well blooded and Carloman well versed in tactical advantage. Odilo was no match.

That was, of course, assuming Carloman's army survived the journey intact. She had heard rumors that the Hessians had greatly weakened his army.

"He who waits for death, soon finds it," a voice called out from behind her.

Trudi turned to find Kovrat striding across the rampart. Her two guards gave way before him, allowing her sword master to stand beside her.

She chuckled. "Then why are you here?"

"I had heard you took your evening hours on the wall. I thought I might join you."

Trudi nodded and turned back to the sunset.

"Are your brothers as good as Charles in battle?"

"No one is as good as Charles in battle. But they are good." She turned back to look Kovrat in the eye. "They're better than Odilo and his generals."

Kovrat frowned. "They will be far from home and weakened before they arrive."

"They will still be better than Odilo and his generals." She couldn't keep the anger from her words. "Our only hope is keeping Pippin from the field. If we fight the two of them, we'll fail."

Kovrat played with his beard. "Strange things can happen in battle. The outcome is never assured. All you can do is to be prepared to take advantage if the Fates show you the way."

"What if the Fates don't care?"

"Then you must trust your guard's preparedness to protect you from the Frankish horde."

Trudi grunted. "That's not who I worry about. I worry about the Alemannians, the Hessians, the Slavs, and even the Bavarians. If Odilo dies – and right now that looks like a strong possibility – I'll be a woman alone with only my child's birthright to protect me. I'm not afraid of our enemies, Kovrat. I'm afraid of our friends."

# CHAPTER
# TWENTY-NINE

*West of Regensburg*

C arloman had sent Hamar through the woods to mount the attack. It would be a difficult journey, especially for the warhorses, but they hoped the element of surprise would make it worth the effort. They had planned for Hamar to reach the enemy's chosen field just as the parley was supposed to commence.

Using heavy cavalry to lead the attack, they hoped to catch the Hessians off-guard, before the pagans could form a decent shield wall. If they succeeded, the Hessians would be too disorganized to defend themselves and Hamar would take their army in a rout. With any luck, the battle would be over before sunset.

With trained Alemannians, however, it was less likely to work. By the time Carloman arrived, he saw that his initial plan had been partly successful. The Hessian infantry was in disarray, unable to form a wall against his cavalry. It was hardly a fight among equals as much of the Hessian infantry was without armor or sword. Boys with sticks fell in droves before Carloman's seasoned warriors.

But Theudebald's return changed the direction of the

battle. He ordered archers into the field to harass the Frankish cavalrymen and shouted for his Alemannian regulars to form a shield wall behind the Hessian front line. He then sent them forward. Caught between Frankish cavalry and the Alemannian shield wall, the Hessians had nowhere to go. They died in droves.

It was a desperate tactic to sacrifice so many men, but the shield wall stabilized their line. Despite his hatred for the man, Carloman was impressed. He had no choice but to recall his cavalry and send forward his own shield wall. Once the two lines met, the fighting slowed to the stabbing and hacking of the lines while the cavalries retreated to protect their respective flanks.

It was grim work and the screams of the men in the wall pierced the air. Carloman's line was at a disadvantage pushing uphill, but his men were more seasoned fighters and the line held. For hours the line of engagement didn't move more than a few feet in either direction as each side reinforced their shield wall.

In time, darkness overtook the battlefield and the Alemannian horns blew, calling for an organized retreat. Both sides fell back to encamp. Carloman sent teams out to recover the wounded and the dead. Theudebald did as well. They would wait until the morning to re-engage. The battle would now be a war of attrition that could take days to decide.

Carloman wasn't sure he had that much time.

❉ ❉ ❉

"The Hessians are the weak point." Hamar had drawn a map of the battlefield in the dirt outside Carloman's tent. "We almost won the day using our heavy cavalry to disrupt their line."

"It won't work again." Drogo brushed out the line for his cavalry. "We took them by surprise. We'll have to find some other way to break their line."

Hamar shook his head. "Fighting uphill? That's asking a lot of our shield wall."

Carloman frowned. He had to find a quicker way to win. "We have the advantage of numbers. We'll spread thin their line and exploit their weakest point."

"Their cavalry will be held in reserve." Hamar said. "We won't get far."

"Then perhaps we can outsmart them." Carloman drew up the plan he had been considering. Although Hamar and Drogo agreed to it, they didn't look pleased.

Carloman slept, but was up before the dawn, surveying the battlefield. Theudebald had chosen well. The Franks again would be fighting uphill as well as into the sun. The field was also narrower than Carloman had remembered, putting into jeopardy his strategy of spreading thin the enemy line.

At the crest of the hill, Theudebald's army formed their ranks just below the edge of the forest line. They were a display in contrasts. The Hessian infantry dressed in animal skins their faces painted to look like demons. They shouted obscenities across the battlefield and exposed their genitals in a display of contempt. By contrast, the Alemannians stood quietly at attention, dressed in uniform armor and tunics.

Carloman wasn't surprised to see the Alemannians take the center of the line. They were clearly the more veteran soldiers, unlikely to panic or flee.

At a barked command the two shield walls, three rows deep, began their orchestrated shuffle forward to the center of the battlefield; left foot first, right foot behind, left shoulders supporting a shield aligned to create an impenetrable wall.

With a piercing battle cry, a group of the Hessians broke ranks and sprinted downhill towards the Frankish line, screaming obscenities. A foolish gambit, thought Carloman, but still he held his breath as the cohort streamed down hill.

To a man, they leapt high above the Frankish pikes and shields in an attempt to bludgeon or hack apart the first line.

Pikes gored them as they leapt, and swords pierced them as they fell. Most were dead before they hit the ground. The Frankish line stepped over them, advancing up the hill as if they had never attacked.

Both armies unleashed their archers and waves of arrows arced over the battlefield. Shields on both sides tilted up to catch the bolts. Not all were successful and dozens in each line fell as arrows found flesh.

As the lines closed on each other, both sides reared backwards to hurl their shields against the other's wall. Five hundred throats roared as the shields slammed against each other.

"Thrust!" A voice shouted, and pikes and blades stabbed above and below the shields into the faces and feet of the enemy. Screams and shouts cut through the crisp morning air as eyes were gouged and feet cut away.

It was grim work. Hours ground by as the shield walls struggled in a game of wills. Periodically, one side or another would use axes and pikes to weaken the enemy wall and take advantage of a break or a fallen man, but always the line would coalesce, and the struggle would continue undeterred.

Carloman ordered his first surprise. Drogo led extra men to the right side of his shield wall in an effort to "wheel" the line. Three new rows pressed into the back of the shield wall, pushing the right side of the line forward. As it surged, the shield wall appeared to spin as the enemy tried to keep its forward line intact. Carloman readied his cavalry to rush the end of the wall as it came into view.

Seeing his line wheel, Theudebald shouted for his own cavalry and entered the fray to shore up their position at the wall's end. He met the first of Carloman's cavalry with fury, chopping off the leg of a warhorse as he passed and slamming into the next with his shield. Hamar moved to join the charge, but by the time he arrived, the wheel had lost its momentum and the Alemannian cavalry had propped up its wall.

The battle returned to the desperate, close-in fighting

along the shield wall.

As time progressed, Carloman could see his men weakening from the effort of pushing uphill. Although he was forced to reinforce his side far more frequently than Theudebald, he was never in doubt that his line would hold; he had plenty of reserves to throw at it, but his overarching problem remained; he needed to end the battle and end it soon.

Carloman called for his second surprise. Hamar rode through their reserve line giving instructions.

"Ready, my Lord."

Carloman gave the order and his archers dipped their arrows in tar and flooded the air with flaming arrows. The arrows arced high above the gathered forces and streamed into the forest directly behind the enemy line. A second volley targeted the infantry and set several men ablaze. Carloman's men started shouting, "Fire! Fire!" They screamed as if in a panic.

The Hessians who had lived through the forest conflagration, began to panic. Theudebald shouted for them to maintain order, but their attention shifted to the woods behind them and their shield wall lost cohesion.

It was enough to do them in. Drogo's cavalry swept into their ranks and the line broke on the wall's left side. The Alemannian regulars tried to fill in the gap, but it was too late. Drogo's cavalry drove through them like a storm. The panic among the Hessians spread and almost as one, the combined army broke and ran.

An Alemannian captain formed their regulars into the four walls of a box to protect against the cavalry charge, but it soon became clear the battle was lost. Carloman's men surrounded what was left of Theudebald's army and ordered his men to halt so that the hopelessness of their position could be realized. The Alemannian captain drove his sword into the ground and ordered his men to lay down their arms.

Theudebald was nowhere to be found. Carloman ordered an extensive search of the captured army and of the dead, offering a bag of solidi to the man who brought him the Alemannian leader. No one came to collect. When the line collapsed, Theudebald and his primary lieutenants had fled to fight another day.

Carloman's Knights in Christ herded the vanquished enemy into makeshift ranks, stripping them of all their weapons. A great mound of armaments grew on the side of the conquered hill. When at last they were weaponless, Carloman ordered the captives to be arranged into three lines. His Knights in Christ erected a makeshift cross before each of the lines. Beside each cross, they placed a large wooden block.

Carloman rode forward. "Rebellion is not tolerated. I have the power and the right to kill you here and now for your insurrection. But, as a merciful man, I offer you one last chance to live. Pledge your vassalage to me and swear an oath of faith to our Lord Jesus Christ. Recognize Him as the one and only true God in heaven and you may return home."

He signaled for the first man to be brought forward. The Hessian struggled against his captors as if the cross was a mortal threat to him. Two of the Knights in Christ dragged him before the cross. Hamar followed sword in hand.

Carloman lifted his voice so that all could hear him clearly. "We believe in one God, the Father Almighty, Maker of heaven and earth and of all things visible and invisible. And in the one Lord, Jesus Christ, the only begotten Son of God, begotten of the father before all the worlds, Light of Light, very God of very God, begotten not made being of one substance of the father, by whom all things were made. If you so testify, signify by kissing the cross. Then may you live to serve me in vassalage."

The Hessian's struggles increased. The Knights in Christ forced him to kneel. The Hessian looked up into Carloman's eyes and spat on the Cross.

Carloman nodded and the Knights took him to the block of wood, draped him over the side, holding his hands behind his back. Hamar swung his sword in a downward arc. The

Hessian tried to buck away from the block, lifting his head at the last second to avoid the blow. He failed. The blow cut his head in two, leaving his brains to spill from his head. A second blow severed the head completely. They dragged his body to the side of the hill.

Carloman nodded and another man was brought forward. Without hesitation, he knelt and kissed the cross and was released to stand in the field behind it. One by one the Knights in Christ herded the Alemannian and Hessian soldiers forward to kiss the foot of the cross and swear allegiance. Few hesitated.

Until Hodar. The Hessian leader was brought forward. He didn't struggle. He strode to the cross with his back straight and his head held high. When he stood before Carloman, he raised his voice so that all men could hear him.

"You violated the blot and now you defame our gods. You have but one god, Carloman, but we have many. They will defeat your God just as we will defeat you."

Carloman showed no emotion. "Either kiss the cross or die."

Hodar turned, walked to the block and placed his own hands behind his back. Carloman nodded and Hodar's head joined the pile on the ground.

Carloman watched as every one of their captives knelt and chose to live or die. In all, only about twenty men chose to meet their fate.

The last to choose was Rasling, the only remaining Hessian chieftain. He stood before the ranks of his men who had kissed the cross and the severed heads of those who had refused. He said nothing to disparage Carloman, bent his knee and kissed the foot of the cross. Carloman took him aside to take him into vassalage and motioned for Rasling to rise.

"Take your men and go home. Rebuild from the fire. If I see you on the field with Odilo, there will be no mercy for you and yours. Do you understand my commands?"

Rasling didn't flinch. "Yes, my Lord."

"Now, get out of my sight."

Hamar, Carloman and Drogo watched the Hessian organize his men into ranks and lead them into the north.

Hamar spat. "You should have killed him."

"We have to leave someone in charge. He obeyed the forms and swore the oaths. It might as well be him. If we killed everyone we defeat, we'd have no one to lead in our absence. They all saw him pledge."

"He doesn't believe in the Lord our God," Drogo objected.

"Yet he kissed the cross. And again, they all watched him do it."

Hamar shook his head. "We'll see him again on the field with Odilo."

"Then he'll meet his fate." Carloman spat. "How badly were we damaged?"

"In two days of battle we lost close to six hundred men - either killed or severely wounded," Hamar estimated. "We're down a thousand soldiers since leaving Paris."

Although it could have been worse, Carloman was still reluctant to face Odilo without Pippin.

"How far away is Odilo?"

"Less than a week away."

"Any news of Pippin?"

Hamar looked dour. "We may have to fight without him."

Carloman frowned. "Maybe not."

"My Lord?"

"Strike camp. We aren't staying here."

# CHAPTER THIRTY

*Paris*

During his exile in Narbonne Childeric had developed a taste for some exotic spices available only from the east. To meet his demand for them, Miette had ordered a case brought north at considerable expense. She had developed a taste for them as well and spent many an afternoon in the kitchen sampling the sauce being prepared for the evening meal.

"A little more of the black pepper." She handed the spoon back to the cook. It was the rarest and most expensive spice of the lot, but the one she favored most. The cook knuckled his head in acknowledgement and Miette was about to move on to selecting the wine – another expensive indulgence upon which Childeric insisted – when she was interrupted by one of the Merovingian's servants.

"Milady, his royal highness summons you to his presence." The servant was a young man who had yet to lose the boyish softness to his face. And although he bowed deeply, it did little to hide the scarlet color rising to his cheeks.

Miette smiled at his embarrassment. She had dropped all pretenses surrounding her affair with the Merovingian. Where once she had hidden the relationship from her husband and the court, she now openly shared Childeric's bed when he called for her. She waved for the boy to lead the way upstairs to Childeric's quarters.

As she walked, her mind drifted to her "affair" with Pippin. She had taken great delight watching Pippin's desire for her grow with each successive meeting. She loved the way his face blushed at the touch of her hand, and how his eyes followed her every move. She relished stretching his desire to the breaking point. She wanted him to ache for her.

She hadn't lied to him. She was attracted to powerful men and, if Pippin was anything, he was powerful. She also got a perverse pleasure in knowing that Pippin could evoke such paralyzing fear in her husband.

Both Childeric and her husband were more than pleased with the information she had obtained from Pippin. Much of it had proven useful. With it, she had dissuaded Childeric from assaulting the palace to assert his right to the throne. The one garrison Pippin had left behind was more than enough to mount a strong defense and the drawings in Pippin's chambers she had copied from memory showed defensive tactics capable of stopping anything Childeric might attempt.

Her husband had joined with her in cautioning Childeric against overt military action, preferring a political solution or an attempt later when the two mayors had been weakened by the war.

At the foot of the stairs, Miette stumbled and the young man guiding her was quick to catch her arm. If possible, he blushed even more deeply. Miette had to restrain a chuckle at his expense.

She stopped outside of Childeric's chambers to prepare herself for the encounter.

Childeric's infatuation with her was based on his inability to completely dominate the relationship. Her beauty gave her power over him, which violated his need to be in control. And the more he desired her, the more he wanted to debase her to prove his dominance. And yet, when she willingly embraced his degradation, she frustrated his sense of control and he became all the more aroused. It was a game of cat and mouse and her survival required her never to give the cat everything he wanted.

But she wondered how far he would go...and how much more she could tolerate. What started as sex play had become something dangerous. Each time with him brought a new indignity that she had to endure, and the defilement was taking its toll on her. Bruises covered her body and she never felt clean, no matter how many baths she had the servants draw.

Childeric waved her into his chambers and with a cruel smirk on his face offered her to two men of his guard that she had never seen before. They were coarse, brutes of the battlefield with ugly scared faces and misshapen teeth. At first, they hesitated, unsure of what Childeric had put them to but soon settled into the job with great delight. When she resisted, they beat her, striking her in the face until she quieted.

For the first time, Miette grew frightened for her life. They took her, both at the same time while Childeric masturbated beside the bed.

She recoiled before their assault, shrinking inside herself to a place they couldn't touch. Although she wanted to beg them to stop, to beg Childeric to stop, her survival relied on her ability to overcome her degradation–to not let him break her. He was watching her, his eyes holding her gaze, reveling in her humiliation.

She knew what she had to do. With every ounce of her will, Miette pretended to wallow in her defilement, begging for more with each violent thrust.

She nearly wept with relief when the brutes climaxed. Childeric stepped forward and Miette held his gaze in triumph while he stroked himself until his semen splashed over her.

He sent her away, his frustration for her resilience plain. She rose from his bed like a queen and walked naked from his quarters through the residence all the way to her chambers. She dismissed her servants, and crawled into bed, wrapping herself in a blanket.

Only then did she unbridle her fear and allow her body to quake. She had been a fool. Childeric would be twice as cruel the next time and the time after that. She had let her pride think she could master him. If she didn't find a way out, one day soon, he would kill her.

❊ ❊ ❊

Childeric sent for her the very next day. Miette was with her husband conferring about some of the nobles at court when the servant arrived with her summons. She couldn't help but groan at the directive. She had spent much of that morning trying to hide the bruises on her face and arms. She didn't think she could suffer through another bout with Childeric so soon.

"What is it?" her husband asked.

"I...I can't." Her eyes filled with tears and she clutched her husband's arm for support. "I can't do it anymore."

Ragomfred looked confused. "You have to go. He is the king."

"It's gone too far. He keeps upping the stakes. He's going to kill me. That's the only way it will end. You have to stop it."

Ragomfred stared at her a long moment as the meaning of her words sank in. He shoved her hand away his eyes alight with indignation. "You were so smug, openly betraying me with your new lover in my own home...and then you dare to complain to me about it?" He cocked his arm towards her with the same gesture she had once taunted him. "You started this game and you're going to have to see it through to the end. There is no exit for you, no savior waiting to absolve you. You will serve the king in any way he desires or I'll have you killed myself."

He stalked out of the room.

The rebuke sobered her. She swore under her breath at her stupidity. Of course, he wouldn't help. Miette shook herself to regain her composure. There had to be another way. She straightened her back, wiped away her tears, and strode down the hall to the king's chambers with all the dignity she could muster. When she entered, she portrayed none of the fear raging inside her.

She curtsied low before the Merovingian.

He motioned for her to rise. "I have an assignment for you."

Miette did her best to smirk and began to disrobe.

"Not that." Childeric waved for her to stop. "Salau has learned that Pippin stopped at the Abbey at Chelles on his way to Regensburg."

"He was likely visting his step-mother, Sunnichild. She was imprisoned there by Carloman."

"Do you know her?"

Miette shook her head. "I wasn't an accepted member of the court then."

"But surely you share acquaintances."

"Yes. Lady Hélène for one."

Childeric's eyes widened. "It was Lady Hélène who aided Pippin's mistress after the ball."

"Yes, they left with Tedbalt of Soissons and her sister."

"Don't you find it odd that their carriage was attacked by three of my men and somehow all four of them survived?"

Miette nodded. "It is odd."

"How well do you know Lady Hélène?"

"She was one of the few women at court who were kind to me before – before your arrival."

Childeric nodded. "That should be enough for you to gain entry. I want you to pay Sunnichild a visit, out of concern for your friend Lady Hélène. See what you can learn about Bertrada's disappearance. A nunnery is a perfect place for women to hide."

"And if I find her?"

"Advise Salau. He'll report back to me and we will discuss what to do. What happens to Bertrada is my responsibility."

Miette bowed to take her leave. While she was relieved to be back playing a political role for the future king, she didn't want to think about what would happen if she actually found Bertrada. She held no acrimony for Bertrada, but that mattered little. She had no choice in the matter. She would have to go to the Abbey.

Still, she recognized part of her hoped to find Bertrada and she was intrigued by the prospect of meeting her. She wanted to know what it was about her that Pippin found so attractive. Was it her brain or her beauty? And why did she end the relationship?

* * *

Miette left the following morning for Chelles. Salau and two armed men accompanied her. It was little more than a day's ride and the weather was warm. It would have been a perfect day if Salau hadn't been with her. She had never been with him outside of the king's presence and the thought frightened her. His eyes held her with the same deadness they always did. If he chose to ravage her, there would be little she could do to defend herself. The thought made her shudder.

"Dreaming of me, milady?"

Miette weighed her response. She certainly didn't want to goad him. "I'm the king's plaything, not yours, Salau."

Salau grunted his dismissal. "So, you tell yourself."

Miette's anger won out over her caution. "Do you think he degrades me for *your* pleasure? Do you think this is about you? He has me fuck the likes of you to humiliate me, to shame me. That's the source of his passion. You're only a tool in his fantasies. I, on the other hand, am the fantasy."

Salau's ghoulish laugh didn't touch his eyes. "Shall we play a game, you and I? Tell me now, how you'd like to service me the next time he summons: by the hand, the mouth, or –

whatever you desire. See if the king doesn't order it so. Then you shall know if you are my plaything or his."

Miette shook her head, refusing to take the bait.

Salau shrugged. "In the ass, then. That way I don't have to look at you."

"You are a pig."

*　*　*

They arrived early that evening. She had never been to an Abbey and was surprised by its size. It was as large as a small city. Rumored to be part haven and part prison for the aging women at court, how one came to be here depended on one's favor. Miette found it hard to imagine that the sole purpose of the sprawling compound and all who lived there was the care of the Abbey's secluded women. She left the three soldiers at the entrance and, after being ushered inside, requested an audience with the abbess.

She waited nearly an hour before the abbess appeared. A large woman with a pronounced accent, the abbess was exceedingly cooperative once Miette used Childeric's name. It affected the woman like a magical command. She stood at once, bowed, and retreated into the Abbey.

After a few minutes, a novice appeared at the door and led her to an exterior courtyard where she was told to wait. She amused herself by watching an ancient gardener tend to the voluminous hedges and plants that surrounded the benches and walkways of the yard. He was a short man with disheveled hair, and he hummed distractedly as he worked. Miette was surprised by his presence as she had assumed that only women would be allowed inside the Abbey.

Although Miette had never met Sunnichild, she knew instinctively that the nun walking towards her was Charles's widow. She wore a long blue habit that covered her completely, creating the illusion that Sunnichild floated, rather than walked, towards her over the stone pathway. A white cowl covered her hair and shoulders so that only her face remained uncovered. She turned it towards the sun, basking in its warmth as she made her way. A tall woman dressed as a postulant accompanied her. She moved like a dancer.

"Lady Ragomfred." Sunnichild held out her hand to Miette.

"Sister." Miette kissed the offered hand.

"I'm a little surprised by your visit. It's not often that I'm visited by anyone from court, let alone the wife of one of my late husband's enemies."

"I try to avoid politics, Sister. I'm here only out of concern for a friend who has gone missing. I believe you are acquainted with her...Lady Hélène?"

It was clear that this was not new information to either woman, but the postulant shifted her feet at the mention of Hélène's name. It was a small thing, yet it struck Miette as significant. It was the kind of shift a soldier would make when threatened.

"I had heard this news." Sunnichild motioned that Miette should join her on one of the benches. The postulate remained standing behind Sunnichild as if charged with her protection. "My son Pippin was here not long ago. He was distressed at the disappearance of both Lady Hélène and Lady Bertrada. How can I help you?"

"There are rumors that both women were attacked and remain in hiding out of fear that their lives are in jeopardy. Since Pippin is known to have paid a visit to the Abbey, I was hopeful that they could be found here."

"I'm sorry to disappoint you." Sunnichild said. "But out of curiosity, what did you hope to accomplish if she was?"

"I'm here with guards loyal to the throne. We could offer them safe passage back to my home where they would be well protected." Miette kept her eyes on Sunnichild but watched for a reaction from the postulate. The woman's face hardened, and her lips pressed into a thin line. She knew enough to be alarmed by the offer.

"As I said, I'm sorry I can be of no help." Sunnichild straightened as if ending the interview. "If I should learn anything you should know about, I'll be happy to send you a message."

Sunni was about to rise when Miette reached out a hand to stop her and did her best to act like a supplicant. "Sister, if I may ask a boon?"

Sunnichild sat and nodded for her to continue.

"I've always wondered about life as a nun. As you know, my husband is an older man, and one who likely will not be long on this earth. As a widow with no heir, my estate will pass to the eldest male in my husband's family. It's likely that I'll need to find refuge and had hoped the Abbey at Chelles would receive me. Might I spend a day or two with you in prayer to prepare for such a day?"

Sunnichild's face froze. Her eyes squinted in concentration. "You'll have to ask the abbess for her permission. Such boons are not mine to give."

"Of course." Miette rose. "By your leave, Sister." She turned to the tall postulate, "My pardon. I did not greet you properly. I am Lady Ragomfred." She held out her hand. The postulate curtsied and kissed her hand. "And you are?"

"Agnès, milady." When Miette waited for more, she said. "Just Agnès."

Her accent alone was suspicious, but a name without attribution? Chelles was an abbey for nobility. What was a peasant doing here? What was she to Sunnichild? Happy to have uncovered a clue worth exploring, Miette rose to take her leave. "It was a pleasure to make your acquaintance."

She turned to Sunnichild, curtsied, and went to find the abbess.

# CHAPTER
# THIRTY-ONE

*Regensburg*

"You can't go." Trudi insisted. "The pope's legate just arrived."

"So has Carloman!" Odilo's face was red with fury. "Reports from Theudebald place him just days from here and without Pippin. If we mobilize now, we can trap Carloman between us."

"Carloman isn't that stupid. By the time you reach him, he'll have bested Theudebald and the Hessians. And in all likelihood Pippin will arrive as well."

"This is our best chance to stop them."

"Sergius is our best chance. As a Legate of the Holy See, he's offering to mediate. He says that without a king, the mayors have no right to subjugate Bavaria. He'll appeal to Carloman to avoid bloodshed until the succession is resolved."

"Do you really believe Carloman will stop for a legate?" Odilo's sarcasm was thick as an infantry shield.

Trudi bit back her retort. Their relationship had cooled since the rape. She just couldn't bring herself to forgive him. He should have protected her. He should have sent Theudebald away. She had done nothing to openly antagonize her husband, far from it; she was courteous and polite, attending him in every way a wife should. She stood by his side at every function, but she withheld her body. She could see the disappointment and frustration in his eyes, but it was unavoidable. She blamed it on the growing child within her, but the truth was Trudi couldn't stand to be touched. She even bristled when Eta attended her bath.

"Carloman listens to the Pope. If the Pope is against this, Carloman will be too."

"You don't believe I can win."

Trudi shook her head. "I don't."

"I wish you held me in the same kind of awe you hold your brothers." Anger made Odilo's voice tremble.

Trudi looked up at him, surprised. It was stupid and irrational, something a boy would say. She saw the hurt and embarrassment on his face. She had held him away and now he wanted to prove to himself that he was man enough for her. If the subject wasn't so serious, she might have laughed. Instead, she thought about how she had lied to Odilo that he was the father of her child. Guilt stabbed at her and she felt her guard fall. She was being unfair.

He was a good man who had embraced her and defended her without question. She remembered their first kiss and his awkwardness in the cave at their "communion." She remembered the eagerness in his eyes and the gentleness of his touch. Warmth for him flooded into her, thawing her distaste.

She knelt and took his hands in hers. "I side with you. I left them for you. You are the man I chose, not because you could rival my brothers, but because I want to spend my life with you. I want to have this baby with you. I want him to become a man like you."

There were tears in her eyes. "I want to stop this madness because I don't want to lose you. I've lived with them the entirety of my life. I've trained with their knights. I've seen up close the size of their army and the skill of their warriors. I love you, Odilo, but I'm sure of one thing: You. Will. Not. Win. And if you die at either of my brothers' hands, I won't live to see this baby born. He'll be taken from my womb before the day is out. If you care for us – for the future of Bavaria as you have named us – you'll listen to Sergius."

Odilo pulled her to her feet took her face in his hands and kissed her. "I will speak to Sergius," he said.

* * *

Trudi had warned Odilo that Sergius was as pompous as he was tall. The Legate towered over Odilo by nearly two hands. Trudi guided him to a seat and offered him some wine, even though it was only mid-morning.

"That would be lovely." Sergius tilted his head in acknowledgement as if talking to a servant. "Something red and dry."

Odilo's face filled with fury.

Trudi interrupted before he could react "Of course. Does your excellency require anything else?"

"If I do, I will be sure to advise you."

Trudi gave a slight bow; she had always hated the man. He had a long patrician nose, hair cut square across the face in the Roman fashion, thick expressive lips, and an air about him that exuded arrogance.

Odilo coughed politely to get everyone's attention. "May we get down to the task at hand?"

Sergius gave a tight smile. "I was relieved to receive Hiltrude's request. For months we've heard rumors of a Bavarian rebellion. And it's plain to my eyes that you've-been building up an army to rival the Franks. I am here to implore you not to use it. We already have the political chaos of an empty throne. A war would reduce the continent to rubble. I have reports that half of Hesse is already up in flames."

"You make the case for rebellion, not against it."

Sergius waved away Odilo's objection. "Foolishness. War will impoverish the kingdom and spawn a thousand uprisings. It will be a nightmare."

"At least we won't wear the yoke."

"Is that what you think this is? Tell me, who did Charles leave in charge of Bavaria?'

"Me."

"So, if you are already in charge, why do you need to rebel?"

"It is more complicated than that."

"You're talking about religion?"

"I'm talking about freedom."

"You're talking about paganism. Don't look so shocked. I know you married Hiltrude beneath the Ash. Did anyone stop you?"

"We were married in a church," Trudi said.

"Words! Nothing but words. You don't fight wars over words. In many ways, you've already won. You have Charles's daughter." He gestured toward Trudi as if she were a chair. "If she bears a boy, he'll have every bit as much a right to Charles's legacy as does Carloman's son. Why fight them now? Just wait a generation and the world will be yours.

"By the way, your marriage has really angered the Lombards. Aistulf is taking out his manly frustration against the Mother Church by encroaching on the Papal lands in Ravenna –"

Odilo cut in. "Your church is not my struggle."

Sergius looked up in anger. "That is where you're mistaken. You think of this as a civil war between Bavaria and Austrasia. Between pagan and Christian. I am here to assure you that it is not. There's a much greater war that we wage, and your rebellion will do nothing but weaken us. Tell me this, if Bavaria and the Franks destroy each other who will be left to pick up the pieces?"

Sergius didn't wait for an answer. "The Saracen. Our true enemy. From the beginning they've been an Arab religion of conquest. They seized Damascus and Antioch and Palestine. They sacked Jerusalem and the Church of the Holy Sepulcher. An army of thirty thousand marched on Mecca and it fell without a fight. They conquered Syria and Iraq, Egypt and Mesopotamia, Persia, Sicily and Cyprus. They laid siege to Constantinople, conquered Iberia and India. They invaded Avignon, Nimes and Narbonne. And, if not for Charles Martel, they would have taken Tours and Paris and eventually all of the kingdom.

"You fight over words. You fight over pagan practices that die on the vine like rotten fruit, but only one thing has kept us from Saracen rule: Charles Martel and a kingdom united under Christianity. Destroy that and you destroy us all."

This is what Trudi wanted. With Sergius making a case against civil war, Carloman would have to side with the Pope and relent. There would be no war. She just had to get Carloman to listen.

Odilo was less convinced. "What does it matter to me that one religion replaces another if neither are my own?"

"As I've said, the Saracens abide by an Arab religion of conquest. As we are not Arabs, that would leave us to be the conquest."

Trudi watched Odilo absorb the discourse, knowing it wouldn't move him. He felt too strongly about the Church to buy an argument that they were better overlords than the Saracen. But all Trudi needed was for Carloman to hear the argument. If he didn't fight, Odilo wouldn't have to.

Odilo nodded. "I don't agree with your logic, Your Excellency, but I will arrange a parley with Carloman."

Trudi gave herself a silent cheer.

\* \* \*

It took Odilo the better part of a day to mobilize his

army. With ten thousand men, it required a lot more time than he expected. Supply wagons had to be packed and the infantry rounded up from the brothels and alehouses of "Trudiville." Just getting his army into defined ranks to march took several hours. When they were finally ready to disembark, the sun was already in the afternoon sky. He was so furious that he kept them marching until nightfall, forcing his men to set pickets in the dark.

He was up before dawn to set an arduous pace. The men had grown soft during the winter months. Encamped for so long at Regensburg, they had grown accustomed to sleeping in beds and eating hot food. Even the Slavs had grown used to the comfort.

They marched for two days along the Danube before scouts returned with news of Theudebald's defeat. Odilo bristled at the accounts of Hessians being forced to convert. More worrisome still was Theudebald's disappearance. Odilo couldn't imagine him running from battle.

Yet, as the next day unfolded, there was no word of his half-brother's whereabouts or a sign of his army. When his scouts returned without a sighting, it became clear that Theudebald had quit the campaign, leaving Odilo to fight Carloman alone.

Although frustrated at the thought, Odilo conceded that Theudebald already might have done enough damage. He would have to wait for scouting reports to assess the status of Carloman's army himself.

As the pace of their progress improved, so did Odilo's mood. Even the Slavs were falling into a disciplined march. He let his gaze drift over the vast army he had built and took a moment's pride in all he had accomplished. He had blended the barbaric fury of the Slavs with Bavarian professionalism to build an army of a size that Carloman had never faced. It made him almost giddy with anticipation. They were going to win! He had never felt so confident. He pushed the men hard, anxious to engage the battle.

They would reach Carloman's last-known position within a day. He sent scouts to pin down Carloman's current location to ensure there were no surprises. He wanted to be as ready as he could possibly be.

As the army closed on the battlefield where Theudebald had met Carloman, Odilo's scouts returned with troubling news; Carloman's army had vanished. Aggressive questioning of local townspeople had the Franks heading west along the Danube. Odilo was stunned. Were they running away? Had Theudebald crippled Carloman's ability to wage war?

It was the only explanation. Filled with euphoria, Odilo pressed onward. It was only a matter of time.

Only it wasn't. An entire day swept by as Odilo advanced west along the Danube finding little sign of Carloman's army. He grew frustrated with his scouts. How could an entire army disappear? They questioned everyone they passed, and no one had seen the Frankish army. Something had changed. But for the life of him, Odilo couldn't figure out what.

It wasn't until they reached Donauwörth that news of Carloman's army came to light. One of his scouts brought a trader in from the marketplace that swore he had seen an army of Franks south of the Danube, encamped by the River Lech. It seemed impossible. How had Carloman's army crossed the river? How had they done it without being seen?

Odilo called his men to a halt and summoned his generals. They would have to make their own way across the river.

# CHAPTER THIRTY-TWO

*Banks of the River Lech*

C arloman leaned back against a boulder, letting the morning sun warm his face and the rich, wet, verdant spring assault his senses. He and Hamar had ridden out to the northernmost picket to await one of his scouts. He couldn't remember the last time he had done something so indulgent as to bask in the sun.

The decision to shift the field of battle had proved to be a good one. It allowed the men to rest, mend their battle wounds, repair their armor and hone their weapons. Carloman had roamed among the campfires the previous night as the soldiers clustered in groups singing bawdy songs and recounting fantastical tales of their battlefield exploits. It had taken only a few days of plentiful food and a victory over Theudebald to restore vitality to his army.

Carloman still didn't believe in luck, but if he did, he would have said it had finally turned in his favor. They had acquired a dozen large boats to ferry his men across the Danube. It was a challenging affair as the Danube's current was swift. It took them the better part of a day for the crossing, but hardly anyone witnessed the feat. People tended to avoid armies when they could and the aftermath of the battle with Theudebald was no exception. Once Hamar had secured the boats they were left alone to make their crossing.

"Without Pippin, we'll still be outnumbered." Hamar picked up a rock and threw it at a nearby rabbit.

"We are better trained. Odilo has recruited the Slavs and people from the east to fill out his ranks. They'll be no match for our regulars."

"Depends on how long the battle drags on. Numbers matter, my lord. They always have."

Carloman nodded. "Pippin will come."

Another rock targeted a passing squirrel. "I just hope he's in time."

A rider approached the picket from the north and the guards on watch waved for him to stop. Carloman and Hamar rose to their feet to move closer. The man's horse was lathered from a hard ride. It was the scout they were expecting. Carloman waved him forward.

"Odilo's army is crossing the Danube, milord. They should be here by late tomorrow."

"How many?"

"Close to twelve thousand men."

"Cavalry?"

"About five hundred."

Carloman and Hamar exchanged a look. Odilo's army was much larger than they had expected.

"Keep me informed as to their progress." Carloman said, dismissing the man with a wave. He turned to Hamar. "It will take Odilo longer than a day to move that many men."

"But surely, no more than two days at the most. That doesn't give Pippin much time to find us."

"Maybe we can improve our odds."

Hamar arched an eyebrow in question.

"Break camp." Carloman clapped his champion on the shoulder. "We're heading west. I want to keep Odilo thinking we're on the run."

"We're not?"

Carloman shook his head, smiling. "We waited here so his scouts could find us. I want him to bring his army here. If we attack from the west, they'll be penned in by the River Lech to the east and the Danube to the north. And it will give Pippin time to find us."

"And if he doesn't?"

Carloman frowned. "Let's just hope that he does."

* * *

Carloman set a leisurely pace, allowing his men to enjoy the mild spring weather. Although the sun had little to temper its direct gaze, a breeze off the Danube kept the infantrymen cool. They marched the better part of a day, camped for the night, waited another day, and then turned around to march back. He wasn't surprised to hear some of his men grumbling at the about face, but it was better to keep them busy than leaving them idle before a battle.

Even Drogo groused at the turn-around.

"Choosing ground is half the battle," Carloman told him. "If they cross the Danube to the east of us, we'll have them at a disadvantage. They'll be caught between the two rivers and us and have nowhere to run."

"Once we best them," Drogo said.

"Do you have doubts?"

"Don't you?"

Carloman grew serious. "Pippin and I have been in many battles, Drogo. Each one is different. They are ugly, brutal affairs that cost us far more than we anticipate in men and treasure. But we win. We always win. We come better trained, with better cavalry, and we seize every advantage available."

"They have a bigger army."

Carloman nodded. "Then we'll have to be smarter. We can't afford a prolonged melee. Their numbers would overwhelm us. We have to use our shields and our cavalry to advantage."

"Gunther says the Slavs are brutal fighters, savages who drink the blood of their enemies."

Carloman smiled at his son. "Gunther likes to tell stories. They are a savage people, but that's a disadvantage when facing a trained fighter. What did Fulrad tell you about your heart during battle?"

"He said to keep it cold. Anger and passion breed mistakes. It's best to be cold and devoid of emotion and let the other man make the mistakes."

"That's right. That's what he taught me. We have to be cold or we can't do what needs to be done."

"Are you ever afraid?"

Carloman thought on this for a moment, and then shook his head. "We are holy warriors. We have no need for fear. Ours is a righteous path. We're nothing but an instrument in His hands. And even if we die, we will be welcomed to His table in heaven."

* * *

They had followed the Danube, using a road that dated back to the days of Rome's legions. It was well built and designed for the rapid movement of troops. Despite Carloman's leisurely pace, they made good time. By late afternoon, Odilo's army came into view. Even with his scout's advance warning, Carloman still was astounded by the size of the rebel force. Their rank and file stretched across the horizon in an impressive array of might.

"They're signaling for a parley," Hamar called out.

"We'll be happy to oblige." Carloman nodded to Hamar and Drogo and the three of them rode forward to meet Odilo and his entourage.

\* \* \*

If Odilo recognized that two rivers penned him in, he didn't show it. He sat confidently in his saddle with a slight sneer on his face. Carloman did his best to contain his surprise at the presence of the pope's legate. How could Sergius side with a pagan? It left him dumbfounded.

Odilo and Carloman greeted each other in a polite exchange before Carloman addressed Sergius directly.

"Does the pope now endorse pagans, Sergius? What could bring you to stand against the Christian Knights of Francia?"

"I was summoned by your sister, Hiltrude." Sergius was as imperious as ever. "As you may recall, she was baptized by the same hand as you."

"To what purpose did she call you?"

"To stop this war. You must recognize – "

"That there's no need for war." Carloman finished, addressing Odilo directly. "If you are here to renew your pledge of fealty and faith, I'll be happy to withdraw."

Odilo said nothing.

"Theudebald stood against me and was vanquished. His army of Hessians and Alemannians kissed the foot of the cross and pledged their fealty to me, just as you once pledged. Yet here you are with an army at your back. Must I make you kneel again?"

"I asked you to avoid this war, Carloman. I begged you to. It was you who broke the terms of succession. It was you who went to war and imprisoned Gripho."

"It couldn't be avoided."

"Of course, it could have been avoided."

"There can be only one religion in Francia."

"You are in Bavaria now, Carloman. By what right–"

"Peace, good sirs!" Sergius held up his hand to forestall

further argument. "I'm here at the behest of His Holiness the Pope. You will listen to his wishes!"

Despite his growing anger, Carloman nodded.

"Surely you both recognize our true enemy," Sergius began. "We are besieged by the Saracen in the south, the west, and in the east. We cannot afford to waste our blood warring amongst ourselves."

"These men are pagan," Carloman protested.

"But they're not Saracen. If you want to save Christianity, Carloman, save this war for another day. None of us can afford its consequences. The church has need of all your armies in the war against Islam. It's been only seven years since your father stopped the Saracen horde at Poitiers, and a year since you beat them back at Narbonne. You were there, Carloman. Have you forgotten them so quickly?"

Carloman's face was a mask. "You of all people should see that there can be no peace without adherence to the faith."

"All in good time, Carloman." Sergius pleaded. "But this...this isn't the time. You rule without a king. You violate your own succession. You have rebellions in the east and west. Let us negotiate a truce until a Merovingian sits on the throne of Francia."

"Will you support the Merovingian, Carloman?" Odilo asked.

"He has yet to be proved legitimate." Carloman knew it was a weak answer, but it was all he had to offer.

Odilo chuckled at his evasion. "And if he is?"

"We'll make a decision at that time."

"The church has already deemed his claim valid." Sergius said. "Unless you have information that contradicts our findings – "

"We will make a decision at that time!"

Odilo grinned. "It's not like you to defy the church, Carloman."

"You don't speak for the church!"

"And you are not a king. If you agree to put the Merovingian on the throne, I'll accept a truce until we have a king to address our grievances."

Sergius was quick with his support. "The church agrees, Carloman. Delay this war. Elevate the Merovingian. Save our might for the true enemy of the church. The pope has made his position very clear. Accept the truce. And I promise the church will act as an arbiter for settling this dispute."

Carloman wasn't happy with this turn of events. Sergius was offering a complication he hadn't considered, and it made him uncomfortable. He understood why the pope might want to intercede, but was it the right choice?

Odilo's army was substantially larger than either he or Pippin had anticipated. Defeating it would be a challenge and the loss of men substantial, but could he afford to leave Odilo's army intact? If he backed down now, they effectively would lose Bavaria and have a hostile enemy to the east. With the Lombards in the south and Waifar in the west, enemies would surround them.

One other factor clouded his thoughts. With Pippin childless, Drogo stood alone to inherit the family's power. He was already old enough to exert his authority. But if Odilo and Trudi had a boy, the child would have every right to claim his legacy as a grandson of Charles and to challenge Drogo's claim. With an army the size of Odilo's, he would be able to enforce it.

Odilo interrupted his thoughts. "You are far from home with half an army. You've been bloodied in battle, while my men are fresh and ready to fight. We have you outnumbered, and the odds are likely that we will prevail."

He paused. "Take the peace, Carloman. It's the right choice."

Carloman shook his head. It wasn't the right choice. They had to fight. It was either war now or split the kingdom and allow paganism to prevail. There was no room for a truce. For the hundredth time since he left Paris, Carloman silently cursed Pippin for his absence in a time of need.

"Either pledge fealty and kiss the cross or I'll see you on the battlefield in the morning."

Sergius swore under his breath.

Odilo nodded. "Until morning, then."

❊ ❊ ❊

As the sun peaked over the horizon it threw long shadows over the field of battle, obscuring Carloman's view of Odilo's troops. He had heard, rather than seen, their march to the battlefield in the pre-dawn hours. It was hard to disguise the sound of an army's approach. Drums counted out the cadence for thousands of synchronized marching steps. Metal clanged against metal and horses whinnied and huffed in the cold morning air.

Carloman watched with Hamar and Drogo as Odilo's infantry marched across the field in four broad phalanxes, each backed by cavalry and archers. He would have preferred to see a single phalanx – two at the most – to avoid stretching thin his own line. Given the superior size of Odilo's army, it was an intelligent strategy. It was what he would have done in the Bavarian's place.

A trickle of mucous ran out of Carloman's damaged nose and he blew it out onto the ground. "Four lines!" he commanded.

"Huh-yah!" Hamar wheeled his horse and gave orders to arrange the troops to mirror Odilo's formation.

Drogo seemed uneasy. "We'll be only two regiments deep."

Carloman nodded. "We'll have to rely on our cavalry."

The two armies marched in formation towards the center of the field. At fifty paces, Odilo raised his arm, calling for a halt. Carloman mirrored the gesture and waited. A single combatant strode forward. He was a giant of a man, dressed in Bavarian armor with broad shoulders and powerful arms. He was screaming, his face contorted in rage, and Carloman had trouble deciphering his words.

"He's challenging our champion." Drogo said. "He says we're women dressed in men's clothes."

Hamar laughed. "Doesn't say much for Bavarian women."

"He says our God is a weak God, a puny man who refused to defend himself."

"Half right." Carloman said.

"He spits on our God."

"That's enough," Carloman said. "Hamar?"

Hamar unsheathed his sword and scissored his legs to dismount. "Happily, milord." He strode to the center of the field with a swagger of confidence. When he stood face-to-face with the challenger it became clear how much smaller Hamar was. He looked like an adolescent next to the challenger.

Drogo's face blanched. "Good Lord, he's big."

The two combatants circled each other. The giant shuffled, adopting the Window Guard stance that held the pommel high against his ear and the sword pointing forward. By contrast, Hamar walked casually, holding his weapon low between his legs in Full Iron Gate.

The giant attacked with a broad sweep of his sword. Hamar stepped back in a fade to avoid the blow. The giant lunged, stabbing for Hamar's midsection, but Hamar deflected the thrust with his own blade and again they circled. Again, the giant lunged. Hamar met the blade and, with a quick riposte under the attack, stabbed the challenger's left shoulder. The man howled in rage and advanced, chopping down with a series of overhand blows. Although Hamar's sword met every one, the power of the blows forced him back. Seizing the moment, the challenger advanced, raining down blow after blow. Hamar continued to retreat, overwhelmed by the assault, his sword flashing to defend against each strike of the challenger's attack.

"He's faltering." Drogo said.

"He's looking for weaknesses," Carloman said with more confidence than he felt.

Hamar regained his footing and, again, the two combatants circled. Hamar struck an overhand blow, which was easily met. He swung a blow meant for the giant's left shoulder, but the huge man parried, and their blades crossed above them. Hamar tried to grapple for the pommel of the man's sword, but the challenger butted Hamar in the face and he staggered away from the attack.

The giant leapt to take advantage. Again, Hamar fell back beneath a series of overhand blows, trying desperately to find space to regain his footing. With a roar the challenger swept his blade in a wide arc designed to cut Hamar's torso in two.

Hamar jumped back to avoid it, then leapt forward in an empty fade, positioning himself behind the giant's sword arm. With a quick lunge, he stabbed up, catching the man in his armpit. When Hamar removed his blade, blood cascaded downward. The giant spun to face him roaring in defiance. He slashed down with his blade in a diagonal cut; Hamar stepped aside to evade it; the man lunged again; Hamar deflected. The giant stumbled; Hamar withheld his attack. The challenger lunged and again Hamar faded backwards, ignoring the opportunity to riposte.

Soon the entire right side of Hamar's opponent was covered in blood and the red liquid pooled at his feet. The giant shuffled two steps, trying to lift his blade, but instead fell to a knee. He looked up in surprise as Hamar raised the pommel of his sword to his head in salute. The Giant pitched forward, face-first into his own blood.

Hamar raised his blade skyward and the Franks roared their appreciation. He turned back to face Odilo's army, and with spread his arms wide, waited for a new challenger.

None came. Instead, at a barked command, all four phalanxes of the Bavarian infantry stepped forward as one. The battle had begun.

# CHAPTER THIRTY-THREE

*The Abbey at Chelles*

T he abbess readily agreed to Miette's request. After telling Salau she would be spending the night, Miette returned to the Abbey where the abbess herself showed her to a dormitory that housed twenty other women. The room she gave to Miette was the size of a small closet, just enough for a bed, a prie-dieu, and a chamber pot.

The abbess was a large woman with a deep Germanic accent that Miette found intimidating.

"You will stay here in this room. You'll wear no gold or jewelry, no makeup, no gown. I've provided you with a robe to wear and a scarf to cover your head. Wear them at all times. Supper is at the seventeenth bell. Vespers one hour later. Collatio at nineteenth and then Compline to end the day. Matins will be at the third bell. After that you are to pray on your own until Terce, at eight. You'll be expected to share in all chores until dinner at the fourteenth bell. Sister Sunnichild will direct you."

Supper was hard bread and cheese. Miette knew enough not to complain. It was something she could live with for a day or two.

Sunnichild sat with her for the meal. "Attendance is required for every mass," she said. "Meals on the other hand are optional. Unlike other abbeys, Chelles offers two meals each day, but neither offers any meat. We eat what we grow."

Miette did her best to look interested but spent much of her time trying to look for Hélène and Bertrada among the faces in attendance. It was hard to distinguish one nun from another given that most were covered with habits and cowls. She studied the faces, dismissing the older and younger nuns and tried to pick distinguishing features on the rest. Unfortunately, Sunnichild made the task more difficult by continuing to make small talk, which forced Miette to pull her eyes away from the search.

Miette decided to turn the table on her. "I have a question for you."

Sunnichild put down her bread and waited.

"I've been having a difficult time believing what happened to Bertrada and her sister. They were in the company of Tedbalt of Soissons at a ball I hosted for the future king. They were offered a ride home by Lady Hélène and on their way, highwaymen attacked the carriage. Afterwards, the driver was found dead as were several of the highwaymen. All four of the nobles escaped."

Sunnichild nodded. "That matches the description that Pippin gave me."

"How is that possible?"

"I don't understand."

"How did two women and one nobleman, defeat three highwaymen?"

"I don't know." Sunnichild shrugged.

"By all accounts, Tedbalt was unarmed when he left."

"Perhaps there were arms in the carriage."

Miette scoffed. "It seems unlikely that he could be so proficient as to best all three – even if he had a sword, especially caught as they were unawares."

"Yet the facts remain."

Whatever else she was, Sunnichild seemed unflappable. Miette took another tack. "How well do you know Lady Hélène?"

"Well enough."

"Some say she was Charles's assassin."

Sunnichild chuckled. "Hélène was one of Charles's lovers. She used the rumor to hide their trysts and to frighten those who liked to gossip."

"You didn't object?"

Sunnichild raised an eyebrow. "Do you object to the young men your husband keeps?"

Miette was taken aback. She hadn't known her husband's secret was known at court.

Sunnichild patted her hand. "We have none of those concerns inside these walls. Here, such things remain in the past. All the passion, the violence, the deceit – it doesn't touch us here."

Miette didn't know about "passion" and "violence," but she was pretty sure "deceit" was no stranger to the Abbey at Chelles.

❊ ❊ ❊

Miette was already awake due to hunger pangs when the bells sounded for Matins. She couldn't imagine how these women survived on so little food. She put on her robe and made use of the chamber pot, pouring its contents out the window when she was finished. Sunnichild found her and they made their way to the chapel for Matins.

Miette tried to stifle a yawn. "It's so dark. Why do they hold Matins at three in the morning?"

"You get used to it after a few weeks."

"Where's Agnès?"

"She'll meet us at the chapel."

Miette tried to keep her voice sounding casual. "Tell me

about her."

"There's not much to tell."

"Why is she here?"

"Part of taking the vows is that we leave our former lives behind. I know little of her history, only that she needed someone to act as a mentor inside these walls."

"She's a peasant," Miette said. "You can hear it in her voice. How did she come to be accepted by such a place as Chelles?"

Sunnichild walked a few paces before responding. "Charity is a cornerstone of the church. Not all our sisters are of nobility."

It was a lie. And Miette became all the more interested in Agnès because of it. The peasant would lead her to Hélène and Bertrada. She was sure of it.

After Matins, the abbess put Miette to work in a garden, planting seeds for the bean crop. While she knelt in the dirt, she searched the faces of the sisters she could see for Bertrada and Hélène. As before, there were too many nuns and their faces too similar. She had spied Agnès early. The peasant woman spent most of the morning fetching water from the well. She brought bucket after bucket into the abbey for those who scrubbed the chapel floors. To Miette's surprise, the woman never tired or broke a sweat, despite the warmth of the day.

After her chores were complete, Miette hurried to stand by the meal hall where the nuns gathered after their daily tasks. Again, she played the supplicant, curtsying for the more aged sisters and greeting the others. It was the closest she had come to many of them and she quickly screened those who filed in for the afternoon meal.

After it became clear that all who were going to dine were in the hall, Miette abandoned her search and took her meal with Sunnichild. They were hiding Bertrada. She could feel it in her heart. Sunnichild was too cautious and Agnès too mysterious. Bertrada was at the Abbey. The question was:

where?

After the meal was finished, Miette returned to the dormitory and gathered her things. Unless they allowed her to search the Abbey, there was little more she could do. She left her room and made for the abbey gate. She ran outside, hoping to find Salau waiting, but he wasn't there. She accosted the first person she saw.

"Where's the nearest inn?"

The man pointed down the street. Miette sprinted until she saw a sign with a bed on it. She ran inside and found Salau and the two soldiers sitting at a table with clay mugs of ale before them. She sat down and took a drink from his mug.

Salau didn't look pleased. "Do you have anything to report?"

"I haven't seen her, but I know Bertrada is there. Sunnichild is definitely hiding something and there's a postulate... a peasant postulate in the Abbey at Chelles!

"We need to send word to Childeric. To find her, we'll need to search the Abbey."

Salau and the two soldiers stood and left the table.

"Wait! Where are you going?" Miette followed them out into the street. They were running for the Abbey gate. She tried to catch up with them but they quickly outpaced her. She walked and ran as best as she could back to the abbey. The gate she had left open was ajar and she made her way back to the meal hall.

Salau was outside, holding a nun by the neck against the wall. "Where did they go? I know they're here."

The nun whimpered. "I don't know."

The hand held a blade that seemed to breeze by the nun as if nothing had touched her. But then her neck opened like a melon and blood poured down her robe. She fumbled for a moment, trying to hold the rift at her throat together, but fell forward to her knees and then toppled sideways to the ground. Salau had already moved into the meal hall.

Miette stared at the horror. Salau wasn't there to escort

her. He was there to kill Hélène and Bertrada. This was her fault; her words led directly to this attack. These nuns were dying at her instigation. Guilt and sorrow assaulted her, followed by a fear that she had soiled herself for eternity. There was screaming coming from the meal hall. Miette stumbled to the door.

Inside the hall, the bodies of two more nuns lay on the floor, their eyes open in vacant shock, their blood pooling around them. Salau held another nun, his knife before her face. "Where did they go?"

"Here." Hélène and Agnès appeared across the meal hall. They had taken off their postulate robes and stood in what looked like men's breeches. They each carried a long staff. Sunnichild and Bertrada – her belly already swollen with child – came in behind them.

Salau grinned and turned to face Hélène and Agnès. His two soldiers spread out behind him, moving to flank their quarry as they drew swords.

Hélène moved forward so fast that Miette couldn't believe it. Like a dancer, she twisted and twirled her staff moving in and out between the three men turning aside their blades and attacking their arms and legs. Agnès followed her into the fray and if anything, she was faster. They leapt in and out of harm's way challenging the swords before them. Neither side had landed a blow as sword challenged staff and staff challenged sword.

And then, with an audible crack, Agnès caught one of the soldiers on the side of his leg and he fell to the knee. Although Hélène was fighting Salau, her staff swung across her body and slammed into the side of the man's face. He fell forward like a rag doll. Now there were two soldiers left to fight.

Salau attacked with a fury, but he couldn't draw close to the women. They spun and twisted away in their macabre dance. The second soldier went down with a blow to the head and then it was Salau fighting alone. He shifted his stance, holding his sword before him in a defensive posture.

He moved carefully, always keeping the two women in front of him. Their staffs swirled before him. Miette couldn't tell what was feint, and what was attack, until the staffs landed.

But Salau was quick and parried most of the blows. The women slowed their attack, as if they recognized more care was needed with him. They kept up the assault, forcing Salau to parry one and then the other. As time passed, he visibly began to tire and his arms dropped lower.

Miette saw no signal, but as one the two women split apart to attack from opposite sides. Salau blocked the blow from Agnès. Hélène's caught him the ribs. He grunted and hunched over that side. He lowered his sword and Agnès went in for the kill. Just as her long staff arced down for his head, Salau's sword tipped up and he drove it through her stomach until it punched out her back. He grinned at the surprised look on her face.

Hélène screamed and reached for Agnès. Salau punched her with his fist and she went down.

"No, no. no. no. no." Miette looked frantically about her for some way to stop him. She saw a knife next to one of the soldiers and grabbed it. She couldn't let him kill her. She couldn't let him win.

Hélène was on the ground trying desperately to fend off Salau. He kept up the attack, so she didn't have time to get back to her feet. He circled left, turning his back to Miette. She hesitated and then with a shout took the knife in both hands and stabbed down at Salau's back. She caught him just above the waist and felt the knife push into his flesh. He arched his back against the pain, and she stabbed again. And again.

Salau straightened awkwardly and turned to find his assailant. He looked at Miette, first with surprise, and then with fury. He backhanded her across the face and she collapsed to the ground. Turning to face her, he raised his sword high above her head. "You, bitch."

Miette knew she was going to die but couldn't seem to move her arms and legs.

Then, from behind, Hélène's long staff came down on his head. With a sickening crunch, the left side of his skull caved in under the blow. Bone and brain matter spewed all over Miette. Salau fell to his knees, the long staff still in his head. Hélène had to kick his head away to free it.

Throwing the staff aside in disgust, Hélène knelt beside Agnès. She pulled the peasant woman into her arms. "No, my love. Not this way. Don't die. Don't leave me."

Agnès lifted her hand to cup Hélène's face. "Ssshhh. I was stupid. It was an old trick. I should have known better."

Blood was everywhere.

Hélène was kissing Agnès on the lips. "Please. Please, don't go."

The color drained from Agnès's face. "I love you," she said and then, "Take care of Patrice." It seemed more of a question than a statement.

Hélène nodded. "Of course, my love." And then Agnès was gone. Hélène held her, rocking the woman back and forth like a child, a growl of rage coming from someplace deep inside her.

Sunnichild stepped forward and put her hand on Hélène's shoulder. The gesture seemed to quiet Hélène. With one final kiss, Hélène lowered Agnès to the ground and closed the woman's eyes.

When she stood up, Hélène turned towards Miette. "You did this. You brought them here."

Still on the floor, Miette backed away until she hit a wall. Hélène's words were a death sentence. Miette could hear it in her voice. "I was just supposed to find her. I didn't know." Miette whimpered. It was a lie, of course. In her heart, she did know, had known. What other end could she have expected? She had just chosen not to think about it. All she had cared about was serving Childeric. "I didn't know," she repeated.

Hélène picked up her long staff but Sunnichild stood in her way. "There's been enough death."

"Just one more," Hélène said.

"It won't be one. Her death will start a civil war with the Neustrians. Let her go."

Hélène didn't move. Bertrada stepped forward from the back of the room. She put her hand on Hélène's shoulder. "She stopped him in the end. She saved your life."

"After she betrayed us."

Bertrada leaned close and whispered. "The path of justice is hard."

It took a moment, but Hélène nodded.

Bertrada took the long staff out of her hands. "You and Agnès saved my life. I'll be forever in your debt. But now we have to go. They've found us."

Hélène stared at Miette long and hard before turning to leave. Miette shuddered; Hélène's eyes were empty, as dead as Salau's.

❄ ❄ ❄

Miette started for the gate only to find two nuns closing it. "Soldiers! Soldiers are coming!" They shut the gate and ran inside. Miette didn't know what to do. Had Salau sent word to the king? She could hear the commotion outside as riders approached. There had to be dozens of them. One of them banged on the gate.

"Open this gate or we'll break it down!"

The abbess and Sunnichild along with half a dozen elderly nuns entered the courtyard. Many clutched each other in distress.

"They're Pippin's men." Sunnichild said to the abbess. "I sent Gunther a message when Lady Ragomfred asked to stay at the Abbey. I'm only sorry that they arrived too late."

The abbess was red in the face. She clearly didn't know what to do.

"Open the gate, Abbess. They *will* knock it down."

After an agonizing moment, the abbess nodded and two

of the nuns opened the gate. Twenty men on horse pushed through it. Pippin's man Gunther was in their lead. For some reason, Miette found it reassuring to see him.

Several of the nuns started screaming, "Murder! Murder!"

"Silence!" Gunther shouted. He looked to the abbess and Sunnichild. "What goes on here?"

Sunnichild stepped forward. "Thank you for coming Gunther."

"Milady – Sister" he corrected himself. "Your message said Bertrada was here. Is she alive?"

"Yes. Thankfully. But the king's men were here." Sunnichild pointed to Miette. "She brought them. Once she confirmed Bertrada was here, they came to kill her. Three nuns – and one postulate – are dead. As are the king's men."

"I didn't know." Miette's voice sounded pathetic, even to her own ears.

Gunther ignored her and focused on Sunnichild. "How did you stop them?"

"It was Hélène."

If Gunther was surprised by her answer, he hid it well. Pippin's man merely stroked his chin and nodded. "Bertrada and Lady Hélène! Get your things. We're going back to the palace."

The abbess tried to protest, but Gunther cut her off. "I don't have time to argue, Abbess. I took enough of a risk leaving the palace for this long. I'll let Pippin sort this out when he returns. Lady Ragomfred, you will be accompanying us as well."

All Miette could manage was a nod. Nothing mattered anymore. Her life was finished.

# CHAPTER THIRTY-FOUR

*The River Lech*

C arloman's shields had stood against Odilo's four columns for over eight hours before the imbalance in their numbers began to show. His right flank was falling back, slowly giving way before the larger Bavarian army. As he had throughout the day, he rotated new men in to replace the wounded and used his cavalry to harass the Bavarians, but it wasn't enough to hold the line.

Carloman diverted men from his left flank to support them, but Odilo quickly took advantage and his left columns were forced to retreat. He was giving up far too much ground. The knowledge was disorienting. He had been in too many battles not to read the signs. He was losing. He had never considered the possibility. If he didn't do something soon, his army would be routed.

Fury and humiliation coursed through him. "Goddamn it!" he shouted. As a holy warrior, he served as the right hand of God. He could not fail. Yet the specter of failure was all around him. Everything he had fought for and everything his father had fought for would fail. How could he face Greta and Drogo? How could he face Pippin? Carloman searched for

Drogo across the battlefield. The boy had such faith in him.

He would be a pariah, a jest in history. The Church would be weakened. Paganism would flourish. Drogo's succession would be challenged; the kingdom split.

Carloman howled in frustration. The sound grew in him, a vehicle for his rage until it became a full-throated battle cry. He could not allow it. He would not allow it.

His horse was moving before the middle of his right flank began to give way. Bavarians and Slavs pushed through the line in a fury trying to break it in two. Carloman kicked his warhorse, driving it into the breach. Those on foot, who had broken through, paid for their audacity. Carloman hacked them into pieces. The cavalry followed him into the fray and the line stiffened, but he knew it wouldn't last. His men were exhausted. He searched the field in desperation. He needed more men. He shouted to Drogo to take his place and turned to the rear. He raced behind the infantry to where the tents held his wounded and rode his horse among them.

"Get up! Get back to the line!" he shouted. "Get back to the line!"

His men looked at him as if he were daft. They were holding bandages to open wounds and severed limbs. Many lay on the ground.

Carloman drew his sword and rode down the nearest man. With a broad sweep of his blade, he cleaved the soldier's head from his body. "Get back to the line! I'll kill every last one of you. Get back to the line!"

Those who could move scrambled to avoid him. He screamed like a demon swinging his sword at anyone who lagged behind. His fury herded nearly a hundred and fifty men back into the battle behind the third and fourth column. Their added weight strengthened the shields and the line reformed. Carloman rode the length of his army screaming every oath he could remember. If his men were to fear anyone, he wanted it to be him.

An hour passed. Then another. And still the line held. As

dusk fell into darkness, the Bavarian horns called for retreat and Carloman let himself believe that they had survived. He knelt on the battlefield and prayed to Saint Michael to intercede for another day's grace. Every soldier left on the field knelt with him.

Hamar met him in his tent. "Five hundred men lost."

Carloman nodded.

"We can't defeat him this way, Carloman. Odilo will win by attrition. Sooner or later, their numbers will overwhelm us."

"What would you have me do? Retreat?"

Hamar's face was cut from stone. "Let's find better ground. We can harass their advance, stretch their supply lines, and use surprise to sap their strength. If we line up in four columns tomorrow, we'll lose."

His words cut deeply into Carloman's pride. He would never run before Odilo's army. He would never look weak and afraid. A leader's weakness fueled his enemy's fire. He had to fight. He had to win. It was his only choice.

"Only a third of Odilo's army is comprised of hardened Bavarian troops. That's what we fought today. The rest are Slavs. They're nothing but savages. With each passing day Odilo will lose his best men. In a day or two, we'll be fighting peasants with sticks. We just have to hold on till then. Our cavalry will keep us whole until Pippin arrives."

Hamar seemed less than convinced. "And if Pippin doesn't?"

Carloman ignored him and went to bed. His night was restless with specters of doubt and failure. He ran over his battle plan again and again, looking for any possible advantage. Sleep came and went of its own in accord, further undermining his sense of reality. For a time, he walked among the battlefield's dead with his father. Charles kept asking, "What have you done?"

❊ ❊ ❊

Carloman rose well before dawn and walked among the tents housing his army. The feeling of dread he had experienced on the battlefield bloomed again inside him. All his life he had fought by his father's side. He had never once doubted the outcome of a battle. The success and failure always had rested with Charles alone. And Charles never lost. Now that the responsibility fell to him, Carloman understood the weight of it. He alone would be given credit for a successful outcome, just as he alone would bear the blame of defeat.

He went to rouse Hamar. His champion was awake in an instant.

"Walk with me." They went out into the feeble light of the morning and with the use of a nearby stick, Carloman drew battle lines in the dirt outside his champion's tent. "Odilo will push hard on our right flank to exploit the weakness he found there yesterday."

Hamar nodded. "I can divert men from the left to shore up our strength."

"Make sure we don't offer Odilo too thin of a line. He needs to see an army full of regulars. Put all the wounded who can fight behind our left flank."

"Huh-yah."

"And then I've got one more strategy I'd like to employ."

*  *  *

Odilo watched the sun creep over the horizon much as it had on the first day of battle, casting long shadows of his men. They shifted uneasily in their lines, waiting for the combat to begin. The sounds of their apprehension – metal shields and armor clanging in their restlessness – only fueled their disquiet.

This time, there would be no call for champions. At Odilo's signal, the horns blew and the Bavarian columns flowed across the field.

Carloman, too, signaled for his men to advance and the distance between the two armies disappeared under the relentless march of infantrymen.

At twenty paces, he raised a signal flag and the first lines of his army's right flank fell to the ground as if they had been slain. Odilo stood up in his saddle to get a better view of what was occurring. It had to be some kind of trick.

Behind the fallen shields stood archers, crossbows cocked at the ready.

"Shields!" Odilo screamed. "Shields!"

The first row of archers triggered their bows and a wave of arrows slammed into Odilo's left column. Scores fell before the onslaught, arrows protruding from their eye sockets and necks. A second volley took a similar toll. His men were screaming and cowering behind their shields. A third volley flew. His line was disintegrating.

Again, and again, they fired, wreaking devastation with each volley.

"Charge!" Odilo put heels to his warhorse. "Charge! Take out the archers!"

His cavalry swept outside the decimated shield wall to run down the archers, buying some much-needed time for his line to reform.

At a command from Carloman, the Franks' archers dropped back, and his shield line reformed as if nothing had happened. They raised pikes against Odilo's cavalry, and the warhorses veered away in panic. The Franks' infantry turned to face Odilo's men. They raised their shields and closed, pushing with such force that Odilo's men fell back, struggling to hold a coherent line. Odilo ordered the cavalry to harass the Franks' progress along the edges, but his entire left flank was giving way under the onslaught.

The fight within the shield wall grew desperate. Odilo took the cavalry to harass Carloman's right flank, hoping to use his presence as a rallying point. Men cheered him as he crashed into Franks' infantry, but their voices were muted.

They were too focused, fighting for their lives. Odilo brought forward the first of his reserves. If he couldn't tactically beat Carloman, he would overwhelm him.

❊ ❊ ❊

Carloman fell back alongside Drogo to see the shape of the battle. While his strategy had worked, it had only succeeded in giving him more time. There were simply too many Bavarians. Odilo had more men to throw into the battle and it took away any advantage he temporarily might have.

An hour passed. Two. Carloman's line was weakening and he had no more reserves to draw upon. His eyes searched the horizon. He wasn't sure they would last until nightfall. The specter of defeat hung over him like a dark cloud. *God help us*, he prayed.

To shore up his line, he ordered his men to fall back in a structured retreat. It was his only choice. As the Bavarians advanced over the battlefield, they stabbed the bodies of the wounded Franks lying in their wake. Helpless to stop it, Carloman offered a prayer for their souls.

The only thing keeping them in the fight was the superiority of his cavalry, but even that couldn't stop the Bavarian advance. Across the field, his line was in retreat. It was only a matter of time before defeat was inevitable.

Carloman pictured the surrender in his mind and knew he couldn't abide it. He wouldn't concede as had Rasling. He would not kneel before Odilo. He would not bow before a pagan god and renounce his faith. He roared his frustration like a wounded animal.

An idea pricked at the corner of his thoughts, its implications so dire that he almost dismissed it out of hand. But as the concept took shape in his mind, he seized hold of it with all his might. In an instant, the din of the battle quieted and the pace of it slowed. His infantry still strained inside the shield wall and his cavalry still pranced on the edges of the fray, but Carloman stood outside the battle.

How little he had accomplished! He was never the man Charles had been and now he would never get the chance. The fate of Francia would be left to Pippin.

The thought of his brother redoubled his fears. Pippin didn't have his faith, his political acumen, or his vision. And he was hardly a match for the Merovingian. Carloman's eyes welled at the thought. He had failed. He had failed everyone he loved.

The sounds of the battle roared back to him and Carloman blinked to clear his eyes. Making the sign of the cross, he called for Hamar.

"We're going to mount a cavalry charge between the third and fourth columns to break their line."

"That's suicide. Their pikes will turn the horses and we'll get cut down."

"Not if we force a break. If we can cut through, and make a run at Odilo, we have a chance to turn the battle."

"Not a good chance. We're better off holding the line until nightfall."

"We won't make it. It's the charge or nothing."

Hamar was no fool. He understood what such a charge meant. "Then I will lead it."

"No, old friend. This is my war. My doing. Its fate rides with me."

Hamar nodded. "As do I."

Carloman put his hand on Hamar's shoulder, an act of intimacy he rarely displayed. "Thank you, my friend."

He then sent for Drogo. It took only a minute for his son to arrive.

"Hamar and I are going to lead a cavalry charge to break their line. You have command of the battle, son."

Tears sprang in Drogo's eyes. He knew it was lunacy. "Is there no other way?"

Carloman shook his head. "The fighting is desperate.

The men won't last much longer. Should we fail, organize an orderly retreat. Show Odilo enough spear and he won't follow you tonight. Fall back until you can join Pippin."

Color blossomed in Drogo's cheeks. "You're the arm of God, Father. You will not fail."

Carloman smiled. "You're a good son, Drogo. Always stand in the light of our Lord." He made the sign of the cross over Drogo's forehead. "I give you the blessing my father gave me."

"Father, no – " Emotion choked off Drogo's voice.

"Our line is sworn to preserve the might of Francia and to champion the will of God. I leave this solemn task in your hands and in the hands of your children and your children's children. Be fearless in the face of our enemies and humble in the hands of the Father. Be true, my son. And may the blessing of God, the Father, the Son, and the Holy Ghost come upon you and remain with you forever."

Although Drogo sat straight in his saddle, tears streamed down his face. Carloman and Hamar turned as one. At a signal from Hamar, the cavalry fell in behind them.

Carloman led them in a long arc behind the line until the cavalry was at full gallop. He drove them straight up through the center of the battle, between the second and third columns, banking on surprise to catch the Bavarian shields before their pikes could be raised. It was a risky move. If they failed, the lead horses would be gored and the charge halted abruptly, leaving the cavalry vulnerable. Even if they were successful, there was a chance that the lead horses could be cut off before the bulk of the cavalry was through the line.

They burst through the opening between the two columns before the pikes were raised and Carloman plowed into the left side of the Bavarian infantry. His horse became a battering ram and Carloman chopped his sword down on any and all that were near him. Hamar rode beside him and together they pushed deep inside the enemy. It took a minute before Carloman realized he was screaming in rage as they drove a wedge into the enemy's forces.

Deeper and deeper, they plunged, spreading death in a wake behind them. Carloman didn't look back to see if the cavalry had broken through behind them. It no longer mattered. He was a dead man either way. Those first through such a breach never survived.

Somehow, this knowledge lifted him, elevating his mind and body in the last moments of life. The battle again slowed around him. His mind seemed three steps ahead of his sword, and all who came before it were swept away.

A blade grazed his shield arm, but Carloman didn't feel it; he was impervious. "I am the arm of God," he screamed as the bodies piled up around him. The power he wielded was euphoric; surely, God's touch was upon him.

A pike gored his horse and Carloman jumped free to avoid being pinned. He wheeled to cut off the arm of the man responsible and laid waste to those around him. He was surrounded and alone on foot. A part of him recognized that those he fought wore only a patchwork of armor and wielded wooden staffs, peasants who had taken up arms. Carloman took their souls as well.

In the distance, horns blared, but the weight of the war no longer held Carloman. All that mattered was happening now in this moment. His sword wove a pattern of blood around him as he wheeled and spun to meet his attackers. He no longer could see Hamar but didn't have time to look for him. He pushed further into the sea of soldiers and they fell before him as he became death incarnate.

He saw the rock before it hit him. He snapped his head away, hoping to soften the blow, but the shock of it jolted through him. He stumbled under its impact but caught his balance before falling. The entire left side of his face grew numb and his sense of grace and euphoria dissipated. The touch of God lifted from him and the battle rushed back to its normal pace.

He found himself alone atop a small hill, blood running

into his eyes and without his shield. He held his sword before him with both hands, trying to see the threat before him. He was encircled, but no one was close enough to strike.

Another rock struck him on the arm. A third hit him in the back.

Carloman staggered under the blow. "Fight, goddamn you!" But they stayed away from his sword. "Cowards!" he shouted, and then realized they were peasants. Of course, they wouldn't fight.

Another rock hit him and another. He blinked, trying to clear his eyes. He sensed movement to his left and swung blindly, hoping to capture one more death in his struggle, but his blade found nothing, and he stumbled off balance.

"Hamar!" He called for his champion. If he was to die, he wanted Hamar to be with him. "HAMAR!" A wooden staff caught him across the back and Carloman went down to a knee. He struggled, trying to get back to his feet.

"HAMAR!!"

Another glancing blow hit his head and Carloman went down. They descended upon him then, beating him and kicking him from all sides. He tried to cover his head with his arms, but it wasn't sufficient. Blow after blow pushed him further and further from consciousness. As the darkness took him, he tried to remember the prayer for extreme unction, but his memory failed him. Instead, he held out his hand in supplication as he had a thousand times to St. Michael.

But his guardian angel didn't answer.

# CHAPTER THIRTY-FIVE

*Regensburg*

By the time Trudi heard about Theudebald's return to Regensburg, the Alemannian had already taken control of the fort's garrison and closed the gates to the city.

According to Hans, after Theudebald lost the battle to Carloman, he rallied together what was left of the Hessians and Alemannians by promising to restore their arms and their dignity. Once the men had reassembled, he had led them directly back to the gates of Regensburg which opened to him as an allied combatant. Theudebald immediately ordered his men to raid the armory and seize the city.

Trudi fought to keep her panic from overwhelming her. It was her worst fear come to call. With Odilo away, she and the city would be at Theudebald's mercy. She had to get away. She had to run.

She didn't even make it to the corridor before the realization hit her. She couldn't run. Not in her condition. "Christ!" Trudi tried to quell her panic.

"Milady?" Hans stood looking at her expectantly.

Trudi returned to her room. "You must secure the palace." She tried to keep her voice calm. "Send to the nobles left in the city for reinforcement and get me a messenger. I need to send word to Odilo."

"Of course, milady." Hans bowed to take his leave, but Trudi grabbed his arm.

"Theudebald must not take the palace. Promise me!"

Hans stood to attention. "You have my word, milady."

The relief she found in his promise, however, was short-lived. A stabbing pain lanced across her stomach, forcing her to grab the back of a chair for support. It took several moments to subside.

"Not now. Not now!" Trudi mumbled under her breath as she made her way to her balcony. From there she had an unimpeded view of the square outside the palace and the road leading up to its gate. The road had an "S" shape to it, as if the Romans who built it were inebriated. She watched as Hans mobilized her guard to reinforce the door and stepped aside as archers raced up the palace stairs to take their places in the highest of the palace windows.

It didn't take long before Theudebald's men arrived.

There were only five of them, a brutish bunch that bullied their way through the square, shoving aside all they encountered. The leader, a broad-chested Alemannian newly dressed in Bavarian armor, waved aside her guard as he approached the gate. He seemed genuinely surprised when they refused.

His tone was imperious. "I have orders to take control of the palace and to place the Lady Hiltrude under guard for her protection."

Hans, to his credit, was calm and professional. "The Lady Hiltrude is already protected and under guard."

"Then fetch her. I'm to take her to Lord Theudebald."

Hans said nothing.

The Alemannian moved to push past him, but stopped when the tips of two spears held by her guards appeared at his throat. He held up his arms and backed away. A crowd began to form in the market.

"Don't be foolish, my friend. I'm here with an army of men under Lord Theudebald's direction. Either let me in or I'll be back with them in minutes to take your palace. And I promise you, if I have to do that, your head will be mounted above that fucking door."

Hans didn't move. "We are the Lady's guard. She rules here."

The brute spat in Hans' face. "I will fuck you in the ass before this is done." He and the other four Alemannians turned to head back the way they had come.

When they were gone, Trudi called from the balcony. "Well done, Hans." She turned to the crowd that had formed in the square below. "The Alemannians have come to usurp Duc Odilo's rule. They've already quit the war, leaving the battlefield to my husband to fight alone against the Franks. Theudebald has only one purpose here. He has come to kill my husband's heir and me. He is here to murder your future Duc. We will stand against him until my husband returns."

She scanned the crowd. They appeared uncertain.

"Give Theudebald no aid, no shelter, no food. The man is godless, a rapist, and a murderer. Go and hide your daughters, your wealth, and your stores. A monster walks among us."

Ten minutes later Theudebald arrived in the market below Trudi's balcony. He had a hundred men with him. They marched into the square, displacing the growing crowd. Her guards no longer patrolled outside. Trudi had called them in, telling Hans to lock the gate and fortify it from the inside.

While Trudi watched, Theudebald sauntered to the center of the market. Fear of the upcoming battle seized her by the throat. To calm herself, she remembered the conversation she had with Kovrat on that same balcony as they planned the palace's defense.

"We can't withstand so many, Kovrat."

"He'll lose four to one storming the palace."

"It will still be close."

"Better to fight him than let him starve you."

"We can store enough to outlast a siege."

"Enough to feed your guard? How many days will they last?

"We just have to last until Odilo returns."

"And if he doesn't?"

Trudi's stomach had lurched at the thought. If Odilo died, nothing would stop Theudebald. But Kovrat had believed she was more vulnerable to a blockade. He had trained the men on a series of maneuvers to defend the palace, saying that battle would better serve her. "Men can't fight if they're starving," he said.

Trudi would have to settle this now while her men were still fresh. She stood to face him from the balcony.

"My lady Hiltrude," Theudebald bowed. He eyed the crowd around him. "What is this foolishness? I'm here as your protector, the protector of all Regensburg. Why have your men denied me entrance?"

"Why aren't you fighting with Odilo?"

"I'm here at his request to guard the city against your brother Carloman's treachery."

"Liar! Your place is with Odilo, unless you've already capitulated."

That jibe seemed to strike a chord. Theudebald's face turned red. She pressed on. "That's it, isn't it? You've already been defeated. Carloman bested you and you've come here to take out your revenge on me."

Theudebald again eyed the growing crowd around him. "You have me wrong, milady. I only have your interests at heart. Open your gates."

"Open them yourself."

Theudebald seemed to assess risk of such an assault. "I have no need. I can just wait here for you to open them. How long before your food stores run low? A few days? A week?"

She needed to goad him into attacking. "Rapist."

Theudebald actually smiled at the charge. "What is the saying? 'Ravaged women share the blame; their bodies be forever stained.'" He lifted his voice so that it carried to the crowd. "Tell me, Hiltrude, daughter of Charles, whose babe do you carry? Did you really think we were so stupid to believe your child is Odilo's? There are so many other suspects, aren't there? Prince Aistulf, the Lombard swordsman, a French knight who followed you to the gates of Regensburg, and a rogue outlaw who kidnapped you. Are we to assume you remained pure for all this time?"

"Odilo was my first love and my last. Your lies shame your own family. You shame the people of Bavaria."

"You shame us!" His shout carried the market. "Your family is a blight on Bavaria."

Trudi frowned. He wasn't taking the bait. "You're weak, Theudebald. It took less than a day for my father to best you on the battlefield. Have you forgotten how he stripped you naked and paraded you through the streets? How long did it take Carloman to beat you? You boasted that you would best both my brothers, but you couldn't even beat one. I'll bet he made you kiss the cross. Did you kneel before him and place your hands in his?"

She could see the fury in Theudebald's face from her balcony.

"You're nothing but an oath breaker, a murderer, and a rapist. You're weak and unskilled in battle. And even now, with all these men, you're afraid of me, a woman large with child. Go back to Alemannia, Theudebald. We only welcome strong men here in Bavaria."

"If you don't come willfully, bitch, I will tear down your palace stone by stone."

Trudi took the sword from one of her guards and lifted it, shoulder high in challenge. "Come and try, Aleman! You couldn't take this palace with ten times as many men. I fight for Bavaria. I fight for its future Duc. And you will die trying to take this palace."

Theudebald spat on the ground. "Not before I cut that child from your belly." He signaled to his men.

The forward line of his army rushed the palace only to find it strongly barricaded. While those nearest to the door tried to force it, the rest crowded around it, waiting to storm the building. Trudi stepped back from the balcony to make room for her archers and found a vantage point at a nearby arrow slit. The bowmen stepped forward and with methodical precision rained bolts down on their attackers. At first those nearest the door didn't recognize the threat, but, as their compatriots fell, shouts filled the square and panic began to spread.

Theudebald waded into the crowd shouting orders to retreat and began pulling his men back away from the market. But he was too slow to maintain order. Dozens died around him and the rest started to run.

A horn sounded and the doors to the palace flew open. Hans led Trudi's guard into the marketplace in a structured charge. Two lines waded into what was left of Theudebald's men, making short work of the melee. When the slaughter was complete Theudebald was nowhere to be found.

Trudi returned to the balcony. Theudebald had underestimated her. Clearly, he had expected to find only a token guard at the palace. He wouldn't make that mistake again.

"Collect their weapons," she called from the balcony to Hans. "And ready the men for a counter-attack."

It took most of an hour for Theudebald to return. When he did, his men came prepared with shields, a battering ram, and archers of their own. Trudi again moved to her arrow slit to watch the battle unfold while her archers advanced to the balcony. Two of them fell dead before they could release an arrow as enemy archers on the ground fired into the balcony. Her remaining archers scrambled for cover. From that point forward, bowmen on both sides played a cat and mouse game of harassment.

Without archers to hinder them, Theudebald's men advanced on the palace. Two lines of Alemannians carried the battering ram forward, swinging it at the end of their approach and smashing it into the door. On the third try, the doors suddenly swung open throwing them off-balance. A column of Trudi's guard stepped forward and its spears decimated the attack. The battering ram lay in the doorway preventing a structured advance, but it also made it impossible for Hans to shut the gate. Theudebald's men swarmed into the corridor, abandoning their shields for hand-to-hand combat.

At first, Trudi's guard fought them to a stalemate. The corridor was too narrow for numbers to be much of an advantage. At a signal from Hans, they began to fall back before the invaders, fighting a structured retreat to slow the attackers' pace. By the time Theudebald's men reached the interior courtyard of the palace, Trudi's archers had taken new positions on the upper floor landings and targeted their slaughter on the troops below. The attackers fell in droves. One or two raised a shield above their heads to ward off the onslaught of arrows, but this left them vulnerable to the guards on the ground. They turned to run, but the press of attackers behind them effectively cut off any avenue of retreat.

A desperate surge by the attackers pushed Hans' men deep into the courtyard. A number of Trudi's guardsmen fell to the ground, leaving an opening to the stairwell. A stream of attackers made for the stairs but was challenged by her personal guard. Using spears, they forced her attackers back down the steps.

Neither side seemed to gain advantage. Bodies of the wounded and dead lay in heaps of flesh throughout the interior courtyard, making it difficult to move. The fighting became desperate, a bloody and intimate struggle of swords, knives, hands, and teeth.

Trudi sent the last of her personal guard into the fray, keeping a sword for herself in case they failed. Her men roared battle cries as they streamed down the stairs. The guards in the courtyard took up the cry and together they beat the attackers back into the corridor. The tide tipped in their favor. With a massive shout, they pushed Theudebald's men out

through the corridor, and out the palace door into the courtyard. A forward column beat back the attack while a second
group drew the battering ram inside the gate. A horn blew and
the forward column retreated back through the gate. They
closed the door and reinforced it with wooden beams.

Theudebald had no one left to fight. He stood facing the
door until one of Trudi's archers hazarded a shot in his direction. He made an obscene gesture towards Trudi's balcony and
then called for a retreat.

Trudi waited until the man was out of sight before returning to her room. She sank into her chair with relief. They
had won the day. But how much of a dent had they put in
Theudebald's army? He would likely return in the morning to
start the attack all over again. Hans appeared in the doorway and after thanking him, Trudi ordered him to see to their
wounded.

❋ ❋ ❋

Overnight, the palace became part barracks, part dining hall, and part hospital. Trudi used Odilo's room as a makeshift command center. They had lost twenty men in the day's
assault. More than seventy Alemannians lay dead in the interior courtyard. Trudi ordered them all to be dumped outside
the palace, like a human shield wall outside the door. She
wanted Theudebald to see how many he lost each day.

Hans rejoined her to sketch out the plans for the expected attack in the morning. "In addition to the attack on the
main entrance, they'll try to gain access to the balconies using
ladders and grappling hooks. We must be ready to repel them.
I've shuttered the second-floor balconies and put men on the
roof with boulders and oil to discourage attack."

"What about the city nobles still in Regensburg?"

"Theudebald's men have cut us off from the rest of the
city. We weren't even able to get a message out to your hus-

band. Each household left behind has a small contingent of soldiers to protect their families, but it's unlikely that they'll rise to your defense. They're too disorganized to rally in defense of the palace."

"What of the troops Odilo left behind to guard the fort?"

Hans shrugged. "We have to assume they stand with Theudebald."

"I can't believe they would let an Alemannian walk in here and seize their royal family without a fight."

"When it comes to our ruling family, we Bavarians have had little stability. Death has followed death in a never-ending succession of heirs. You can't blame people for waiting to see who will survive before proclaiming their loyalty."

"And I thought there was hope for my son."

"Ah, but there is." Hans's face brightened. "It's the one thing that can bring us together. But if he's never born?" Hans shrugged again. "It will be hard to fight for an empty chair."

"Let's hope for our sake the local nobles come to my aid. Otherwise, it will be a long day tomorrow."

\* \* \*

As the morning cast a myriad of shadows inside the fortress, Trudi climbed the stairs to her balcony on the third floor to discover what kind of attack Theudebald planned to mount against her. She moved slowly, fearing another contraction to her belly. The randomness and severity of the attacks had left her exhausted and fearful of any kind of exertion that might trigger another.

She didn't have to wait long for Theudebald. He rode into the square leading over five hundred soldiers. At a sign from him, they broke into two columns and surrounded the palace compound.

When his men had come to a halt, Theudebald addressed Trudi in a voice that carried throughout the square. "We Alemannians and Bavarians are cousins by blood. I will waste no more of it on a Frankish bastard, milady. In a few days, you and your guard will have a choice. You can either starve or open the door. Either way, that bastard in your belly will die by my hand."

Trudi stood to face him. "Once again, you are the coward, Theudebald. You're too weak to take the palace with strength. We have prepared for you, rapist. We have stores enough to feed our men for weeks to come. And you don't have weeks, do you? Once the battle with Carloman is done, Odilo will return and your little revolt will be over. You're finished Theudebald. You just haven't figured it out yet."

Theudebald spat on the ground and turned to address a captain. His voice was loud enough to carry the square. "No one goes into the palace or comes out, unless they bring out the Duchesse...either dead or in chains." He turned his horse away and cantered out of the square.

Having already rationed their food stores, there was little for Trudi to do in response to the blockade. Hans changed the guards every four hours to keep the men fresh and forbade all strong drink; he didn't want the men filling their stagnant hours with mead and ale.

After four days, however, there was food spoilage in one of the smoked meat stores. It forced Trudi to cut rations, much to the dismay of her guard. When she tried to cut her own rations, however, Hans reprimanded her, saying his men wouldn't hear of her sharing in on their sacrifice. "You must maintain the young Duc's strength, Milady."

Begrudgingly, she agreed. Without a healthy baby, her future would be lost. And she had reasons to be worried as the pains in her stomach didn't disappear.

She had her doctor examine her and could see by his face he was worried.

"It's too soon to deliver, milady. You must hold out for several more weeks. I suggest you remain in bed for the duration of your condition."

"I'll take more rest but can't be restricted to bed. Theudebald is too impatient to wait in siege. He'll attack and we must be ready."

"If you're not careful, milady, you'll give Theudebald exactly what he wants. 'A dead child.'"

Trudi nodded. "I'll try to stay abed."

And she did. She used the bed in Odilo's chambers – their command center – to preside over the palace's defense during the day and retired to her own chambers on the third floor to sleep at night. She overruled Eta's objections to this arrangement, knowing in her heart that Theudebald would attack. Two days later, the Alemannian proved her right.

# CHAPTER THIRTY-SIX

*The Road to Regensburg*

P ippin had travelled light and slept little catching up with Childebrand and his army. He and his small cohort of men had left Paris at a hellish pace, stopping only to rest their mounts and to sleep. Even so, several of their horses grew lame from the exertion. He pushed onward, leaving behind those who were stranded rather than slow the party down.

He had set aside all thoughts of Bertrada. She had distracted him long enough. She was safe. That was all that he needed to know. He had a battle to fight and a rebellion to quash.

The countryside rolled by in a blur. They travelled east from the easy, sloping hillsides in Neustria to the low country of the Loire valley. They skirted the Vosges Mountains by heading south to Strasbourg. Pippin took his party north on the Old Roman Road east and south again towards the broad valley near Canstatt.

There, Pippin's party was forced to slow due to the number of refugees on the road fleeing the devastation of a fire in the east. A never-ending stream of destitution filled the road.

Families in pitiful conditions, still covered in soot, scowled at Pippin as if he were to blame for their plight.

Once they reached the Danube, Pippin left the Roman road to follow the path of the river east towards Ingolstat. This was the most pleasant part of the journey. The weather was unshakably cool with bright blue skies and endless sunshine. Although Arnot begged him, Pippin refused to ease their pace. He had received reports that Carloman's army had suffered from its battle with Theudebald and was being hounded by Odilo along the southern banks of the Danube.

One of Childebrand's scouts found them in route and guided them to the army's encampment outside Ingolstat. They arrived at dusk, covered in ten days' worth of dust and sweat. Pippin laughed out loud as he crested the hill overlooking his army's encampment. Childebrand had raised more than eight thousand men, substantially more than Carloman had brought to the battle.

Pippin greeted Childebrand with a bear hug. "How did you recruit so many?"

"Gold has a way of solving most problems."

"We're going to need every one of them." Pippin said. "Odilo has a much larger army than we anticipated."

Childebrand nodded. "They're camped by the River Lech. Our scouts saw them cross the Danube a day ago. It's not yet clear where Carloman is. Last report we had, he defeated Theudebald and then his army disappeared."

"If we find Odilo, we'll find Carloman. He won't be far."

Childebrand shook his head. "Theudebald weakened him. Carloman may be on the run. We have to consider that we may have to fight Odilo alone."

Pippin shook his head. "Carloman started this war. He's not going to let me fight it for him."

They left in the morning and marched a day before crossing the Danube at Donauwörth. Upon learning that the battle was already underway, Pippin hastened their pace, but it still took the better part of another day before they arrived at the battlefield.

* * *

They marched into chaos. The lines on both sides of the battle had disintegrated into a horrific melee. Thousands of bodies from both armies lay strewn across the field in a massive sea of dead. Carloman's cavalry had been dispersed and was fighting in pockets. There was no sign of Carloman, Drogo, or the Frankish command.

Pippin pushed aside the implications. "Sound the horn. Take the infantry and drive them towards the river." He called to his uncle. "I'll take the cavalry around their flank and attack the rear."

Pippin didn't wait for confirmation. He led his cavalry in a wide arc around the melee and drove straight for the heart of Odilo's rear guard.

He heard the roar from Childebrand's infantry as it swarmed across the battlefield like a cloud of locusts, devouring everything before them. Without a formed line, the Bavarians were helpless to stop the charge. Their trumpets called for order, and then retreat but the battle had disintegrated too far into chaos. There was no line to stop them. They swept over the battlefield in a concentrated wave of destruction.

As Pippin circled the battlefield in search of Odilo, a phalanx of enemy fighters caught his attention. They alone were advancing against his army, cutting a path through it like a wet knife. They were superior swordsmen, dressed in exotic armor that Pippin had last seen in the east. They fought with an orchestrated vehemence that was defying his line.

He sent Arnot forward with half the cavalry and took the rest towards the enemy phalanx. They were driving a section of Childebrand's line backward. It should have become a rallying point for Odilo's troops, but they were in too much disarray to respond. Without support the enemy phalanx would soon drive too deep into Pippin's line and become surrounded.

Pippin used his cavalry to cut the phalanx off from Odilo's army, and then he rammed his warhorse into their rear guard, riding over several of the enemy soldiers on foot. He hacked down his blade on those near him as he plunged deeper into their ranks. The swordsmen closed in behind him, taking away his exit. The only way out was forward.

Pippin kicked the flanks of his warhorse and pushed onward. The fighting seemed to collapse on itself in the phalanx as his infantry closed in around them. The enemy swordsmen were being cut down around him. In the end, their leader fought alone. He was a blur of technique, stepping into and out of harm's way with his blade moving with violent grace as it took those who challenged him.

Pippin signaled for his men to back away until the man stood alone.

With the phalanx no longer a threat, Childebrand's line swept forward unimpeded, churning through what was left of the Bavarians.

"Fight me!" The swordsman called to Pippin.

Pippin saluted him with his sword from his warhorse. "I bow to your superior skill. I haven't seen a man fight like that since Fulrad was young."

"He was good." The swordsman spat. "I am better."

"You are from the east. Why are you fighting with the Bavarians?"

"I'm an Avar, a gift of my Kagan to Odilo."

"Odilo will be finished before the day is done. May I have your name?"

"Kovrat."

"I am Pippin, son of Charles."

"The mayor. I've met your sister."

"She is well?"

"Well protected."

Pippin frowned. "I would suggest a truce between us. As

you can see, Odilo will not carry the day and I would rather not kill a swordsman so valuable."

Kovrat seemed to weigh his options before giving a shrug. "I'm a gift of my Kagan, but not a stupid gift. I agree to your truce."

"Do I have your word as a knight?"

Kovrat nodded.

"Then you may keep your sword."

The Bavarian rear guard was better organized than its infantry. By the time Pippin arrived, Odilo had formed a square with pikes to turn aside Arnot's cavalry. All Pippin could do was make it impossible for Odilo to mobilize support for the Bavarian infantry in the field. He ordered a series of feints and flanking moves to harass the Bavarian column, effectively isolating Odilo from the battle.

Pippin searched the battlefield for some sign of Carloman. He saw pockets of cavalry battling across the field, but nothing of his brother's standard. The same was true of Hamar and Drogo. They were nowhere to be found.

It took two more hours for the battle to be decided. With Odilo's cavalry isolated from the battle, the Franks' cavalry had the freedom to fall on the Bavarian infantry across the field. In the end they tried to run, but with the River Lech behind them, they had nowhere to go. The Frankish cavalry waded into the melee and the battle became slaughter.

Pippin turned to Odilo, who was still trapped inside his boxed square, and shouted. "End this!"

Odilo looked away.

"End this! How many more men have to die?"

The Frankish cavalry had become butchers, methodically carving wide swaths of blood through the Bavarians on foot. Most of those left fighting were peasants and no match for armored cavalry. Screams echoed across the battlefield.

Disgusted, Pippin shouted again to Odilo. "Yield, goddamn you! Yield!"

With fury on his face, Odilo threw his sword into the

dirt. Horns signaled their surrender and those Bavarians and Slavs who were still fighting across the battlefield lay down their arms.

Childebrand rode up to join Pippin. He was a figure out of a nightmare. His two-meter frame towered over everyone like a demon. His armor was bathed in blood and his eyes still carried his rage from the battle. Seeing Odilo, he spurred his warhorse forward. Odilo's generals moved to intercede.

"Hold, uncle!" Pippin intercepted him. "He has yielded."

"It took him long enough! I find no honor in killing peasants."

"He has yielded." It was a command. With a grunt, Childebrand sheathed his sword. Pippin turned to the Bavarians. "Odilo?"

Odilo's face was red with rage, but the rebel dismounted and strode forward with a straight back. He stopped in front of Pippin.

"Kneel." Pippin commanded.

Odilo knelt. "I will not kiss your cross."

The statement surprised Pippin. He hadn't thought to make Odilo kiss the cross. But having raised the subject, it forced Pippin into a choice. Carloman certainly would have insisted upon it. And he would have killed Odilo if the man refused. So too, would most of his commanders, especially those who were Knights in Christ.

On the other hand, killing Odilo would leave Bavaria without a Duke. Their nobility was already in shambles. If Odilo didn't lead, there would likely be a civil war and Pippin would have to return to restore order.

And then there was Trudi. Pippin didn't think he could kill his sister's husband. There were limits to what he would do for religion. He drew his sword and watched the rebel's eyes widen. Pippin stabbed it into the ground before Odilo so that the hilt was level with the man's face.

"You will honor my commands and prohibitions," Pippin said.

It took only a moment before Odilo put his hands on the pommel of Pippin's sword. "I will."

Pippin covered the Bavarian's hands with his own. "You acknowledge my right to punish the transgression of my commands and prohibitions."

"I do."

*　*　*

They found Carloman hours later. His body was beneath Hamar's. His champion had fought to where Carloman had fallen and butchered those attacking him. He then stood over Carloman's body, alone atop the small hill, fighting until he too was struck down. Several deep wounds covered his body and his right shoulder had been nearly severed from his torso.

His effort to save Carloman, however, had been successful. They found Pippin's brother alive, but unconscious. He was so bloodied and bruised that he looked as if he had been dragged behind a horse. Only three of his wounds were of any significance: one to his arm, one to his back, and one to the head. They dressed his arm and back but could only pray for him to regain consciousness.

Drogo, too, was alive. He had been isolated with one of the pockets of cavalry fighting across the field. After tending to his father, he gave Pippin a summary of the battle in a hollow voice.

"Father's cavalry charge broke the Bavarian line. But their pikes split our cavalry and our infantry was too weak to seize the advantage. Without organized lines, the battle disintegrated into melee. At first, I thought their greater numbers doomed us, but they kept most of their cavalry in reserve to protect Odilo. Their infantry was no match for our regulars. The fighting disintegrated into chaos. Only Odilo's rear guard held its formation. If he had led them in a charge, it would have ruined us. For some reason, he held back, perhaps thinking his numbers were enough to win the day."

"It was suicide to lead a cavalry charge." Pippin said. "What was Carloman thinking?"

"He thought the battle lost. It was a forlorn hope."

Pippin stared at his nephew in silence. The accusation was plain. He had come too late and forced Carloman into a desperate situation. It was his fault.

"He gave me his blessing before he charged." Drogo's eyes held Pippin's. The boy was angry. "He wouldn't let himself be taken by those pagans. He refused to acknowledge their God. He was willing to sacrifice his life for the Church. And you didn't even make Odilo kiss the cross."

Pippin frowned. "It's more complicated than that."

"Is it?"

# CHAPTER THIRTY-SEVEN

*Regensburg*

A single solider dressed in black with a coil of rope over his shoulder scaled the eastern wall of the palace using nothing but his hands and feet and the natural crevices in the palace's stone walls. A dozen men waited silently below in the warm night air.

Nicknamed "Scales," he was a legend for doing this sort of thing. He would take bets that he could climb any tower or a wall without a rope or a stake to help him, with the higher the tower the larger the bet. Those in his platoon knew never to wager against him.

Having learned of his unique capability, Theudebald bet Scales a solidus he couldn't climb to the second-floor balcony of the palace. Scales hesitated, but only because the feat had to be accomplished at night. Theudebald doubled the offer and Scales readily nodded his head. He'd bet his mother for two solidi.

He had already bypassed the shuttered first floor balcony and was making slow but persistent progress towards the second when he hit a snag.

He had leveraged a toehold to push himself close, but

when he tried to find a handhold using his right hand – the one closest to the balcony – there were none within reach. Shifting his weight to his other foot, he searched with his left hand.

A worn edge of a stone block provided a grip, and he took it, knowing it drew him away from the second-floor balcony, but hoping that it would provide him a path above it. It did. He found a quick succession of toeholds and handholds and within seconds was elevated four feet above the targeted balcony. His only problem was he had no leverage with which to make the jump. His right hand searched for a new crevice or a natural ledge to grasp, but again he found nothing. He retreated to his prior handhold and searched with his foot. After some effort, he found a small outcropping – no more than a half-inch wide – and shifted his weight to it.

The outcropping tore from the wall and all his weight followed. His right handgrip ripped away from the wall and his momentum dislodged his left foot. He dangled from the wall by three fingers and they strained as his body flailed thirty feet above the ground. He bounced once against the wall and then became still. With a concerted effort, he threw his weight to his right, searching with his free hand for any kind of purchase. Sweat stung his eyes and he blinked to clear them. He tried again and, at last, his right hand found a crevice to hold. He breathed a sigh of relief and searched to find a foothold, first for the right foot, and then the left.

He took a moment to rest, knowing he had to start the process all over again. He shook his left hand to get some feeling back into it and then searched with his right foot for a higher anchor point. He found one, but it was much higher than he wanted, almost to the level of his waist. It was, however, the only chance he had of making the balcony. If it didn't hold when he put his weight into it, he wouldn't be able to stop from falling. He found a handhold high above his head and swung his right foot up to the small shelf. He pulled and pushed until he was upright but didn't wait to see if the shelf would hold. He leapt for the balcony rail.

Halfway into the leap, he knew it was too far. His body slammed against the side of the balcony sending a shock of pain through his chest and he began to fall backward. Out of desperation, he made one last swipe with his right arm and caught a gutter spout below the balcony. His body swung crazily as he tried to hold on.

His hands started to slip, and panic filled him. He clawed desperately for any purchase, but each hand slipped on the smooth stone. He was losing ground, sliding farther down the gutter spout. A lip at the end of the outlet saved him. Using it for leverage, he hauled himself up until he could throw an arm through the railing and from there climbed up onto the second-floor balcony. He paused for several seconds, knife in hand, fearing that the noise from his jump had raised an alarm. When he was confident that all remained quiet, he secured the rope to the railing and let it down to the men waiting below.

One by one the other soldiers scaled the rope until four stood with him. The balcony would fit no more; the others would have to follow after they gained entry. Scales edged into the window opening. He poked his head through for just a second to check for guards. There was one stationed about twenty paces down the hallway to his left.

Scales flipped a rock into the opening and heard it clatter down the hall. In the stillness of the early hours, the sound echoed. The guard walked past the window to investigate and Scales scraped his knife against the stone wall. When the guard poked his head out of the window Scales buried his knife in the man's eye. He caught the body as it fell and drew him out onto the balcony.

They were told that the Duchess's rooms were on the third floor, so the Alemannians scurried down the hall as quietly as possible looking for a stairway to the next level. After they turned the first corner, they found it. Unfortunately, three armed guards were descending towards them.

"To the stairs! The stairs!" one shouted. "*We are invaded! To the stairs!*" Each of the soldiers had a spear and they lowered them to fend off the invaders. Thinking the guards might cost him his two solidi, Scales was first into the fray. He prayed that the men outside would hurry.

\* \* \*

Trudi heard the commotion and rolled out of bed. By the time she got to her door, the guard stationed there had already joined the battle on the stairs. It took only seconds for her to assess the danger. Although the narrowness of the stairway would temporarily keep Theudebald's men at bay, it wouldn't stop them as more kept arriving through the window. Trudi fled deeper into the palace.

"*To the stairs!*" she shouted. The only other guards on her floor were those from her personal retinue. All four of them poured into the hallway in their nightshirts and raced down the hallway to the fight.

Two of Trudi's nursemaids and her doctor also lived on her floor and Trudi ran to warn them. She found the nursemaids already out of bed. One even had a robe on.

"Get to my room!" She ordered and fled down the hall to the doctor's room. She found him still asleep.

"Get up, you old fool! We're under attack!" The man didn't move. She rolled him over. "Get up!"

A dozen stab wounds covered his chest, his stomach and neck. There was blood everywhere. Trudi stared into his unseeing eyes and fought back the urge to vomit.

She ran back to her room, panic assaulting her every step. It was the safest place, she told herself. They had rebuilt the door to be strong and it would buy them time until the guards on the lower level stopped the attack.

But who killed the doctor? The question leapt into Trudi's mind as she barreled down the corridor to her room. The fighting had backed up to the head of the stairs. Only two of her guards remained standing.

She turned the corner into her room and swung the heavy wooden door closed. She lifted the wooden beam into the brackets. When it fell into place, she breathed a sigh of relief and let her head fall against the thick wood that stood between her and the attackers.

She heard a whimper behind her and turned to find one of the two nursemaids lying in a pool of blood on the floor.

The other nursemaid stood facing Trudi with a knife in hand. "Bitch! Did you think we would buy your Frankish lies? Did you think we were too stupid to see your treachery?"

"You killed the doctor." Her words sounded naïve, even to Trudi, but she was trying to make sense of the night's violence.

"And now I'm going to kill you."

Trudi wrestled with the logic. "The soldiers?"

The nursemaid licked her lips. "My way out."

Something heavy slammed into the door, startling both women.

Trudi circled to her right to give herself some room. "No one is leaving here tonight. You'll be caught."

The nursemaid shook her head. "I'll claim the soldiers did it. No one will ever know.

"Why the doctor?"

"So, no one would save you."

Trudi's hand went behind her back. When she brought it forward, it held a blade of her own. She enjoyed the shock on the nursemaid's face.

Another blow shook the door.

A horrible contraction seized her. With a groan, Trudi doubled over, clutching her belly. The nursemaid seized the moment to attack, rushing across the room with her blade held high. Despite the pain she felt, Trudi's training responded to the threat. More out of instinct than intent, she ducked beneath the attack and grabbed the woman's wrist. Using the blade's momentum, she pulled the wrist up sharply behind the woman's back until she heard the dull crack of a bone breaking. The nursemaid screamed and dropped her knife.

Trudi clouted her on the head with the butt of her knife and the woman dropped like a sack of flour. She lay on the floor without a twitch.

Again, something crashed into the door. Trudi heard shouts in the hallway and scuffling outside her door. The fighting continued for a minute and then abruptly ended. A voice called through the door.

"Milady? Are you well?" It was Hans. With a groan, Trudi lifted the wooden beam from its brackets and opened the door.

Hans and a dozen soldiers behind him crowded the door. He looked from the two women on the floor to the blade in her hand. "Milady?"

"I'm fine, Hans. Arrest her." She pointed to the unconscious nursemaid. "And get Eta to help the other. The doctor is dead."

"But-

"I said I'm fine."

He was staring at her shift. Trudi looked down. From the waist down her shift was wet. It took her a moment to process this newest development. "Oh, Christ! I'm having the babe."

\* \* \*

Theudebald had had enough of Regensburg. He had planned to bury the Frankish whore and be on his way. He didn't count on needing a siege to do it. She had surprised him by anticipating the attack. And now, he was running out of time. Sooner or later either Odilo or Carloman would return and he couldn't afford to be in Regensburg when they did.

He had had high hopes for the midnight raid. He had been sure that one of the two attacks would have succeeded. Yet, here he was, another day dawning and the bitch was still alive. He took a company of men and rode to the palace to inspect his blockade. As he drew near the square, he was surprised to see crowds of people surrounding the palace.

He was even more surprised to find his siege abandoned. In its place were a hundred men lined up in formation.

"What is this?"

An elderly knight rode forward. "Lord Theudebald, I am Helig of the Agilolfings. These men are the household retainers of the noble families of Regensburg, all sworn subjects of Duc Odilo. We will allow no further attacks on the palace."

"And you think one hundred men can stop me?"

"Perhaps not, but we won't stand aside. The Duchesse is giving birth to the heir as we speak."

A murmur rose from the crowd as it digested the news.

"Helig, I'll give you one chance to stand aside before I cut your tongue from your head." As Theudebald spoke, one of his soldiers broke ranks and ran to join Helig.
Before he could react, a dozen more had followed.

"Bavarians, my lord." One of his captains said.

"You've run out of time, Lord Theudebald." Helig turned to join the column of men. "Reports have been received that Odilo has been defeated and that Carloman and Pippin are coming. I doubt very much that they will appreciate your plans for their sister."

Doubt stabbed through Theudebald. Perhaps it was a bluff. Perhaps the old man was playing a game with him. But if Helig wasn't bluffing, he didn't have enough time to tarry. Moving an army was a slow business.

*Damn that bitch!* He felt a trickle of sweat roll down his back. *That cunt!*

It would take days if not a week to take the palace, even without Helig's men to guard it. He would have to leave Trudi for another time. And he would have to find some way to prevent the Franks from giving chase. The crowd was growing reckless with shouting and shoving. Men with rakes and shovels made a great show of leaving the square to stand with

Helig's men. It was a pathetic display of bravery. Such men would be the first to die and they would die quickly at the hands of trained soldiers. They mistook his deliberation as a weakness.

But he didn't have time. He turned his horse to leave, thinking through the steps he'd take to get away. A cheer went up in the crowd and Theudebald stopped. Ten years earlier such a response would have provoked their slaughter. But he was wiser now. He didn't have time to spare for it.

A man in the crowd spit in his direction. Theudebald considered him. *I could still kill them,* he thought. *It would take half a day and I could leave before sunset.*

The crowd started to taunt him, whistling and laughing derisively. Theudebald drew his sword and rode into the crowd, straight at the man who had spit. He took off the peasant's head with one blow. The panicked shouts of the crowd sent a thrill of joy jolting through him, but he knew better than to waste his time on them. He turned his back on the crowd and rode away.

# CHAPTER THIRTY-EIGHT

*Regensburg*

P ippin was glad to finally break camp. It had taken two full days to bury the dead. Drogo had insisted that two sets of graves be dug, one for the Christians and one for the pagans so that the Christian soldiers could be properly buried. He had assigned the grisly task to Odilo's men, who laid out the bodies, head to foot and foot to head. Once the corpses were covered, a priest provided extreme unction and blessed the ground where the Christians were buried. No one spoke over the massive pagan grave.

The battle seemed like a distant dream to Pippin. He had spent so much time worrying about the rebellion and planning for it that it seemed impossible that it could be over so quickly. Once he had arrived at the battle, it had taken only a day to overwhelm the rebel army. His men had tipped the scales and won the day, but they had paid little of the ultimate cost. He had to remind himself that Carloman had battled for days before he arrived.

And the toll to his brother's army had been heavy. Of the six thousand who had started out on the campaign from Paris, fewer than three thousand remained. An entire swath of

Carloman's commanders had lost their lives, including many of his Knights in Christ.

Pippin escorted Odilo and what was left of the Bavarian army back to Regensburg. He wanted to provide a lasting image of their victory over Odilo, insisting that Odilo ride between him and Drogo. The Duc had barely spoken to Pippin since offering his hands in acclamation. He looked furious with humiliation and refused to meet Pippin's eye. As long as he did what he was ordered to do, Pippin left the man alone.

They carried Carloman's unconscious body in a cart accompanied by his doctor. Color had returned to his brother's face and his heartbeat was strong, but nothing could rouse him.

As they drew near Regensburg, a scout arrived at full gallop, his eyes wide in alarm. "An army just vacated the city. They've set it on fire!"

"Quick march!" Pippin shouted. The shout was repeated down the line and the army surged into a faster pace. Pippin turned to the scout. "What army?"

"Theudebald."

Drogo spat at the mention of the name. "What is that bastard doing here?"

The answer hit Pippin and Odilo at the same time. They both shouted, "Trudi!" Odilo spurred his horse forward. Pippin turned to Drogo. "Take charge of the fire!"

Drogo shook his head. "I'm chasing Theudebald?"

Pippin frowned. The boy had a point. If they put out the fire, Theudebald would get away. "Not today. We'll have to chase him later."

Pippin said, "Save the city." With that, he gave his warhorse a kick and took off after Odilo for the fortress gate. If anything had happened to Trudi, he swore he would hunt down Theudebald and flay the bastard alive.

❊ ❊ ❊

Trudi was exhausted. She had nothing left to give. The pain had been overwhelming, far worse than anything she had imagined. She had screamed and screamed, holding onto Eta's arms. When the babe's head finally pushed through, she nearly lost consciousness from the pain. The rest of him followed in a liquid rush that seemed to take her with it. It was such an overwhelming release that she found herself laughing and crying at the same time.

Eta cut the cord and took the baby from her while the rest of the nursemaids stayed to await the afterbirth. They prodded Trudi's stomach and gently pulled onto the cord until a spasm shook her and the cord gave way. There was so much blood! For a while, she lost consciousness.

When she awoke, the nursemaids were cleaning her up, changing her sheets and leaving a rolled-up towel between her legs. They made her drink a glass of ale for strength before Eta brought the baby to her. She showed Trudi how to hold her nipple to help the baby suckle. Trudi did as she was told, wondering how much more of her there was left to give.

"Theudebald?"

"He's gone, milady." She could tell there was more news but didn't have the strength to ask.

When the babe had taken its fill, Eta took him from her and informed her that Odilo and Pippin had arrived. She tried to sit up but couldn't quite find the strength. Two of the nursemaids propped her up in bed. Eta waited for her to nod and then opened the door to let her husband and brother in.

No one had to tell Trudi that Pippin had won the battle; he wouldn't have come if he had lost. No one had to tell her that Odilo had offered his hands to Pippin; Odilo wouldn't be alive if he hadn't. She had known this would happen before he left. The only question had been: would her husband return alive or dead?

When she saw him, a sob took her unexpectedly. She was so relieved. All the grief and pain and fear she had suffered in his absence came pouring out of her. She didn't care that

Pippin was in the room. She held out her arms to Odilo and he came to her and buried his face in her shoulder. A new fear struck her, and she shook him off, frantically searching his body with her hands. "Are you wounded?"

"I am whole."

"Thank God." It was all she could manage to say. Her emotions cut off her words. She gathered him into her arms and wept.

Eta brought the baby beside the bed, wrapped in a blanket.

"It is a son, Duc Odilo." Eta pulled back the blanket to display the baby's genitals. "The future Duc of Bavaria!"

The baby wailed at the indignity.

"We have a son," she whispered.

"An heir." Odilo said. He let out a grunt of a laugh when Eta handed him the child. He cradled it carefully, holding it in the crook of his arm. And then he smiled; it wasn't much, but it was a smile. Trudi wiped the tears from her eyes, trying to contain her emotions.

Pippin reached out his hand to stroke the baby's head. The gesture startled Odilo, and he pulled away defensively; but after a moment he held the baby out for his brother-in-law to caress. Pippin pushed what little hair the boy had away from his forehead. And then his face grew serious. "I need to have a moment with my sister."

"This is hardly the time." Odilo protested, but Pippin's face brooked no argument.

Trudi interceded. "It's alright, husband. He's no threat to me."

Odilo looked furious but took the babe with as he left the room.

Trudi waited until the door was closed before holding out her hand to her brother. "Come sit beside me on the bed."

Pippin took off his sword and sat.

Trudi hugged him, holding on as if her life depended on it. "Thank you for not killing my husband."

Pippin laughed and kissed her on the forehead. "That was never my wish."

"I know." Trudi frowned, suddenly. "Where is Carloman?"

"Alive, but unconscious. He was wounded on the battlefield. Hamar gave his life to protect him. We can only hope Carloman will awaken."

Pippin seemed reluctant to speak. When he finally did, his voice was full of restrained fury. "Why was Theudebald here?"

She wanted to tell him everything. She wanted Pippin to chase down the bastard and torture him to the farthest edge of sanity before killing him. And if she told Pippin of the rape, he would do it. Of that she had no doubt. But she couldn't tell him. The shame of it was too great. It would never leave her.

"He wanted to kill my baby," she blurted. It was some of the truth, but it would suffice. Pippin would make the bastard pay. Her brother had always protected her...even when they were on opposing sides. She felt safe with him, just as she had felt safe with Charles. It took her a moment to realize she hadn't felt that way in a long time, even with Odilo. A wave of shame and gratitude washed over her. And again, unable to help herself, she started to cry.

Pippin held her in his arms. "I will find him."

All Trudi could do was nod against his chest. She let him hold her until she had gained some measure of control over herself and sat up to wipe away the tears on her face.

"I did my best to stop the war, but it happened anyway. Even the church couldn't stop it."

"The Church was wrong. Further delay only would have made Odilo stronger and a greater threat. He wouldn't be turned away from his rebellion."

"You could have made peace with him. He only wanted Gripho's claim satisfied."

Pippin shook his head. "Carloman was right about

Odilo. Your husband wanted more than that. He wanted a pagan state, as did Gripho. Charles would never have allowed that. and neither would Carloman."

"And you?"

Pippin shrugged. "Like Charles, I'm happy to let the pagans have their religion as long as it doesn't divide the kingdom. But Odilo used it to sow the seeds of rebellion. He made paganism his rallying cry. He made it our enemy."

Trudi took Pippin's hand in hers. "What did you really want to talk about?"

He seemed to be weighing his words as if they were precious. "Carloman already has a son. And now, so do you. One day, God willing, I will as well."

"Of course, you will."

"As grandsons of Charles, each of our children will have a claim to succession as mayor. Each of them will have a base of power to assert their claim. If left alone, they'll destroy each other and everything that Charles has accomplished."

"Surely, you exaggerate."

"The events of the past year prove that I'm not."

"What is it that you want from me?"

"I want you to promise me that your son will never claim to be mayor of the palace."

"Are you saying he can never rule?"

"He can rule Bavaria." Then Pippin shook his head slowly. "But he can't be mayor."

"Odilo will never agree to that."

"That's why I'm asking you."

*  *  *

Carloman awoke the next day and had a hard time believing he was alive. He felt disoriented, had trouble standing up, and was prone to lapses in concentration. His initial relief that Pippin's arrival had turned the tide of the battle was short-lived as accounts of Hamar's loss were relayed. The death of his champion so grieved Carloman that he wept openly in front of his men.

As he regained his equilibrium, Carloman came to the realization that something profound had changed within him. For one thing, he had a hard time holding in his emotions. His passions and fervency were so strong that they unnerved him. He also saw the world around him with renewed clarity. He had always been calculating – playing out every scenario before making a move – but now he possessed a sense of surety that infused him with great confidence.

He tried to tell Pippin about his last charge, how he had been prepared to die, and how, for a time, the touch of God had made him invincible. He wanted to tell Pippin that the outcome of battle was never really assured and that they only thought it was because Charles had always won. He tried to say that they could lose, and that he almost did.

His brother had listened, but it was obvious that Pippin was only humoring him. Carloman knew he sounded daft, even to himself. He wondered if his newfound surety came from being so close to death, but soon became convinced that it was the hand of God upon him. He, Carloman, was blessed… in a state of grace…holy in the eyes of God.

He gathered the remaining Knights in Christ together in the church that Boniface had consecrated in Regensburg and together they held a vigil for their fallen brethren. He prayed all night, and in the morning announced several decisions. He elevated Drogo to be mayor of Thuringia, Alemannia, and Bavaria. He vowed to chase down Theudebald and hold him accountable. But his final decision required a conversation with Pippin. He waited until he and his brother were alone.

"We must elevate the Merovingian."

"No." Pippin's face was resolute.

"The Church is behind him and it will end the rebellions. We have to elevate him."

Pippin grunted derisively. "We just finished ending the

rebellion."

"The eastern rebellion. We can't rule by military force alone. It's the Church that gives power to the king. And he, in turn, gives us power to rule. Without the king, we are nothing."

"Without us, the king is nothing. Childeric isn't who you think he is. He isn't even a man of God. He's dangerous and cruel. He should never be allowed to rule."

"It's we who should not rule! We've gone too far, Pippin. We are Knights in Christ, not kings."

"No."

"At least, consider it."

Pippin shook his head. "I won't hear any more about the Merovingian. I won't discuss it. Now or ever."

Carloman was stunned. Pippin could be difficult but never this obstinate. "It is God's will."

"You have not met Childeric. I have. I've looked into his eyes. The man is mad. I won't elevate him."

*  *  *

Pippin left the next morning for Chelles and Carloman wasn't sorry to see him go. His brother's absence made things easier. With his newfound surety, Carloman wanted to move quickly to put the kingdom in order and Pippin's interference would only slow him down.

Fortunately, Boniface arrived in Regensburg. The bishop had ridden for days after receiving a pigeon from the papal legate and was delighted to find the rebellion ended and all of Charles's children among the living.

Carloman cornered him soon after his arrival. "I'm going to elevate the Merovingian."

"And your brother?"

"He refuses." Carloman waved off Boniface's protest. "I'll do it alone. Nothing says we have to be united in this."

"It would be preferable."

"But not necessary."

The bishop nodded. "Not necessary, but preferable."

"When you get back to Paris, I want it announced immediately. We'll have a coronation ceremony when I return."

"How will you deal with Pippin?"

Carloman wasn't sure he was ready to take Boniface into his confidence. But he was so sure he was right. "In truth, I don't need him anymore. We've put down the rebellion. The church is behind me. Once I elevate the Merovingian, I will rule on his behalf. Pippin will still have his territories and I will have mine, but I alone will serve in the name of the king. I have a son to succeed me while Pippin remains childless. Who do you think the nobles will follow?"

Boniface looked surprised, but after a long moment nodded his consent.

Carloman wasn't finished. "I also want you to baptize Trudi's babe. I want it done before the entire citizenry before I leave."

"Have you spoken to your sister and Odilo?"

"Odilo is in no position to object. If he refuses to attend, I'll see him hanged."

Again, Boniface's face registered surprise, but he nodded. "God's will be done."

❃ ❃ ❃

Trudi's face blotched red, a clear sign she was furious. Carloman braced himself for her onslaught.

"How dare you barge into our rooms to demand such a thing of Odilo?" She stood to face Carloman, leaving Odilo to sit alone at the table. "It would be one thing for him to grant you such a boon in private. It's another to humiliate the man in front of all Bavaria."

"It's not a request."

"We won't do it." Trudi poked her finger at his chest. It wasn't lost on Carloman that Odilo had yet to speak. The Bavarian looked deep in thought, rubbing his hand over his chin.

Carloman turned his attention to Trudi. "You're in no position to negotiate. He pledged his hands."

"To Pippin, not you. And neither of us agreed to such a demand."

"I'm afraid, I must insist. I was shocked that Pippin didn't make your husband kiss the cross after his defeat. This is my way of correcting that mistake."

"It will humiliate him and weaken his hold on the city."

"I will kill him if the baby isn't baptized."

That shocked her into silence. Carloman could see that she looked at him as if he were a stranger. In many ways, he mused, she was right. He no longer felt like the same man. He searched for some feeling for his sister...and couldn't find any.

"Did Pippin agree to this?" Trudi asked in a small voice.

"He doesn't have to. He's no longer here and I don't care to argue the matter."

"We won't agree to it."

Odilo stood. "Yes. We will. We'll baptize the baby in the church. I will attend, and do what's required."

Trudi looked incredulous. "Why would you do that?"

"It's the only way. They won the day. I no longer set the terms. If I baptize the baby, they'll leave and I'll remain Duc of Bavaria and can raise my child. If I don't, our child loses his father. We'll raise him as a Christian."

Having what he came for, Carloman bowed to take his leave.

＊ ＊ ＊

Trudi waited until the door closed behind Carloman to turn on her husband. "Why would you agree to that?"

"If our son is to rule all of Francia one day, he'll need to be Christian."

Trudi's heart skipped in her chest. "If he is to rule?"

"He will have as much right to the succession as will Drogo."

She couldn't believe it. Odilo had acquiesced to fight another day. He would use his son to gain power. "Carloman's son is a grown man. He's already a mayor. If you pit our son against Drogo, he'll lose."

"Just like I lost?" There was hurt in her husband's voice. "Our son has rights."

"Like Gripho had rights? Gripho is in prison because he tried to assert his rights."

"Drogo isn't immortal. If he dies, our child will be the obvious choice."

"Unless Pippin has a son. This is exactly what Pippin warned me about! If we pit our children against each other, they will destroy each other and the kingdom."

"Is that what Pippin wanted to discuss with you alone?"

Trudi nodded.

"Then he discussed it with the wrong person. Ruling is my job. You are only my wife."

His words stung. She hadn't talked to Pippin to undermine him. "Odilo, please-"

"It's bad enough that I have to live under Carloman's thumb, I didn't think you would join in."

Trudi fought to keep her voice calm. "Husband, I chose you. I married you under the ash and gave you an heir. I love you. But Pippin is right. If we set our children against each other, they'll tear each other and the kingdom apart."

"I have a duty to protect the interests of my family."

"Like you protected me from Theudebald?"

"At least he stood with me against Carloman!"

Trudi was stunned into silence. All the rage she had suffered roiled inside her. She opened her mouth to speak, but nothing came forth. Frustrated, humiliated, and angered by her impotence, she turned to go. She made it to the door before she stopped. She couldn't walk away. In a small voice she said the words.

"He raped me."

"What did you say?"

She rounded on him, finally able to give voice to her anger. "He held a knife to my throat and raped me. Right there on the table next to you in the great hall. While you snored from too much drink, your brother ravaged me. That night you broke down my door? That was the night of my violation. That was the night he ruined me."

Odilo reached out for her but Trudi recoiled from his touch.

"I told you I didn't want him in this house, but you insisted he stay. You brought him under our roof and he took your bed. You thought you could control him? He couldn't wait to fight Carloman. He wasn't doing it for you. He was doing it to hurt me. When you went off to fight? He came back here to kill our baby. He wanted to cut the baby from my womb. Ask anyone in the city. He shouted it in the square."

"This can't be true."

Trudi let her silence weigh on him. "You know in your heart it is. You know what that man is capable of doing. You closed your eyes to his evil because it served the interests of your rebellion. You looked the other way because your ambition was stronger than your sense. You didn't start this war because of Gripho. You started it because of your own lust for power. I begged you to find another way, knowing this would be the outcome."

"Your family took away our power – "

"Don't you ever talk to me about defending your family! You know nothing of family. You never had one."

# CHAPTER
# THIRTY-NINE

*Regensburg*

T he baptism was everything Carloman wanted. Crowds lined the street to catch a glimpse of the new heir. Boniface led the procession carrying the cross and a half-dozen priests blessed the crowds as they passed. At every turn, Odilo raised his son skyward and the people bellowed their support. Odilo and Trudi were presenting their new son to the population of Regensburg as a Christian. It would reinforce the church's role at the center of Bavarian life.

No longer would Odilo use paganism to foment rebellion. No longer would he undermine his rule or his faith. He had placed soldiers along the side of the road to ensure there were no attempts at violence. But rather than the belligerence he expected, Carloman found the crowd to be surprisingly cooperative. Most of the peasants followed the soldiers' instructions to kneel as Boniface and the procession drew before them. After the first fifty feet, the soldiers didn't even have to demonstrate as the crowd could see what was expected. Many – Carloman assumed they were already Christian – made the sign of the cross on their own.

The celebration inside the church would be far less welcoming. All the remaining Bavarian nobles who survived the battle were gathered there to witness the holy rite. Carloman could understand the hostility they held for him. Many carried wounds from the battle or had lost beloved sons and husbands. Instead of celebrating the newly born Duc-in-waiting, they would greet him and the procession with silence.

Boniface and the priests mounted the steps up to the door of the church and then turned. Carloman and his knights stepped to the side, snapped to attention and turned to observe Odilo and Trudi as they advanced to Boniface. They stopped on the step below him.

"Who do you bring to the church for baptism?" Boniface demanded in a voice that carried throughout the square.

"Our son." Odilo held the baby aloft.

"And what name do you give him?"

The crowd silenced in anticipation.

Odilo held the child aloft and proclaimed in a loud voice. "Tassilo, son of Odilo, son of Godefred."

He handed the babe to Trudi and the crowd roared its approval. Boniface took a pinch of salt and pushed it into the babe's mouth as Tassilo squirmed in Trudi's grasp. The bishop then took a cluster of basil and dipped it in a bowl of holy water and splashed it over the infant, still tainted by original sin.

"I exorcise thee, unclean spirit...accursed one, damned and to be damned...in the name of the Father and of the Son and of the Holy Ghost, that thou goest out and depart from this servant of God, Tassilo, son of Odilo, son of Godefred. For God the Almighty commands thee, accursed one, He who walked upon the sea, and stretched out His right hand to Peter about to sink. Therefore, accursed devil, acknowledge thy sentence and give honor to the one living and true God: give honor to Jesus Christ His Son, and to the Holy Ghost; and depart from this servant of God, Tassilo. Because God and our Lord Jesus Christ hath vouchsafed to call him to His holy grace and benediction and to the font of Baptism."

Carloman and his knights barked, "Amen."

Boniface turned and led them into the church and up to the altar where they bowed and turned to take their assigned seats: Carloman and his Knights in Christ in the first pews, Odilo, Trudi, and the baby on the altar.

As Carloman turned into the pew, he bowed in greeting to the gathered Bavarian nobles. He restrained an urge to grin at their obvious anger.

As the mass wore on, Boniface wrapped up his Latin prayers and made his way to the baptismal font. He turned to Carloman.

"May we have the Bonpère? Carloman rose and joined him on the altar. Trudi and Odilo followed holding the baby. "Take the infant," Boniface instructed. Carloman took Tassilo from Trudi's hands and held him over the holy water. Boniface dipped his thumb in the baptismal font and made the sign of the cross on the baby. With the Bible in his left hand, he extended his right over the child's forehead.

"Do you renounce the devil and all his angels?" Boniface asked.

"I renounce them," Carloman and Trudi responded.

Carloman caught Boniface's eye.

"Do you renounce all his works and his schemes?"

"I renounce them," Trudi and Carloman replied.

"Do you believe that Jesus Christ is the Son of God?"

"I do." Again, only Trudi and Carloman responded.

Boniface held Odilo's gaze. "You must declare it."

Odilo looked briefly towards the congregation where the Bavarian nobility sat.

"You didn't say I had to swear," Odilo whispered.

"It is required." Boniface matched his whisper.

"Just finish the ceremony. You've got what you want."

With his newfound clarity, Carloman didn't hesitate. He knew what to do to bring the pagan in line. He kept his voice low. "Say the words."

Odilo shook his head.

Carloman lowered the baby towards the font of holy water, dipping his head into the fluid.

"Carloman!" Trudi exclaimed.

"Carloman?" This time it was Boniface

Carloman whispered to Odilo. "I am the hand of God here on earth. From this day forward, you will kneel before the cross. You will accept the holy Eucharist and you will bathe your children in the baptismal font."

Carloman lowered the baby's head deeper into the font, his eyes never leaving Odilo.

"Carloman, don't!" Trudi begged.

"Stop it!" Odilo whispered.

"Give me your vow!" The baby's head was almost covered, and it struggled in Carloman's hands. "If not, his next breath will be his last."

"I give it!"

Carloman lifted the baby out of the font and bowed to Boniface. "I beg your forgiveness, Bishop, for the moment of confusion."

After that, it all proceeded as Carloman had asked. Odilo bent his knee before the cross, bowed his head in reverence to the Eucharist, and dipped the crown of his baby's head into the baptismal font. Carloman was named the child's compater when the blessing was delivered, sending a clear message that should Odilo and Trudi die before Tassilo reached maturity, Carloman would claim pater familias and take the child into his household.

As the mass ended, Boniface blessed the congregation from the altar. Carloman turned to observe the Bavarian nobles. Although grim-faced, they were all kneeling.

He had won.

# CHAPTER FORTY

*Paris*

Bertrada felt like a prisoner. Gunther had brought her, Hélène and the Lady Ragomfred back to the palace on the Île de la Cité and forbade any travel outside the compound until Pippin or Carloman returned. The palace itself was locked down as if in siege. Guards monitored every entrance and exit and patrolled regularly along the ramparts.

Gunther found quarters for each of the three women, made sure they had servants seeing to their needs, and then promptly ignored them.

Their presence created quite a stir amongst the nobles at court, especially when Lord Ragomfred insisted that his wife be returned to him. A delegation approached the gate and demanded Miette's return, threatening a siege if she wasn't freed. Gunther ignored their entreaties and calmly told them where they could put further complaint. After a half-day of arguing outside the gate, the delegation left.

Bertrada spent most of her days in prayer. The palace chapel was quite small and used primarily for family services. Ceremonial services for the court typically took place at Saint Germain des Prés. She preferred to pray in a small alcove dedicated to the Blessed Mother.

After the first week, however, she grew bored. She

wasn't finding the same spiritual solace she had found at Chelles. She had seen little of Hélène since their arrival. Her protector had remained in her room, taking meals there instead of in the main hall.

By contrast, the Lady Ragomfred – who insisted on being called Miette – was constantly underfoot. She sought out Bertrada at mealtimes and even accosted her during prayers. Knowing it would likely never stop, Bertrada agreed to provide her an audience in an effort to attend to whatever the young woman needed to get off her chest.

"I didn't know." Miette said. It had been the opening sentence of every attempt at conversation since the attack. "The king merely requested that I find you. Salau acted on his own. He wasn't supposed to kill you or Agnes. If he was, no one told me. You must believe me! If I were in league with him, why would I try to kill him?"

Bertrada kept her face neutral. She believed the woman up to a point. It was true that Miette had stabbed Salau, possibly even saving Hélène's life, but it wasn't the whole truth. Miette was holding something back. She wasn't stupid. She must have suspected that Salau was there to murder her, even if Miette wasn't specifically told about it.

"Why does the king want to kill me?" Bertrada asked Miette.

"I honestly don't know, milady."

Bertrada let the lie stand for a moment. "If I'm to believe you, you must first tell me the whole truth. Despite your age, you're far from naïve. Sunnichild warned me that you're more perceptive than you let on. If your objective is to gain my allegiance in advance of Pippin's arrival, you would be smart to discard this façade. I have little tolerance for fools or anyone pretending to be one."

She waited, watching Miette closely. The wide-eyed innocence that had dominated the woman's demeanor faded with a nod. In its place, a cunning intelligence occupied the place behind Miette's eyes. She shrugged, as if the explanation was obvious. "You're with child. If it's a boy, your child will be in line for succession as mayor."

"Childeric would kill a child?"

"Now who is being naïve?"

"How did he know I was pregnant at the ball? I didn't even know myself."

"That I cannot say. As Pippin's consort, you're a game piece in your own right. Childeric might have wanted to take you off the table to unsettle the mayor. You drew his notice at the ball when you called out to Pippin. You stopped the mayor from pledging his hands. Childeric would kill you for that alone."

"I am no longer Pippin's consort."

Miette grunted. "That only makes you more vulnerable."

A cold trickle of dread seeped into Bertrada's stomach, making her queasy. If this woman were right, she would always be vulnerable. "Did you know that Salau was sent to kill me?"

Miette paused before answering. "The words were never spoken. I was told to report back to Childeric when we found you." She wrung her hands. "But I suspected. I knew it was a possibility. I just didn't let myself think it all the way through. And then Salau acted so fast."

"Why did you stop him?"

"If I was as cold and calculating as you think I am, I wouldn't have."

"Then why did you?"

"I – I didn't want you to die."

Bertrada didn't know what to make of this woman. She seemed a contradiction. She *was* cold and calculating and yet, at that moment, she seemed quite vulnerable.

"Why?" Bertrada insisted.

Miette's handwringing grew intense. "I'm no killer and...I couldn't do that to Pippin."

Bertrada was dumbfounded. It didn't make sense. "Do

you even know Pippin?"

A wan smile stole across Miette's face. "So it has been rumored."

Bertrada had to walk away from the woman to avoid slapping her. The idea that that Miette had some sort of relationship with Pippin infuriated her. *When did that start? Before the Ragomfred ball? After I went missing?*

Either way, it was an insult. Here she was carrying Pippin's child while he was out flirting with the first woman who threw herself in his direction. It was disgusting! Worse, it was embarrassing.

\* \* \*

After asking some of the noble women at court, Bertrada found out that there were rumors circulating about Pippin and Miette during the time Pippin supposedly was searching for her. The idea made her want to retch. She tried to find out as much about Miette as she could but was hampered by being locked away in the palace until Pippin returned.

The only person who seemed to know about Miette in any detail was Lady Hélène. Bertrada went to visit her rooms and found her protector in the company of an elegant older woman.

"My sister Catherine," Hélène explained. "She was taken hostage by Pippin after he sacked her husband's castle at Loches."

"I'm pleased to make your acquaintance, my lady," Catherine said.

"At this point, I'm a postulant. Calling me Sister will suffice."

Catherine raised an eyebrow but nodded her acceptance. "Then Sister it is, although, I must say I'm surprised. I had the distinct impression at the Ragomfred ball that you were in love with our mayor."

Bertrada felt her face flush with anger. "Not that it's any of your affair, but much has happened since then."

Hélène reached out to her, laying a reassuring hand on her arm. "Catherine is the reason I followed to protect you. She saw the danger Childeric presented and asked me to watch out for you."

Bertrada flushed even further, this time with embarrassment. "Then I must thank you. I believe you saved my life."

"I believe it's Hélène who saved your life. I just saw the danger."

"How did you know I was with child?"

Catherine shrugged. "I have a good eye for details. I hope you recognize that you are still in grave danger, my lady."

"Sister," Bertrada corrected. Although she hadn't yet taken her vows, she wasn't about to let this woman patronize her.

Catherine again nodded, although Bertrada had the distinct impression she was being humored. She turned to Hélène. "What do you know about Lady Ragomfred?"

"She's a merchant's daughter. She married Lord Ragomfred for his title. He married her for her dowry. An intelligent young woman, anxious to be accepted at court."

"I would say she has succeeded," Catherine said. "She's been the talk of the court since I arrived."

"Did Pippin sleep with her?"

Catherine frowned. "That's a question for the mayor."

"But surely you've heard the rumors."

"I have."

"Are they true?"

"I don't know. It was clearly in Childeric's interest to spread them. She made her supposedly secret visits to the palace very visible."

Bertrada was growing frustrated. "Did he sleep with her?"

"I don't know." Catherine said.

"You could tell across a crowded room that I was with

child but can't deduce whether or not Pippin seduced Lord Ragomfred's wife?"

Catherine sighed. "I must admit that he's quite an enigma to me. That he loves you, I'm certain. Just as I can see that you love him." She waved away Bertrada's protest. "Please, my dear, I may be old but I'm not blind. But as to Lady Ragomfred, I really don't know. Your Pippin is ruled by emotions so strong that sometimes he's lost to them. I watched him nearly kill a man for having the audacity to interrupt our conversation. I also know that Lady Ragomfred is a very attractive young woman and quite aware of her power over men...a dangerous combination. And you, my lady, as I recall, abandoned him. What claim can you make on his affections if you released him from his commitment?"

"He might have waited more than a month."

Catherine frowned. "It's been several months since you severed the relationship. And...he is without an heir. Whether you know it or not that makes him vulnerable. Carloman has a son. His sister is with child. Without an heir, Pippin's rule will eventually come into question."

"That won't matter for years."

"Childeric certainly thought it did. The game of kings is a long one."

"But Lady Ragomfred? She's already married."

Catherine scoffed. "Have you met her husband? Hardly one to consummate a marriage! I doubt Pippin would have difficulty getting it annulled."

Bertrada didn't like the way the conversation was going. If she didn't want Pippin herself, then why was she arguing? What was to be gained?

"You're right." Bertrada said, angry with herself. "Who am I to question what Pippin does?"

"You're going to be the mother of his child. That will never change. I'm sure that will be enough to ensure your safety. In all likelihood, that will mean you have to remain part of his household, so you had best resign yourself to being present for his future indiscretions."

Bertrada shuddered at the thought of such an arrangement.

Catherine stood. "Speaking of children, it's time I checked on mine. They don't like being cooped up in this palace all day."

Bertrada waited for the older woman to leave before addressing Hélène. "Is she always so blunt?"

Hélène laughed. "Always. She sees things from a different perspective. And she's usually right. She has had her way with me since birth." Her face grew serious. "I suppose I should have listened to her years ago."

"About what?"

Hélène shook her head as tears welled in her eyes. "She told me that I was choosing the iron path for the wrong reason."

"Why did you?"

"Because I was afraid to love Agnès."

❋ ❋ ❋

Time slowed to a crawl inside the palace. Bertrada tried to rededicate herself to a life of God, emulating her days at Chelles and using the daily masses to keep time.

But instead of quieting her mind, the solitude only sent her thoughts raging down corridors of doubt. Why was she really abandoning her life? Was she right to condemn Pippin's use of violence? She had felt thankful for Hélène's protection when the king's men had attacked and would be forever in debt to Agnès, so why did she judge Pippin so harshly?

Round and round her thoughts went trying to uncover what had set her on her path to God. The answers eluded her. She sought out Hélène, hoping the older woman would find a way to distract her. She found her protector in the practice yard, working through the slow careful movements that

Hélène and Agnès had taught her out on the farm.

"Join me."

Bertrada nodded and took her place alongside Hélène. It didn't take long before the forms returned to her and she could move from one to the next without a pause. Her body of course was different, as the babe had grown large in her womb, but the slow progression of poses forced her mind to concentrate on something other than Pippin. When they were done, she felt quite relaxed, almost exuberant.

Hélène was smiling. "Feeling better?"

Bertrada nodded. "I should do this every day."

"You're welcome to join me."

"I'd like that." She smiled.

"Oh, my lord, what's that?" Hélène seemed alarmed.

"What is what?"

"It almost looks like a smile! Where did that come from?"

Bertrada laughed, enjoying the moment, despite being embarrassed. "I enjoy your company." A sudden thought struck her, destroying the mood. "Hélène, what will you do when Pippin returns?"

"That depends on the man he is when he returns."

"I don't understand."

"I asked him a question when he came to the Abbey. He's had plenty of time to consider his answer."

Bertrada shook her head. None of that made sense to her. "I meant, what about me? I've grown quite dependent on you."

"Pippin will protect you."

"It's more than that. I've grown quite fond of you."

"Again, that will depend on the man Pippin is when he returns."

"What kind of man do you want him to be?"

"One who will bring justice to the kingdom."

Miette stepped into the practice yard, her voice cutting through their conversation like a sword. "What about Carloman? Isn't he the Holy Warrior and the Arm of God?"

Bertrada could barely control her fury at the woman's interruption. "How long have you been listening?" She felt like a farm animal next to Miette's diminutive beauty. Sweaty and dirty after her practice, Bertrada couldn't help but notice that Miette looked as if she had just bathed. Her hair, skin, and clothes looked fresh and delicate next to Bertrada's girth and shorn hair. She could see why Pippin might prefer Miette.

"The two aren't the same thing." Hélène answered the question as if Miette had always been part of the conversation. In fact, Hélène's eyes seemed alight with an inner fire. "You serve the wrong master, Lady Ragomfred. The time of Clovis is at an end. The Merovingians no longer serve Francia. They only serve themselves."

"How do you know whom I serve?" Miette's voice took on a coquette's charm.

"I serve justice," Hélène said. "You serve power. The two are not the same."

"What if I served Pippin?" Miette looked directly at Bertrada. "What if I were to bear his child?"

"You hedgehog!" Bertrada took a step only to be halted by Hélène's raised hand. It had an authority that wouldn't be denied. Hélène faced Miette with such power and strength that her very posture was an implied threat. When she spoke, her voice was barely a whisper but still carried all the severity of a gaoler.

"Only time will tell whom you serve, milady. Perhaps you still have a role to play. Know only this: if Pippin is to serve justice – if he is who I believe he is destined to be – betraying him will be your death."

A thrill leapt through Bertrada at the look of utter fright that crossed Miette's petite face. Yet the young woman recovered quickly, so quickly in fact that Bertrada almost believed she hadn't seen the change at all. With a short, but dignified curtsy Miette left the room.

Bertrada was about to speak when Hélène turned to face

her, the threat still on her face. "Does that answer your question?"

* * *

Pippin rode into Paris late in the year with the army at his back, squandering any doubts that he was weakened by the rebellion. Bertrada watched from the ramparts as he crossed the bridge to the palace gate, hoping that he would have time for her. She had much to discuss with him.

But from the moment he arrived, Pippin barked out a whirlwind of orders that sent most of the palace jumping to obey. Servants rushed to pack clothes, equipment and all the accouterments of his household into carts, Bertrada's things included. The palace was in an uproar.

Pippin was so preoccupied with Gunther, Childebrand and Arnot that he barely acknowledged her presence. Rumors ran rampant in the chaos: She heard that Carloman was dead; Hamar was dead. Trudi was dead. No one knew what to believe.

When Pippin finally called for her, she found him pacing in the throne room, surrounded by Gunther, Childebrand, and the Lady Catherine. A furious look marred his face.

She stepped towards him. "Pippin – "

He held up a hand to silence her. "Sister, please wait until the others are here."

It was as if she were a stranger! She could feel her cheeks flush with anger but did as he requested wondering what "others" were to arrive.

Within a moment Hélène and Miette were ushered into the room. They were a study in contrasts; Hélène, tall and exuding power, strode into the room like a soldier. She even had a sword on her back. Miette, dark and diminutive, entered like a cat, cautious but curious, taking care to be sure of her exits.

Pippin wasted no time on pleasantries. "Lady Hélène,

please tell me what happened at Chelles."

Hélène spoke with a calm professionalism. "The Lady Ragomfred arrived with three of the king's men. She entered the Abbey for the purpose of finding the Lady Bertrada. Once she became convinced of our presence, she notified the guards who attacked the Abbey. They killed several of the sisters and Agnès, a close friend of mine."

"This was Salau?" Pippin said.

Hélène nodded. "Agnès and I fought and defeated two of them. But after Agnès fell, I faced Salau alone. At least I did until Lady Ragomfred stabbed him from behind with one of the guards' knives. It was that wound that allowed me to finish him."

Pippin turned to Miette. "Why did you stab him?"

"Couldn't we discuss this in private?"

"No banter, milady. Not today."

Bertrada could have cheered the way Pippin shut out Miette. Much as she had with Bertrada, Miette squared her shoulders and her coquettish persona dropped away. She addressed Pippin directly. "It's true that I was sent to find Bertrada. But that was all I was told. Perhaps I should have guessed Childeric's plan. In truth, I probably should have. But in the end, I couldn't stand by while they killed her. I couldn't be part of her murder. I," Miette hesitated. "I couldn't do that to you."

Pippin swore under his breath, his anger seething from him. "You must realize that you're still complicit in killing the nuns at Chelles."

"Unknowingly, yes. But consider this, the only knife I raised was in defense of Hélène and Bertrada."

Pippin scowled.

Catherine cleared her throat before speaking. "While you would be right to administer justice, my lord, this is perhaps not the most opportune time to do so. You can ill afford to start a civil war over the girl. Since she came to her senses – albeit late in the day – perhaps discretion might be the best course in this particular instance."

Both Childebrand and Gunther nodded their heads in agreement.

"Very well." Pippin addressed Miette. "Your act to save them has, in turn, saved yourself. You'll be returned to your husband."

Bertrada felt a thrill at his words, but Miette looked so frightened that for once she almost felt sorry for her. "Please, Pippin, let me stay. They'll kill me."

Pippin was unmoved. "They don't know what happened. Tell them what you want...that Gunther killed him."

"Let me stay as your hostage. If you let me go, they'll know I betrayed them. Tell them that I couldn't bring myself to kill you...that our affair saved your life."

Bertrada felt her whole body grow cold. So, it was true! And Pippin wasn't even embarrassed to admit it.

"Please!" Miette begged, tears welling in her eyes.

Pippin's face was a mask. Even Bertrada couldn't read it. *Did he admit the affair? Did he care how she would feel about it?*

Miette must have realized her pleas would go unanswered. Although she wept, she straightened her shoulders and curtsied. "As you will, milord." She turned to take her leave and walked regally from the room.

Bertrada looked up to find Pippin staring at her. "Sister, you will travel with me to Quierzy. I can't afford to have my child threatened again. I'm sorry for your plans at the Abbey, but they're no longer possible."

Bertrada noticed that he had said "my child" and not "you." It was almost as if she didn't exist, save as a vessel for his progeny. She felt tears of humiliation coming and angrily pushed them aside. She refused to show less control than Miette. Ignoring the irony of it, she curtsied and said, "As you will, milord." She left the room with as much dignity as she could muster and followed Miette out the door.

\* \* \*

The next morning, Pippin was roused early. Servants had found Miette's body outside the palace gate on the far side of the bridge. She had been beaten so badly that she was barely recognizable. Both eyes and her left cheek were swollen and bruised. Blood caked about her nose, her mouth, and one eye. Although she still drew breath, she was close to death.

Pippin cursed himself when he saw her. He should have listened to her. He should have believed her. He had dismissed her fears and she had paid the price. He lifted her into his arms, cradling her like a child, and carried her inside the palace. He shouted for his doctors and took Miette up to his room.

Once he had her situated on the bed, Pippin grabbed a towel and doused it with ale leftover from the previous night and tried to clean away the blood on Miette's face. She groaned at his touch, but her eyes fluttered open, two small slits in the bruising. When she saw him, she tried to smile.

"I'm sorry, Miette. I should have believed you."

"No," she whispered through cracked lips. "My fault."

"What did he do to you?"

Her eyes misted with tears and she looked away from him. "He broke me."

\* \* \*

An armed delegation arrived at the gates of the palace two days later led by Bishop Boniface that included Childeric and Lord Ragomfred. Pippin met them in the throne room with Childebrand and Lady Hélène beside him.

The fact that Pippin sat on the throne clearly wasn't lost on any of his guests. The cheeks on Boniface's face splotched red and Childeric's eyes grew dark and menacing. The delegation crossed the room and stopped several feet before the throne.

"Forgive me, Lord Mayor." Boniface stressed the title when he spoke. "I expected a much warmer reception."

Pippin was in no mood for pleasantries. "Are you here at my brother's request?"

Boniface looked over his shoulder at his companions. "I'm here on behalf of the Church."

Pippin rocked back in the oversized throne and banged the back of his head against it...not once, but twice. He felt like he had been here before. Boniface was here to corral him like a wild horse, hobble him so that Carloman's grand plan would succeed. They had drawn him into the fight with Odilo and now they came to draw him into Childeric's ascendancy.

All his life, Pippin had been the dutiful soldier, the dutiful son, and brother. He had fallen into line whenever Charles or Carloman had called him to. Time and time again, he had compromised his interests for the greater good.

But now, Carloman was betraying him. He had been clear with Carloman about Childeric and yet here was Boniface presenting the bastard for elevation. He wouldn't do this without Carloman's blessing. The implication was clear. They no longer needed his approval.

For some reason, Pippin thought of Catherine. If she were here, she would ask him what Charles would do. With sudden clarity, he realized it was the wrong question. Charles wouldn't have been put in this position because Boniface would never have tried to coerce him. Charles had been his own man from the very beginning.

"Say what you have to say, Boniface."

The Bishop cleared his throat. "Tomorrow, the Holy Catholic Church will announce that Childeric, son of Chilperic will assume the throne. He'll be anointed with the holy oil at St. Denis with the blessing of Carloman, mayor of the palace. I'm here to ask for your blessing for his elevation."

"No."

"I beg you to think about this, Pippin. Your father struggled for most of his life to unite the kingdom and yet here you are splitting it apart."

"Don't speak to me of my father! He would have nothing

to do with this. It's Carloman who chooses this path."

"The Church agrees with him."

"I will not serve this man."

Childeric stepped forward, his manner dripping in haughtiness. It was as if he already had been crowned. "In the end, you will. It's but a matter of time. Most of the Neustrian nobility support me. Your brother and his son Drogo support me. The church supports me. Your opposition is meaningless. You'll be a voice crying out of the wilderness."

"You are no king."

"On the contrary. I am the last of the royal blood, a direct descendent of Clovis. And you? Your father was a bastard who had to steal his mother's treasure to purchase an army. Soldiers may follow you, Pippin, but will a kingdom? I think not. And what of the nobles who support you now? Will they continue their allegiance when I'm crowned their king? Treason is punishable by death. I doubt you'll have an army six months after I'm crowned.

"Save us all the blood and treasure and anguish your pride will cost us, Pippin. Kneel now and unite the land under its legitimate king. Pledge your hands to me and we'll rule together."

Pippin held in his mind the image of Miette, broken and bruised by the side of the road and Bertrada hiding in a nunnery to protect her life. Childeric wasn't a man; he was a monster. And with the divine right of kings, he would become a very powerful monster.

Rather than reply to Childeric, Pippin addressed Lord Ragomfred. "And your wife, Lord Ragomfred? How does she fare?"

Ragomfred was so angry he stuttered through his response. "How – How dare you speak of my wife!"

Boniface stepped forward, holding up a calming hand. "We are also here on her account, Pippin. Lord Ragomfred has accused you of adultery – of lying with his wife. He has asked the Church to excommunicate you."

Pippin was incredulous. "Me? You condemn me?"

"Do you deny it?" Lord Ragomfred charged. "It's been the talk of the court for months."

"Of course, I deny it! As will she. It was an illusion to mislead Childeric."

"She's a fallen woman." Ragomfred said. "She's been turned out of my house. Her word means nothing."

"She lies within these walls...grievously wounded. If she dies, I will see you hung."

Ragomfred was indignant. "There's your proof, Bishop. She came running to him!"

"She was left on the side of the road to die." Pippin assessed Ragomfred. "But you didn't beat her, did you?" His eyes found Childeric. "You did. She ran to you and you left her to die."

Boniface interrupted. "Adultery is a serious charge, Pippin. Unless it's withdrawn, the church can't ignore it. You may be excommunicated."

"And if I support Childeric?"

"The charge," Ragomfred answered, suddenly looking very smug, "will be withdrawn."

Pippin stood. The guards with Childeric and Ragomfred stiffened, their hands moving to their swords. Pippin stood directly in front of Boniface.

"You've lost your way, Bishop. That you were once my father's friend, I have no doubt. But this isn't what he wanted for Francia. And it isn't what I want. I didn't spend my entire life in battle so that you could tell me who will be king."

Pippin next turned to Ragomfred. He leaned into the older man's face so that their noses almost touched. He was so furious that he had to stop himself from killing Ragomfred on the spot. "If Miette dies. I'll come for you."

"Do you plan to kill us all?" Childeric said, haughty as ever.

Pippin knew he was being baited. He let his anger cool so he could think clearly. Childeric wanted him isolated with his leadership in doubt. A threat on Childeric's life coupled with a charge of adultery would undermine his legitimacy as mayor and threaten the support of the nobles who served him.

Pippin caught a look from Boniface. It was a face he had seen throughout his youth when the bishop had taught him the catechism. The older man's eyebrow was arched like he was waiting for him to figure out an obvious answer. He was telling him silently that there was only one logical way for this saga to play out.

But Pippin was no longer his pupil and no longer interested in the bishop's lessons. From this day forward, he would be his own man. He would decide his path and let others adjust theirs. He unfastened a money purse from his belt and pulled out two gold solidi.

"Here," he said tossing them to Childeric. "These are for you."

"It's a start." Childeric smiled and made a show out of biting them to ensure their legitimacy. "Whatever are they for?"

"To cover the eyes of your corpse."

# CHAPTER
# FORTY-ONE

*St. Denis*

B ishop Boniface waited as the crowd gathered outside the palace at the end of the bridge. With a nod from Carloman, he signaled for the procession to begin.

Two trumpeters mounted the rampart and lifted their horns in regal fanfare. The palace gates opened, revealing Carloman, sitting tall upon his warhorse and leading two rows of his commanders – all Knights in Christ, wearing their red and white doublets.

Boniface came next dressed in ceremonial robes holding aloft the cross of Christ. With practiced command, he paused to hold the crowd's attention before stepping into the street. Behind him marched twenty priests carrying thuribles of burning incense that clinked and clanked as they waved the pungent smoke before the procession.

As they had planned, cheering crowds lined the streets, throwing dyed flour into the air as infantry soldiers marched from the gate in formation, banging their shields in rhythm with their steps. The court's nobles and their retinues followed, each flying their family banners. At the end of the procession, twenty young women, dressed in white, waved palm leaves before a primitive, two-wheeled, ox-cart that made its way through the streets. Childeric, dressed in a plain white robe rode within the cart, waving blessings upon the crowd as he made his way on the three-hour journey to St. Denis.

To Boniface, it looked like the triumphant return of Jesus to Jerusalem, the future king of Francia was headed to claim his crown.

It was a long march, but the road was crowded save for small gaps between towns. The three hours passed quickly, although the attention of the twenty young women often seemed to flag.

As they approached the entrance to St. Denis, Boniface led the priests in a ritual chant, calling upon the saints to pray for the future king. His voice projected far into the crowd. "Kyrie, eleison."

The priests chorused. "*Kyrie, eleison.*"

"Christe, eleison!

"*Christe, eleison.*"

"Kyrie, eleison!"

When Carloman entered the square before the cathedral Boniface saw him lift his arm in salute and the crowd bellowed their support.

"Spiritus Sancte Deus,"

"*Miserere nobis.*"

"Sancte Trinitas, unus Deus,"

"*Miserere nobis.*"

As his priests approached the cathedral, Carloman and his Knights stood aside as Boniface and his priests mounted the stairs.

"Sancta Virgo Virginum."

"*Ora pro nobis.*"

"Sancte Michaeli Archangelo,

"*Ora pro nobis.*"

"Sancte Gabriel"

"*Ora pro nobis*"

The cheers grew louder as the end of the procession

neared and the crowd surrounding the cathedral spied their future king. Carloman waited for Childeric at the base of the stairs and offered his hand. Childeric took it to descend from the cart. Instead of letting go, the Merovingian raised Carloman's hand above his head in celebration and the crowd roared its approval. Carloman bowed to the king and Childeric strode regally up the steps to the cathedral.

Together, they stood at the back of the cathedral bathed in the light of alabaster-laced windows until a fanfare announced them. As one they walked down the aisle.

Bishops Boniface and Aidolf awaited them on the altar.

"I'd say this is going well," Aidolf mused. "No one seems to notice Pippin's absence."

"It's not the peasants I worry about," Boniface said. "His absence, and the absence of his army, suggests civil war. He's taken his army and much of the court to Quierzy."

"Carloman seems content. As does Childeric."

"Carloman believes that once Childeric is anointed with the holy oil, Pippin will fall in line."

"You don't?"

Boniface frowned. "Carloman has a habit of underestimating his brother."

"Surely you can guide them towards reconciliation."

"I don't know." Boniface grimaced. "Pippin is resolute and Carloman has changed since the rebellion."

"The Church has never had a more devout champion than Carloman."

Boniface nodded, but weakly. He had growing reservations about Carloman. The man's behavior at Tassilo's baptism had unnerved him. The careful, thoughtful man Carloman once had been was gone. This man was ruthless and arrogant.

As Carloman and Childeric approached the altar, Aidolf bowed and ushered Childeric to his seat facing the congregation. The Merovingian sat on it like it was already his throne. Carloman stood behind him like a proud parent. Boniface returned to the altar to begin the mass.

The Latin came easily to his lips. He had led the service so often than he could do it from memory. As his body went through the introductory rites, the liturgies and communion, his thoughts chased down the reasons for his growing unease.

He had been so sure that raising the Merovingian had been the best course of action that he had never once questioned his own judgment. Now, he wasn't so sure. He had believed both brothers would fall into line before elevating the king. Carloman's decision to preempt Pippin was a mistake. It only had hardened his brother's position.

And why *was* Pippin so adamant that Childeric not be crowned? What had he seen that was worth risking a civil war? Pippin's objections didn't seem to be based on coveting the throne. Just the opposite, he simply didn't want Childeric to have it.

And what about Lady Ragomfred? He had never known Pippin to lie. For some reason Boniface felt like the fate of the kingdom hung in the balance of such questions.

He had just put away the Eucharist and was reveling in the quiet that surrounded his routine of cleaning the chalice when Bishop Aidolf interrupted.

"Bishop?"

Boniface was embarrassed to find that he had lost his place in the ceremony. Aidolf had stepped in with the holy oil for anointing the Merovingian.

"Yes, of course." Boniface whispered. Whatever his misgivings were, they were too late now. The course of events had moved too quickly. Boniface dipped his thumb into the oil and turned to make the sign of the cross on Childeric's forehead. The congregation of nobles rose as Boniface extended his hand.

"As the holy dove brought the oil to christen Clovis on the day he became king, so we baptize thee as king."

The moment his thumb pressed against the man's skin, a dove behind the altar was released and flew up into the rafters above the nave. "In the name of the Father, the Son, and the Holy Ghost..."

Aidolf next offered the crown to Boniface. Boniface lifted it, saying, "As Legate of the Holy See, I crown thee King Childeric III."

As Boniface lowered the crown, a wave of foreboding passed through him that was so strong, his hands shook. The crown slipped and would have fallen save for Carloman steadying the circlet with his two hands. Together, they set the crown on Childeric's head.

The applause from the congregants was deafening. All Boniface felt was dread.

# EPILOGUE

*Quierzy*

After a month at Quierzy, Bertrada began to feel like herself again. It reminded her of the years she had spent there as Pippin's consort. A day's ride from Paris, the massive hunting estate had been one of Charles's favorite residences. To her it was like a second home.

The weather cooled as winter settled in at the country estate. Bertrada ordered the villa to be decorated with greenery for the holidays. With Sunnichild gone, the servants had turned to her for direction and she had fallen into the role of running the household.

Pippin's court had taken up residence at the estate and there was much to do. She had doled out rooms for each of the nobles, laid in food stores for the winter, and had enough trees cut down to ensure the Quierzy villa would stay warm for the winter.

In truth, she found great joy in the role. It gave her purpose and allowed her to forget about the future implications of bearing Pippin's child. None of the nobles at court seemed to question her role. In fact, it seemed like they expected this behavior from her.

She had grown large with child. Although she had continued to train each morning with Hélène, rising early to avoid the eyes of Pippin's court, her belly had grown to the point of discomfort. Her skin was so tight it felt like the head of a drum. And the babe had a habit of kicking her late at night, impeding her ability to sleep. Her only solace was that the nausea no longer plagued her.

Pippin, too, seemed to enjoy Quierzy. Once he had decided that his army would camp there until the Spring Assembly, he and the nobles began to enjoy themselves hunting and drinking their way through the winter months. She had taken to walking with him around the grounds during the early afternoon so that she could update him on the household needs of the palace.

He was always polite on these walks, asking after her health and her comfort. He was always deferential, referring to her as Sister. But as the weeks flew by, and their familiarity returned, so did his mischievous side. He teased her like the old days to make her laugh and she was glad to have this time with him.

She had taken charge of Miette's recovery, ensuring that her wounds were clean and that her bandages were replaced on a daily basis. Early on, she even had fed her rival with a spoon as Miette's jaw was too swollen to eat solid food. As the bruising healed, Miette's face began to take on its former beauty, but the woman's eyes remained haunted, giving her a ghost-like quality.

Bertrada kept up most of the conversation during their time together. This was by necessity in the early days, as Miette could barely speak. But as time moved on, the pattern continued. Bertrada was willing to share a greater burden of the discussion and, for the most part, Miette seemed content to listen.

"Why are you helping me?" Miette asked one morning.

"Because you need help."

"But why you? Why are you the mistress here?"

"I don't know. Perhaps you should ask Pippin."

"Perhaps I will." Miette smiled, wickedly. "Maybe I'll

apply for the role."

It was a silly statement, meant in humor, but the thought pained Bertrada. Despite their familiarity, there was still a wide gulf between her and Pippin. And she wasn't sure she wanted it bridged. She liked things the way they were. But the thought of Miette sleeping in his bed appalled her.

As Miette's wounds continued to heal, she became more mobile and began to explore the town of Quierzy. On several occasions, Bertrada saw Miette and Pippin together in the town. He had given her an allowance to use for replacing the wardrobe and personal items she had lost when Lord Ragomfred had turned her out.

Their playfulness set Bertrada on edge. She pictured Miette touching his arm, laughing at his jokes. And Pippin was so vulnerable to her wiles! He would tease Miette just as he'd teased her and then one day they would kiss and Bertrada was sure it would be a short hop into Miette's bed.

She began to resent Miette's beauty. How could she compete with that? She wanted to feel pretty again. She wanted to see the light in Pippin's eyes when he smiled at her. She wanted to make him eager to take her in his arms. But she argued with herself: did she really want that? She wasn't sure, but as her time neared, she grew more and more anxious about him.

She rose one morning and walked to the kitchen to ensure the morning meal was on schedule. A frost covered the ground, and the air was thick and cold, and it smelled like snow. She made a mental note to check the wood supply when a pain lanced across her belly, doubling her over. After a minute it subsided, and she returned to her chores. A second pain lashed out at her and this time, she had to sit. The third time it hit, she knew.

She told one of the cooks to fetch the midwives and to advise Pippin that her time had come. She then tried to make her way back to her room, wobbling awkwardly across the yard. She was no more than halfway there when liquid splashed down her legs. She was running out of time. She soldiered on, leaving a trail of fluid behind her.

She reached her chambers and climbed into bed. The lead midwife and Pippin arrived soon afterwards and took care to make her comfortable. She was about to make a joke about her timing when a wave of pain hit her. She tried to hold back from crying out from the pain.

Pippin was on his knees beside the bed, holding her hand. "Is there anything I can do for you, Sister? Anything?"

She looked up at him, his face so open and vulnerable. He loved her. It was obvious. And in that moment, she knew she loved him too. She held onto the thought, liking the way it made her feel. She reached out to touch his face, caressing it with her hand.

She was surprised to see his eyes well up with tears. She must have made a face, because he grew embarrassed and brushed them away.

"I'm sorry, Sister. I was carried away."

"Stop!" she said. "As the father of this child, from now on, you must promise that you will do one thing for me."

"Anything. Just name it."

"Please, call me Bertrada."

He laughed and stroked her hair. She took his hand in hers and squeezed it with all her might. A look of pain lanced across his face, but it was tiny compared to the cramping in her stomach. She cried out, needing to push the baby out. Again, and again the pain took her, and she pushed and pushed until it felt like her body was splitting in two and then she had to push all the more.

❋ ❋ ❋

When they gave the boy to him, Pippin was afraid to hold it. Although the midwife had wrapped it in a blanket, the babe was still half covered in mucous and screaming like a banshee. Pippin tried to seek help from the midwife, but she was too focused on Bertrada. It was then he noticed that all of the midwives were surrounding Bertrada and none of them were smiling.

He tried to move into the circle around the bed, but the lead midwife shooed him away. There was something wrong. Bertrada lay back on the bed, she was pale and nearly unconscious. "What is it?" he asked. *"What's wrong?!"*

"She's bleeding too much," one of the midwives said. "We're trying to stop it."

Pippin knelt beside the bed, holding the babe in his arms. "No, Bertie. Not now. Stay with me. The babe needs you. I need you."

Bertrada's head lolled toward him and she looked at him through delirious eyes. "You love me," she smiled and then her eyes rolled back into her head as she lost consciousness.

The midwives pushed Pippin aside and propped Bertrada's legs open. Using towels, they tried to staunch the blood that seeped from her. Pippin nearly wept at the sight of it. It was as if her life was pouring from her.

He retreated to the back of the room, still holding the child. It twisted and squirmed in his arms. A crippling fear took hold of him. Although he hadn't prayed alone to God in half his lifetime, Pippin bent his knee.

It took several hours before the midwives said with any confidence that Bertrada would live. When she was ready, Pippin brought the babe to her. Bertrada looked weak and pale. With a small smile, she opened her robe to let the babe feed. She seemed grateful to have the child in her arms.

They sat in silence simply watching the infant together until the babe had finished. Bertrada handed it to Pippin while the midwives covered her. Once she was presentable, others crowded into the room, including, Childebrand, Gunther, Arnot, Catherine, and Hélène.

Pippin displayed the child for his new audience. "A

boy!" Everyone in the room applauded. "He'll be named after my father, Charles."

Gunther produced mugs and handing them around the room, poured drinks from a large flagon.

"He should have an epithet," Childebrand said, "Charles the Hammer has been taken and we need one that is better than the child's father's."

Gunther chuckled. "It's not hard to surpass Pippin the Short."

They all looked to Bertrada expectantly. She held out her arms for the baby and Pippin gave the infant back to her. As she looked down into his face, the baby opened his eyes and turned his head as if looking for her. When their eyes met, he smiled. Bertrada's cheeks flushed with emotion.

"He's magnificent," she said.

Catherine chuckled. "That's perfect. Le magne! 'The magnificent' it shall be."

Gunther raised his mug. "To Charles *le Magne!*

They drank to the babe's health.

####

# AUTHOR'S NOTE

Although this story is drawn from history and set in a very real time and place with many real characters and real events, it is fiction...pure and simple. Please don't take offense if I have treated a beloved personage harshly or seek to "set the record straight" if I've made a character come to life in a way that you find inaccurate or offensive. I make no claims to know the personalities of those who lived over twelve hundred years ago.

History for this period is sketchy at best. Most of what was recorded was written long after the fact and usually by those who prevailed in the conflicts of the day. As a result, their biased perspectives defined what was "true."[1] Most historians readily recognize this fundamental flaw and work hard to piece together the record from what limited sources exist into a common thread of what happened and what did not. And even then, they don't always agree.

For those who are interested in knowing which pieces of these stories come from that common thread of facts versus my fiction, I offer the following:

## General Plot Outline

For much of Frankish history, the power behind the Merovingian Kings was ensconced in the office of the "mayor of the palace." Mayors were men who commanded the military and ran the government over one or more of three primary states in the Frankish Kingdom (Neustria, Austrasia and Burgundy) much akin to the way the Shogun in Japanese history ruled in the name of a "divine" emperor.

Other states within Francia operated somewhat more independently as "duchies." These included Alemannia, Bavaria, Thuringia, Hesse and Aquitaine, all related through agreements and fealty to the offices of mayor, although some more than others. Often passed from father to son, the office of the mayor created powerful families that ruled large territories over the course of many generations. By the beginning of the eighth century the power of the mayors had coalesced into two regions, Austrasia and Neustria, and increased so substantially that the Merovingian kings of this time are often referred to as "puppet" or "shadow" kings.[2]

Much of this consolidation of power was due to the military and diplomatic machinations of Pippin II of Herstal. After seizing power and the title of mayor through force of arms in Austrasia in 675, Pippin and his family spent much of the next twelve years battling for control over neighboring Neustria. Following a rash of assassinations and a decisive battle at Tetry in 687, Pippin succeeded and ultimately took the title of mayor in Neustria as well. By the time of his death in 714, Pippin's influence dwarfed considerably the power of dukes in the other states of the Frankish territories.

Pippin and his wife, Plectrude (from a powerful Austrasian family) had a son named Grimoald who stood to inherit the bulk of this power. Unfortunately, Grimoald was murdered in the chapel of his patron saint, Saint Lambert, shortly after Pippin's death.

Grimoald's assassination set off a cascade of events: Plectrude sought to retain control over both states by naming Grimoald's six year-old son, Theudoald, mayor of Neustria and another grandson, Arnulf, mayor of Austrasia; She imprisoned Charles, the 26 year-old bastard son of her late husband to prevent him asserting a claim; The Neustrians revolted, displaced Theudoald and named their own mayor; Charles escaped, battled Plectrude and her allies, seized his father's treasure and named himself mayor. Ultimately, this displaced both his nephews as mayor and pulled much of Francia into a civil war. One by one, Charles fought the states within the Frankish kingdom to assert his claim as mayor and re-conquered what today constitutes Western Europe.[3]

Historically, Charles is most famous for the battle of Poitiers in 732. There, he stopped an invasion of the Saracen (Muslim) army under Abd ar-Rachman, then governor of Spain. The Saracens' advance threatened Tours, which was where many of the kingdom's holy relics were kept. Charles' army stepped in to arrest the Saracen progress north. The battle ended in the death of Abd ar-Rachman and the rout of the Saracen army. It was for this battle that Charles was named, "Charles Martel" or "Charles the Hammer." For over a thousand years, historians credited him with saving Christianity in Europe.[4]

Charles reigned as mayor of the palace for 27 years. His power grew so great that in the last years of his reign, he openly ignored the rights of succession of the Merovingian Kings. When Theuderic IV died in 737, Charles refused to elevate another Merovingian to the throne and led the kingdom himself, without a king, for four more years until his death.

Charles Martel had four (legitimate) children. His eldest two sons, Carloman and Pippin, were born of his first wife, Chlotrude, who also gave Charles a daughter named Hiltrude. After Chlotrude's death, Charles had a third son, Gripho, from a second marriage to a Bavarian princess from the powerful Agilolfing family. Her name was Sunnichild (*also seen as Swannahilde*).

After putting down a rebellion by Maurontus in Septemia and Provence, Charles Martel died at home in his villa in Quierzy on September 22, 741. No cause is listed for his death. Just before he died, he named all of his sons mayor and divided the kingdom equally among them.

History shows that upon Charles' death his two eldest sons warred against the younger Gripho and his mother, laying siege to them at the city of Laon where they had taken up residence. Sunnichild and Gripho were captured and imprisoned. Gripho was sent to Neufchateau and Sunnichild to the nunnery at Chelles. Questions have arisen among historians as to whether the two older brothers were actually united in this endeavor. Later events clearly indicate that the two may have disagreed on the treatment of Gripho as well on the question of raising another Merovingian to the throne. There is no question, however, that the two brothers divided Gripho's territories between them. [5]

The succession was immediately renounced by Hunoald, Duke of Aquitaine and his son Waifar.[6] A challenge to the succession was also raised at the time by Theudoald, the above-mentioned grandson of Pippin of Herstal and Plectrude. I have suggested that he may have been aided in this by Bishop Wido of St. Wandrille. Given Theudoald's lineage, his claim would have had considerable merit. His challenge for the office failed, however, due to his untimely death. One text indicates that Theudoald may have been killed but did not specify by whom or why.[7] The poor man died so suddenly that year, however, one must wonder at the turn of events.

A scandal during that time involving Charles' daughter Hiltrude plagued the family well into the ninth century. Much to the consternation of her two older brothers and their court, Hiltrude fled to Regensburg following Charles' death to marry Duke Odilo of Bavaria, the uncle of Sunnichild. Hiltrude met Odilo during a prolonged visit he had made to Charles' court. Further complicating matters, Odilo was suspected of fomenting rebellion among the states of the Frankish empire and leading the kingdom into civil war.[8]

## Religion

None of the texts I have read refer to the civil war and rebellions that followed Charles's death in religious terms. The Church had long had a strong hold on the ruling aristocracy of the Franks. The Merovingians had been Christian since Clovis was baptized by bishop Remigius of Reims in 496 (after a military victory against the Alemans). Most of the regions of Francia are believed to have been Christian by the mid 700's. Recognized exceptions to this are few. In Spain, the Saracen ruled and paganism prevailed in the Frisian and the Saxon territories.

That being said, there is evidence that Christianity's hold over Europe was not so comprehensive in the mid-eighth century, particularly in the eastern regions. And given the role that religion has played and continues to play in violently dividing peoples, I felt comfortable in sowing the seeds of rebellion in a clash of faiths. For the skeptics, I offer the following:

St. Boniface was a missionary who spent most of his life in the eastern Germanic countries converting the pagan to Christianity...particularly in Frisia, Hesse and Bavaria. The bishopric at Regensburg, which Boniface founded, was not established until 739, two years before the story in ANVIL begins. If Europe were already Christian, this life's work would not have been so worthy of Boniface's attention let alone the papal recognition he received for it.

Another indication of Christianity's tentative hold on Bavaria is the lack of Christian symbols buried along with its dead. Prior to 800 (nearly sixty years after our story), few in the Regensburg region were buried with crosses or other symbols of Christianity. In fact, most corpses were buried with treasured artifacts and enough wealth to sustain them through the afterlife. Christians need no such help in the Kingdom of Heaven. According to a leading archeologist of the region, this practice stopped abruptly and almost entirely after 800 A.D. This indicates that Christianity's reach into the countryside was still new to the region and that Christianity wasn't dominant among the populace until years later, during Charlemagne's time.[9]

There is also ample evidence that the Church was very concerned over the continuing practice of pagan rituals throughout the kingdom. As late as 830, Haltigar, bishop of Cambrai produced a handbook for confessors. It was an example of the questions a confessor should ask a penitent about specific beliefs and practices.[10] The church issued specific warnings about pagan practices (it was in part upon these that I drew the rituals I describe in the novels). These infractions involved penances so light that one must assume that the practices were still widespread at the time.

Two other facts pushed me into the direction of having religion be a critical factor for the rebellion following Charles' death. When ANVIL's story begins, Trudi presses Sunni about Charles' intervention in Bavaria and recounts a tale of how Sunni's uncles married the same woman and practiced pagan rituals to heal their dying and hexed son. This story is documented history. [11] Clearly, if the nobles of Bavaria were practicing Christians, they were still only "practicing" and were not above resorting to paganism when they felt the circumstances warranted it.

Much of the pagan faith I describe in ANVIL and WHEEL originates in the Nordic and Germanic countries. The use of runes and the mythology surrounding them I pulled from a short book on runes by Nigel Pennick.[12] As mentioned above, I also drew upon the Church's condemnation of pagan practices which matched the practices Bishop Haltigar describes.

Finally, I drew from an older religion that likely preceded the Norse Gods to Eastern Europe, namely Hinduism and particularly Tantrism. For the Tantric rituals, I drew on several sources, but primarily on a book by André Van Lysebeth on Tantrism.[13] Since older religious practices and rites are often "adopted" by newer religions as is evident in the adoption of Greek mythology into that practiced by the Romans and also Christianity's adoption of rites and symbols from many cultures, I felt comfortable merging some aspects of the older Tantric faith with the "newer" Nordic religion.

## Characters
### Carloman

As Charles' eldest son, Carloman was actively involved

with his father's rise to power and was considered a formidable military force as mayor. Tutored by St. Boniface, Carloman was also greatly influenced by religion throughout his life. In the novel, I credited Carloman with founding a religious military order called the "Knights in Christ." I have no evidence that such organization existed at the time. Given the later rise of several formal religious orders among the knights (The Templars etc.), I felt at liberty to define the "Knights in Christ" as an early prototype under Carloman's care.

After Charles' death, Carloman laid siege to his half-brother Gripho and his stepmother Sunnichild at the walled city of Laon. After they capitulated, Sunnichild was sent to take orders at the Abbey at Chelles and Gripho imprisoned at Neufchateau. The hanging of Duke Heden's son depicted in ANVIL during the siege of Laon is a fiction I created for dramatic purposes.

In 742 Carloman did indeed lead an army eastward across the Rhine, help Bishop Boniface found a monastery in Fulda, and then ravage "with fire and sword" the breadth of the Alemannic duchy to the banks of the Danube where the Aleman Duke Theudebald capitulated.[14]

This conflict, along with the combined brothers' effort to put down Duc Odilo's rebellion in Bavaria (which actually happened in 743), formed the basis of Book II. I condensed the timeline for plot simplicity and because Theudebald participated in both events.

A new Merovingian – the last – Childeric III was also raised to the throne in 743. It has been argued that Carloman – not Pippin – raised the king. Historians surmised that this was a political move necessitated by the year-round military operations of both brothers requiring large masses of troops to fight on several fronts at once.[15]

*Pippin*

Having been on campaign with his father from early

adolescence, Charles' second son, Pippin (also referred to by historians as Pepin) would have been a well-blooded warrior in 741 (he was 27 at the time of Charles' death). Unlike Carloman, however, Pippin left Charles' court for several years to live with the Lombards on the Roman Peninsula in what today is Italy. Pippin was, in fact, "an adopted son" of King Liutbrand and would have been a contemporary of Prince Aistulf. Pippin's sojourn to the Roman Peninsula would have likely diminished Boniface's role in his upbringing. Therefore, I've portrayed Pippin as the less religious of the two older brothers.

Throughout ANVIL and WHEEL, I portray Pippin as a more reluctant partner in Carloman's wars. There is plenty of debate over this in the histories as it is unclear that Pippin actually participated in or approved of the siege of Laon and the raising of Childeric III to the Merovingian throne. Of the two charters that remain from Childeric III's reign, he only sites Carloman, "who placed us on the throne."[16]

Pippin did try to repay Duke Hunoald's treason by conquering the castles in northern reaches of Aquitaine. The two brothers met at Vieux Poitiers to split the kingdom after the imprisonment of their half-brother Gripho.[17] Later Pippin agreed to join Carloman in defeating Duc Odilo of Bavaria by the River Lech in 743.[18]

The history also shows that Pippin fathered a son with Bertrada, daughter of the Compte de Laon, early in his adulthood who as the story suggests becomes Charlemagne, Emperor of the Holy Roman Empire. The timing of his birth, however, has been greatly debated as some suggest he might have been born as early as 742.[19] I chose to agree with this scenario and it forms the basis of much of the story in Book III.

### Bertrada

As noted above Bertrada, the daughter of the Compte de Laon had a long relationship with Pippin starting in their early years. The fight in the novel between Bertrada and Pippin is purely fictional as is her attack on the King's road and her flight from the king's men. I was led to this in part by the need for some romantic tension in the novel, but also because Pippin didn't join Carloman on his campaign in Alemannia. I needed some reason for him to stay in Paris.

## Hiltrude

As described above, Hiltrude left Charles Martel's Court without permission to marry Duke Odilo of Bavaria in 741. This became what was considered the "scandal of the eighth century" in part because Duke Odilo promptly led a rebellion against Pippin and Carloman following the death of Charles.

In the novel, Trudi is carrying the child of another man when she arrives in Regensburg to marry Odilo. This is fiction and part of a romantic narrative I developed for ANVIL. She did give birth after marrying the Duke to a son named Tassilo.

I portrayed Hiltude as opposing Odilo's rebellion primarily because of the presence of a Papal Legate named Sergius. The histories show Sergius trying to make peace between the Franks and the Bavarians before the war. Hiltrude would have had access to and the ear of the Pope, so I chose to have her solicit this intercession.

After the fact, Pippin is reported to have given a speech in which he lectures Sergius on the justice of the Frankish cause. The two brothers spent more time justifying this battle than any other conquest made [20] and it may have been done in part out of concern for their sister.

## Boniface

Boniface (née Winfred) now St. Boniface, held great sway over Charles Martel and at least Carloman. A legate of the Pope, Boniface personally ministered to Charles' family, was godfather to Charles' sons, and a close advisor to the family. A passionate missionary who spent much of his early life converting the pagans, Boniface was named by the pope a "bishop at large." Boniface held enormous influence over the other bishops of the region and was partly responsible for gathering the synods to address Charles' taking of Church lands.

As noted in the story he also founded a monastery in Fulda, Hesse in 742. The story of Boniface felling Thor's tree in Fritzlar is well-known in ecclesiastic circles and is described much as I have portrayed it the novel. To this day, there is a memorial depicting Boniface cutting down the tree in dowtown Fritzlar.

### Theudebald

A son of Godefred of Alemannia, Theudebald had made an enemy of Charles Martel when he expelled Bishop Eto from Alemannia "because of a hatred for Charles." A year later, Charles returned to expel Theudebald.[21] There is no evidence that Theudebald paraded Eto naked through the streets or vice versa. That is my fiction.

As noted above, Theudebald does resurface after Charles death to lead a rebellion in Alemannia in 742, where he was defeated by Carloman. He later joined with Odilo in 743 at the battle of River Lech.

His rape of Hiltrude is pure fiction. Although it was a cruel way to treat her character after she finally arrives in Regensburg to marry Odilo, it helped to portray the sense of isolation she would have suffered as the daughter of Charles Martel in rebel territory. Later events (to be covered in book III) also suggest a substantial dislike for Theudebald among her brothers, so I felt it justified in keeping the storyline intact.

### Odilo

Duke Odilo of Bavaria came to power following Charles' intervention in the "civil unrest" there nearly twenty years before the story in WHEEL begins. As he had blood ties in Alemannia, I named him a relative of Theudebald. Odilo survived the battle at the River Lech and for a time continued to rule

Bavaria in the name of the Franks. As mentioned above, he and Hiltrude had a son named Tassilo.

### Fictional characters

Lady Hélène, her sister Catherine and Agnès are fictional characters. Lady Hélène played a significant role in ANVIL and, enjoying her character, I kept her around for Book II. To my surprise, her sister appeared in the early drafts of WHEEL as Catherine of Loches. This required me to write some back-story for the two which led to the development of Agnès's character.

Pippin's lieutenant Gunther is also a fictional character as is Carloman's champion Hamar. Childebrand, however, is a very real person. He was Charles half-brother and Pippin's uncle.

### Other personages

Where I could, I used the real names of the Dukes and warlords of the time. Hunoald and Waifar of Aquitaine existed and were a constant thorn in the side of the Carolingians. King Liutbrand and Aistulf ruled the Lombards on the Roman Peninsula and did indeed threaten Pope Gregory. Aistulf was also a renowned swordsman who won prizes at the Spoleto tournaments much as is described in ANVIL.

There is also no record of the name of Carloman's wife, so I supplied one. The fact of this, I find odd. As the wife of the mayor and the mother of Drogo, she should have been important enough for her name to be recorded.

### Places

Little construction exists today that existed in the eighth century. Charles' palace at Quierzy along the river Oise is gone. Quierzy still exists. It is a very small farming community with little remaining historical reference (although I did find a civic building there named the "salle de Charlemagne"). The walled city of Laon still stands atop a ridge northeast of Soissons. Although the city has grown and protects far newer buildings than were present in the mid-eighth century, it is still possible to stand on the southern wall and imagine Carloman's army approaching across the vast plain below the city. Dozens of tunnels beneath the city have recently been excavated. Many were created to protect the wealth of its residents.

The basilica of St. Denis was built in 451 above a Gallo-Roman cemetery. The monastic community there was founded in the seventh century. The church that stands there today was built after the turn of the millennium and post-dates the story in ANVIL. The tombs that housed the remains of French kings, sadly, were sacked during the French revolution. St. Germain des Prés, the church Carloman visits in ANVIL during his stay at Isle de la Cité still stands, although the portion of the church that existed during that time is closed to the public. There is no evidence that Carloman was married or received his first communion at St. Germain des Prés.

The Abbey at Chelles was founded in 658 at the site of a Merovingian royal villa in Val-de-Marne near Paris. It was primarily used as a retreat for noble women who had become widowed or wished to take orders. Unfortunately, it was destroyed down during the French Revolution and no longer stands.

Danauwörth and Regensburg still stand along the southern banks of the Danube. Little is left of the Roman fort I described that was built in Regensburg during the 1st century after Christ. Part of one tower and one half of a double-arched entryway still exist, as does a portion of the southeastern wall. I was greatly helped in visualizing it by a schematic drawing of what the fort should have looked like, provided by Dr. Boors, chief archeologist of the Regensburg museum. Dr. Boors gave me a guided tour of the museum and what was left of the fort walls. He was also kind enough to show me those artifacts from the region attributed to the eighth cen-

tury. The value of this tour was extremely helpful in that it resolved several open questions in my mind. These included the
use of Roman coin during this time period (Dr. Boors showed
me a treasure trove of solidi and denarii), the existence of
spurs and more importantly the Christian artifacts (or rather
the lack thereof) among grave sites in the region.

As can be deduced from the footnotes, I have relied
heavily on Paul Fouracare's account of the period which is detailed in *The Age of Charles Martel* published by Pearson Education Limited in 2000. Much of the summary I've recounted
above I pulled from his text, specifically the pages that dealt
with church's influence and the death of Charles Martel (pp.
160 – 176). It is one of the clearest texts on this period that I
have read and magically appeared on the bookstore shelf just
in time for the research phase of ANVIL. For that I am eternally grateful. I did not always take his lead, however, and
have tried to cite some of the other choices I made throughout
this note. I provided Fouracre with a copy of ANVIL, which he
was kind enough to read and to give the following feedback:

> "I initially jibbed every time you filled in gaps with
> your imagination - a no no for historians, but a must
> for novelists! But eventually I just went with the nar
> rative flow and found that you captured the spirit or
> the essence of the issues (personal and political) ra
> ther nicely. I have always been struck by the drama of
> Hiltrude's flight to Odilo and Bavaria."

## Bibliography

I also drew heavily on the writings of Ian Wood *The
Merovingian Kingdoms* 450 – 751 and Edward Bachrach's *Early
Carolingian Warfare, Prelude to Empire,* the latter of which was
extremely helpful in characterizing battle armor and tactics
of the time.

Other important texts upon which I relied include:

- *Carolingian Chronicles, the Royal Frankish Annals and Nithard's Histories*, translated by Scholz and Rogers (The University of Michigan Press, 1992)
- *Two Lives of Charlemagne* by Einhard and Notker the Stammerer, (Penguin Classics 1979)
- *Frankish Institutions Under Charlemagne* by Francois Louis Ganshof (Norton Library 1970)
- *Sieges of the Middle Ages* by Philip Warner (Pen & Sword Military Classics 2004)
- *Witchcraft in Europe 400 – 1700* edited by Alan Charles Kors and Edward Peters (University of Pennsylvania Press 2001)
- *Charlemagne* by Mathias Becher (Yale University Press 2003)
- *Charlemagne* by Roger Collins (University of Toronto Press 1998)
- *Charlemagne, Father of a Continent* by Alessandro Barbero and translated by Allan Cameron (University of California Press 2004)
- *Complete Illustrated Guide to Runes*, Nigel Pennick (HarperCollins Publishers 2002)
- *TANTRA, The Cult of the Feminine*, Andre Van Lysebeth (Weiser Books, Boston, MA 1995).

## Footnotes

[1]     *The Age of Charles Martel*, Paul Fouracre, (Pearson Education Limited 2000) Introduction p.6: "Modern scholarship has picked away at this picture of unqualified Carolingian success by taking on board the fact that the sources reveal only one point of view, and that late-eighth century and early ninth century writers were, in the main, working under the patronage of the Carolingian family itself."

[2]     *The Merovingian Kingdoms 450-751*, Ian Wood (Pearson Education Limited, 1994) Chapter 15 p. 287

[3]     *The Merovingian Kingdoms 450-751*, Ian Wood (Pearson

Education Limited, 1994) Chapters 15 – 16 pp. 270-275

[4]     *The Age of Charles Martel*, Paul Fouracre (Pearson Education Limited 2000) Introduction p. 2

[5]     *The Merovingian Kingdoms 450-751*, Ian Wood (Pearson Education Limited 1994) Chapter 16 pp. 289-290

[6]     *Early Carolingian Warfare, Prelude to Empire*, Bernard S. Bachrach (University of Pennsylvania Press 2001) Chapter 1 p.37

[7]     *Charlemagne*, Roger Collins (University of Toronto Press 1998) Chapter 2 p. 31 citing *Annales Laureshamenses* 741, ed. Pertz, MGH SS, 2, p. 24

[8]     *The Age of Charles Martel*, Paul Fouracre (Pearson Education Limited 2000) Chapter 6 pp. 167-168

[9]     Interview with Dr. Andreas Boos M.A. Archeologist, Historisches Museum der Stadt Regensburg, May 2005

[10]    *Witchcraft in Europe 400-1700*, ed. Alan Charles Kors and Edward Peters (University of Pennsylvania Press) Chapter 1 pp.55-57; Source: *Medieval Handbooks of Penance*, McNeill and Gamer, (New York 1938, rpt. 1990) pp. 305-306

[11]    *Age of Charles Martel*, Paul Fouracre (Pearson Education Limited 2000) Chapter 3 pp. 108-109

[12]    *Complete Illustrated Guide to Runes*, Nigel Pennick (HarperCollins Publishers 2002)

[13]    *TANTRA, The Cult of the Feminine*, Andre Van Lysebeth (Weiser Books, Boston, MA 1995)

[14]    *Early Carolingian Warfare, Prelude to Empire*, Bernard S. Bachrach (University of Pennsylvania Press 2001) Chapter 1 p.33 referencing the *Chronicles of Fredegar* chapter 25

[15]    *Ibid.* Chapter 1 p.40

[16]    *Age of Charles Martel*, Paul Fouracre (Pearson Education Limited 2000) Chapter 3 p.168

[17]    *Early Carolingian Warfare, Prelude to Empire*, Bernard S. Bachrach (University of Pennsylvania Press 2001) Chapter 1 p.39

[18]    Ibid. Chapter 1 p.39

[19]    *Two Lives of Charlemagne*, Einhard and Notker the Stam-

merer, (Penguin Classics 1969) Translation and introduction by Lewis Thorpe p.3

[20]     *Age of Charles Martel,* Paul Fouracre (Pearson Education Limited 2000) Chapter 3 pp. 168-169 referencing the *Earlier Annals of Metz*

[21]     *Age of Charles Martel,* Paul Fouracre (Pearson Education Limited 2000) Chapter 3 pp. 106-107 referencing the *Chronicon Herimanni Augiensis*

# BOOKS IN THIS SERIES

*The Carolingian Chronicles*
Based on a true story, the Carolingian Chronicles recounts the rise of one of the most influential families in the history of western civilization.

## Anvil Of God, Book One Of The Carolingian Chronicles

After conquering a continent for the Merovingian kings, only one things stands between Charles the Hammer and the throne - he's dying. Anvil of God is a whirlwind of love, honor, sacrifice and betrayal that follows a bereaved family's relentless quest for power and destiny.

## Wheel Of The Fates, Book Two Of The Carolingian Chronicles

Wheel of the Fates picks up where the award-winning Anvil of God left off - chronicling the lives of Charles the Hammer's children as they vie for power in what's left of the kingdom...and their family

Made in the USA
Monee, IL
12 August 2021